PRAISE FOR THE NOVELS OF
#1 *NEW YORK TIMES* BESTSELLING AUTHOR
Nicholas Sparks

Safe Haven

"[The] Paganini of the heartstrings."   —*Miami Herald*

"Suspenseful."   —*Wichita Sunday Eagle*

"Gives readers a unique feature by displaying a glimpse of human behavior and insight into psychological instability... although Sparks strayed from his usual style, it was every bit as satisfying as his other novels, and exactly what I looked for."
—*Sacramento Book Review*

"Sparks has written another wonderful love story that makes you see true love in its simplest form and believe in it...a fantastic book about relationships, love, trust, and friendships."
—BestsellersWorld.com

"Sparks has a well-founded reputation for being able to craft romantic stories that touch people's hearts."   —Patheos.com

"A gripping tale of love and survival...a riveting 'read all night' page-turner...Fans know what to expect from Nicholas Sparks: a compelling love story centered on two appealing individuals. In SAFE HAVEN, readers find that—and much more...Sparks's bevy of fans will be wowed. But this book will attract many new admirers with its crossover into thriller territory."   —BookReporter.com

"If you love a good book about relationships, then you will want to be sure and read SAFE HAVEN by Nicholas Sparks...The story helps us realize that we should appreciate the people in our lives and the simple things we do with them."

—Examiner.com

"Delves into the depths of complicated relationships...Stepping to the plate once again, the North Carolina author has launched another one over the outfield wall. SAFE HAVEN is definitely a home run!" —BookLoons.com

"Looking for a love story? Read SAFE HAVEN."

—*Women's World*

THE LAST SONG

"Romance, betrayal, and youthful discovery...Fans of *The Notebook, Message in a Bottle*, etc., will gobble it up."

—*Entertainment Weekly*

"4½ stars! Readers will be invested in this story from the beginning. That it's never too late to strengthen relationships with loved ones is a central focus, and it's exemplified by comparing life to a song. Another emotional blockbuster!"

—*RT Book Reviews*

"A very enjoyable read...a plot that allows his characters to learn and grow from their experiences...Sparks is at his best."
—*Greensboro News-Record* (NC)

"Raw emotion, young love, family angst, and—ultimately—sweet resolution...[from] the reigning champ of the contemporary family drama/love story." —*BookPage*

"A beautifully scripted story...Though it's a book about a summer at the shore, *The Last Song* is no light summer romp. It will challenge you to view the world outside your comfort zone and examine your own responses to life's twists and turns."

—FictionAddict.com

THE LUCKY ONE

"A tale of redemption...holds readers in suspense until the final chapter...it will test readers' beliefs in the power of destiny and fate, and how they relate to choices one makes in life."

—*Chattanooga Times Free Press*

"A tender tale." —*BookPage*

"An emotional roller coaster...The book is great...it will introduce you to a great storyteller."

—*Navajo Times* (AZ)

"In true Nicholas Sparks fashion, the reader is engaged from the first to last page. The characters are authentic and the plot is engrossing and emotionally charged. Sparks is a talented storyteller who is adept at tugging the reader's heartstrings."

—BookLoons.com

"Sparks gives his many fans another reason to adore him with this tale of a once-in-a-lifetime quest for true romance...a grand, destined love story...Romance fans will consider themselves more than fortunate to have discovered *The Lucky One*."

—TeenReads.com

"Builds up to a breathtaking climax and satisfying epilogue."

—Suite101.com

THE CHOICE

"A tender and moving love story."

—*Publishers Weekly*

"Provides subtle lessons in love and hope...reinforces the theory that all choices, no matter how seemingly unimportant...often have far-reaching, rippling effects. Sparks has become a favorite storyteller because of his ability to take ordinary people, put them in extraordinary situations, and create unexpected outcomes." —BookReporter.com

"A heartrending love story...will have you entranced. And if *The Notebook* left you teary-eyed, his latest will have the same effect." —*Myrtle Beach Sun News*

"Will unleash a torrent of tears...But the emotion will be emotionally cleansing for it involves a choice each of us is likely to face one day. This is the stuff of serious romance novels."

—ContemporaryLit.About.com

DEAR JOHN

"Beautifully moving...Has tremendous emotional depth, revealing the true meaning of unconditional love."

—*RT Book Reviews*

"Full of pathos." —*Roanoke Times*

"For Sparks, weighty matters of the day remain set pieces, furniture upon which to hang timeless tales of chaste longing and harsh fate." —*Washington Post Book World*

"Sparks lives up to his reputation...a tribute to courageous and self-sacrificing soldiers."   —*Booklist*

AT FIRST SIGHT

"An ending that surprises."   —*New York Times Book Review*

"Engrosses readers from the first page to the last."
—*RT Book Reviews*

"Nicholas Sparks is one of the best-known writers in America and overseas for good reason: He has written stories that reveal the yearning for our most prized possession: love."
—*Mobile Register* (AL)

"Highly recommended. Nicholas Sparks can take a simple plot and turn it into a masterwork of art...Be prepared for a surprise ending."   —BestsellersWorld.com

"A tender, poignant tale...Never expect the expected when you pick up a Nicholas Sparks novel...Prepare to laugh, cry, and fall in love all over again!"   —RoundTableReviews.com

TRUE BELIEVER

"Time for a date with Sparks...The slow dance to the couple's first kiss is a two-chapter guilty pleasure."   —*People*

"For romance fans, *True Believer* is a gem."
—EDGEBoston.com

"Another winner...a page-turner...has all the things we have come to expect from him: sweet romance and a strong sense of place."   —*Charlotte Observer*

"A story about taking chances and following your heart. In the end, it will make you, too, believe in the miracle of love."

—BusinessKnowhow.com

"Sparks does not disappoint his readers. He tells a fine story that entertains us."

—*Oklahoman*

THE WEDDING

"Sweet but packs a punch... There is a twist that pulls everything together and makes you glad you read this."

—*Charlotte Observer*

"A slice of life readers will take to their hearts."

—*Tulsa World*

"Sparks tells his sweet story... [with] a gasp-inducing twist at the very end. Satisfied female readers will close the covers with a sigh."

—*Publishers Weekly*

THE GUARDIAN

"An involving love story... an edge-of-your-seat, unpredictable thriller."

—*Booklist*

"Nicholas Sparks is a top-notch writer. He has created a truly spine-tingling thriller exploring love and obsession with a kind of suspense never before experienced in his novels."

—RedBank.com

"Fans of Sparks won't be disappointed."

—*Southern Pines Pilot* (NC)

NIGHTS IN RODANTHE

"Bittersweet...romance blooms...You'll cry in spite of yourself."   —*People*

"Passionate and memorable...smooth, sensitive writing...This is a novel that can hold its own."   —Associated Press

"Extremely hard to put down...a love story, and a good love story at that."   —*Boston Herald*

A BEND IN THE ROAD

"Sweet, accessible, uplifting."   —*Publishers Weekly*

"A powerful tale of true love."   —*Booklist*

"Don't miss it; this is a book that's light on the surface but with subtle depths."   —BookLoons.com

THE RESCUE

"A romantic page-turner...Sparks's fans won't be disappointed."
                                                           —*Glamour*

"All of Sparks's trademark elements—love, loss, and small-town life—are present in this terrific read."   —*Booklist*

A WALK TO REMEMBER

"An extraordinary book...touching, at times riveting...a book you won't soon forget."   —*New York Post*

"A sweet tale of young but everlasting love."

—*Chicago Sun-Times*

"Bittersweet...a tragic yet spiritual love story."   —*Variety*

MESSAGE IN A BOTTLE

"The novel's unabashed emotion—and an unexpected turn—will put tears in your eyes."   —*People*

"Glows with moments of tenderness...delve[s] deeply into the mysteries of eternal love."   —*Cleveland Plain Dealer*

"Deeply moving, beautifully written, and extremely romantic."

—*Booklist*

THE NOTEBOOK

"Nicholas Sparks...will not let you go. His novel shines."

—*Dallas Morning News*

"Proves that good things come in small packages...a classic tale of love."   —*Christian Science Monitor*

"The lyrical beauty of this touching love story...will captivate the heart of every reader and establish Nicholas Sparks as a gifted novelist."   —*Denver Rocky Mountain News*

Safe Haven

NICHOLAS SPARKS

Safe Haven

GRAND CENTRAL
PUBLISHING

NEW YORK   BOSTON

Copyright © 2010 by Nicholas Sparks
Reading Group Guide copyright © 2011 by Hachette Book Group
All rights reserved. In accordance with the U.S. Copyright Act of 1976, the scanning, uploading, and electronic sharing of any part of this book without the permission of the publisher is unlawful piracy and theft of the author's intellectual property. If you would like to use material from the book (other than for review purposes), prior written permission must be obtained by contacting the publisher at permissions@hbgusa.com. Thank you for your support of the author's rights.

Grand Central Publishing
Hachette Book Group
237 Park Avenue
New York, NY 10017
www.HachetteBookGroup.com

Printed in the United States of America

Originally published in hardcover by Grand Central Publishing.

First trade edition: August 2011
First trade media tie-in edition: December 2012
10 9 8 7 6 5 4 3 2

Grand Central Publishing is a division of Hachette Book Group, Inc.
The Grand Central Publishing name and logo is a trademark of Hachette Book Group, Inc.

The Hachette Speakers Bureau provides a wide range of authors for speaking events. To find out more, go to www.hachettespeakersbureau.com or call (866) 376-6591.

The publisher is not responsible for websites (or their content) that are not owned by the publisher.

LCCN: 2010932492
ISBN 978-1-4555-2355-9 (pbk.)
ISBN 978-1-4555-2941-4 (Scholastic edition)

In loving memory of Paul and Adrienne Cote.
My wonderful family. I miss you both already.

Acknowledgments

At the completion of every novel, I always find myself reflecting on those people who've helped me along the way. As always, the list begins with my wife, Cathy, who not only has to put up with the creative moodiness that sometimes plagues me as a writer, but has lived through a very challenging year, one in which she lost both her parents. I love you and wish there were something I could have done to lessen the loss you feel. My heart is with you.

I'd also like to thank my children—Miles, Ryan, Landon, Lexie, and Savannah. Miles is off in college, my youngest are in the third grade, and watching all of them grow is always a source of joy.

My agent, Theresa Park, always deserves my thanks for all she does to help me write the best novel I possibly can. I'm lucky to work with you.

Ditto for Jamie Raab, my editor. She's taught me much about writing, and I'm thankful for her presence in my life.

Denise DiNovi, my Hollywood friend and producer of a number of my films, has been a source of joy and friendship over the years. Thank you for all you've done for me.

David Young, the CEO of Hachette Book Group, is both

smart and terrific. Thanks for tolerating the fact that I'm end-lessly late on delivering my manuscripts.

Howie Sanders and Keya Khayatian, my film agents, have worked with me for years, and I owe much of my success to their hard work.

Jennifer Romanello, my publicist at Grand Central Publishing, has worked with me on every novel I've written, and I consider myself lucky for all she does.

Edna Farley, my other publicist, is professional and diligent, and is fabulous at helping to make my tours run smoothly. Thank you.

Scott Schwimer, my entertainment attorney, is not only a friend, but also exceptional at negotiating the finer points of my contracts. I'm honored to work with you.

Abby Koons and Emily Sweet, a couple of cohorts at Park Literary Group, deserve my thanks for all they do with my foreign publishers, my website, and any contracts that come my way. You're the best.

Marty Bowen and Wyck Godfrey, who did a terrific job as the producers of *Dear John*, deserve my thanks for the work they did. I appreciate the care they showed the project.

Likewise Adam Shankman and Jennifer Gibgot, the producers of *The Last Song*, were terrific to work with. Thanks for all you did.

Courtenay Valenti, Ryan Kavanaugh, Tucker Tooley, Mark Johnson, Lynn Harris, and Lorenzo di Bonaventura all showed great passion for the films adapted from my novels, and I want to thank you all for everything you've done.

Thanks also to Sharon Krassney, Flag, and the team of copy-editors and proofreaders who had to work late evenings to get this novel ready to print.

Jeff Van Wie, my screenwriting partner on *The Last Song*, deserves my thanks for his passion and effort in crafting screen-plays, along with his friendship.

Safe Haven

1

As Katie wound her way among the tables, a breeze from the Atlantic rippled through her hair. Carrying three plates in her left hand and another in her right, she wore jeans and a T-shirt that read *Ivan's: Try Our Fish Just for the Halibut*. She brought the plates to four men wearing polo shirts; the one closest to her caught her eye and smiled. Though he tried to act as though he was just a friendly guy, she knew he was watching her as she walked away. Melody had mentioned the men had come from Wilmington and were scouting locations for a movie.

After retrieving a pitcher of sweet tea, she refilled their glasses before returning to the waitress station. She stole a glance at the view. It was late April, the temperature hovering just around perfect, and blue skies stretched to the horizon. Beyond her, the Intracoastal was calm despite the breeze and seemed to mirror the color of the sky. A dozen seagulls perched on the railing, waiting to dart beneath the tables if someone dropped a scrap of food.

Ivan Smith, the owner, hated them. He called them rats-with-wings, and he'd already patrolled the railing twice wielding a wooden plunger, trying to scare them off. Melody had leaned toward Katie and confessed that she was more worried about where the plunger had been than she was about the seagulls. Katie said nothing.

She started another pot of sweet tea, wiping down the station. A moment later, she felt someone tap her on the shoulder. She turned to see Ivan's daughter, Eileen. A pretty, ponytailed nineteen-year-old, she was working part-time as the restaurant hostess.

"Katie—can you take another table?"

Katie scanned her tables, running the rhythm in her head. "Sure." She nodded.

Eileen walked down the stairs. From nearby tables Katie could hear snippets of conversations—people talking about friends or family, the weather or fishing. At a table in the corner, she saw two people close their menus. She hustled over and took the order, but didn't linger at the table trying to make small talk, like Melody did. She wasn't good at small talk, but she was efficient and polite and none of the customers seemed to mind.

She'd been working at the restaurant since early March. Ivan had hired her on a cold, sunny afternoon when the sky was the color of robins' eggs. When he'd said she could start work the following Monday, it took everything she had not to cry in front of him. She'd waited until she was walking home before breaking down. At the time, she was broke and hadn't eaten in two days.

She refilled waters and sweet teas and headed to the kitchen. Ricky, one of the cooks, winked at her as he always did. Two days ago he'd asked her out, but she'd told him that she didn't want to date anyone at the restaurant. She had the feeling he would try again and hoped her instincts were wrong.

"I don't think it's going to slow down today," Ricky commented. He was blond and lanky, perhaps a year or two younger than her, and still lived with his parents. "Every time we think we're getting caught up, we get slammed again."

"It's a beautiful day."

"But why are people here? On a day like today, they should

be at the beach or out fishing. Which is exactly what I'm doing when I finish up here."

"That sounds like a good idea."

"Can I drive you home later?"

He offered to drive her at least twice a week. "Thank you, no. I don't live that far."

"It's no problem," he persisted. "I'd be glad to do it."

"Walking's good for me."

She handed him her ticket and Ricky pinned it up on the wheel and then located one of her orders. She carried the order back to her section and dropped it off at a table.

Ivan's was a local institution, a restaurant that had been in business for almost thirty years. In the time she'd been working there, she'd come to recognize the regulars, and as she crossed the restaurant floor her eyes traveled over them to the people she hadn't seen before. Couples flirting, other couples ignoring each other. Families. No one seemed out of place and no one had come around asking for her, but there were still times when her hands began to shake, and even now she slept with a light on.

Her short hair was chestnut brown; she'd been dyeing it in the kitchen sink of the tiny cottage she rented. She wore no makeup and knew her face would pick up a bit of color, maybe too much. She reminded herself to buy sunscreen, but after paying rent and utilities on the cottage, there wasn't much left for luxuries. Even sunscreen was a stretch. Ivan's was a good job and she was glad to have it, but the food was inexpensive, which meant the tips weren't great. On her steady diet of rice and beans, pasta and oatmeal, she'd lost weight in the past four months. She could feel her ribs beneath her shirt, and until a few weeks ago, she'd had dark circles under her eyes that she thought would never go away.

"I think those guys are checking you out," Melody said, nodding toward the table with the four men from the movie studio. "Especially the brown-haired one. The cute one."

"Oh," Katie said. She started another pot of coffee. Anything

she said to Melody was sure to get passed around, so Katie usually said very little to her.

"What? You don't think he's cute?"

"I didn't really notice."

"How can you not notice when a guy is cute?" Melody stared
at her in disbelief.

"I don't know," Katie answered.

Like Ricky, Melody was a couple of years younger than Katie,
maybe twenty-five or so. An auburn-haired, green-eyed minx,
she dated a guy named Steve who made deliveries for the home
improvement store on the other side of town. Like everyone
else in the restaurant, she'd grown up in Southport, which she
described as being a paradise for children, families, and the elderly, but the most dismal place on earth for single people. At
least once a week, she told Katie that she was planning to move
to Wilmington, which had bars and clubs and a lot more shopping. She seemed to know everything about everybody. Gossip,
Katie sometimes thought, was Melody's real profession.

"I heard Ricky asked you out," she said, changing the subject,
"but you said no."

"I don't like to date people at work." Katie pretended to be
absorbed in organizing the silverware trays.

"We could double-date. Ricky and Steve go fishing together."

Katie wondered if Ricky had put her up to it or whether it was
Melody's idea. Maybe both. In the evenings, after the restaurant
closed, most of the staff stayed around for a while, visiting over
a couple of beers. Aside from Katie, everyone had worked at
Ivan's for years.

"I don't think that's a good idea," Katie demurred.

"Why not?"

"I had a bad experience once," Katie said. "Dating a guy from
work, I mean. Since then, I've kind of made it a rule not to do
it again."

Melody rolled her eyes before hurrying off to one of her tables. Katie dropped off two checks and cleared empty plates. She kept busy, as she always did, trying to be efficient and invisible. She kept her head down and made sure the waitress station was spotless. It made the day go by faster. She didn't flirt with the guy from the studio, and when he left he didn't look back.

Katie worked both the lunch and dinner shift. As day faded into night, she loved watching the sky turning from blue to gray to orange and yellow at the western rim of the world. At sunset, the water sparkled and sailboats heeled in the breeze. The needles on the pine trees seemed to shimmer. As soon as the sun dropped below the horizon, Ivan turned on the propane gas heaters and the coils began to glow like jack-o'-lanterns. Katie's face had gotten slightly sunburned, and the waves of radiant heat made her skin sting.

Abby and Big Dave replaced Melody and Ricky in the evening. Abby was a high school senior who giggled a lot, and Big Dave had been cooking dinners at Ivan's for nearly twenty years. He was married with two kids and had a tattoo of a scorpion on his right forearm. He weighed close to three hundred pounds and in the kitchen his face was always shiny. He had nicknames for everyone and called her Katie Kat.

The dinner rush lasted until nine. When it began to clear out, Katie cleaned and closed up the wait station. She helped the busboys carry plates to the dishwasher while her final tables finished up. At one of them was a young couple and she'd seen the rings on their fingers as they held hands across the table. They were attractive and happy, and she felt a sense of déjà vu. She had been like them once, a long time ago, for just a moment. Or so she thought, because she learned the moment was only an illusion. Katie turned away from the blissful couple, wishing that she could erase her memories forever and never have that feeling again.

2

The next morning, Katie stepped onto the porch with a cup of coffee, the floorboards creaking beneath her bare feet, and leaned against the railing. Lilies sprouted amid the wild grass in what once was a flower bed, and she raised the cup, savoring the aroma as she took a sip.

She liked it here. Southport was different from Boston or Philadelphia or Atlantic City, with their endless sounds of traffic and smells and people rushing along the sidewalks, and it was the first time in her life that she had a place to call her own. The cottage wasn't much, but it was hers and out of the way and that was enough. It was one of two identical structures located at the end of a gravel lane, former hunting cabins with wooden-plank walls, nestled against a grove of oak and pine trees at the edge of a forest that stretched to the coast. The living room and kitchen were small and the bedroom didn't have a closet, but the cottage was furnished, including rockers on the front porch, and the rent was a bargain. The place wasn't decaying, but it was dusty from years of neglect, and the landlord offered to buy the supplies if Katie was willing to spruce it up. Since she'd moved in, she'd spent much of her free time on all fours or standing on chairs, doing exactly that. She scrubbed the bathroom until it sparkled; she washed the ceiling with a damp cloth. She wiped the windows with vinegar and spent hours on her hands and knees, trying her best to remove the rust and grime from the linoleum in the kitchen. She'd filled holes in the walls with Spackle and then sanded the Spackle until it was smooth. She'd painted the walls in the kitchen a cheery yellow and put glossy white paint on the cabinets. Her bedroom was now a light blue, the living room was beige, and last week, she'd put a new slipcover on the couch, which made it look practically new again.

With most of the work now behind her, she liked to sit on the front porch in the afternoons and read books she'd checked out from the library. Aside from coffee, reading was her only indulgence. She didn't have a television, a radio, a cell phone, or a microwave or even a car, and she could pack all her belongings in a single bag. She was twenty-seven years old, a former long-haired blond with no real friends. She'd moved here with almost nothing, and months later she still had little. She saved half of her tips and every night she folded the money into a coffee can she kept hidden in the crawl space beneath the porch. She kept that money for emergencies and would rather go hungry than touch it. Simply the knowledge that it was there made her breathe easier because the past was always around her and might return at any time. It prowled the world searching for her, and she knew it was growing angrier at every passing day.

"Good morning," a voice called out, disrupting her thoughts. "You must be Katie."

Katie turned. On the sagging porch of the cottage next door, she saw a woman with long, unruly brown hair, waving at her. She looked to be in her mid-thirties and wore jeans and a button-up shirt she'd rolled to her elbows. A pair of sunglasses nested in tangled curls on her head. She was holding a small rug and she seemed to be debating whether or not to shake it before finally tossing it aside and starting toward Katie's. She moved with the energy and ease of someone who exercised regularly.

"Irv Benson told me we'd be neighbors."

The landlord, Katie thought. "I didn't realize anyone was moving in."

"I don't think he did, either. He about fell out of his chair when I said I'd take the place." By then, she'd reached Katie's porch and she held out her hand. "My friends call me Jo," she said.

"Hi," Katie said, taking it.

"Can you believe this weather? It's gorgeous, isn't it?"

"It's a beautiful morning," Katie agreed, shifting from one foot to the other. "When did you move in?"

"Yesterday afternoon. And then, joy of joys, I pretty much spent all night sneezing. I think Benson collected as much dust as he possibly could and stored it at my place. You wouldn't believe what it's like in there."

Katie nodded toward the door. "My place was the same way."

"It doesn't look like it. Sorry, I couldn't help sneaking a glance through your windows when I was standing in my kitchen. Your place is bright and cheery. I, on the other hand, have rented a dusty, spider-filled dungeon."

"Mr. Benson let me paint."

"I'll bet. As long as Mr. Benson doesn't have to do it, I'll bet he lets me paint, too. He gets a nice, clean place, and I get to do the work." She gave a wry grin. "How long have you lived here?"

Katie crossed her arms, feeling the morning sun begin to warm her face. "Almost two months."

"I'm not sure I can make it that long. If I keep sneezing like I did last night, my head will probably fall off before then." She reached for her sunglasses and began wiping the lenses with her shirt. "How do you like Southport? It's a different world, don't you think?"

"What do you mean?"

"You don't sound like you're from around here. I'd guess somewhere up north?"

After a moment, Katie nodded.

"That's what I thought," Jo went on. "And Southport takes awhile to get used to. I mean, I've always loved it, but I'm partial to small towns."

"You're from here?"

"I grew up here, went away, and ended up coming back. The oldest story in the book, right? Besides, you can't find dusty places like this just anywhere."

Katie smiled, and for a moment neither said anything. Jo seemed content to stand in front of her, waiting for her to make the next move. Katie took a sip of coffee, gazing off into the woods, and then remembered her manners.

"Would you like a cup of coffee? I just brewed a pot."

Jo put the sunglasses back on her head, tucking them into her hair. "You know, I was hoping you'd say that. I'd *love* a cup of coffee. My entire kitchen is still in boxes and my car is in the shop. Do you have any idea what it's like to face the day without caffeine?"

"I have an idea."

"Well, just so you know, I'm a genuine coffee addict. Especially on any day that requires me to unpack. Did I mention I hate unpacking?"

"I don't think you did."

"It's pretty much the most miserable thing there is. Trying to figure out where to put everything, banging your knees as you bump around the clutter. Don't worry—I'm not the kind of neighbor who asks for that kind of help. But coffee, on the other hand . . ."

"Come on." Katie waved her in. "Just keep in mind that most of the furniture came with the place."

After crossing the kitchen, Katie pulled a cup from the cupboard and filled it to the brim. She handed it to Jo. "Sorry, I don't have any cream or sugar."

"Not necessary," Jo said, taking the cup. She blew on the coffee before taking a sip. "Okay, it's official," she said. "As of now, you're my best friend in the entire world. This is soooo good."

"You're welcome," she said.

"So Benson said you work at Ivan's?"

"I'm a waitress."

"Is Big Dave still working there?" When Katie nodded, Jo went on. "He's been there since before I was in high school. Does he still make up names for everyone?"

"Yes," she said.

"How about Melody? Is she still talking about how cute the customers are?"

"Every shift."

"And Ricky? Is he still hitting on new waitresses?"

When Katie nodded again, Jo laughed. "That place never changes."

"Did you work there?"

"No, but it's a small town and Ivan's is an institution. Besides, the longer you live here, the more you'll understand that there are no such things as secrets in this place. Everyone knows everyone's business, and some people, like, let's say . . . Melody . . . have raised gossip to an art form. It used to drive me crazy. Of course, half the people in Southport are the same way. There isn't much to do around here but gossip."

"But you came back."

Jo shrugged. "Yeah, well. What can I say? Maybe I like the crazy." She took another sip of her coffee and motioned out the window. "You know, as long as I'd lived here, I wasn't even aware these two places existed."

"The landlord said they were hunting cottages. They used to be part of the plantation before he turned them into rentals."

Jo shook her head. "I can't believe you moved out here."

"You did, too," Katie pointed out.

"Yes, but the only reason I considered it was because I knew I wouldn't be the only woman at the end of a gravel road in the middle of nowhere. It's kind of isolated."

Which is why I was more than happy to rent it, Katie thought to herself. "It's not so bad. I'm used to it by now."

"I hope I get used to it," she said. She blew on the coffee, cooling it off. "So what brought you to Southport? I'm sure it wasn't the exciting career potential at Ivan's. Do you have any family around here? Parents? Brothers or sisters?"

"No," Katie said. "Just me."

"Following a boyfriend?"

"No."

"So you just . . . moved here?"

"Yes."

"Why on earth would you do that?"

Katie didn't answer. They were the same questions that Ivan and Melody and Ricky had asked. She knew there were no ulterior motives behind the questions, it was just natural curiosity, but even so, she was never quite sure what to say, other than to state the truth.

"I just wanted a place where I could start over."

Jo took another sip of coffee, seemingly mulling over her answer, but surprising Katie, she asked no follow-up questions. Instead, she simply nodded.

"Makes sense to me. Sometimes starting over is exactly what a person needs. And I think it's admirable. A lot of people don't have the courage it takes to do something like that."

"You think so?"

"I know so," she said. "So, what's on your agenda today? While I'm whining and unpacking and cleaning until my hands are raw."

"I have to work later. But other than that, not much. I need to run to the store and pick up some things."

"Are you going to visit Fisher's or head into town?"

"I'm just going to Fisher's," she said.

"Have you met the owner there? The guy with gray hair?"

Katie nodded. "Once or twice."

Jo finished her coffee and put the cup in the sink before sighing. "All right," she said, sounding less than enthusiastic. "Enough procrastinating. If I don't start now, I'm never going to finish. Wish me luck."

"Good luck."

Jo gave a little wave. "It was nice meeting you, Katie."

From her kitchen window, Katie saw Jo shaking the rug she'd set aside earlier. She seemed friendly enough, but Katie wasn't sure whether she was ready to have a neighbor. Although it might be nice to have someone to visit with now and then, she'd gotten used to being alone.

Then again, she knew that living in a small town meant that her self-imposed isolation couldn't last forever. She had to work and shop and walk around town; some of the customers at the restaurant already recognized her. And besides, she had to admit she'd enjoyed chatting with Jo. For some reason, she felt that there was more to Jo than met the eye, something . . . trustworthy, even if she couldn't explain it. She was also a single woman, which was a definite plus. Katie didn't want to imagine how she would have reacted had a man moved in next door, and she wondered why she'd never even considered the possibility.

Over by the sink, she washed out the coffee cups then put them back into the cupboard. The act was so familiar—putting two cups away after coffee in the morning—and for an instant, she felt engulfed by the life she'd left behind. Her hands began to tremble, and pressing them together she took a few deep breaths until they finally stilled. Two months ago, she wouldn't have been able to do that; even two weeks ago, there had been little she could do to stop it. While she was glad that these bouts of anxiety no longer overwhelmed her, it also meant she was getting comfortable here, and that scared her. Because being comfortable meant she might lower her guard, and she could never let that happen.

Even so, she was grateful to have ended up in Southport. It was a small historic town of a few thousand people, located at the mouth of the Cape Fear River, right where it met the Intracoastal. It was a place with sidewalks and shade trees and flowers that bloomed in the sandy soil. Spanish moss hung from the tree branches, while kudzu climbed the wizened trunks. She had watched kids riding their bikes and playing kick ball in the streets, and had marveled at the number of churches, one on nearly every corner. Crickets and frogs sounded in the evening, and she thought again that this place had felt right, even from the beginning. It felt *safe*, as if it had somehow been beckoning to her all along, promising sanctuary.

Katie slipped on her only pair of shoes, a pair of beat-up Converse sneakers. The chest of drawers stood largely empty and there was almost no food in the kitchen, but as she stepped out of the house and into the sunshine and headed toward the store, she thought to herself, *This is home*. Drawing in a deeply scented breath of hyacinth and fresh-cut grass, she knew she hadn't been happier in years.

3

His hair had turned gray when he was in his early twenties, prompting some good-natured ribbing from his friends. It hadn't been a slow change, either, a few hairs here and there gradually turning to silver. Rather, in January he'd had a head of black hair and by the following January, there was scarcely a single black hair left. His two older brothers had been spared, though in the last couple of years, they'd picked up some silver in their sideburns. Neither his mom nor his dad could explain it; as far as they knew, Alex Wheatley was an anomaly on both sides of the family.

Strangely, it hadn't bothered him. In the army, he sometimes suspected that it had aided in his advancement. He'd been with Criminal Investigation Division, or CID, stationed in Germany and Georgia, and had spent ten years investigating military crimes, everything from soldiers going AWOL, to burglary, domestic abuse, rape, and even murder. He'd been promoted regularly, finally retiring as a major at thirty-two.

After punching his ticket and ending his career with the military, he moved to Southport, his wife's hometown. He was newly married with his first child on the way, and though his immediate thought was that he would apply for a job in law enforcement, his father-in-law had offered to sell him the family business.

It was an old-fashioned country store, with white clapboard siding, blue shutters, a sloped porch roof, and a bench out front, the kind of store that enjoyed its heyday long ago and had mostly disappeared. The living quarters were on the second floor. A massive magnolia tree shaded one side of the building, and an oak tree stood out front. Only half of the parking lot was asphalt—the other half was gravel—but the lot was seldom empty. His father-in-law had started the business before Carly was born, when there wasn't much more than farmland surrounding him. But his father-in-law prided himself on understanding people, and he wanted to stock whatever they happened to need, all of which lent a cluttered organization to the place. Alex felt the same way and kept the store largely the same. Five or six aisles offered groceries and toiletries, refrigerator cases in the back overflowed with everything from soda and water to beer and wine, and as in every other convenience store, this one had racks of chips, candy, and the kind of junk food that people grabbed as they stood near the cash register. But that's where the similarity ended. There was also assorted fishing gear along the shelves, fresh bait, and a grill manned by Roger Thompson, who'd once worked on Wall Street and had moved to Southport in search of a simpler life. The grill offered burgers, sandwiches, and hot dogs as well as a place to sit. There were DVDs for rent, various kinds of ammunition, rain jackets and umbrellas, and a small offering of bestselling and classic novels. The store sold spark plugs, fan belts, and gas cans, and Alex was able to make duplicates of keys with a machine in the back room. He had three gasoline pumps, and another pump on the dock for any boats that needed to fill up, the only place to do so aside from the marina. Rows of dill pickles, boiled peanuts, and baskets of fresh vegetables sat near the counter.

Surprisingly, it wasn't hard to keep up with the inventory.

Some items moved regularly, others didn't. Like his father-in-law, Alex had a pretty good sense of what people needed as soon as they walked in the store. He'd always noticed and remembered things that other people didn't, a trait that had helped him immeasurably in his years working CID. Nowadays he was endlessly tinkering with the items he stocked, in an attempt to keep up with the changing tastes of his customers.

Never in his life had he imagined doing something like this, but it had been a good decision, if only because it allowed him to keep an eye on the kids. Josh was in school, but Kristen wouldn't start until the fall, and she spent her days with him in the store. He'd set up a play area behind the register, where his bright and talkative daughter seemed most happy. Though only five, she knew how to work the register and make change, using a step stool to reach the buttons. Alex always enjoyed the expressions on strangers' faces when she started to ring them up.

Still, it wasn't an ideal childhood for her, even if she didn't know anything different. When he was honest with himself, he had to admit that taking care of kids and the store took all the energy he had. Sometimes, he felt as though he could barely keep up—making Josh's lunch and dropping him off at school, ordering from his suppliers, meeting with vendors, and serving the customers, all while keeping Kristen entertained. And that was just for starters. The evenings, he sometimes thought, were even busier. He tried his best to spend time doing kid things with them—going on bike rides, flying kites, and fishing with Josh, but Kristen liked to play with dolls and do arts and crafts, and he'd never been good at those things. Add in making dinner and cleaning the house, and half the time, it was all he could do to keep his head above water. Even when he finally got the kids in bed, he found it nearly impossible to relax because there was always something else to do. He wasn't sure if he even knew how to relax anymore.

After the kids went to bed, he spent the rest of his evenings alone. Though he seemed to know most everyone in town, he had few real friends. The couples that he and Carly sometimes visited for barbecues or dinners had slowly but surely drifted away. Part of that was his own fault—working at the store and raising his kids took most of his time—but sometimes he got the sense that he made them uncomfortable, as if reminding them that life was unpredictable and scary and that things could go bad in an instant.

It was a wearying and sometimes isolating lifestyle, but he remained focused on Josh and Kristen. Though less frequent than it once had been, both of them had been prone to nightmares with Carly gone. When they woke in the middle of the night, sobbing inconsolably, he would hold them in his arms and whisper that everything was going to be all right, until they were finally able to fall back asleep. Early on, all of them had seen a counselor; the kids had drawn pictures and talked about their feelings. It hadn't seemed to help as much as he'd hoped it would. Their nightmares continued for almost a year. Once in a while, when he colored with Kristen or fished with Josh, they'd grow quiet and he knew they were missing their mom. Kristen sometimes said as much in a babyish, trembling voice, while tears ran down her cheeks. When that happened, he was sure he could hear his heart breaking, because he knew there was nothing he could do or say to make things any better. The counselor had assured him that kids were resilient and that as long as they knew they were loved, the nightmares would eventually stop and the tears would become less frequent. Time proved the counselor right, but now Alex faced another form of loss, one that left him equally heartbroken. The kids were getting better, he knew, because their memories of their mom were slowly but surely fading away. They'd been so young when they'd lost her—four and three—and it meant that the day would come when their mother would become more an idea than a person to them. It was inevitable, of course, but somehow it didn't seem right to Alex that they would never remember the sound of Carly's laughter, or the tender way she'd held them as infants, or know how deeply she'd once loved them.

He'd never been much of a photographer. Carly had always been the one who reached for the camera, and consequently, there were dozens of photographs of him with the kids. There were only a few that included Carly, and though he made it a point to page through the album with Josh and Kristen while he told them about their mother, he suspected that the stories were becoming just that: stories. The emotions attached to them were like sand castles in the tide, slowly washing out to sea. The same thing was happening with the portrait of Carly that hung in his bedroom. In their first year of marriage, he'd arranged to have her portrait taken, despite her protests. He was glad for that. In the photo, she looked beautiful and independent, the strong-willed woman who'd captured his heart, and at night, after the kids were in bed, he would sometimes stare at his wife's image, his emotions in turmoil. But Josh and Kristen barely noticed the photo at all.

He thought of her often, and he missed the companionship they'd once shared and the friendship that had been the bedrock of their marriage at its best. And when he was honest with himself, he knew he wanted those things again. He was lonely, even though it bothered him to admit it. For months after they lost her, he simply couldn't imagine ever being in another relationship, let alone consider the possibility of loving someone again. Even after a year, it was the kind of thought he would force from his mind. The pain was too fresh, the memory of the aftermath too raw. But a few months ago, he'd taken the kids to the aquarium and as they'd stood in front of the shark tank, he'd struck up a conversation with an attractive woman standing next to him. Like him, she'd brought her kids, and like him, she wore no ring on her finger. Her children were the same ages as Josh and Kristen, and while the four of them were off point-

ing at the fish, she'd laughed at something he'd said and he'd
felt a spark of attraction, reminding him of what he had once
had. The conversation eventually came to an end and they
went their separate ways, but on the way out, he'd seen her
once more. She'd waved at him and there'd been an instant
when he contemplated jogging over to her car and asking for
her phone number. But he didn't, and a moment later, she was
pulling out of the parking lot. He never saw her again.

That night, he waited for the wave of self-reproach and regret
to come, but strangely, it didn't. Nor did it feel *wrong*. Instead,
it felt . . . okay. Not affirming, not exhilarating, but okay, and
he somehow knew it meant he was finally beginning to heal.
That didn't mean, of course, that he was ready to rush headlong
into the single life. If it happened, it happened. And if it didn't?
He figured he'd cross that bridge when he came to it. He was
willing to wait until he met the right person, someone who not
only brought joy back into his life, but who loved his kids as
much as he did. He recognized, however, that in this town, the
odds of finding that person were tiny. Southport was too small.
Nearly everyone he knew was either married or retired or at-
tending one of the local schools. There weren't a lot of single
women around, let alone women who wanted a package deal,
kids included. And that, of course, was the deal breaker. He
might be lonely, he might want companionship, but he wasn't
about to sacrifice his kids to get it. They'd been through enough
and would always be his first priority.

Still . . . there was one possibility, he supposed. Another
woman interested him, though he knew almost nothing about
her, aside from the fact that she was single. She'd been coming
to the store once or twice a week since early March. The first
time he'd seen her, she was pale and gaunt, almost desperately
thin. Ordinarily, he wouldn't have given her a second glance.
People passing through town often stopped at the store for
sodas or gasoline or junk food; he seldom saw such people again.

But she wanted none of those things; instead, she kept her head down as she walked toward the grocery aisles, as if trying to remain unseen, a ghost in human form. Unfortunately for her, it wasn't working. She was too attractive to go unnoticed. She was in her late twenties, he guessed, with brown hair cut a little unevenly above her shoulder. She wore no makeup and her high cheekbones and round, wide-set eyes gave her an elegant if slightly fragile appearance.

At the register, he realized that up close she was even prettier than she'd been from a distance. Her eyes were a greenish-hazel color and flecked with gold, and her brief, distracted smile vanished as quickly as it had come. On the counter, she placed nothing but staples: coffee, rice, oatmeal, pasta, peanut butter, and toiletries. He sensed that conversation would make her uncomfortable so he began to ring her up in silence. As he did, he heard her voice for the first time.

"Do you have any dry beans?" she asked.

"I'm sorry," he'd answered. "I don't normally keep those in stock."

As he bagged her items after his answer, he noticed her staring out the window, absently chewing her lower lip. For some reason, he had the strange impression that she was about to cry.

He cleared his throat. "If it's something you're going to need regularly, I'd be happy to stock them. I just need to know what kind you want."

"I don't want to bother you." When she answered, her voice barely registered above a whisper.

She paid him in small bills, and after taking the bag, she left the store. Surprising him, she kept walking out of the lot, and it was only then he realized she hadn't driven, which only added to his curiosity.

The following week, there were dry beans in the store. He'd stocked three types: pinto, kidney, and lima, though only a single bag of each, and the next time she came in, he made a point of mentioning that they could be found on the bottom shelf in the corner, near the rice. Bringing all three bags to the register, she'd asked him if he happened to have an onion. He pointed to a small bag he kept in a bushel basket near the door, but she'd shaken her head. "I only need one," she murmured, her smile hesitant and apologetic. Her hands shook as she counted out her bills, and again, she left on foot.

Since then, the beans were always in stock, there was a single onion available, and in the weeks that followed her first two visits to the store, she'd become something of a regular. Though still quiet, she seemed less fragile, less nervous, as time had gone on. The dark circles under her eyes were gradually fading, and she'd picked up some color during the recent spate of good weather. She'd put on some weight—not much, but enough to soften her delicate features. Her voice was stronger, too, and though it didn't signal any interest in him, she could hold his gaze a little longer before finally turning away. They hadn't proceeded much beyond the *Did you find everything you needed?* followed by the *Yes, I did. Thank you* type of conversation, but instead of fleeing the store like a hunted deer, she sometimes wandered the aisles a bit, and had even begun to talk to Kristen when the two of them were alone. It was the first time he'd seen the woman's defenses drop. Her easy demeanor and open expression spoke of an affection for children, and his first thought was that he'd glimpsed the woman she once had been and could be again, given the right circumstances. Kristen, too, seemed to notice something different about the woman, because after she left, Kristen had told him that she'd made a new friend and that her name was Miss Katie.

That didn't mean, however, that Katie was comfortable with him. Last week, after she'd chatted easily with Kristen, he'd seen her reading the back covers of the novels he kept in stock. She didn't buy any of the titles, and when he offhandedly asked as she was checking out if she had a favorite author, he'd seen a flash of the old nervousness. He was struck by the notion that he shouldn't have let slip that he'd been watching her. "Never mind," he added quickly. "It's not important." On her way out the door, however, she'd paused for a moment, her bag tucked in the crook of her arm. She half-turned in his direction and mumbled, *I like Dickens*. With that, she opened the door and was gone, walking up the road.

He'd thought about her with greater frequency since then, but they were vague thoughts, edged with mystery and colored by the knowledge that he wanted to get to know her better. Not that he knew how to go about it. Aside from the year he courted Carly, he'd never been good at dating. In college, between swimming and his classes, he had little time to go out. In the military, he'd thrown himself into his career, working long hours and transferring from post to post with every promotion. While he'd gone out with a few women, they were fleeting romances that for the most part began and ended in the bedroom. Sometimes, when thinking back on his life, he barely recognized the man he used to be, and Carly, he knew, was responsible for those changes. Yes, it was sometimes hard, and yes, he was lonely. He missed his wife, and though he never told anyone, there were still moments when he could swear he felt her presence nearby, watching over him, trying to make sure he was going to be all right.

Because of the glorious weather, the store was busier than usual for a Sunday. By the time Alex unlocked the door at seven, there were already three boats tied at the dock waiting for the pump to be turned on. As was typical, while paying for the gas, the boat owners loaded up on snacks and drinks and bags of ice to stow in their boats. Roger—who was working the grill, as always—hadn't had a break since he'd put on his apron, and the tables were crowded with people eating sausage biscuits and cheeseburgers and asking for tips about the stock market.

Usually, Alex worked the register until noon, when he would hand over the reins to Joyce, who, like Roger, was the kind of employee who made running the store much less challenging than it could be. Joyce, who'd worked in the courthouse until her retirement, had "come with the business," so to speak. His father-in-law had hired her ten years ago and now, in her seventies, she hadn't showed any signs of slowing down. Her husband had died years earlier, her kids had moved away, and she viewed the customers as her de facto family. Joyce was as intrinsic to the store as the items on the shelves.

Even better, she understood that Alex needed to spend time with his children away from the store, and she didn't get bent out of shape by having to work on Sundays. As soon as she showed up, she'd slip behind the register and tell Alex he could go, sounding more like the boss than an employee. Joyce was also his babysitter, the only one he trusted to stay with the kids if he had to go out of town. That wasn't common—it had happened only twice in the past couple of years when he'd met up with an old army buddy in Raleigh—but he'd come to view Joyce as one of the best things in his life. When he'd needed her most, she'd always been there for him.

Waiting for Joyce's arrival, Alex walked through the store, checking the shelves. The computer system was great at tracking inventory, but he knew that rows of numbers didn't always tell the whole story. Sometimes, he felt he got a better sense by actually scanning the shelves to see what had sold the day before. A successful store required turning over the inventory as frequently as possible, and that meant that he sometimes had to offer items that no other stores offered. He carried homemade jams and jellies; powdered rubs from "secret recipes" that flavored beef and pork; and a selection of locally canned fruits and vegetables. Even people who regularly shopped at the Food Lion or Piggly Wiggly often dropped by on their way home from the store to pick up the local specialty items Alex made a point of stocking.

Even more important than an item's sales volume, he liked to know *when* it sold, a fact that didn't necessarily show up in the numbers. He'd learned, for instance, that hot dog buns sold especially well on the weekends but only rarely during the week; regular loaves of bread were just the opposite. Noting that, he'd been able to keep more of both in stock when they were needed, and sales rose. It wasn't much but it added up and enabled Alex to keep his small business afloat when the chain stores were putting most local shops out of business.

As he perused the shelves, he wondered idly what he was going to do with the kids in the afternoon and decided to take them for a bike ride. Carly had loved nothing more than strapping them into the bike stroller and hauling them all over town. But a bike ride wasn't enough to fill the entire afternoon. Maybe they could ride their bikes to the park . . . they might enjoy that.

With a quick peek toward the front door to make sure no one was coming in, he hurried through the rear storeroom and poked his head out. Josh was fishing off the dock, which was far and away his favorite thing to do. Alex didn't like the fact that Josh was out there alone—he had no doubt that some people would regard him as a bad father for allowing it—but Josh always stayed within visual range of the video monitor behind the register. It was a rule, and Josh had always adhered to it. Kristen, as usual, was sitting at her table in the corner behind the register. She'd separated her American Girl doll clothing into different piles, and she seemed content to change her doll from one outfit to the next. Each time she finished, she would look up at him with a bright, innocent expression and ask her daddy how he thought her doll looked now, as if it were possible he would ever say he didn't like it.

Little girls. They could melt the toughest hearts.

Alex was straightening some of the condiments when he

heard the bell on the front door jingle. Raising his head over the aisle, he saw Katie enter the store.

"Hi, Miss Katie," Kristen called out, popping up from behind the register. "How do you think my doll looks?"

From where he was standing, he could barely see Kristen's head above the counter, but she was holding . . . Vanessa? Rebecca? Whatever the doll with brown hair was called, high enough for Katie to notice.

"She's beautiful, Kristen," Katie answered. "Is that a new dress?"

"No, I've had it for a while. But she hasn't worn it lately."

"What's her name?"

"Vanessa," she said.

Vanessa, Alex thought. When he complimented Vanessa later, he would sound like a much more attentive father.

"Did you name her?"

"No, she came with the name. Can you help me get her boots on, though? I can't get them on all the way."

Alex watched as Kristen handed Katie the doll and she began to work on the soft plastic boots. From his own experience, Alex knew it was harder than it looked. There wasn't a chance a little girl could somehow muscle them on. He had trouble putting them on, but somehow Katie made it seem easy. She handed the doll back and asked, "How's that?"

"Perfect," Kristen said. "Do you think I should put a coat on her?"

"It's not that cold out."

"I know. But Vanessa gets cold sometimes. I think she needs one." Kristen's head vanished behind the counter and then popped up again. "Which one do you think? Blue or purple?"

Katie brought a finger to her mouth, her expression serious. "I think purple might be good."

Kristen nodded. "That's what I think, too. Thanks."

Katie smiled before turning away, and Alex focused his attention on the shelves before she caught him staring. He moved jars of mustard and relish toward the front of the shelf. From the corner of his eye, he saw Katie scoop up a small shopping basket before moving toward a different aisle.

Alex headed back to the register. When she saw him, he offered a friendly wave. "Good morning," he said.

"Hi." She tried to tuck a strand of hair behind her ear, but it was too short to catch. "I just have to pick up a few things."

"Let me know if you can't find what you need. Sometimes things get moved around."

She nodded before continuing down the aisle. As Alex stepped behind the register, he glanced at the video screen. Josh was fishing in the same spot, while a boat was slowly docking.

"What do you think, Daddy?" Kristen tugged on his pant leg as she held up the doll.

"Wow! She looks beautiful." Alex squatted down next to her. "And I love the coat. Vanessa gets cold sometimes, right?"

"Yup," Kristen said. "But she told me she wants to go on the swings, so she's probably going to change."

"Sounds like a good idea," Alex said. "Maybe we can all go to the park later? If you want to swing, too."

"I don't want to swing. Vanessa does. And it's all pretend, anyway, Daddy."

"Oh," he said, "okay." He stood again. *Scratch going to the park*, he thought.

Lost in her own world, Kristen began to undress the doll again. Alex checked on Josh in the monitor just as a teenager entered the store, wearing nothing but board shorts. He handed over a wad of cash.

"For the pump at the dock," he said before dashing out again.

Alex rang him up and set the pump as Katie walked to the register. Same items as always, with the addition of a tube of sunscreen. When she peeked over the counter at Kristen, Alex noticed the changeable color of her eyes.

"Did you find everything you needed?"

"Yes, thank you."

He began loading her bag. "My favorite Dickens novel is *Great Expectations*," he said. He tried to sound friendly as he put the items in her bag. "Which one is your favorite?"

Instead of answering right away, she seemed startled that he remembered that she'd told him she liked Dickens.

"*A Tale of Two Cities*," she answered, her voice soft.

"I like that one, too. But it's sad."

"Yes," she said. "That's why I like it."

Since he knew she'd be walking, he double-bagged the groceries.

"I figured that since you've already met my daughter, I should probably introduce myself. I'm Alex," he said. "Alex Wheatley."

"Her name is Miss Katie," Kristen chirped from behind him. "But I already told you that, remember?" Alex glanced over his shoulder at her. When he turned back, Katie was smiling as she handed the money to him.

"Just Katie," she said.

"It's nice to meet you, Katie." He tapped the keys and the register drawer opened with a ring. "I take it you live around here?"

She never got around to answering. Instead, when he looked up, he saw that her eyes had gone wide in fright. Swiveling around he saw what she'd caught on the monitor behind him: Josh in the water, fully clothed and arms flailing, in panic. Alex felt his throat suddenly close and he moved on instinct, rushing out from behind the counter and racing through the store and into the storeroom. Bursting through the door, he knocked over a case of paper towels, sending it flying, but he didn't slow down.

He flung open the back door, adrenaline surging through his system as he hurdled a row of bushes, taking a shortcut to the dock. He hit the wooden planks at full speed. As he launched himself from the dock, Alex could see Josh choking in the water, his arms thrashing.

His heart slamming against his rib cage, Alex sailed through the air, hitting the water only a couple of feet from Josh. The water wasn't deep—maybe six feet or so—and as he touched the soft, unsettled mud of the bottom, he sank up to his shins. He fought his way to the surface, feeling the strain in his arms as he reached for Josh.

"I've got you!" he shouted. "I've got you!"

But Josh was struggling and coughing, unable to catch his breath, and Alex fought to control him as he pulled him into shallower water. Then, with an enormous heave, he carried Josh up onto the grassy bank, his mind racing through options: CPR, stomach pumping, assisted breathing. He tried to lay Josh down, but Josh resisted. He was struggling and coughing, and though Alex could still feel the panic in his own system, he had enough presence of mind to know that it probably meant that Josh was going to be okay.

He didn't know how long it took—probably only a few seconds, but it felt a lot longer—until Josh finally gave a rattling cough, emitting a spray of water, and for the first time was able to catch his breath. He inhaled sharply and coughed again, then inhaled and coughed again, though this time it settled into something that sounded like he was clearing his throat. He drew a few long breaths, still panic-stricken, and only then did the boy seem to realize what had happened.

He reached for his dad and Alex folded him tightly in his arms. Josh began to cry, his shoulders shuddering, and Alex felt sick to his stomach at the thought of what might have been. What would have happened had he not noticed Katie staring at the monitor? What if another minute had passed? The answers to those questions left him shaking as badly as Josh.

In time, Josh's cries began to slow and he uttered the first words since Alex had pulled him from the water.

"I'm sorry, Daddy," he choked out.

"I'm sorry, too," Alex whispered in return, and still, he held on to his son, afraid that somehow, if he let go, time would start to run backward, but this time, the outcome would be different.

When he was finally able to loosen his hold on Josh, Alex found himself gazing at a crowd behind the store. Roger was there, as were the customers who'd been eating. Another pair of customers craned their necks, probably just having arrived. And of course, Kristen was there, too. Suddenly he felt like a terrible parent again, because he saw that his little girl was crying and afraid and needed him, too, even though she was nestled in Katie's arms.

It wasn't until both Josh and Alex had changed into dry clothes that Alex was able to piece together what had happened. Roger had cooked both kids hamburgers and fries, and they were all sitting at a table in the grill area, though neither of them showed any interest in eating.

"My fishing line got snagged on the boat as it was pulling out, and I didn't want to lose my fishing rod. I thought the line would snap right away but it pulled me in and I swallowed a bunch of water. Then I couldn't breathe and it felt like something was holding me down." Josh hesitated. "I think I dropped my rod in the river."

Kristen was sitting beside him, her eyes still red and puffy. She'd asked Katie to stay with her for a while, and Katie had remained at her side, holding her hand even now.

"It's okay. I'll head out there in a little while and if I can't find it, I'll get you a new one. But next time, just let go, okay?"

Josh sniffed and nodded. "I'm really sorry," he said.

"It was an accident," Alex assured him.

"But now you won't let me go fishing."

And risk losing him again? Alex thought. Not a chance. "We'll talk about that later, okay?" Alex said instead.

"What if I promise to let go the next time?"

"Like I said, we'll talk about it later. For now, why don't you eat something?"

"I'm not hungry."

"I know. But it's lunchtime and you've got to eat."

Josh reached for a French fry and took a small bite, chewing mechanically. Kristen did the same. At the table, she almost always mimicked Josh. It drove Josh crazy, but he didn't seem to have the energy right now to protest.

Alex turned to Katie. He swallowed, feeling suddenly nervous. "Can I talk to you for a minute?"

She stood up from the table and he led her away from the kids. When they were far enough away that he was sure they wouldn't hear, he cleared his throat. "I want to thank you for what you did."

"I didn't do anything," she protested.

"Yes," he said. "You did. Had you not been looking at the monitor, I wouldn't have known what was happening. I might not have reached him in time." He paused. "And also, thank you for taking care of Kristen. She's the sweetest thing in the world, but she's sensitive. I'm glad you didn't leave her alone. Even when we had to go up and change."

"I did what anyone would do," Katie insisted. In the silence that followed, she suddenly seemed to realize how close they were standing and took a half step backward. "I should really be going."

"Wait," Alex said. He walked toward the refrigerated cases at the rear of the store. "Do you like wine?"

She shook her head. "Sometimes, but—"

Before she could finish, he turned around and opened the case. He reached up and pulled out a bottle of chardonnay.

"Please," he said, "I want you to have it. It's actually a very good wine. I know you wouldn't think you could get a good bottle of wine here, but when I was in the army, I had a friend who introduced me to wine. He's kind of an amateur expert, and he's the one who picks what I stock. You'll enjoy it."

"You don't need to do that."

"It's the least I can do." He smiled. "As a way to say thank you."

For the first time since they'd met, she held his gaze. "Okay," she finally said.

After gathering her groceries, she left the store. Alex returned to the table. With a bit more cajoling, Josh and Kristen finished their lunches, while Alex went to the dock to retrieve the fishing pole. By the time he got back, Joyce was already slipping on her apron, and Alex took the kids for a bike ride. Afterward, he drove them to Wilmington, where they saw a movie and had pizza, the old standbys when it came to spending time with kids. The sun was down and they were tired when they got home, so they showered and put on their pajamas. He lay in bed between them for an hour, reading stories, before finally turning out the lights.

In the living room, he turned on the television and flipped through the channels for a while, but he wasn't in the mood to watch. Instead, he thought about Josh again, and though he knew that his son was safe upstairs, he felt a ripple of the same fear he'd felt earlier, the same sense of failure. He was doing the best he could and no one could love their kids more than he did, but he couldn't help feeling that somehow it wasn't enough.

Later, long after Josh and Kristen had fallen asleep, he went to the kitchen and pulled out a beer from the refrigerator. He nursed it as he sat on the couch. The memories of the day played in his mind, but this time, his thoughts were of his daughter and the way she'd clung to Katie, her little face buried in Katie's neck.

The last time he'd seen that, he reflected, was when Carly had been alive.

4

April gave way to May and the days continued to pass. The restaurant got steadily busier and the stash of money in Katie's coffee can grew reassuringly thick. Katie no longer panicked at the thought that she lacked the means to leave this place if she had to.

Even after paying her rent and utilities, along with food, she had extra money for the first time in years. Not a lot, but enough to make her feel light and free. On Friday morning, she stopped at Anna Jean's, a thrift shop that specialized in second-hand clothes. It took most of the morning to sift through all the clothing, but in the end, she bought two pairs of shoes, a couple of pairs of pants, shorts, three stylish T-shirts, and a few blouses, most of which were name brands of one sort or another and looked almost new. It amazed Katie to think that some women had so many nice clothes that they could donate what would probably cost a small fortune in a department store.

Jo was hanging a wind chime when Katie got home. Since that first meeting, they hadn't talked much. Jo's job, whatever it was, seemed to keep her busy and Katie was working as many shifts as she could. At night, she'd notice that Jo's lights were on, but it was too late for her to drop by, and Jo hadn't been there the previous weekend.

"Long time, no talk," Jo said with a wave. She tapped the wind chime, making it ding before crossing the yard.

Katie reached the porch and put the bags down. "Where've you been?"

Jo shrugged. "You know how it goes. Late nights, early mornings, going here and there. Half the time, I feel like I'm being pulled in every direction." She motioned to the rockers. "You mind? I need a break. I've been cleaning all morning and I just hung that thing. I like the sound, you know."

"Go ahead," Katie said.

Jo sat and rolled her shoulders, working out the kinks. "You've been getting some sun," she commented. "Did you go to the beach?"

"No," Katie said. She scooted one of the bags aside to make room for her foot. "I picked up some extra day shifts the past couple of weeks and I worked outside on the deck."

"Sun, water . . . what else is there? Working at Ivan's must be like being on vacation."

Katie laughed. "Not quite. But how about you?"

"No sun, no fun for me these days." She nodded toward the bags. "I wanted to drop by and mooch a cup of coffee this morning, but you were already gone."

"I went shopping."

"I can tell. Did you find anything you liked?"

"I think so," Katie confessed.

"Well, don't just sit there, show me what you bought."

"Are you sure?"

Jo laughed. "I live in a cottage at the end of a gravel road in the middle of nowhere and I've been washing cabinets all morning. What else do I have to excite me?"

Katie pulled out a pair of jeans and handed them over. Jo held them up, turning them from front to back. "Wow!" she said. "You must have found these at Anna Jean's. I love that place."

"How did you know I went to Anna Jean's?"

"Because it's not like any of the stores around here sell things this nice. This came from someone's closet. A rich woman's closet. A lot of the stuff is practically new." Lowering the jeans, Jo ran her finger over the stitching on the pockets. "These are great. I love the designs!" She peeked toward the bag. "What else did you get?"

Katie handed over the items one by one, listening as Jo raved about every piece. When the bag was empty, Jo sighed. "Okay, it's official. I'm jealous. And let me guess, there's nothing like any of this left in the store, is there?"

Katie shrugged, feeling suddenly sheepish. "Sorry," she said. "I was there for a while."

"Well, good for you. These are treasures."

Katie nodded toward Jo's house. "How's it coming over there?" she asked. "Have you started painting?"

"Not yet."

"Too busy at work?"

Jo made a face. "The truth is, after I got the unpacking done and I cleaned the place from top to bottom, I sort of ran out of energy. It's a good thing you're my friend, since that means I can still come over here where it's bright and cheery."

"You're welcome anytime."

"Thanks. I appreciate that. But evil Mr. Benson is going to deliver some cans of paint tomorrow. Which also explains why I'm here. I'm dreading the very idea of spending my entire weekend covered in splatter."

"It's not so bad. It goes fast."

"Do you see these hands?" Jo said, holding them up. "These were made for caressing handsome men and meant to be adorned with pretty nails and diamond rings. They're not made for paint rollers and paint splatter and that kind of manual labor."

Katie giggled. "Do you want me to come over and help?"

"Absolutely not. I'm an expert in procrastination, but the last thing I want you to think is that I'm incompetent, too. Because I'm actually pretty good at what I do."

A flock of starlings broke from the trees, moving in an almost musical rhythm. The motion of the rockers was making the porch creak slightly.

"What *do* you do?" Katie asked.

"I'm a counselor of sorts."

"For the high school?"

"No," she said, shaking her head. "I'm a grief counselor."

"Oh," Katie said. She paused. "I'm not sure what that is."

Jo shrugged. "I visit with people and try to help them. Usually, it's because someone close to them has died." She paused, and when she went on, her voice was softer. "People react in a lot of different ways and it's up to me to figure out how to help them accept what happened—and I hate that word, by the way, since I've yet to meet anyone who *wants* to *accept it*—but that's pretty much what I'm supposed to do. Because in the end, and no matter how hard it is, acceptance helps people move on with the rest of their lives. But sometimes . . ."

She trailed off. In the silence, she scratched at a piece of flaking paint on the rocker. "Sometimes, when I'm with someone, other issues come up. That's what I've been dealing with lately. Because sometimes people need help in other ways, too."

"That sounds rewarding."

"It is. Even if it has challenges." She turned toward Katie. "But what about you?"

"You know I work at Ivan's."

"But you haven't told me anything else about yourself."

"There's not much to tell," Katie protested, hoping to deflect the line of questioning.

"Of course there is. Everyone has a story." She paused. "For instance, what really brought you to Southport?"

"I already told you," Katie said. "I wanted to start over."

Jo seemed to stare right through her as she studied the answer. "Okay," she finally said, her tone light. "You're right. It's not my business."

"That's not what I said . . ."

"Yes, you did. You just said it in a nice way. And I respect your answer because you're right; it isn't my business. But just so you know, when you say you wanted to start over, the counselor in me wonders why you felt the need to start over. And more important, what you left behind."

Katie felt her shoulders tense. Sensing her discomfort, Jo went on.

"How about this?" she asked gently. "Forget I even asked the question. Just know that if you ever want to talk, I'm here, okay? I'm good at listening. Especially with friends. And believe it or not, sometimes talking helps."

"What if I can't talk about it?" Katie said in an involuntary whisper.

"Then how about this? Ignore the fact that I'm a counselor. We're just friends, and friends can talk about anything. Like where you were born or something that made you happy as a kid."

"Why is that important?"

"It isn't. And that's the point. You don't have to say anything at all that you don't want to say."

Katie absorbed her words before squinting at Jo. "You're very good at your job, aren't you?"

"I try," Jo conceded.

Katie laced her fingers together in her lap. "All right. I was born in Altoona," she said.

Jo leaned back in her rocking chair. "I've never been there. Is it nice?"

"It's one of those old railroad towns," she said, "you know the kind. A town filled with good, hardworking people who are just trying to make a better life for themselves. And it was pretty, too, especially in the fall, when the leaves began to change. I used to think there was no place more beautiful in the world." She lowered her eyes, half lost in memories. "I used to have a friend named Emily, and together we'd lay pennies on the railroad tracks. After the train went past, we'd scramble around trying to find them, and when we did, we'd always marvel at how any trace of engraving would be completely gone. Sometimes the pennies were still hot. I remember almost burning my fingers one time. When I think back on my childhood, it's mostly about small pleasures like that."

Katie shrugged, but Jo remained silent, willing her to go on.

"Anyway, that's where I went to school. All the way through. I ended up graduating from high school there, but by then, I don't know . . . I guess I was tired of . . . all of it, you know? Small-town life, where every weekend was the same. The same people going to the same parties, the same boys drinking beer in the beds of their pickup trucks. I wanted something more, but college didn't work out and, long story short, I ended up in Atlantic City. I worked there for a while, moved around a bit, and now, years later, here I am."

"In another small town where everything stays the same."

Katie shook her head. "It's different here. It makes me feel . . ."

When she hesitated, Jo finished the thought for her.

"Safe?"

When Katie's startled gaze met hers, Jo seemed bemused. "It's not that hard to figure out. Like you said, you're starting over and what better place to start over than a place like this? Where nothing ever happens?" She paused. "Well, that's not quite true. I heard there was a little excitement a couple of weeks back. When you dropped by the store?"

"You heard about that?"

"It's a small town. It's impossible not to hear about it. What happened?"

"It was scary. One minute, I was talking to Alex, and when I saw what was happening on the monitor, I guess he noticed my expression because in the next instant, he was racing past me. He moved through that store like lightning, and then Kristen saw the monitor and started to panic. I scooped her up and followed her dad. By the time I got out there, Alex was already out of the water with Josh. I'm just glad he was okay."

"Me, too." Jo nodded. "What do you think of Kristen? Isn't she just the sweetest thing?"

"She calls me Miss Katie."

"I love that little girl," Jo said, drawing her knees up to her chest. "But it doesn't surprise me that the two of you get along. Or that she reached for you when she was scared."

"Why would you say that?"

"Because she's a perceptive little thing. She knows you've got a good heart."

Katie made a skeptical face. "Maybe she was just scared about her brother, and when her dad took off I was the only one there."

"Don't sell yourself short. Like I said, she's perceptive." Jo pressed on. "How was Alex? Afterward, I mean?"

"He was still shaken up, but other than that, he seemed all right."

"Have you talked to him much since then?"

Katie gave a noncommittal shrug. "Not too much. He's always nice when I come into the store, and he stocks what I need, but that's about it."

"He's good about things like that," Jo said with assurance.

"You sound like you know him pretty well."

Jo rocked a little in her chair. "I think I do."

Katie waited for more, but Jo was silent.

"You want to talk about it?" Katie inquired innocently. "Because talking sometimes helps, especially with a friend."

Jo's eyes sparkled. "You know, I always suspected you were a lot craftier than you let on. Throwing my own words back at me. You should be ashamed."

Katie smiled but said nothing, just as Jo had done with her. And, surprising her, it worked.

"I'm not sure how much I should say," Jo added. "But I can tell you this: he's a good man. He's the kind of man you can count on to do the right thing. You can see that in how much he loves his kids."

Katie brought her lips together for a moment. "Did you two ever see each other?"

Jo seemed to choose her words carefully. "Yes, but maybe not in the way you're thinking. And just so we're clear: it was a long time ago and everyone has moved on."

Katie wasn't sure what to make of her answer but didn't want to press it. "What's his story, by the way? I take it he's divorced, right?"

"You should ask him."

"Me? Why would I want to ask him?"

"Because you asked me," Jo said, arching an eyebrow. "Which means, of course, that you're interested in him."

"I'm not interested in him."

"Then why would you be wondering about him?"

Katie scowled. "For a friend, you're kind of manipulative."

Jo shrugged. "I just tell people what they already know, but are afraid to admit to themselves."

Katie thought about that. "Just so we're clear, I'm officially taking back my offer to help you paint your house."

"You already said you'd do it."

"I know, but I'm taking back the offer."

Jo laughed. "Okay," she said. "Hey, what are you doing tonight?"

"I have to go to work in a little while. Actually, I should probably start getting ready."

"How about tomorrow night? Are you working?"

"No. I have the weekend off."

"Then how about I bring over a bottle of wine? I'm sure I'm going to need it, and I really don't want to be inhaling the paint fumes any longer than I have to. Would that be okay?"

"Actually, that sounds like fun."

"Good." Jo unfolded herself from the chair and stood. "It's a date."

5

Saturday morning dawned with blue skies, but soon clouds began rolling in. Gray and thick, they swirled and twisted in the ever-rising wind. The temperature began to plummet, and by the time Katie left the house, she had to wear a sweatshirt. The store was a little shy of two miles from her house, maybe half an hour's walk at a steady pace, and she knew she'd have to hurry if she didn't want to get caught in a storm.

She reached the main road just as she heard the thunder rumbling. She picked up the pace, feeling the air thickening around her. A truck sped past, leaving a blast of dust in its wake, and Katie moved onto the sandy median. The air smelled of salt carried from the ocean. Above her, a red-tailed hawk floated intermittently on updrafts, testing the force of the wind.

The steady rhythm of her footfalls set her mind adrift and she found herself reflecting on her conversation with Jo. Not the stories she'd told, but some of the things Jo had said about Alex. Jo, she decided, didn't know what she was talking about. While she was simply trying to make conversation, Jo had twisted her words into something that wasn't quite true. Granted, Alex seemed like a nice guy, and as Jo said, Kristen was as sweet as could be, but she wasn't *interested* in him. She barely knew him. Since Josh had fallen in the river, they hadn't said more than a few words to each other, and the last thing she wanted was a relationship of any kind.

So why had it felt like Jo was trying to bring them together?

She wasn't sure, but honestly, it didn't matter. She was glad Jo was coming over tonight. Just a couple of friends, sharing some wine . . . it wasn't that special, she knew. Other people, other women, did things like that all the time. She wrinkled her brow. All right, maybe not *all* the time, but most of them probably felt like they could do it if they wanted to, and she supposed that was the difference between her and them. How long had it been since she'd done something that felt normal?

Since her childhood, she admitted. Since those days when she'd put pennies on the track. But she hadn't been completely truthful with Jo. She hadn't told her that she often went to the railroad tracks to escape the sound of her parents arguing, their slurred voices raging at each other. She didn't tell Jo that more than once, she'd been caught in the crossfire, and that when she was twelve, she'd been hit with a snow globe that her father had thrown at her mother. It made a gash in her head that bled for hours, but neither her mom nor her dad had shown any inclination to bring her to the hospital. She didn't tell Jo that her dad was mean when he was drunk, or that she'd never invited anyone, even Emily, over to her house, or that college hadn't worked out because her parents thought it was a waste of time and money. Or that they'd kicked her out of the house on the day she graduated from high school.

Maybe, she thought, she'd tell Jo about those things. Or maybe she wouldn't. It wasn't all that important. So what if she hadn't had the best childhood? Yes, her parents were alcoholics and often unemployed, but aside from the snow-globe incident, they'd never hurt her. No, she didn't get a car or have birthday parties, but she'd never gone to bed hungry, either, and in the fall, no matter how tight things were, she always got new clothes for school. Her dad might not have been the greatest, but he hadn't snuck into her bedroom at night to do awful things, things she knew had happened to her friends. At eighteen, she didn't consider herself scarred. A bit disappointed about college, maybe, and nervous about having to make her own way in the world, but not damaged beyond repair. And she'd made it. Atlantic City hadn't been all bad. She'd met a couple of nice guys, and she could remember more than one evening she spent laughing and talking with friends from work until the early hours of the morning.

No, she reminded herself, her childhood hadn't defined her, or had anything to do with the real reason she'd come to Southport. Even though Jo was the closest thing to a friend that she had in Southport, Jo knew absolutely nothing about her. No one did.

"Hi, Miss Katie," Kristen piped up from her little table. No dolls today. Instead, she was bent over a coloring book, holding crayons and working on a picture of unicorns and rainbows.

"Hi, Kristen. How are you?"

"I'm good." She looked up from her coloring book. "Why do you always walk here?"

Katie paused, then came around the corner of the counter and squatted down to Kristen's level. "Because I don't have a car."

"Why not?"

Because I don't have a license, Katie thought. *And even if I did, I can't afford a car.* "I'll tell you what. I'll think about getting one, okay?"

"Okay," she said. She held up the coloring book. "What do you think of my picture?"

"It's pretty. You're doing a great job."

"Thanks," she said. "I'll give it to you when I'm finished."

"You don't have to do that."

"I know," she said with charming self-assurance. "But I want to. You can hang it on your refrigerator."

Katie smiled and stood up. "That's just what I was thinking."

"Do you need help shopping?"

"I think I can handle it today. And that way, you can finish coloring."

"Okay," she agreed.

Retrieving a basket, she saw Alex approaching. He waved at her, and though it made no sense she had the feeling that she was really seeing him for the first time. Though his hair was gray, there were only a few lines around the corners of his eyes, but they added to, rather than detracted from, an overall sense of vitality. His shoulders tapered to a trim waist, and she had the impression that he was a man who neither ate nor drank to excess.

"Hey, Katie. How are you?"

"I'm fine. And yourself?"

"Can't complain." He grinned. "I'm glad you came in. I wanted to show you something." He pointed toward the monitor and she saw Josh sitting on the dock holding his fishing pole.

"You let him go back out there?" she asked.

"See the vest he's wearing?"

She leaned closer, squinting. "A life jacket?"

"It took me awhile to find one that wasn't too bulky, or too hot. But this one is perfect. And really, I had no choice. You have no idea how miserable he was, not being able to fish. I can't tell you how many times he begged me to change my mind. I couldn't take it anymore, and I thought this was a solution."

"He's okay with wearing it?"

"New rule—it's either wear it, or don't fish. But I don't think he minds."

"Does he ever catch any fish?"

"Not as many as he'd like, but, yes, he does."

"Do you eat them?"

"Sometimes." He nodded. "But Josh usually throws them back. He doesn't mind catching the same fish over and over."

"I'm glad you found a solution."

"A better father probably would have figured it out before-hand."

For the first time, she looked up at him. "I get the sense you're a pretty good father."

Their eyes held for a moment before she forced herself to turn away. Alex, sensing her discomfort, began rummaging around behind the counter.

"I have something for you," he said, pulling out a bag and placing it on the counter. "There's a small farm I work with that has a hothouse, and they can grow things when other people can't. They just dropped off some fresh vegetables yesterday. Tomatoes, cucumbers, some different kinds of squash. You might want to try them out. My wife swore they were the best she'd ever tasted."

"Your wife?"

He shook his head. "I'm sorry. I still do that sometimes. I meant my late wife. She passed away a couple of years ago."

"I'm sorry," she murmured, her mind flashing back to her conversation with Jo.

What's his story?

You should ask him, Jo had countered.

Jo had obviously known that his wife had died, but hadn't said anything. Odd.

Alex didn't notice that her mind had wandered. "Thank you," he said, his voice subdued. "She was a great person. You would have liked her." A wistful expression crossed his face. "But anyway," he finally added, "she swore by the place. It's organic, and the family still harvests by hand. Usually, the produce is gone within hours, but I set a little aside for you, in case you wanted to try some." He smiled. "Besides, you're a vegetarian, right? A vegetarian will appreciate these. I promise."

She squinted up at him. "Why would you think I'm a vegetarian?"

"You're not?"

"No."

"Oh," he said, pushing his hands into his pockets. "My mistake."

"It's okay," she said. "I've been accused of worse."

"I doubt that."

Don't, she thought to herself. "Okay." She nodded. "I'll take the vegetables. And thank you."

6

As Katie shopped, Alex fiddled around the register, watching her from the corner of his eye. He straightened the counter, checked on Josh, examined Kristen's picture, and straightened the counter again, doing his best to seem busy.

She'd changed in recent weeks. She had the beginnings of a summer tan and her skin had a glowing freshness to it. She was also growing less skittish around him, today being a prime example. No, they hadn't set the world on fire with their scintillating conversation, but it was a start, right?

But the start of what?

From the very beginning, he'd sensed she was in trouble, and his instinctive response had been to want to help. And of course she was pretty, despite the bad haircut and plain-Jane attire. But it was seeing the way Katie had comforted Kristen after Josh had fallen in the water that had really moved him. Even more affecting had been Kristen's response to Katie. She had reached for Katie like a child reaching for her mother.

It had made his throat tighten, reminding him that as much as he missed having a wife, his children missed having a mother. He knew they were grieving, and he tried to make up for it as best he could, but it wasn't until he saw Katie and Kristen together that he realized that sadness was only part of what they were experiencing. Their loneliness mirrored his own.

It troubled him that he hadn't realized it before.

As for Katie, she was something of a mystery to him. There was a missing element somewhere, something that had been gnawing at him. He watched her, wondering who she really was and what had brought her to Southport.

She was standing near one of the refrigerator cases, something she'd never done before, studying the items behind the glass. She frowned, and as she was debating what to buy, he noticed the fingers of her right hand twisting around her left ring finger, toying with a ring that wasn't there. The gesture triggered something both familiar and long forgotten.

It was a habit, a tic he'd noticed during his years at CID and sometimes observed with women whose faces were bruised and disfigured. They used to sit across from him, compulsively touching their rings, as though they were shackles that bound them to their husbands. Usually, they denied that their husband had hit them, and in the rare instances they admitted the truth, they usually insisted it wasn't his fault; that they'd provoked him. They'd tell him that they'd burned dinner or hadn't done the wash or that he'd been drinking. And always, always, these same women would swear that it was the first time it had ever happened, and tell him that they didn't want to press charges because his career would be ruined. Everyone knew the army came down hard on abusive husbands.

Some were different, though—at least in the beginning—and insisted that they wanted to press charges. He would start the report and listen as they questioned why paperwork was more important than making an arrest. Than enforcing the law. He would write up the report anyway and read their own words back to them before asking them to sign it. It was then, sometimes, that their bravado would fail, and he'd catch a glimpse of the terrified woman beneath the angry surface. Many would end up not signing it, and even those who did would quickly change their minds when their husbands were brought in. Those cases went forward, no matter what the woman decided. But later, when a wife wouldn't testify, little punishment was meted out. Alex came to understand that only those who pressed charges ever became truly free, because the life they were leading was a prison, even if most of them wouldn't admit it.

Still, there was another way to escape the horror of their lives, though in all his years he'd come across only one who actually did it. He'd interviewed the woman once and she'd taken the usual route of denial and self-blame. But a couple of months later, he'd learned that she'd fled. Not to her family and not to her friends, but somewhere else, a place where even her husband couldn't find her. Her husband, lost in his fury that his wife had left, had exploded after a long night of drinking and had bloodied an MP. He ended up in Leavenworth, and Alex remembered grinning in satisfaction when he'd heard the news. And when thinking of the man's wife, he smiled, thinking, *Good for you.*

Now, as he watched Katie toying with a ring that wasn't there, he felt his old investigative instincts kick in. There'd been a husband, he thought; her husband was the missing element. Either she was still married or she wasn't, but he had an undeniable hunch that Katie was still afraid of him.

The sky exploded while she was reaching for a box of crackers. Lightning flashed, and a few seconds later thunder crackled before finally settling into a loud, angry rumble. Josh dashed inside right before the downpour started, clutching his tackle box and fishing reel as he entered the store. His face was red and he was panting like a runner crossing the finish line.

"Hey, Dad."

Alex looked up. "Catch anything?"

"Just the catfish again. The same one I catch every time."

"I'll see you in a little bit for lunch, okay?"

Josh vanished back into the storeroom and Alex heard him padding up the steps to the house.

Outside, the rain came down hard and the wind whipped sheets of water against the glass. Branches bent in the wind, bowing to a higher power. The dark sky flashed bright with lightning, and thunder boomed, loud enough to shake the windows. From across the store, Alex saw Katie flinch, her face a mask of surprise and terror, and he found himself wondering whether it was the same way her husband had once seen her.

The door of the store opened and a man rushed in, trailing water on the old wood flooring. He shook rivulets of rain from his sleeves and nodded at Alex before finally moving toward the grill.

Katie turned back to the shelf that held crackers. He didn't have a big selection, just Saltines and Ritz, the only two that sold regularly, and she reached for the Ritz.

She selected her usual items as well and carried her basket to the register. When he finished ringing up and bagging her items, Alex tapped the bag he'd put on the counter earlier.

"Don't forget the vegetables."

She glanced at the total on the register. "Are you sure you rang them up?"

"Of course."

"Because the total isn't any more than it usually is."

"I gave you the introductory price."

She frowned, wondering whether to believe him, then finally reached into the bag. She pulled out a tomato and brought it to her nose.

"It smells good."

"I had some last night. They're great with a touch of salt, and the cucumbers don't need anything."

She nodded but her gaze was focused on the door. The wind was driving rain against it in furious waves. The door creaked open, the water fighting to get inside. The world beyond the glass was blurry.

People lingered in the grill. Alex could hear them mumbling to themselves about waiting for the storm to break.

Katie drew a fortifying breath and reached for her bags.

"Miss Katie!" Kristen cried, sounding almost panicked. She stood, brandishing the picture she'd colored. She'd already torn it from the book. "You almost forgot your picture."

Katie reached for it, brightening as she examined the picture. Alex noted how—at least for an instant—everything else in the world seemed to be forgotten.

"This is beautiful," she murmured. "I can't wait to hang it up."

"I'll color another one for you the next time you come in."

"I'd like that very much," she said.

Kristen beamed before sitting at the table again. Katie rolled up the picture, making sure not to wrinkle it, and then tucked it into the bag. Lightning and thunder erupted, almost simultaneously this time. Rain hammered the ground and the parking lot was a sea of puddles. The sky was as dark as northern seas.

"Do you know how long the storm is supposed to last?" she asked.

"I heard it was supposed to last most of the day," Alex answered.

She stared out the door. As she debated what to do, she toyed again with the nonexistent ring. In the silence, Kristen tugged at her dad's shirt.

"You should drive Miss Katie home," she told him. "She doesn't have a car. And it's raining hard."

Alex looked at Katie, knowing she'd overheard Kristen. "Would you like a ride home?"

Katie shook her head. "No, that's okay."

"But what about the picture?" Kristen said. "It might get wet."

When Katie didn't answer immediately, Alex came out from

behind the register. "Come on." He motioned with his head. "There's no reason to get soaked. My car's right out back."

"I don't want to impose . . ."

"You're not imposing." He patted his pocket and pulled out his car keys before reaching for the bags. "Let me get those for you," he said, taking them. "Kristen, sweetie? Will you run upstairs and tell Josh I'll be back in ten minutes?"

"Sure, Daddy," she said.

"Roger?" he called out. "Watch the store and the kids for a bit, would you?"

"No problem." Roger waved.

Alex nodded toward the rear of the store. "You ready?" he asked.

They made a frantic dash for the jeep, wielding bent umbrellas against the gale-force winds and blankets of rain. Lightning continued to flash, making the clouds blink. Once they had settled into their seats, Katie used her hand to wipe the condensation from the window.

"I didn't think it would be like this when I left the house."

"No one ever does, until the storm hits, anyway. We get a lot of *the sky is falling* on the weather reports, so when something big does hit, people never expect it. If it's not as bad as the reports predicted, we complain. If it's worse than expected, we complain. If it's just as bad as predicted, we complain about that, too, because we'll say that the reports are wrong so often, there was no way to know they'd be right this time. It just gives people something to complain about."

"Like the people in the grill?"

He nodded and grinned. "But they're basically good people. For the most part, they're hardworking, honest, and as kind as the day is long. Any one of them would have been glad to watch the store for me if I'd asked, and they'd account for every penny.

It's like that down here. Because deep down, everyone here knows that in a small town like this, we all need one another. It's great, even if it did take some time for me to get used to it."

"You're not from here?"

"No. My wife was. I'm from Spokane. When I first moved here, I remember thinking that there wasn't a chance I'd ever stay in a place like this. I mean, it's a small Southern town that doesn't care what the rest of the world thinks. It takes a little getting used to, at first. But then . . . it grows on you. It keeps me focused on what's important."

Katie's voice was soft. "What's important?"

He shrugged. "Depends on the person, doesn't it? But right now, for me, it's about my kids. This is home for them, and after what they've been through, they need predictability. Kristen needs a place to color and dress her dolls and Josh needs a place to fish, and they both need to know that I'm around whenever they need me. This place, and the store, gives them that, and right now, that's what I want. It's what I need."

He paused, feeling self-conscious about talking so much. "By the way, where am I going, exactly?"

"Keep going straight. There's a gravel road that you'll have to turn on. It's a little bit past the curve."

"You mean the gravel road by the plantation?"

Katie nodded. "That's the one."

"I didn't even know that road went anywhere." He wrinkled his forehead. "That's quite a walk," he said. "What is it? A couple of miles?"

"It's not too bad," she demurred.

"Maybe in nice weather. But today, you'd have to swim home. There's no way you could have walked this far. And Kristen's picture would have been ruined."

He noted the flicker of a smile at Kristen's name but she said nothing.

"Someone said you work at Ivan's?" he prompted.

She nodded. "I started in March."

"How do you like it?"

"It's okay. It's just a job, but the owner has been good to me."

"Ivan?"

"You know him?"

"Everyone knows Ivan. Did you know he dresses up like a Confederate general every fall to reenact the famed Battle of Southport? When Sherman burned the town? Which is fine, of course . . . except that there was never a Battle of Southport in the Civil War. Southport wasn't even called Southport back then, it was called Smithville. And Sherman was never within a hundred miles of here."

"Seriously?" Katie asked.

"Don't get me wrong. I like Ivan—he's a good man, and the restaurant is a fixture in this town. Kristen and Josh love the hush puppies there, and Ivan's always welcoming whenever we show up. But sometimes, I've wondered what drives him. His family arrived from Russia in the fifties. First generation, in other words. No one in his extended family has probably even heard of the Civil War. But Ivan will spend an entire weekend pointing his sword and shouting orders right in the middle of the road in front of the courthouse."

"Why have I never heard about this?"

"Because it's not something the locals like to talk about. It's kind of . . . eccentric, you know? Even locals, people who really like him, try to ignore him. They'll see Ivan in the middle of downtown and they'll turn away and start saying things like, *Can you believe how beautiful those chrysanthemums are by the courthouse?*"

For the first time since she'd been in the car, Katie laughed. "I'm not sure I believe you."

"It doesn't matter. If you're here in October, you'll see for yourself. But again, don't get me wrong. He's a nice guy and the restaurant is great. After a day at the beach, we almost always stop in there. Next time we come in, we'll ask for you."

She hesitated. "Okay."

"She likes you," Alex said. "Kristen, I mean."

"I like her. She's a bright spirit—a real personality."

"I'll tell her you said that. And thanks."

"How old is she?"

"She's five. When she starts school in the fall, I don't know what I'm going to do. It'll be so quiet around the store."

"You'll miss her," Katie observed.

He nodded. "A lot. I know she'll enjoy school, but I kind of like having her around."

As he spoke, rain continued to sheet against the windows. The sky flashed on and off like a strobe, accompanied by an almost continuous rumble.

Katie peered out the passenger-side window, lost in her thoughts. He waited, somehow knowing she would break the silence.

"How long were you and your wife married?" Katie finally asked.

"Five years. We dated for a year before that. I met her when I was stationed at Fort Bragg."

"You were in the army?"

"Ten years. It was a good experience and I'm glad I did it. At the same time, I'm glad I'm done."

Katie pointed through the windshield. "There's the turn up ahead," she said.

Alex turned onto Katie's road and slowed down. The rough gravel surface had flooded during the downpour, and water splashed up to the windows and over the windshield. As he focused on steering the car through the deep puddles, Alex was suddenly struck by the thought that this was the first time he'd been alone in a car with a woman since his wife had died.

"Which one is it?" he asked, squinting at the outline of two small cottages.

"The one on the right," she said.

He turned into the makeshift drive and pulled as close to the house as he could. "I'll bring the groceries to the door for you."

"You don't have to do that."

"You don't know the way I was raised," he said, jumping out before she could object. He grabbed the bags and ran them to her porch. By the time he set them down and began to shake off, Katie was hurrying toward him, the umbrella Alex had lent her clutched in her hands.

"Thanks," she called out over the noise of the downpour.

When she offered him the umbrella, he shook his head. "Keep it for a while. Or forever. It doesn't matter. If you walk a lot around here, you're going to need it."

"I can pay you—" she began.

"Don't worry about it."

"But this is from the store."

"It's okay," he said. "Really. But if you don't think you should, then just settle up the next time you're in the store, okay?"

"Alex, really—"

He didn't let her finish. "You're a good customer, and I like to help my customers."

It took a moment for her to answer. "Thank you," she finally said, her eyes, now dark green, fixed on his. "And thanks for driving me home."

He tipped his head. "Anytime."

What to do with the kids: it was the endless, sometimes unanswerable question he faced on weekends, and as usual, he had absolutely no idea.

With the storm in full fury and showing no signs of letting up, doing anything outside was out of the question. He could take them to a movie, but there was nothing playing that they'd both be interested in. He could simply let them entertain themselves for a while. He knew lots of parents operated that way. On the other hand, his kids were still young, too young to be left completely to their own devices. More important, they were already on their own a lot, improvising ways to keep themselves entertained, simply because of his long hours at the store. He pondered the options as he made grilled cheese sandwiches, but he soon found his thoughts drifting to Katie. While she was obviously doing her best to maintain a low profile, he knew it was almost impossible in a town like this. She was too attractive to blend in, and when people caught on to the fact that she walked everywhere, it was inevitable that talk would start and questions would be asked about her past.

He didn't want that to happen. Not for selfish reasons, but because she was entitled to the kind of life she'd come here to find. A normal life. A life of simple pleasures, the kind that most people took for granted: the ability to go where she wanted when she wanted and live in a home where she felt safe and secure. She also needed a way to get around.

"Hey, kids," he said, putting their sandwiches on plates. "I have an idea. Let's do something for Miss Katie."

"Okay!" Kristen agreed.

Josh, always easygoing, simply nodded.

7

Wind-driven rain blew hard across dark North Carolina skies, sweeping rivers against the kitchen windows. Earlier that afternoon, while Katie did her laundry in the sink and after she had taped Kristen's picture to the refrigerator, the ceiling in the living room had begun to leak. She'd placed a pot beneath the drip and had already emptied it twice. In the morning, she planned to call Benson, but she doubted whether he'd get around to repairing the leak right away. If, of course, he ever got around to fixing it at all.

In the kitchen, she sliced small cubes from a block of cheddar cheese, nibbling as she moved about. On a yellow plastic plate were crackers and slices of tomatoes and cucumbers, although she couldn't arrange them to look the way she wanted. Nothing looked quite the way she wanted. In her previous home, she'd had a pretty wooden serving board and a silver cheese knife with an engraving of a cardinal, and a full set of wineglasses. She'd had a dining room table made of cherry, and sheer curtains in the windows, but here the table wobbled and the chairs didn't match, the windows were bare, and she and Jo would have to drink wine from coffee mugs. As horrible as her life had been, she'd loved assembling the pieces of her household, but as with everything she'd left behind, she now viewed them as enemies that had gone over to the other side.

Through the window, she saw one of Jo's lights blink out. Katie made her way to the front door. Opening it, she watched as Jo splashed through puddles on the way to her house, umbrella in one hand and a bottle of wine in the other. Another couple of stomps and she was on the porch, her yellow slicker dripping wet.

"Now I understand how Noah must have felt. Can you believe this storm? I've got puddles all over my kitchen."

Katie motioned over her shoulder. "My leak is in the living room."

"Home sweet home, right? Here," she said, handing over the wine. "Just like I promised. And believe me, I'm going to need it."

"Rough day?"

"Like you couldn't imagine."

"Come on in."

"Let me leave my coat out here or you're going to have two puddles in your living room," she said, shimmying out of her slicker. "I got soaked in the few seconds I was out there."

Jo tossed her coat on the rocker along with the umbrella and followed Katie inside as she led the way to the kitchen.

Katie immediately set the wine on the counter. As Jo wandered to the table, Katie pulled open the drawer by the refrigerator. From the back of the drawer, she pulled out a rusted Swiss Army knife and readied the opener.

"This is great. I'm starved. I haven't eaten all day."

"Help yourself. How did it go with the painting?"

"Well, I got the living room done. But after that, it wasn't such a good day."

"What happened?"

"I'll tell you about it later. I need wine first. How about you? What did you do?"

"Nothing much. Ran to the store, cleaned up, did my laundry."

Jo took a seat at the table and reached for a cracker. "In other words, memoir material."

Katie laughed as she began to twist the corkscrew. "Oh, yeah. Real exciting."

"Do you want me to get that?" Jo asked.

"I think I've got it."

"Good." Jo smirked. "Because I'm the guest, and I expect to be pampered."

Katie propped the bottle between her legs and the cork came out with a pop.

"Seriously, though, thanks for having me over." Jo sighed. "You have no idea how much I've been looking forward to this."

"Really?"

"Don't do that."

"Don't do what?" Katie asked.

"Act surprised that I wanted to come over. That I wanted to bond over a bottle of wine. That's what friends do." She raised an eyebrow. "Oh, and by the way, before you start wondering whether or not we're actually friends and how well we know each other, trust me when I say that yes, absolutely. I consider you a friend." She let that sink in before going on. "Now how about some wine?"

The storm finally broke in the early evening, and Katie opened the kitchen window. The temperature had dropped and the air felt cool and clean. While pockets of mist rose from the ground, rolling clouds drifted past the moon, bringing light and shadow in equal measures. Leaves turned from silver to black and silver again as they shimmered in the evening breeze.

Katie drifted dreamily on the wine, the evening breeze, and Jo's easy laughter. Katie found herself savoring every bite of the buttery crackers and sharp, rich cheese, remembering how hungry she once had been. There was a time when she'd been as thin as a heated strand of blown glass.

Her thoughts were wandering. She remembered her parents, not the hard times but the good ones, when the demons were sleeping: when her mom made eggs and bacon, the aroma filling the house, and she'd seen her father glide into the kitchen, toward her mother. He would pull aside her hair and kiss the side of her neck, making her giggle. Once, she remembered, her dad had brought them to Gettysburg. He'd taken her hand as they walked around, and she could still recall the rare sensation of strength and gentleness in his grasp. He was tall and broad-shouldered with dark brown hair and there was a navy tattoo on his upper arm. He'd served on a destroyer for four years and had been to Japan, Korea, and Singapore, though he said little else about his experience.

Her mom was petite with blond hair and had once competed in a beauty pageant, finishing as the second runner-up. She loved flowers, and in the spring she would plant bulbs in ceramic flowerpots she placed in the yard. Tulips and daffodils, peonies and violets, would explode in colors so bright they almost made Katie's eyes ache. When they moved, the flowerpots would be placed on the backseat and fastened with seat belts. Often, when she cleaned, her mother would sing to herself, melodies from childhood, some of them in Polish, and Katie would listen secretly from another room, trying to make sense of the words.

The wine Jo and Katie were drinking had hints of oak and apricots, and it tasted wonderful. Katie finished her cup and Jo poured her another. When a moth began to dance around the light above the sink, fluttering with purpose and confusion, both of them began to giggle. Katie cut more cheese and added more crackers to the plate. They talked about movies and books, and Jo shrieked with pleasure when Katie said her favorite movie was *It's a Wonderful Life*, claiming that it was her favorite movie, too. When she was younger, Katie remembered asking her mom for a bell, so she could help angels get their wings. Katie finished her second glass of wine, feeling as light as a feather on a summer breeze.

Jo asked few questions. Instead, they stuck to superficial topics, and Katie thought again that she was happy for Jo's company. When silver highlighted the world beyond the window, Katie and Jo stepped out onto the front porch. Katie could feel herself swaying slightly and she took hold of the railing. They sipped their wine as the clouds continued to break, and all at once, the sky was filled with stars. Katie pointed out the Big Dipper and Polaris, the only stars she could name, but Jo began naming dozens of others. Katie stared at the sky in wonder, amazed at how much Jo knew about the constellations, until she noticed the names Jo was reciting. "That one's called Elmer Fudd, and over there, right above that pine tree, you can make out Daffy Duck." When Katie finally realized that Jo knew as little about the stars as she did, Jo started to giggle like a mischievous kid.

Back in the kitchen, Katie poured the last of the wine and took a sip. It was warm in Katie's throat and made her feel dizzy. The moth continued to dance around the light, though if she tried to focus on it, there seemed to be two of them. She felt happy and safe and thought again how enjoyable the evening had been.

She had a friend, a real friend, someone who laughed and made jokes about the stars, and she wasn't sure if she wanted to laugh or cry because it had been so long since she'd experienced something so easy and natural.

"Are you okay?" Jo asked.

"I'm fine," Katie answered. "I was just thinking that I'm glad you came over."

Jo peered at her. "I think you might be tipsy."

"I think you might be right," Katie agreed.

"Well, okay then. What do you want to do? Since you're obviously tipsy and ready for fun."

"I don't know what you mean."

"Do you want to do something special? Head into town, find someplace exciting?"

Katie shook her head. "No."

"You don't want to meet people?"

"I'm better off alone."

Jo ran her finger around the rim of the mug before saying anything. "Trust me on this: no one is better off alone."

"I am."

Jo thought about Katie's answer before leaning closer. "So you're telling me that—assuming you had food, shelter, and clothing and anything else you needed to simply survive— you'd rather be stranded on a desert island in the middle of nowhere, all alone, forever, for the rest of your life? Be honest."

Katie blinked, trying to keep Jo in focus. "Why would you think I wouldn't be honest?"

"Because everybody lies. It's part of living in society. Don't get me wrong—I think it's necessary. The last thing anyone wants is to live in a society where total honesty prevails. Can you imagine the conversations? *You're short and fat*, one person might say, and the other might answer, *I know. But you smell bad.* It just wouldn't work. So people lie by omission all the time. People will tell you most of the story . . . and I've learned that the part they neglect to tell you is often the most important part. People hide the truth because they're afraid."

With Jo's words, Katie felt a finger touch her heart. All at once, it seemed hard to breathe.

"Are you talking about me?" she finally croaked out.

"I don't know. Am I?"

Katie felt herself pale slightly, but before she could respond, Jo smiled.

"Actually, I was thinking about my day today. I told you it was hard, right? Well, what I just told you is part of the problem. It gets frustrating when people won't tell the truth. I mean, how am I supposed to help people if they hold things back? If I don't really know what's going on?"

Katie could feel something twisting and tightening in her chest. "Maybe they want to talk about it but they know there's nothing you can do to help," she whispered.

"There's always something I can do."

In the moonlight shining through the kitchen window, Jo's skin glowed a luminous white, and Katie had the sense that she never went out in the sun. The wine made the room move, the walls buckle. Katie could feel tears beginning to form in her eyes and it was all she could do to blink them back. Her mouth was dry.

"Not always," Katie whispered. She turned to face the window. Beyond the glass, the moon hung low over the trees. Katie swallowed, suddenly feeling as if she were observing herself from across the room. She could see herself sitting at the table with Jo, and when she began to speak, her voice didn't seem to be her own. "I had a friend once. She was in a terrible marriage and she couldn't talk to anyone. He used to hit her, and in the beginning, she told him that if it ever happened again, she would leave him. He swore that it wouldn't and she believed him. But it only got worse after that, like when his dinner was cold, or when she mentioned that she'd visited with one of the neighbors who was walking by with his dog. She just chatted with him, but that night, her husband threw her into a mirror."

Katie stared at the floor. Linoleum was peeling up in the corners, but she hadn't known how to fix it. She'd tried to glue it, but the glue hadn't worked and the corners had curled again.

"He always apologized, and sometimes he would even cry because of the bruises he'd made on her arms or legs or her back. He would say that he hated what he'd done, but in the next breath tell her she'd deserved it. That if she'd been more careful, it wouldn't have happened. That if she'd been paying attention or hadn't been so stupid, he wouldn't have lost his temper. She tried to change. She worked hard at trying to be a better wife and to do things the way he wanted, but it was never enough."

Katie could feel the pressure of tears behind her eyes and though she tried again to stop them, she felt them sliding down her cheek. Jo was motionless across the table, watching her without moving.

"And she loved him! In the beginning, he was so sweet to her. He made her feel safe. On the night they met, she'd been working, and after she finished her shift, two men were following her. When she went around the corner, one of them grabbed her and clamped his hand over her mouth, and even though she tried to get away, the men were so much stronger and she didn't know what would have happened except that her future husband came around the corner and hit one of them hard on the back of the neck and he fell to the ground. And then he grabbed the other one and threw him into the wall, and it was over. Just like that. He helped her up and walked her home and the next day he took her out for coffee. He was kind and he treated her like a princess, right up until she was on her honeymoon."

Katie knew she shouldn't be telling Jo any of this, but she couldn't stop. "My friend tried to get away twice. One time, she came back on her own because she had nowhere else to go. And the second time she ran away, she thought she was finally free. But he hunted her down and dragged her back to the house. At home, he beat her and put a gun to her head and told her that if she ever ran away again, he'd kill her. He'd kill any man she cared for. And she believed him, because by then, she knew he was crazy. But she was trapped. He never gave her any money, he never allowed her to leave the house. He used to drive by the house when he was supposed to be working, just to make sure she was there. He monitored the phone records and called all the time, and he wouldn't let her get a driver's license. One time, when she woke up in the middle of the night, she found him standing over the bed, just staring at her. He'd been drinking and holding the gun again and she was too scared to say anything other than to ask him to come to bed. But that was when she knew that if she stayed, the husband would eventually kill her."

Katie swiped at her eyes, her fingers slick with salty tears. She could barely breathe but the words kept coming. "She started to steal money from his wallet. Never more than a dollar or two, because otherwise he would notice. Normally, he locked his wallet up at night, but sometimes, he would forget. It took so long to get enough money for her to escape. Because that's what she had to do. Escape. She had to go someplace where he would never find her, because she knew he wouldn't stop searching for her. And she couldn't tell anyone anything, because her family was gone and she knew the police wouldn't do anything. If he so much as suspected anything, he would kill her. So she stole and saved and found coins in the sofa cushions and in the washing machine. She hid the money in a plastic bag that she put beneath a flowerpot, and every time he went outside she was sure he would find it. It took so long to get the money she needed because she had to have enough to get far away so that he'd never find her. So that she could start over again."

Katie wasn't aware of when it had happened, but she realized that Jo had taken her hand and she was no longer watching herself from across the room. She could taste salt on her lips and imagined that her soul was leaking out. She wanted desperately to sleep.

In the silence Jo continued to hold her gaze. "Your friend has a lot of courage," she said quietly.

"No," Katie said. "My friend is scared all the time."

"That's what courage is. If she weren't scared, she wouldn't need courage in the first place. I admire what she did." Jo gave her hand a squeeze. "I think I'd like your friend. I'm glad you told me about her."

Katie glanced away, feeling utterly drained. "I probably shouldn't have told you all that."

Jo shrugged. "I wouldn't worry too much. One thing you'll learn about me is that I'm good with secrets. Especially when it comes to people I don't know, right?"

Katie nodded. "Right."

Jo stayed with Katie for another hour, but steered the conversation toward easier ground. Katie talked about working at Ivan's and some of the customers she was getting to know. Jo asked about the best way to get the paint out from under her fingernails. With the wine gone, Katie's dizziness began to fade, leaving in its wake a sense of exhaustion. Jo, too, began to yawn, and they finally rose from the table. Jo helped Katie clean up, though there wasn't much to do aside from washing a couple of dishes, and Katie walked her to the door.

As Jo stepped onto the porch, she paused. "I think we had a visitor," she said.

"What are you talking about?"

"There's a bicycle leaning against your tree."

Katie followed her outside. Beyond the yellow glow of the porch light, the world was dark and the outlines of the distant pine trees reminded Katie of the ragged edge of a black hole. Fireflies mimicked the stars, twinkling and blinking, and Katie squinted, realizing that Jo was right.

"Whose bicycle is that?" Katie asked.

"I don't know."

"Did you hear anyone come up?"

"No. But I think someone left it for you. See?" She pointed. "Isn't that a bow on the handlebars?"

Katie squinted, spotting the bow. A woman's bike, it had

wire baskets on each side of the rear wheel, as well as another wire basket on the front. A chain was wrapped loosely around the seat, with the key still in the lock. "Who would bring me a bicycle?"

"Why do you keep asking me these questions? I don't know what's going on any more than you do."

Katie and Jo stepped off the porch. Though the puddles had largely vanished, sinking into the sandy loam, the grass held on to the rain and dampened the tips of her shoes as Katie moved through it. She touched the bicycle, then the bow, rubbing the ribbon between her fingers like a rug merchant. A card was tucked beneath it, and Katie reached for it.

"It's from Alex," she said, sounding baffled.

"Alex the store guy Alex, or another Alex?"

"The store guy."

"What does it say?"

Katie shook her head, trying to make sense of it before holding it out. *I thought you might enjoy this.*

Jo tapped the note. "I guess that means he's as interested in you as you are in him."

"I'm not interested in him!"

"Of course not." Jo winked. "Why would you be?"

8

Alex was sweeping the floor near the coolers when Katie entered the store. He had guessed that she would show up to talk to him about the bicycle first thing in the morning. After leaning the broom handle against the glass, he retucked his shirt and ran a quick hand through his hair. Kristen had been waiting for her all morning and she'd already popped up before the door had even closed.

"Hey, Miss Katie!" Kristen said. "Did you get the bicycle?"

"I did. Thank you," Katie answered. "That's why I'm here."

"We worked really hard on it."

"You did a great job," she said. "Is your dad around?"

"Uh-huh. He's right over there." She pointed. "He's coming."

Alex watched as Katie turned toward him.

"Hey, Katie," he said.

When he was close, she crossed her arms. "Can I talk to you outside for a minute?"

He could hear the coolness in her voice and knew she was doing her best not to show her anger in front of Kristen.

"Of course," he said, reaching for the door. Pushing it open, he followed her outside and found himself admiring her figure as she headed toward the bicycle.

Stopping near the bike, she turned to face him. In the front basket was the umbrella she'd borrowed the day before. She patted the seat, her face serious. "Can I ask what this is about?"

"Do you like it?"

"Why did you buy it for me?"

"I didn't buy it for you," he said.

She blinked. "But your note . . ."

He shrugged. "It's been in the shed collecting dust for the last couple of years. Believe me, the last thing I'd do is buy you a bicycle."

Her eyes flashed. "That's not the point! You keep giving me things and you've got to stop. I don't want anything from you. I don't need an umbrella or vegetables or wine. And I don't need a bike!"

"Then give it away." He shrugged. "Because I don't want it, either."

She fell silent and he watched as confusion gave way to frustration, then finally futility. In the end, she shook her head and turned to leave. Before she could take a step, he cleared his throat. "Before you go, though, would you at least do me the favor of listening to my explanation?"

She glared at him over her shoulder. "It doesn't matter."

"It might not matter to you, but it matters to me."

Her eyes held his, wavering before they finally dropped. When she sighed, he motioned to the bench in front of the store. He'd originally placed it there, wedged between the ice maker and a rack of propane tanks, as a joke, knowing that it would sit unused. Who would want to stare at a parking lot and the road out front? To his surprise, on most days it was almost always occupied; the only reason it was empty now was because it was so early.

Katie hesitated before taking a seat, and Alex laced his fingers together in his lap.

"I wasn't lying about the fact that the bike has been collecting dust for the last couple of years. It used to belong to my wife," Alex said. "She loved that bike and she rode it all the time. Once, she even rode it all the way to Wilmington, but of course, by the time she got there, she was tired and I had to go pick her up, even though I didn't have anyone to mind the store. I literally had to close the place up for a couple of hours." He paused. "That was the last ride she took on it. That night, she had her first seizure and I had to rush her to the hospital. After that, she got progressively sicker, and she never rode again. I put the bike in the garage, but every time I see it, I can't help but think back on that horrible night." He straightened up. "I know I should have already gotten rid of it, but I just couldn't give it to someone who'd ride it once or twice and then forget about it. I wanted it to go to someone who would appreciate it as much as she did. To someone who was going to use it. That's what my wife would have wanted. If you'd known her, you'd understand. You'd be doing me a favor."

When she spoke, her voice was subdued. "I can't take your wife's bike."

"So you're still giving it back?"

When she nodded, he leaned forward, propping his elbows on his knees. "You and I are a lot more alike than you realize. In your shoes, I would have done exactly the same thing. You don't want to feel like you owe anyone anything. You want to prove to yourself that you can make it on your own, right?"

She opened her mouth to answer but said nothing. In the silence, he went on.

"After my wife died, I was the same way. For a long time. People would drop by the store and a lot of them would tell me to call them if I ever needed anything. Most of them knew I didn't have any family here and they meant well, but I never called anyone because it just wasn't me. Even if I did want something, I wouldn't have known how to ask, but most of the time, I didn't even know what it was that I wanted. All I knew was that I was at the end of my rope, and to continue the metaphor, for a long time, I was barely hanging on. I mean, all at once, I had to take care of two young kids as well as the store, and the kids were younger then and needed even more attention than they do now. And then one day, Joyce showed up." He looked at her. "Have you met Joyce yet? Works a few afternoons a week including Sundays, older lady, talks to everyone? Josh and Kristen love her."

"I'm not sure."

"It's not important. But anyway, she showed up one afternoon, maybe around five or so, and she simply told me that she was going to take care of the kids while I spent the next week at the beach. She'd already arranged a place for me and she told me that I didn't have a choice in the matter because, in her opinion, I was heading straight for a nervous breakdown."

He pinched the bridge of his nose, trying to stifle the memory of those days. "I was upset about it at first. I mean, they're my kids, right? And what kind of father was I to make people think that I couldn't handle being a father? But unlike anyone else, Joyce didn't ask me to call if I needed anything. She knew what I was going through and she went ahead and did what she thought was right. The next thing I knew, I was on my way to the beach. And she was right. The first two days, I was still a wreck. But over the next few days, I went for long walks, read some books, slept late, and by the time I got back, I realized that I was more relaxed than I'd been in a long time . . ."

He trailed off, feeling the weight of her scrutiny.

"I don't know why you're telling me this."

He turned toward her. "Both of us know that if I'd asked if you wanted the bicycle, you would have said no. So, like Joyce did with me, I just went ahead and did it because it was the right thing to do. Because I learned that it's okay to accept some help every now and then." He nodded toward the bike.

"Take it," he said. "I have no use for it, and you have to admit that it would make getting to and from work a whole lot easier."

It took a few seconds before he saw her shoulders relax and she turned to him with a wry smile. "Did you practice that speech?"

"Of course." He tried to look sheepish. "But you'll take it?"

She hesitated. "A bike might be nice," she finally admitted. "Thank you."

For a long moment, neither of them said anything. As he stared at her profile, he noted again how pretty she was, though he had the sense that she didn't think so. Which only made her even more appealing.

"You're welcome," he said.

"But no more freebies, okay? You've done more than enough for me already."

"Fair enough." He nodded toward the bike. "Did it ride okay? With the baskets, I mean?"

"It was fine. Why?"

"Because Kristen and Josh helped me put them on yesterday. One of those rainy-day projects, you know? Kristen picked them out. Just so you know, she also thought you needed sparkly handlebar grips, too, but I drew the line at that."

"I wouldn't have minded sparkly handlebar grips."

He laughed. "I'll let her know."

She hesitated. "You're doing a good job, you know. With your kids, I mean."

"Thank you."

"I mean it. And I know it hasn't been easy."

"That's the thing about life. A lot of the time, it isn't easy at all. We just have to try to make the best of it. Do you know what I mean?"

"Yeah," she said. "I think I do."

The door to the store opened, and as Alex leaned forward he saw Josh scanning the parking lot, Kristen close behind him. With brown hair and brown eyes, Josh resembled his mom. His hair was a riotous mess, and Alex knew he'd just crawled out of bed.

"Over here, guys."

Josh scratched his head as he shuffled toward them. Kristen beamed, waving at Katie.

"Hey, Dad?" Josh asked.

"Yeah?"

"We wanted to ask if we're still going to the beach today. You promised to take us."

"That was the plan."

"With a barbecue?"

"Of course."

"Okay," he said. He rubbed his nose. "Hi, Miss Katie."

Katie waved at Josh and Kristen.

"Do you like the bike?" Kristen chirped.

"Yes. Thank you."

"I had to help my dad fix it," Josh informed her. "He's not too good with tools."

Katie glanced at Alex with a smirk. "He didn't mention that."

"It's okay. I knew what to do. But he had to help me with the new inner tube."

Kristen fixed her gaze on Katie. "Are you going to come to the beach, too?"

Katie sat up straighter. "I don't think so."

"Why not?" Kristen asked.

"She's probably working," Alex said.

"Actually, I'm not," she said. "I have a couple of things to do around the house."

"Then you have to come," Kristen cried. "It's really fun."

"That's your family time," she insisted. "I wouldn't want to be in the way."

"You won't be in the way. And it's really fun. You can watch me swim. Please?" Kristen begged.

Alex stayed quiet, loath to add pressure. He assumed Katie would say no, but surprising him, she nodded slightly. When she spoke, her voice was soft.

"Okay," she finally said.

9

After getting back from the store, Katie parked the bike at the back of the cottage and went inside to change. She didn't have a bathing suit, but she wouldn't have worn one even if she did. As natural as it was for a teenager to walk around in front of strangers in the equivalent of underwear and a bra, she wasn't comfortable wearing something like that in front of Alex on a day out with his kids. Or frankly, even without the kids.

Though she resisted the idea, she had to admit he intrigued her. Not because of the things he'd done for her, as touching as that was. It had more to do with the sad way he smiled sometimes, the expression on his face when he'd told her about his wife, or the way he treated his kids. There was a loneliness within him that he couldn't disguise, and she knew that in some way it matched her own.

She knew he was interested in her. She'd been around long enough to recognize when men found her attractive; the clerk at the grocery store talking too much or a stranger glancing her way, or a waiter at a restaurant checking on their table just a bit too frequently. In time, she'd learned to pretend she was oblivious to the attention of those men; in other instances, she showed obvious disdain, because she'd known what would happen if she didn't. Later. Once they got home. Once they were alone.

But that life was gone now, she reminded herself. Opening the drawers, she pulled out a pair of shorts and the sandals she'd picked up at Anna Jean's. The night before, she'd had wine with a friend, and now she was going to the beach with Alex and his family. These were ordinary events in an ordinary life. The concept felt alien, like she was learning the customs of a foreign land, and it left her feeling strangely elated and wary at exactly the same time.

As soon as she finished dressing, she saw Alex's jeep coming up the gravel road and she drew a long breath as he pulled to a stop in front of her house. Now or never, she thought to herself as she stepped out onto the porch.

"You need to put on your seat belt, Miss Katie," Kristen said from behind her. "My dad won't drive unless you're wearing it."

Alex looked over at her, as if to say, *Are you ready for this?* She gave him her bravest smile.

"Okay," he said, "let's go."

They reached the coastal town of Long Beach, complete with saltbox houses and expansive views of the sea, in less than an hour. Alex pulled into a small parking lot nestled against the dunes; saw grass billowed nearby in the stiff sea breeze. Katie got out of the car and stared at the ocean, breathing deeply.

The kids climbed out and immediately made for the path between the dunes.

"I'm going to check the water, Dad!" Josh shouted, holding up his mask and snorkel.

"Me, too!" Kristen added, trailing behind.

Alex was busy unloading the back of the jeep. "Hold up," he called out. "Just wait, okay?"

Josh sighed, his impatience obvious as he shifted from one foot to the other. Alex began pulling out the cooler.

"Do you need some help?" Katie asked.

He shook his head. "I can handle this. But would you mind putting some sunscreen on the kids and keeping an eye on them for a few minutes? I know they're excited to be here."

"That's fine," she said, turning to Kristen and Josh. "Are you two ready?"

Alex spent the next few minutes ferrying the items from the car, setting up camp near the picnic table closest to the dune, where high tide wouldn't encroach. Though there were a few other families, for the most part they had this section of beach to themselves. Katie had slipped off her sandals and was standing at the water's edge as the kids splashed in the shallows. Her arms were crossed and even from a distance, Alex noticed a rare expression of contentment on her face.

He slung a couple of towels over his shoulder as he approached. "It's hard to believe there was a storm yesterday, isn't it?"

She turned at the sound of his voice. "I forgot how much I missed the ocean."

"Been awhile?"

"Too long," she said, listening to the steady rhythm of the waves as they gently rolled ashore.

Josh ran in and out of the waves, while off to the side Kristen crouched, searching for collectible seashells.

"It must be hard sometimes, raising them on your own," Katie observed.

Alex hesitated, considering it. When he spoke, his voice was soft. "Most of the time, it isn't so bad. We kind of get into a rhythm, you know? In our daily lives? It's when we do things like this—where there is no rhythm—that it sometimes gets frustrating." He kicked briefly at the sand, making a small furrow at their feet. "When my wife and I talked about having a third child, she tried to warn me that a third child would mean moving from 'man-to-man' to 'zone' defense. She used to joke that she wasn't sure I was up to it. But here I am, in zone defense every day . . ." he trailed off, shaking his head. "Sorry. I shouldn't have said that."

"Said what?"

"It seems like every time I talk to you, I end up talking about my wife."

For the first time, she turned to him. "Why shouldn't you talk about your wife?"

He pushed a pile of sand back and forth, smoothing over the ditch he'd just made. "Because I don't want you to think that I can't talk about anything else. That all I do is live in the past."

"You loved her very much, didn't you?"

"Yes," he answered.

"And she was a major part of your life and the mother of your kids, right?"

"Yes."

"Then it's okay to talk about her," she said. "You should talk about her. She's part of who you are."

Alex flashed a grateful smile but couldn't think of anything to say. Katie seemed to read his mind, and when she spoke, her voice was gentle. "How did the two of you meet?"

"We met in a bar, of all places. She was out with some girl-friends celebrating someone's birthday. It was hot and crowded and the lights were low and the music was loud, and she just . . . stood out. I mean, all her friends were a little out of control and it was obvious that all of them were having a good time, but she was as cool as can be."

"I'll bet she was beautiful, too."

"That goes without saying," he said. "So, swallowing my nervousness, I wandered over and proceeded to use every ounce of charm I had at my disposal."

When he paused, he noticed the smile playing at the corners of her lips.

"And?" she asked.

"And it still took me three hours to get so much as a name and phone number from her."

She laughed. "And let me guess. You called the next day, right? And asked her out?"

"How would you know that?"

"You seem like the type."

"Spoken like someone who's been hit on more than a few times."

She shrugged, leaving it open to interpretation. "Then what?"

"Why do you want to hear this?"

"I don't know," she admitted. "But I do."

He studied her. "Fair enough," he finally said. "So anyway— as you already magically knew—I asked her out to lunch and we spent the rest of the afternoon talking. That weekend, I told her that the two of us would get married one day."

"You're kidding."

"I know it sounds crazy. Believe me, she thought it was crazy, too. But I just . . . knew. She was smart and kind and we had a lot in common and we wanted the same things in life. She laughed a lot and she made me laugh, too . . . honestly, of the two of us, I was the lucky one."

Rollers continued to ride the ocean breeze, pushing over her ankles. "She probably thought she was lucky, too."

"That's only because I was able to fool her."

"I doubt that."

"That's because I'm able to fool you, too."

She laughed. "I don't think so."

"You're just saying that because we're friends."

"You think we're friends?"

"Yeah," he said, holding her gaze. "Don't you?"

He could tell by her expression that the idea surprised her, but before she could answer, Kristen came splashing toward them, holding a fistful of seashells.

"Miss Katie!" she cried. "I found some really pretty ones!"

Katie bent lower. "Can you show me?"

Kristen held them out, dumping them into Katie's hand before turning toward Alex. "Hey, Daddy?" she asked. "Can we get the barbecue started? I'm really hungry."

"Sure, sweetie." He took a few steps down the beach, watching his son diving in and out of the waves. As Josh popped back up, Alex cupped his mouth. "Hey, Josh?" he shouted. "I'm going to start the coals, so why don't you come in for a while."

"Now?" Josh shouted back.

"Just for a little while."

Even from a distance, he saw his son's shoulders droop. Katie must have noticed it as well, because she was quick to speak up.

"I can stay down here if you want," she assured him.

"You sure?"

"Kristen's showing me her seashells," she said.

He nodded and turned back to Josh. "Miss Katie's going to watch you, okay? So don't go out too far!"

"I won't!" he said, grinning.

10

A little while later, Katie led a shivering Kristen and excited Josh back toward the blanket Alex had spread out earlier. The grill had been set up and the briquettes were already glowing white on the edges.

Alex unfolded the last of the beach chairs onto the blanket and watched them approach. "How was the water, guys?"

"Awesome!" Josh answered. His hair, partially dried, was pointing in every direction. "When's lunch?"

Alex checked the coals. "Give me about twenty minutes."

"Can me and Kristen go back to the water?"

"You just got out of the water. Why don't you take a break for a few minutes?"

"We don't want to swim. We want to build sand castles," he said.

Alex noted Kristen's chattering teeth. "Are you sure you want to do that? You're purple."

Kristen nodded vehemently. "I'm okay," she said shivering. "And we're supposed to build castles at the beach."

"All right. But let's throw shirts on you two. And stay right there where I can see you," he said, pointing.

"I know, Dad." Josh sighed. "I'm not a little kid anymore."

Alex rummaged through a duffel bag and helped both Josh and Kristen put their shirts on. When he was finished, Josh grabbed a bag full of plastic toys and shovels and ran off, stopping a few feet from the water's edge. Kristen trailed behind him.

"Do you want me to head down there?" Katie asked.

He shook his head. "No, they'll be okay. This is the part they're used to. When I'm cooking, I mean. They know to stay out of the water."

Moving to the cooler, he squatted down and opened the lid. "Are you getting hungry, too?" he asked.

"A little," she said before realizing that she hadn't eaten anything since the cheese and wine she'd had the evening before. On cue, she heard her stomach growl and she crossed her arms over it.

"Good, because I'm starved." As Alex began rummaging through the cooler, Katie noticed the sinewy muscles of his forearm. "I was thinking hot dogs for Josh, a cheeseburger for Kristen, and for you and me, steaks." He pulled out the meat and set it aside, then leaned over the grill, blowing on the coals.

"Can I help with anything?"

"Would you mind putting the tablecloth on the table? It's in the cooler."

"Sure," Katie said. She pulled one of the bags of ice out of the cooler and simply stared. "There's enough food for half a dozen families in here," she said.

"Yeah, well, with kids, my motto has always been bring too much rather than not enough, since I never know exactly what they'll eat. You can't imagine how many times we've come out here and I've forgotten something and have had to load the kids back up and run to the store. I wanted to avoid that today."

She unfolded the plastic tablecloth and, at Alex's direction, secured the corners with paperweights he had somehow thought to bring.

"What next? Do you want me to put everything else on the table?"

"We've got a few minutes. And I don't know about you, but I'm ready for a beer," he said. Reaching into the cooler, he pulled out a bottle. "You?"

"I'll take a soda," she said.

"Diet Coke?" he asked, reaching back in.

"Great."

When he passed the can to her, his hand brushed against hers, though she wasn't sure he even noticed.

He motioned to the chairs. "Would you like to sit?"

She hesitated before taking a seat next to him. When he'd set them up, he'd left enough distance between them so that they wouldn't accidentally touch. Alex twisted the cap from his beer and took a pull. "There's nothing better than a cold beer on a hot day at the beach."

She smiled, slightly disconcerted at being alone with him. "I'll take your word for it."

"You don't like beer?"

Her mind flashed to her father and the empty cans of Pabst Blue Ribbon that usually littered the floor next to the recliner where he sat. "Not too much," she admitted.

"Just wine, huh?"

It took her a moment to remember that he'd given her a bottle. "I had some wine last night, as a matter of fact. With my neighbor."

"Yeah? Good for you."

She searched for a safe topic. "You said you were from Spokane?"

He stretched his legs out in front of him, crossing them at the ankles. "Born and raised. I lived in the same house until I went to college." He cast a sidelong glance at her. "University of Washington, by the way. Go, Huskies."

She smiled. "Do your parents still live there?"

"Yes."

"That must make it hard for them to visit the grandkids."

"I suppose."

Something in his tone caught her attention. "You suppose?"

"They're not the kind of grandparents who would come by, even if they were closer. They've seen the kids only twice, once when Kristen was born and the second time at the funeral." He shook his head. "Don't ask me to explain it," he went on, "but my parents have no interest in them, aside from sending them cards on their birthdays and gifts at Christmas. They'd rather travel or do whatever it is they do."

"Huh?"

"What can I do? And besides, I can't say they were all that different with me, even though I was their youngest child. The first time they visited me in college was graduation day, and even though I swam well enough to get a full scholarship, they saw me race only twice. Even if I lived across the street from them, I doubt they'd want to see the kids. That's one of the reasons I stayed here. I might as well, right?"

"What about the other set of grandparents?"

He scratched at the label on his bottle of beer. "That's trickier. They had two other daughters who moved to Florida, and after they sold me the store, they moved down there. They come up once or twice a year to visit for a few days, but it's still hard for them. And they won't stay at the house, either, because I think it reminds them of Carly. Too many memories."

"In other words, you're pretty much on your own."

"It's just the opposite," he said, nodding toward the kids. "I have them, remember?"

"It has to be hard sometimes, though. Running the store, raising your kids."

"It's not so bad. As long as I'm up by six in the morning and don't go to bed until midnight, it's easy to keep up."

She laughed easily. "Do you think the coals are getting close?"

"Let me check," he said. After setting the bottle in the sand, he stood up from his chair and walked over to the grill. The briquettes were white and heat rose in shimmering waves. "Your timing is impeccable," he said. He threw the steaks and the hamburger patty on the grill while Katie went to the cooler and started bringing the endless array of items to the table: Tupperware containers of potato salad, coleslaw, pickles, a green bean salad, sliced fruit, two bags of chips, slices of cheese, and assorted condiments.

She shook her head as she started arranging everything, thinking that Alex somehow forgot that his kids were still little. There was more food here than she'd kept in her house the entire time she'd lived in Southport.

Alex flipped the steaks and the hamburger patty and then added the hot dogs to the grill. As he did, he found his gaze drifting to Katie's legs as she moved around the table, noting again how attractive she was.

She seemed to realize he was staring. "What?" she asked.

"Nothing," he said.

"You were thinking about something."

He sighed. "I'm glad you decided to come today," he finally said. "Because I'm having a great time."

As Alex hovered over the grill, they settled into easy conversation. Alex gave her an overview of what it was like to run a country store. He told her how his in-laws had started the business and described with affection some of the regulars, people who could best be described as eccentric, and Katie silently wondered whether she would have been included in that description had he brought someone else to the beach.

Not that it would have mattered. The more he talked, the more she realized that he was the kind of man who tried to find the best in people, the kind of man who didn't like to complain. She tried and failed to imagine what he'd been like when he was younger, and gradually she steered the conversation in that direction. He talked about growing up in Spokane and the long, lazy weekends he spent riding bikes along the Centennial Trail with friends; he told her that once he discovered swimming, it quickly became an obsession. He swam four or five hours a day and had Olympic dreams, but a torn rotator cuff in his sophomore year of college put an end to those. He told her about the fraternity parties he'd attended and the friends he'd made in college, and admitted that nearly all of those friendships had slowly but surely drifted away. As he talked, Katie noticed that he didn't seem to either embellish or downplay his past, nor did he appear to be overly preoccupied with what others thought of him.

She could see the traces of the elite athlete he once had been, noting the graceful, fluid way he moved and the easy way he smiled, as if long accustomed to both victory and defeat. When he paused, she worried that he would ask about her past, but he seemed to sense that it would make her uncomfortable and would instead launch into another story.

When the food was ready, he called the kids and they came running. They were covered in sand, and Alex had them stand to the side while he brushed them off. Watching him, she knew he was a better father than he gave himself credit for; good, she suspected, in all the ways that mattered.

Once the kids got to the table, the conversation shifted. She listened as they chattered on about their sand castle and one of the shows on the Disney Channel they both enjoyed. When they wondered aloud about the s'mores they were supposed to have later—marshmallows, chocolate bars, and graham crackers, warmed until melting—it was clear that Alex had created special, fun traditions for his kids. He was different, she thought, from the men she'd met in her past, different from anyone she'd met before, and as the conversation rambled on, any vestiges of the nervousness she'd once felt began to slip away.

The food was delicious, a welcome change from her recent

austere diet. The sky remained clear, the blue expanse broken only by an occasional seabird passing overhead. The breeze rose and fell, enough to keep them cool, and the steady rhythm of the waves added to the sense of calm.

When they finished eating, Josh and Kristen helped clear the table and pack away the uneaten items. A few items that wouldn't spoil—the pickles and the chips—were left on the table. The kids wanted to go boogie boarding, and after Alex reapplied their suntan lotion, he slipped off his shirt and followed them into the waves.

Katie carried her chair to the water's edge and spent the next hour watching as he helped the kids through the breakers, moving one and then the other into position to catch the waves. The kids were squealing with delight, obviously having the time of their lives. She marveled at the way Alex was able to make each of them feel like the center of attention. There was a tenderness in the way he treated them, a depth of patience that she hadn't quite expected. As the afternoon wore on and the clouds began to drift in, she found herself smiling at the thought that for the first time in many years, she felt completely relaxed. And not only that, she knew she was having as much fun as the kids.

11

After they got out of the water, Kristen declared that she was cold and Alex led her to the bathroom to help her change into dry clothes. Katie stayed with Josh on the blanket, admiring the way the sunlight rippled on the water while Josh scooped sand into little piles.

"Hey, do you want to help me fly my kite?" Josh suddenly asked.

"I don't know that I've ever flown a kite before . . ."

"It's easy," he insisted, digging around in the pile of toys Alex had brought and pulling out a small kite. "I can show you how. C'mon."

He took off running down the beach, and Katie jogged a few steps before settling back into a brisk walk. By the time she reached him, he was already beginning to unwind the string and he handed her the kite. "Just hold this above your head, okay?"

She nodded as Josh started to back up slowly, continuing to loosen the string with practiced ease.

"Are you ready?" he shouted as he finally came to a stop. "When I take off running and yell, just let go!"

"I'm ready!" she shouted back.

Josh started running, and when Katie felt the tension in the kite and heard him shout, she released it immediately. She wasn't sure the breeze was strong enough, but the kite shot straight to the sky within seconds. Josh stopped and turned around. As she walked toward him, he let out even more line.

Reaching his side, she shielded her eyes from the sun as she watched the slowly rising kite. Black and yellow, the distinctive Batman logo was visible even from a distance.

"I'm pretty good at flying kites," he said, staring up at it. "How come you've never flown one?"

"I don't know. It just wasn't something I did as a kid."

"You should have. It's fun."

Josh continued to stare upward, his face a mask of concentration. For the first time, Katie noticed how much Josh and Kristen looked alike.

"How do you like school? You're in kindergarten, right?"

"It's okay. I like recess best. We have races and stuff."

Of course, she thought. Since they had arrived at the beach, he'd barely stopped moving. "Is your teacher nice?"

"She's really nice. She's kind of like my dad. She doesn't yell or anything."

"Your dad doesn't yell?"

"No," he said with great conviction.

"What does he do when he gets mad?"

"He doesn't get mad."

Katie studied Josh, wondering if he was serious before realizing that he was.

"Do you have a lot of friends?" he asked.

"Not too many. Why?"

"Because my dad says that you're his friend. That's why he brought you to the beach."

"When did he say that?"

"When we were in the waves."

"What else did he say?"

"He asked us if it bothered us that you came."

"Does it?"

"Why should it?" He shrugged. "Everybody needs friends, and the beach is fun."

No argument there. "You're right," she said.

"My mom used to come with us out here, you know."

"She did?"

"Yeah, but she died."

"I know. And I'm sorry. That must be hard. You must miss her very much."

He nodded and for an instant, he looked both older and younger than his age. "My dad gets sad sometimes. He doesn't think I know, but I can tell."

"I'd be sad, too."

He was quiet as he thought about her answer. "Thanks for helping me with my kite," he said.

"You two seemed to be having a good time," Alex observed.

After Kristen had changed, Alex helped her get her kite in the air and then went to stand with Katie on the compact sand near the water's edge. Katie could feel her hair moving slightly in the breeze.

"He's sweet. And more talkative than I thought he'd be."

As Alex watched his kids managing their kites, she had the sense that his eyes missed nothing.

"So this is what you do on weekends after you leave the store. You spend time with the kids?"

"Always," he said. "I think it's important."

"Even though it sounds like your parents felt differently?"

He hesitated. "That would be the easy answer, right? I felt slighted somehow and made a promise to myself to be different? It sounds good, but I don't know if it's totally accurate. The truth is that I spend time with them because I enjoy it. I enjoy them. I like watching them grow up and I want to be part of that."

As he answered, Katie found herself remembering her own childhood, trying and failing to imagine either of her parents echoing Alex's sentiments.

"Why did you join the army after you got out of school?"

"At the time, I thought it was the right thing to do. I was up for a new challenge, I wanted to try something different, and joining gave me an excuse to leave Washington. With the exception of a couple of swim meets here and there, I'd never even left the state."

"Did you ever see . . . ?"

When she trailed off, he finished her sentence. "Combat? No, I wasn't that kind of army. I was a criminal justice major in college and I ended up in CID."

"What's that?"

When he told her, she turned toward him. "Like the police?"

He nodded. "I was a detective," he said.

Katie said nothing. Instead, she turned away abruptly, her face closing down like a gate slamming shut.

"Did I say something wrong?" he asked.

She shook her head without answering. Alex stared at her, wondering what was going on. His suspicions about her past surfaced almost immediately.

"What's going on, Katie?"

"Nothing," she insisted, but as soon as the word came out, he knew she wasn't telling the truth. In another place and time, he would have followed up with another question, but instead, he let it drop.

"We don't have to talk about it," he said quietly. "And besides, it's not who I am anymore. Believe me when I say I'm a lot happier running a general store."

She nodded, but he sensed a trace of lingering anxiety. He could tell she needed space, even if he wasn't sure why. He motioned over his shoulder with his thumb. "Listen, I forgot to add more briquettes to the grill. If the kids don't get their s'mores, I'll never hear the end of it. I'll be right back, okay?"

"Sure," she answered, feigning nonchalance. When he jogged off, Katie exhaled, feeling like she'd somehow escaped. *He used to be a police officer*, she thought to herself, and she tried to tell herself that it didn't matter. Even so, it took almost a minute of steady breathing before she felt somewhat in control again. Kristen and Josh were in the same places, though Kristen had bent over to examine another seashell, ignoring her soaring kite.

She heard Alex approaching behind her.

"Told you it wouldn't take long," he said easily. "After we eat the s'mores, I was thinking about calling it a day. I'd love to stay out until the sun sets, but Josh has school tomorrow."

"Whenever you want to go is fine with me," she said, crossing her arms.

Noting her rigid shoulders and the tight way she'd spoken the words, he furrowed his brow. "I'm not sure what I said that bothered you, but I'm sorry, okay?" he finally said. "Just know that I'm here if you want to talk about it."

She nodded without answering, and though Alex waited for more, there was nothing. "Is this the way it's going to be with us?" he asked.

"What do you mean?"

"I feel like I'm suddenly walking on eggshells around you, but I don't know why."

"I'd tell you but I can't," she said. Her voice was almost inaudible over the sound of the waves.

"Can you at least tell me what I said? Or what I did?"

She turned toward him. "You didn't say or do anything wrong. But right now, I can't say any more than that, okay?"

He studied her. "Okay," he said. "As long as you're still having a good time."

It took some effort, but she finally managed a smile. "This is the best day I've spent in a long time. Best weekend in fact."

"You're still mad about the bike, aren't you?" he said, narrowing his eyes in mock suspicion. Despite the tension she felt, she laughed.

"Of course. It's going to take a long time for me to recover from that," she said, pretending to pout.

Turning his gaze to the horizon, he seemed relieved.

"Can I ask you something?" Katie asked, turning serious again. "You don't have to answer if you don't want to."

"Anything," he said.

"What happened to your wife? You said she had a seizure, but you haven't told me why she was sick."

He sighed, as if he'd known all along she was going to ask but still had to steel himself to answer. "She had a brain tumor," he began slowly. "Or, more accurately, she had three different types of brain tumors. I didn't know it then, but I learned that's fairly common. The one that was slow-growing was just what you'd think; it was about the size of an egg and the surgeons were able to take most of it out. But the other tumors weren't so simple. They were the kind of tumors that spread like spider legs, and there was no way to remove them without removing part of her brain. They were aggressive, too. The doctors did the best they could, but even when they walked out of surgery and told me that it had gone as well as it could, I knew exactly what they meant."

"I can't imagine hearing something like that." She stared down at the sand.

"I admit I had trouble believing it. It was so . . . unexpected. I mean, the week before, we were a normal family, and the next thing I knew, she was dying and there was nothing I could do to stop it."

Off to the side, Kristen and Josh were still concentrating on their kites but Katie knew that Alex could barely see them.

"After surgery, it took a few weeks for her to get back on her feet and I wanted to believe that things were okay. But after that, week by week, I began to notice little changes. The left side of her body started to get weaker and she was taking longer and longer naps. It was hard, but the worst part for me was that she began to pull away from the kids. Like she didn't want them to remember her being sick; she wanted them to remember the way she used to be." He paused before finally shaking his head. "I'm sorry. I shouldn't have told you that. She was a great mom. I mean, look how well they're turning out."

"I think their father has something to do with that, too."

"I try. But half the time, it doesn't feel like I know what I'm doing. It's like I'm faking it."

"I think all parents feel like that."

He turned toward her. "Did yours?"

She hesitated. "I think my parents did the best they could." Not a ringing endorsement, but the truth.

"Are you close with them?"

"They died in a car accident when I was nineteen."

He stared at her. "I'm sorry to hear that."

"It was tough," Katie said.

"Do you have any brothers and sisters?"

"No," she said. She turned toward the water. "It's just me."

A few minutes later, Alex helped the kids reel in their kites and they headed back to the picnic area. The coals weren't quite ready and Alex used the time to rinse the boogie boards and shake sand from the towels before pulling out what he needed for the s'mores.

Kristen and Josh helped pack up most of their things and Katie put the rest of the food back into the cooler while Alex began ferrying items to the jeep. By the time he was finished, only a blanket and four chairs remained. The kids had arranged them in a circle while Alex handed out long prongs and the bag of marshmallows. In his excitement, Josh ripped it open, spilling a small pile onto the blanket.

Following the kids' lead, Katie pushed three marshmallows onto the prong and the four of them stood over the grill, twirling the prongs, while the sugary puffs turned golden brown. Katie held hers a little too close to the heat and two of the marshmallows caught on fire, which Alex quickly blew out.

When they were ready, Alex helped the kids finish the treat: chocolate on the graham cracker, followed by the marshmallow and topped with another cracker. It was sticky and sweet and the best thing Katie had eaten in as long as she could remember.

Sitting between his kids, she noticed Alex struggling with his crumbling s'more, making a mess, and when he used his fingers to wipe his mouth, it made matters only worse. The kids found it hilarious, and Katie couldn't help giggling as well, and she felt a sudden, unexpected surge of hope. Despite the tragedy they'd all gone through, this was what a happy family looked like; this, she thought, is what a loving family did when they were together. For them, it was nothing but an ordinary day on an ordinary weekend, but for her, there was something revelatory about the notion that wonderful moments like these existed. And that maybe, just maybe, it would be possible for her to experience similar days in the future.

12

Then what happened?"

Jo was sitting across from her at the table, the kitchen glowing yellow, illuminated only by the light above the stove. After Katie had returned, she'd come over, specks of paint in her hair. Katie had started a pot of coffee and two cups were on the table.

"Nothing, really. After finishing the s'mores, we walked down the beach one last time, then got in the car and drove home."

"Did he walk you to the door?"

"Yes."

"Did you invite him in?"

"He had to get the kids back home."

"Did you kiss him good night?"

"Of course not."

"Why not?"

"Weren't you listening? He was bringing his kids to the beach and he invited me along. It wasn't a date."

Jo raised her coffee cup. "It sounds like a date."

"It was a family day."

Jo considered that. "It sounded like the two of you spent a lot of time talking."

Katie leaned back in her chair. "I think you wanted it to be a date."

"Why would I want that?"

"I have no idea. But ever since we've met, in every conversation, you bring him up somehow. It's like you've been trying to . . . I don't know. Make sure I notice him."

Jo swirled the contents of her cup before setting it back on the table. "And have you?"

Katie threw up her hands. "See what I mean?"

Jo laughed before shaking her head. "All right. How about this?" She hesitated, then went on. "I've met a lot of people, and over time I've developed instincts that I've learned to trust. As we both know, Alex is a great guy, and once I got to know you, I felt the same way about you. Other than that, I haven't done anything more than tease you about it. It's not like I dragged you to the store and introduced the two of you. Nor was I around when he asked you to go to the beach, an invitation you were more than willing to accept."

"Kristen asked me to go . . ."

"I know. You told me that," Jo said, arching an eyebrow. "And I'm sure that's the only reason you went."

Katie scowled. "You have a funny way of twisting things around."

Jo laughed again. "Did you ever think that it's because I'm envious? Oh, not that you went with Alex, but that you got to go to the beach on a perfect day, while I was stuck inside painting . . . for the second day in a row? If I never touch a paint roller again in my life, it'll still be too soon. My arms and shoulders are *sore*."

Katie stood up from the table and went to the counter. She poured another cup of coffee for herself and held up the pot. "More?"

"No, thank you. I need to sleep tonight and the caffeine

would keep me up. I think I'm going to order some Chinese food. You want any?"

"I'm not hungry," Katie said. "I ate too much today."

"I don't think that's possible. But you did get a lot of sun. It looks good on you, even if it'll lead to wrinkles later."

Katie snorted. "Thanks for that."

"What are friends for?" Jo stood and gave a catlike stretch. "And listen, I had a good time last night. Although, I have to admit, I paid for it this morning."

"It was fun," Katie agreed.

Jo took a couple of steps before turning around. "Oh, I forgot to ask you. Are you going to keep the bike?"

"Yes," Katie said.

Jo thought about it. "Good for you."

"What do you mean by that?"

"Just that I don't think you should give it back. You obviously need it and he wanted you to have it. Why shouldn't you keep it?" She shrugged. "Your problem is that you sometimes read too much into things."

"Like with my manipulative friend?"

"Do you really think I'm manipulative?"

Katie thought about it. "Maybe a little."

Jo smiled. "So what's your schedule like this week? Are you working a lot?"

Katie nodded. "Six nights and three days."

Jo made a face. "Yuck."

"It's okay. I need the money and I'm used to it."

"And, of course, you had a great weekend."

Katie paused. "Yeah," she said. "I did."

13

The next few days passed uneventfully, which only made them feel longer to Alex. He hadn't spoken to Katie since he'd dropped her off on Sunday evening. It wasn't completely unexpected, since he knew she was working a lot this week, but more than once he found himself wandering out of the store and staring up the road, feeling vaguely disappointed when he didn't see her.

It was enough to squash the illusion that he'd dazzled her to the point that she couldn't resist stopping by. He was surprised, though, by the almost teenage-like enthusiasm he felt at the prospect of seeing her again, even if she didn't feel the same way. He pictured her on the beach, her chestnut hair fluttering in the breeze, her delicately boned features, and eyes that seemed to change color every time he saw them. Little by little, she'd relaxed as the day had worn on, and he had the sense that going to the beach had softened her resistance somehow.

He wondered not only about her past, but about all the other things he still didn't know about her. He tried to imagine what kind of music she liked, or what she thought about first thing in the morning, or whether or not she'd ever attended a baseball game. He wondered whether she slept on her back or on her side and, if given the choice, whether she preferred a shower to a bath. The more he wondered, the more curious he became.

He wished she would trust him with the details of her past, not because he was under the illusion that he could somehow rescue her or felt that she even needed to be rescued, but because giving voice to the truth of her past meant opening the door to the future. It meant they would be able to have a real conversation.

By Thursday, he was debating whether to drop by her cottage. He wanted to and had once even reached for his keys, but in the end he'd stopped because he had no idea what to say once he got there. Nor could he predict how she might respond. Would she smile? Or be nervous? Would she invite him inside or ask him to leave? As much as he tried to imagine what might happen, he couldn't, and he'd ended up putting the keys aside.

It was complicated. But then again, he reminded himself, she was a mysterious woman.

It didn't take long before Katie admitted that the bicycle was a godsend. Not only was she able to come home between her shifts on the days she pulled doubles, but for the first time, she felt as though she could really begin to explore the town, which was exactly what she did. On Tuesday, she visited a couple of antique stores, enjoyed the watercolor seascapes at a local art gallery, and rode through neighborhoods, marveling at the broad sweeping porches and porticos adorning the historic homes near the waterfront. On Wednesday, she visited the library and spent a couple of hours browsing the shelves and reading the flaps of books, loading the bicycle baskets with novels that interested her.

In the evenings, though, as she lay in bed reading the books she'd checked out, she sometimes found her thoughts drifting to Alex. Sifting through her memories, those from Altoona, she realized he reminded her of her friend Callie's father. In her sophomore year in high school, Callie had lived down the street from her and though they didn't know each other that well—Callie was a couple of years younger—Katie could remember sitting on her porch steps every Saturday morning. Like clockwork, Callie's dad would open the garage, whistling as he rolled the lawn mower into place. He was proud of his yard—it was easily the most manicured in the neighborhood—and she'd watch as he pushed the mower back and forth with military precision. He stopped every so often to move a fallen branch out of the way, and in those moments, he would wipe his face with a handkerchief he kept in his back pocket. When he was finished, he would lean against the hood of the Ford in his driveway, sipping a glass of lemonade that his wife always brought to him. Sometimes, she would lean on the car alongside him, and Katie would smile as she saw him pat his wife's hip whenever he wanted to get her attention.

There was something contented in the way he sipped his drink and touched his wife that made her think he was satisfied with the life he was leading and that all his dreams had somehow been fulfilled. Often, as Katie studied him, she wondered how her life would have been had she been born into that family.

Alex had the same air of contentment about him when his kids were around. Somehow he not only had been able to move past the tragedy of losing his wife but had done so with enough strength to help his kids move past the loss as well. When he'd spoken about his wife, Katie had listened for bitterness or self-pity, but there hadn't been any. There'd been sorrow, of course, and a loneliness in his expression as he spoke of her, but at the same time, he'd told Katie about his wife without making her feel like he'd been comparing the two of them. He seemed to accept her, and though she wasn't sure exactly when it had happened, she realized that she was attracted to him.

Beyond that, her feelings were complicated. Not since At-lantic City had she lowered her guard enough to let someone else get so close, and that ended up being a nightmare. But as hard as she'd tried to remain aloof, it seemed that every time she saw Alex, something happened to draw them together. Sometimes by accident, like when Josh fell in the river and she'd stayed with Kristen, but sometimes it seemed almost pre-ordained. Like the storm rolling in. Or Kristen wandering out and pleading with her to come to the beach. To this point, she'd had enough sense to volunteer little about herself, but that was the thing. The more time she spent with Alex, the more she had the sense that he knew far more than he was let-ting on, and it frightened her. It made her feel naked and vul-nerable and it was part of the reason she'd avoided going to the store at all this week. She needed time to think, time to decide what, if anything, she was going to do about it.

Unfortunately, she'd spent too much time dwelling on the way the fine lines at the corners of his eyes crinkled when he grinned or the graceful way he'd emerged from the surf. She thought about how Kristen would reach for his hand and the absolute trust Katie saw in that simple gesture. Early on, Jo had said something along the lines that Alex was a good man, the kind of man who would do the right thing, and though Katie couldn't claim to know him well, her instincts told her he was a man she could trust. That no matter what she told him, he would support her. That he would guard her secrets and never use what he knew to hurt her.

It was irrational and illogical and it went against everything she'd promised herself when she'd moved here, but she realized that she wanted him to know her. She wanted him to under-stand her, if only because she had the strange sense that he was the kind of man she could fall in love with, even if she didn't want to.

14

———— ❧ ————

$\mathbf{B}$utterfly hunting.

The notion had popped into his head soon after waking on Saturday morning, even before he'd gone downstairs to open the store. Strangely, as he'd been pondering the possibilities of what to do with the kids that day, he'd remembered a project he'd done in the sixth grade. The teacher had asked the students to make an insect collection. He flashed to a memory of running through a grassy field at recess, chasing after everything from bumblebees to katydids. He was certain that Josh and Kristen would enjoy it, and feeling proud of himself for coming up with something exciting and original to occupy a weekend afternoon, he sifted through the fishing nets he had in the store, choosing three that were about the right size.

When he told them at lunch, Josh and Kristen were less than enthusiastic about the idea.

"I don't want to hurt any butterflies," Kristen protested. "I like butterflies."

"We don't have to hurt them. We can let them go."

"Then why catch them in the first place?"

"Because it's fun."

"It doesn't sound fun. It sounds mean."

Alex opened his mouth to respond, but he wasn't sure what to say. Josh took another bite of his grilled cheese sandwich.

"It's pretty hot already, Dad," Josh pointed out, talking as he chewed.

"That's okay. Afterward, we can swim in the creek. And chew with your mouth closed."

Josh swallowed. "Why don't we just swim in the creek now?"

"Because we're going butterfly hunting."

"Can we go to a movie instead?"

"Yeah!" Kristen said. "Let's go to a movie."

Parenting, Alex thought, could be exasperating.

"It's a beautiful day and we're not going to spend it sitting inside. We're going butterfly hunting. And not only that, you're going to enjoy it, okay?"

After lunch, Alex drove them to a field on the outskirts of town that was filled with wildflowers. He handed them their nets and sent them on their way, watching as Josh sort of dragged his net while Kristen held hers tucked against her, in much the same way she held her dolls.

Alex took matters into his own hands and jogged ahead of both of them, his net at the ready. Up ahead, fluttering among the wildflowers, he spotted dozens of butterflies. When he got close enough, he swung his net, capturing one. Squatting down, he carefully began to shift the net, allowing the orange and brown colors to show through.

"Wow!" he shouted, trying to sound as enthusiastic as he could. "I got one!"

The next thing he knew, Josh and Kristen were peering over his shoulder.

"Be careful with it, Daddy!" Kristen cried.

"I will, baby. Look at how pretty the colors are."

They leaned in even closer.

"Cool!" Josh shouted, and a moment later, he was off and running, swinging the net with abandon.

Kristen continued to study the butterfly. "What kind is it?"

"It's a skipper," Alex said. "But I don't know exactly what kind."

"I think he's scared," Kristen said.

"I'm sure he's fine. But I'll let him go, okay?"

She nodded as Alex carefully pulled the net inside out. In the open air, the butterfly clung to the net before taking off in flight. Kristen's eyes went wide with wonder.

"Can you help me catch one?" she asked.

"I'd love to."

They spent a little more than an hour running among the flowers. They caught about eight different kinds of butterflies, including a buckeye, though the vast majority were skippers like the first. By the time they finished, the kids' faces were red and shiny, so Alex drove them to get ice cream cones before heading to the creek behind the house. The three of them jumped off the dock together—Josh and Kristen wearing life preservers—and floated downstream in the slow-moving water. It was the kind of day he'd spent as a kid. By the time they got out of the water, he was contented by the thought that, aside from going to the beach, it was the best weekend they'd had in a while.

But it was tiring, too. Afterward, once the kids had showered, they wanted to watch a movie, and Alex popped in *Homeward Bound*, a movie they'd seen a dozen times but were always willing to watch again. From the kitchen, he could see them on the couch, neither one moving in the slightest, staring at the television in that dazed way particular to exhausted children.

He wiped the kitchen counters and loaded the dirty dishes into the dishwasher, started a load of laundry, straightened up the living room, and gave the kids' bathroom a good scrubbing before finally sitting beside them on the couch for a while. Josh curled up on one side, Kristen on the other. By the time the movie ended, Alex could feel his own eyelids beginning to droop. After working at the store and playing with the kids and cleaning the house, it felt good to simply relax for a while.

The sound of Josh's voice jarred him awake.

"Hey, Dad?"

"Yeah?"

"What's for dinner? I'm starved."

From the waitress stand, Katie peered out at the deck and then turned back again, staring as Alex and the kids followed the hostess to an open table near the railing. Kristen smiled and waved as soon as she saw Katie, and hesitated only a second before scooting between the tables and hurtling directly for her. Katie bent down as the little girl threw her arms around her.

"We wanted to surprise you!" Kristen said.

"Well, you did. What are you doing here?"

"My dad didn't want to cook for us tonight."

"He didn't?"

"He said he was too tired."

"There's more to the story," Alex announced. "Trust me."

Katie hadn't heard him come up, and she stood.

"Oh, hey," she said, blushing against her will.

"How are you?" Alex asked.

"Good." She nodded, feeling a bit flustered. "Busy, as you can tell."

"It seems like it. We had to wait before they could seat us in your section."

"It's been like that all day."

"Well, we won't keep you. C'mon, Kristen. Let's go to the table. We'll see you in a few minutes or whenever you're ready."

"Bye, Miss Katie." Kristen waved again.

Katie watched them walk to the table, strangely excited by their visit. She saw Alex open the menu and lean forward to help Kristen with hers, and for an instant, she wished she were sitting with them.

She retucked her shirt and glanced at her reflection in the stainless steel coffeepot. She couldn't make out much, only a blurry image, but it was enough to make her run a hand through her hair. Then, after a quick check to make sure her shirt hadn't been stained—nothing she could do about it, of course, but she still wanted to know—she walked over to the table.

"Hey, guys," she said, addressing the kids. "I hear your dad didn't want to cook dinner for you."

Kristen giggled but Josh simply nodded. "He said he was tired."

"That's what I heard," she said.

Alex rolled his eyes. "Thrown under the bus by my own kids. I just can't believe it."

"I wouldn't throw you under the bus, Daddy," Kristen said seriously.

"Thank you, sweetie."

Katie smiled. "Are you thirsty? Can I get you something to drink?"

They ordered sweet teas all around, along with a basket of hush puppies. Katie brought the drinks to the table and as she walked away, she felt Alex's gaze on her. She fought the urge to peek over her shoulder, though she desperately wanted to.

For the next few minutes, she took orders and cleared plates from other tables, delivered a couple of meals, and finally returned with the basket of hush puppies.

"Be careful," she said. "They're still hot."

"That's when they're the best," Josh said, reaching into the basket. Kristen reached for one as well.

"We went butterfly hunting today," she said.

"You did?"

"Yep. But we didn't hurt them. We let them go."

"That sounds like fun. Did you have a good time?"

"It was awesome!" Josh said. "I caught, like, a hundred of them! And then we went swimming."

"What a great day," Katie said sincerely. "No wonder your dad is tired."

"I'm not tired," both Josh and Kristen said, almost simultaneously.

"Maybe not," Alex said, "but you're both still going to bed early. Because your poor old dad needs to go to sleep."

Katie shook her head. "Don't be so hard on yourself," she said. "You're not poor."

It took him a moment to realize she was teasing, and he laughed. It was loud enough for the people at the next table to notice, though he didn't seem to care.

"I come in here to relax and enjoy my dinner, and I end up getting picked on by the waitress."

"It's a tough life."

"You're telling me. Next thing I know, you'll be telling me that I might want to order from the kids' menu, seeing as how I'm gaining weight."

"Well, I wasn't going to say anything," she said with a pointed glance at his midsection. He laughed again, and when he looked at her she saw an appreciative gleam in his eye, reminding her that he found her attractive.

"I think we're ready to order now," he said.

"What can I get you?"

Alex ordered for them and Katie jotted it down. She held his gaze for a moment before leaving the table and dropping the order off in the kitchen. As she continued to work the tables in her station—as quickly as people left, they were replaced—she found excuses to swing by Alex's table. She refilled their waters and their teas, she removed the basket when they were done with the hush puppies, and she brought Josh a new fork after his had dropped on the floor. She chatted easily with Alex and the kids, enjoying every moment, and eventually brought them their dinners.

Later, when they were through, she cleared the table and dropped off the check. By then, the sun was getting lower and Kristen had begun to yawn, and if anything, the restaurant had gotten busier. She had time for only a quick good-bye as the kids scrambled down the stairs, but when Alex hesitated, she had the sense that he was about to ask her out. She wasn't sure how she was going to handle it, but before he could get the words out, one of her customers spilled a beer. The customer stood quickly from the table, bumping it, and two more glasses toppled over. Alex stepped back, the moment broken, knowing she had to go.

"See you soon," he said, waving as he trailed after his kids.

The following day, Katie pushed open the door to the store only half an hour after opening.

"You're here early," Alex said, surprised.

"I was up early and just thought I'd get my shopping out of the way."

"Did it ever slow down last night?"

"Finally. But a couple of people have been out this week. One went to her sister's wedding, and another called in sick. It's been crazy."

"I could tell. But the food was great, even if the service was a little slow."

When she fixed him with an irate expression, he laughed. "Just getting you back for teasing me last night." He shook his head. "Calling me old. I'll have you know my hair went gray before I was thirty."

"You're very sensitive about that," she noted with a teasing tone. "But trust me. It looks good on you. It lends a certain air of respectability."

"Is that good or bad?"

She smiled without giving an answer before reaching for a basket. As she did, she heard him clear his throat. "Are you working as much this coming week?"

"Not as much."

"How about next weekend?"

She thought about it. "I'm off Saturday. Why?"

He shifted his weight from one foot to the other before meeting her eyes. "Because I was wondering if I might be able to take you to dinner. Just the two of us this time. No kids."

She knew they were at a crossroads, one that would change the tenor of things between them. At the same time, it was the reason she'd come to the store as early as she had. She wanted to figure out whether she'd been mistaken about what she'd seen in his expression the previous evening, because it was the first time she knew for certain that she wanted him to ask.

In the silence, though, he seemed to misread what she was thinking. "Never mind. It's not that big of a deal."

"Yes," she said, holding his gaze. "I'd love dinner. But on one condition."

"What's that?"

"You've already done so much for me that I'd rather do something for you this time. How about I make you dinner instead? At my house."

He smiled, relieved. "That sounds perfect."

15

On Saturday, Katie woke later than usual. She'd spent the past few days frantically shopping and decorating her house—a new sheer lace curtain for the living room window, some inexpensive prints for the walls, a few small area rugs, and real place mats and glasses for their dinner. Friday night she'd worked until after midnight, plumping up her new throw pillows and giving the house a final cleaning. Despite the sun that slanted through her windows and striped her bed, she woke only when she heard the sounds of someone hammering. Checking the clock, she saw it was already after nine.

Stumbling out of bed, Katie yawned and then walked toward the kitchen to hit the switch on the coffeepot before stepping out onto the porch, squinting in the brightness of the morning sun. Jo was on her front porch, the hammer poised for another whack, when she spotted Katie.

Jo put the hammer down. "I didn't wake you, did I?"

"Yeah, but that's okay. I had to get up anyway. What are you doing?"

"I'm trying to keep the shutter from falling off. When I got home last night, it was hanging cockeyed, and I was sure it was going to give way in the middle of the night. Of course, thinking that the crash might wake me up any minute kept me from falling asleep for hours."

"Do you need some help?"

"No, I've just about got it."

"How about coffee?"

"Sounds great. I'll be over in a few minutes."

Katie went to her bedroom, slipped out of her pajamas, and threw on a pair of shorts and a T-shirt. She brushed her teeth and hair, just enough to get the tangles out. Through the window, she saw Jo walking toward the house. She opened the front door.

Katie poured two cups of coffee and handed one to Jo as soon as she entered the kitchen.

"Your house is really coming together! I love the rugs and the pictures."

Katie gave a modest shrug. "Yeah, well . . . Southport is starting to feel like home, I guess. I figured I should start making this house into something more permanent."

"It's really amazing. It's like you're finally beginning to nest."

"How's your place coming?"

"It's getting better. I'll bring you by when it's ready."

"Where've you been? I haven't seen you around lately."

Jo gave a dismissive wave. "I was out of town for a few days on business, and then I went to visit someone last weekend, and then I was working. You know the drill."

"I've been working a lot, too. I've had a ton of shifts lately."

"You working tonight?"

Katie took a sip of her coffee. "No. I'm having someone over for dinner."

Jo's eyes lit up. "Do you want me to guess who it could be?"

"You already know who it is." Katie tried to stop the slow flush that was creeping up her neck.

"I knew it!" she said. "Good for you. Have you decided what you're going to wear?"

"Not yet."

"Well, no matter what you decide, you'll look beautiful, I'm sure. And you're going to cook?"

"Believe it or not, I'm actually a fairly good cook."

"What are you going to make?"

When Katie told her, Jo raised her eyebrows.

"Sounds yummy," Jo said. "That's great. I'm happy for you. Both of you, actually. Are you excited?"

"It's only dinner . . ."

"I'll take that as a yes." She winked. "It's too bad I can't stick around to spy on the two of you. I'd love to watch how it all unfolds, but unfortunately, I'm heading out of town."

"Yes," Katie said. "That's really too bad you're not going to be here."

Jo laughed. "Sarcasm doesn't become you, by the way. But just so you know, I'm not going to let you off the hook. As soon as I get back, I'm going to need the full play-by-play."

"It's just dinner," Katie said again.

"Which means that you won't have any trouble telling me all about it."

"I think you need another hobby."

"Probably," Jo agreed. "But right now, I'm having plenty of fun living vicariously through you since my love life is pretty much nonexistent. A girl needs to be able to dream, you know?"

Katie's first stop was the hair salon. There, a young woman named Brittany trimmed and styled her hair, chatting nonstop the entire time. Across the street was the only women's boutique in Southport, and Katie stopped there next. Though she'd ridden past the store, she'd never been inside before. It had been one of the stores she'd never imagined herself either wanting or needing to go into, but as she began to browse, she was pleasantly surprised not only by the selections, but by some of the prices. Well, on the sale items, anyway, which was where Katie focused her attention.

It was an odd experience to shop alone in a clothing store like this. She hadn't done such a thing in a long time, and as she changed in the dressing room, she felt more carefree than she had in years.

She bought a couple of sale items, including a tan formfitting blouse with beading and stitching that scooped a bit in the front, not dramatically but enough to accent her figure. She also found a gorgeous patterned summer skirt that complemented the blouse perfectly. The skirt was a little too long, but she knew she could fix that. After paying for her purchases, she wandered two doors down, to what she knew was the only shoe store in town, where she picked up a pair of sandals. Again, they were on sale and although ordinarily she would have felt almost frantic about shopping, the tips had been good over the last few days and she'd decided to splurge. Within reason, of course.

From there, she went first to the drugstore to buy a few things and then finally rode across town to the grocery store. She took her time, content to browse the aisles, feeling the old, troubling memories trying and failing to reassert themselves.

When she was finished, she rode her bicycle home and started the preparations for dinner. She was making shrimp stuffed with crabmeat, cooked in a scampi sauce. She had to recall the recipe from memory, but she'd made it a dozen times over the years and was confident she hadn't forgotten anything. As side dishes, she'd decided on stuffed peppers and corn bread, and as an appetizer, she wanted to make a bacon-wrapped Brie, topped with a raspberry sauce.

It had been a long time since she'd prepared such an elaborate meal, but she'd always loved to cut recipes from magazines, even from a young age. Cooking was the one enthusiasm she'd been able to share occasionally with her mom.

She spent the rest of the afternoon hurrying. She mixed the bread and put it in the oven, then readied the ingredients for the stuffed peppers. Those went into the refrigerator along with the bacon-wrapped Brie. When the corn bread was done, she placed it on the counter to cool and started the raspberry sauce. Not much to it—sugar, raspberries, and water—but by the time it was ready, the kitchen smelled heavenly. That went into the fridge as well. Everything else could wait until later.

In her bedroom, she shortened the skirt to just above the knee, then made a last tour of the house to make sure everything was in place. Finally, she began to undress.

As she slipped into the shower, she thought about Alex. She visualized his easy smile and the graceful way he moved, and the memory started a slow burn in her belly. Despite herself, she wondered whether he was taking a shower at the same time she was. There was something erotic in the idea, the promise of something exciting and new. It was just dinner, she reminded herself again, but even then, she knew she wasn't being completely honest with herself.

There was another force at work here, something she'd been trying to deny. She was attracted to him more than she wanted to admit, and as she stepped out of the shower she knew she had to be careful. He was the kind of man she knew she could fall for, and the notion frightened her. She wasn't ready for that. Not yet, anyway.

Then again, she heard a voice inside her whisper, maybe she was.

After toweling off, she moisturized her skin with a sweet-smelling body lotion, then put on her new outfit, including the sandals, before reaching for the makeup she'd purchased from the drugstore. She didn't need much, just some lipstick, mascara, and a trace of eye shadow. She brushed her hair and then put on a pair of dangly earrings she'd bought on a whim. When she was finished, she stepped back from the mirror.

That's it, she thought to herself, that's all I've got. She turned one way, then the other, tugging at the blouse before finally smiling. She hadn't looked this good in a long time.

Though the sun had finally moved toward the western sky, the house was still warm and she opened the kitchen window. The breeze was enough to keep her cool as she set the table. Earlier in the week, as she'd been leaving the store, Alex had asked her if he could bring a bottle of wine, and Katie put a couple of glasses out. In the center of the table, she placed a candle and as she stepped back, she heard the sound of an engine approaching. She saw from the clock that Alex was right on time.

She drew a deep breath, trying to calm her nerves. Then, after walking across the room and opening the door, she stepped out onto the porch. Dressed in jeans and a blue shirt rolled up to his elbows, Alex was standing at the driver's-side door and leaning into the car, obviously reaching for something. His hair was still a little damp near his collar.

Alex pulled out two bottles of wine and turned around. Seeing her, he seemed to freeze, his expression one of disbelief. She stood surrounded by the last rays of the setting sun, perfectly radiant, and for a moment all he could do was stare.

His wonder was obvious, and Katie let it wash over her, knowing she wanted the feeling to last forever.

"You made it," she said.

The sound of her voice was enough to break the spell, but Alex continued to stare. He knew he should say something witty, something charming to break the tension, but instead he found himself thinking, *I'm in trouble. Serious trouble.*

He wasn't exactly sure when it had happened. Or even when it started. It may have been the morning when he'd seen Kristen

holding Katie after Josh had fallen in the river, or the rainy afternoon when he'd driven her home, or even during the day
they had spent at the beach. All he knew for sure was that right
here and now, he was falling hard for this woman, and he could
only pray that she was feeling the same way.

In time, he was finally able to clear his throat. "Yeah," he
said. "I guess I did."

16

The early evening sky was a prism of colors as Katie led Alex through the small living room and toward the kitchen.

"I don't know about you, but I could use a glass of wine," she said.

"Good idea," he agreed. "I wasn't sure what we were having, so I brought both a sauvignon blanc and a zinfandel. Do you have a preference?"

"I'll let you pick," she said.

In the kitchen, she leaned against the counter, one leg crossed over the other while Alex twisted the corkscrew into the cork. For once, he seemed more nervous than she was. With a series of quick movements, he opened the bottle of sauvignon blanc. Katie set the glasses on the counter next to him, conscious of how close together they were standing.

"I know I should have said it when I first got here, but you look beautiful."

"Thank you," she said.

He poured some wine, then set the bottle aside and handed her a glass. As she took it, he could smell the coconut-scented body lotion she'd used.

"I think you'll like the wine. At least, I hope so."

"I'm sure I'll love it," she said, raising her glass. "Cheers," she offered, clinking her glass against his.

Katie took a sip, feeling inordinately pleased about everything: how she looked and felt, the taste of the wine, the lingering scent of the raspberry sauce, the way Alex kept eyeing her while trying not to be obvious about it.

"Would you like to sit on the porch?" she suggested.

He nodded. Outside, they each sat in one of the rockers. In the slowly cooling air, the crickets began their chorus, welcoming the coming night.

Katie savored the wine, enjoying the fruity tang it left on her tongue. "How were Kristen and Josh today?"

"They were good." Alex shrugged. "I took them to a movie."

"But it was so pretty outside."

"I know. But with Memorial Day on Monday, I figure we can still spend a couple of days outside."

"Is the store open on Memorial Day?"

"Of course. It's one of the busiest days of the year, since everyone wants to spend the holiday on the water. I'll probably work until one o'clock or so."

"I'd say I feel sorry for you, but I'm working, too."

"Maybe we'll come in and bother you again."

"You didn't bother me at all." She peered at him over the top of her wineglass. "Well, the kids didn't bother me, anyway. As I recall, you were complaining about the quality of service."

"Us old guys will do that," he quipped.

She laughed before rocking back in the chair. "When I'm not working, I like to sit out here and read. It's just so quiet, you know? Sometimes I feel like I'm the only one around for miles."

"You are the only one around for miles. You live in the sticks."

She playfully slapped his shoulder. "Watch it. I happen to like my little house."

"You should. It's in better shape than I thought it would be. It's homey."

"It's getting there," she said. "It's a work in progress. And best of all, it's mine, and no one's going to take it away."

He looked over at her then. She was staring out over the gravel road, into the grassy field beyond.

"Are you okay?" he asked.

She took her time before answering. "I was just thinking that I'm glad you're here. You don't even know me."

"I think I know you well enough."

Katie said nothing to that. Alex watched as she lowered her gaze.

"You think you know me," she whispered, "but you don't."

Alex sensed that she was scared to say any more. In the silence, he heard the porch creaking as he rocked back and forth. "How about I tell you what I think I know, and you tell me if I'm right or wrong? Would that be okay?"

She nodded, her lips compressed. When Alex went on, his voice was soft.

"I think you're intelligent and charming, and that you're a person with a kind heart. I know that when you want to, you can look more beautiful than anyone I've ever met. You're independent, you've got a good sense of humor, and you show surprising patience with children. You're right in thinking that I don't know the specifics of your past, but I don't know that they're all that important unless you want to tell me about them. Everyone has a past, but that's just it—it's in the past. You can learn from it, but you can't change it. Besides, I never knew that person. The person I've come to know is the one I want to get to know even better."

As he spoke, Katie gave a fleeting smile. "You make it sound so simple," she said.

"It can be."

She twisted the stem of her wineglass, considering his words. "But what if the past isn't in the past? What if it's still happening?"

Alex continued to stare at her, holding her gaze. "You mean . . . what if he finds you?"

Katie flinched. "What did you say?"

"You heard me," he said. He kept his voice steady, almost conversational, something he'd learned in CID. "I'm guessing that you were married once . . . and that maybe he's trying to find you."

Katie froze, her eyes going wide. It was suddenly hard to breathe and she jumped up from the chair, spilling the rest of her wine. She took a step away from Alex, staring, feeling the blood drain from her face.

"How do you know so much about me? Who told you?" she demanded, her mind racing, trying to piece it together. There was no way he could know those things. It wasn't possible. She hadn't told anyone.

Except for Jo.

The realization was enough to leave her breathless and she glanced at the cottage next door. Her neighbor, she thought, had betrayed her. Her *friend* had betrayed her—

As fast as her mind was working, Alex's was working as well. He could see the fear in her expression, but he'd seen it before. Too many times. And, he knew, it was time to stop playing games if they wanted to be able to move forward.

"No one told me," he assured her. "But your reaction makes it clear that I'm right. That's not the important question. I don't know that person, Katie. If you want to tell me about your past, I'm willing to listen and help in any way I can, but I'm not going to ask you about it. And if you don't want to tell me, that's okay, too, because, again—I never knew that person. You must have a good reason for keeping it secret, and that means I'm not going to tell anyone, either. No matter what happens, or doesn't happen, between us. Go ahead and make up a brand-new history if you want and I'll back you up word for word. You can trust me on that."

Katie stared at him as he spoke, confused and scared and angry, but absorbing every word.

"But . . . how?"

"I've learned to notice things that other people don't," he went on. "There was a time in my life when that was all I did. And you're not the first woman I've met in your position."

She continued to stare at him, wheels turning. "When you were in the army," she concluded.

He nodded, holding her gaze. Finally, he stood from the chair and took a cautious step toward her. "Can I pour you another glass of wine?"

Still in turmoil, she couldn't answer, but when he reached for her glass, she let him take it. The porch door opened with a squeak and closed behind him, leaving her alone.

She paced to the railing, her thoughts chaotic. She fought the instinct to pack a bag and grab her coffee can full of money and leave town as soon as she could.

But what then? If Alex could figure out the truth simply by watching her, then it was possible for someone else to figure it out, too. And maybe, just maybe, they wouldn't be like Alex.

Behind her, she heard the door squeak open again. Alex stepped onto the porch, joining her at the railing. He set the glass in front of her.

"Did you figure it out yet?"

"Figure what out?"

"Whether you're going to take off to parts unknown as soon as you can?"

She turned to him, her face registering shock.

He held open his hands. "What else would you be thinking? But just so you know, I'm curious only because I'm kind of hungry. I'd hate for you to leave before we eat."

It took her a moment to realize he was teasing, and though she wouldn't have believed it possible considering the last few minutes, she found herself smiling in relief.

"We'll have dinner," she said.

"And tomorrow?"

Instead of answering, she reached for her wine. "I want to know how you knew."

"It wasn't one thing," he said. He mentioned a few of the things he'd noticed before finally shaking his head. "Most people wouldn't have put it all together."

She studied the depths of her glass. "But you did."

"I couldn't help it. It's kind of ingrained."

She thought about it. "That means you've known for a while, then. Or at least had suspicions."

"Yes," he admitted.

"Which is why you never asked about my past."

"Yes," he said again.

"And you still wanted to go out with me?"

His expression was serious. "I've wanted to go out with you from the first moment I saw you. I just had to wait until you were ready."

With the last of the sunlight fading from the horizon, twilight descended, turning the flat, cloudless sky a pale violet. They stood at the railing and Alex watched as the southern breeze gently lifted wayward strands of her hair. Her skin took on a peachy glow; he saw the subtle rise and fall of her chest as she breathed. She gazed into the distance, her expression unreadable, and Alex felt something catch in his throat as he wondered what she was thinking.

"You never answered my question," he finally said.

She stayed quiet for a moment before a shy smile finally appeared.

"I think I'm going to stay in Southport for a while, if that's what you're asking," she answered.

He breathed in her scent. "You can trust me, you know."

She leaned into him, feeling his strength as he slipped his arm around her. "I guess I'm going to have to, aren't I?"

* * *

They returned to the kitchen a few minutes later. Katie set her glass of wine aside as she slid the appetizer and stuffed peppers into the oven. Still reeling from Alex's disturbingly accurate assessment of her past, she was glad for tasks to keep her busy. It was hard to fathom that he *still* wanted to spend an evening with her. And more important, that she wanted to spend an evening with him. Deep in her heart, she wasn't sure she deserved to be happy, nor did she believe that she was worthy of someone who seemed . . . normal.

That was the dirty secret associated with her past. Not that she'd been abused but that somehow she felt that she deserved it because she'd let it happen. Even now, it shamed her, and there were times when she felt hideously ugly, as though the scars that had been left behind were visible to everyone.

But here and now, it mattered less than it once had, because she somehow suspected that Alex understood her shame. And accepted that, too.

From the refrigerator, she pulled out the raspberry sauce she'd made earlier, and began spooning it into a small saucepan to reheat. It didn't take long, and after setting it aside, she pulled the bacon-wrapped Brie from the oven, topped it with the sauce, and brought the cheese to the table. Suddenly remembering, she retrieved her wine from the counter and joined Alex at the table.

"This is just to start," she said. "The peppers are going to take a little longer."

He leaned toward the platter. "It smells amazing."

He moved a piece of Brie to his plate and took a bite. "Wow," he said.

She grinned. "Good, huh?"

"It's delicious. Where did you learn to do this?"

"I was friends with a chef once. He told me this would wow just about anyone."

He cut another piece with his fork. "I'm glad you're staying in Southport," he said. "I can easily imagine myself eating this regularly, even if I have to barter items at my store to get it."

"The recipe isn't complicated."

"You haven't seen me cook. I'm great with kid food, but after that, it starts going downhill fast."

He reached for his glass and took a sip of wine. "I think the cheese might go better with the red. Do you mind if I open the other bottle?"

"Not at all."

He walked over to the counter and opened the zinfandel while Katie went to the cupboard and removed two more glasses. Alex poured wine into each and handed one to her. They were standing close enough to brush up against each other and Alex had to fight the urge to pull her close and wrap his arms around her. Instead, he cleared his throat.

"I want to tell you something, but I don't want you to take it the wrong way."

She hesitated. "Why don't I like the sound of this?"

"I just wanted to tell you how much I've been looking forward to tonight. I mean . . . I've been thinking about it all week."

"Why would I take that the wrong way?"

"I don't know. Because you're a woman? Because it makes me sound desperate and women don't like desperate men?"

For the first time that evening, she laughed easily. "I don't think you're desperate. I get the sense you might be a bit overwhelmed at times because of the business and the kids, but it's not like you've been calling me every day."

"That's only because you don't have a phone. But anyway, I wanted you to know that it means a lot to me. I don't have a lot of experience in things like this."

"Dinner?"

"Dating. It's been a while."

Join the club, she thought to herself. But it made her feel

good anyway. "Come on," she said, motioning to the appetizer. "It's better when it's warm."

When the appetizer was finished, Katie rose from the table and went to the oven. She peeked at the peppers before rinsing the saucepan she'd used earlier. She gathered the ingredients for the scampi sauce and got that started, then began to sauté the shrimp. By the time the shrimp were done, the sauce was ready as well. She put a pepper on each of their plates and added the main course. Then, after dimming the lights, she lit the candle she'd placed at the center of the table. The aroma of butter and garlic and the flickering light against the wall made the old kitchen feel almost new with promise.

They ate and talked while, outside, the stars emerged from hiding. Alex praised the meal more than once, claiming that he'd never tasted anything better. As the candle burned lower and the wine bottle emptied, Katie revealed bits and pieces about her life growing up in Altoona. While she'd held back about telling Jo the whole truth about her parents, she gave Alex the unvarnished version: the constant moves, her parents' alcoholism, the fact that she'd been on her own since she'd turned eighteen. Alex stayed silent throughout, listening without judgment. Even so, she wasn't sure what he thought about her past. When she finally trailed off, she found herself wondering whether she'd said too much. But it was then that he reached over and placed his hand on hers. Though she couldn't meet his gaze, they held hands across the table, neither of them willing to let go, as if they were the only two people remaining in the world.

"I should probably start cleaning the kitchen," Katie said finally, breaking the spell. She pushed back from the table. Alex heard her chair scrape against the floor, aware that the moment had been lost and wanting nothing more than to get it back.

"I want you to know I've had a wonderful time tonight," he began.

"Alex . . . I . . ."

He shook his head. "You don't have to say anything—"

She didn't let him finish. "I want to, okay?" She stood near the table, her eyes glittering with some unknown emotion. "I've had a wonderful time, too. But I know where this is leading, and I don't want you to get hurt." She exhaled, steeling herself for the words that were coming next. "I can't make promises. I can't tell you where I'll be tomorrow, let alone a year from now. When I first ran, I thought I'd be able to put everything behind me and start over, you know? I'd live my life and simply pretend that none of it ever happened. But how can I do that? You think you know me, but I'm not sure that even I know who I am anymore. And as much as you know about me, there's a lot you don't know."

Alex felt something collapse inside him. "Are you saying that you don't want to see me again?"

"No." She shook her head vehemently. "I'm saying all this because I do want to see you and it scares me because I know deep in my heart that you deserve someone better. You deserve someone you can count on. Someone your kids can count on. Like I said, there are things you don't know about me."

"Those things don't matter," Alex insisted.

"How can you say that?"

In the silence that followed, Alex could hear the faint hum of the refrigerator. Through the window, the moon had risen and hung suspended over the treetops.

"Because I know me," he finally said, realizing that he was in love with her. He loved the Katie he'd come to know and the Katie he'd never had the chance to meet. He rose from the table, moving closer to her.

"Alex . . . this can't . . ."

"Katie," he whispered, and for a moment, neither of them moved. Alex finally put a hand on her hip and pulled her closer. Katie exhaled, as if setting down an age-old burden, and when she looked up at him, it was suddenly easy for her to imagine that her fears were pointless. That he would love her no matter what she told him, and that he was the kind of man who loved her already and would love her forever.

And it was then she realized that she loved him, too.

With that, she let herself lean into him. She felt their bodies come together as he raised a hand to her hair. His touch was gentle and soft, unlike anything she'd known before, and she watched in wonder as he closed his eyes. He tilted his head, their faces drawing close.

When their lips finally came together, she could taste the wine on his tongue. She gave herself over to him then, allowing him to kiss her cheek and her neck, and she leaned back, reveling in the sensation. She could feel the moisture of his lips as they brushed against her skin, and she slid her arms around his neck.

This is what it feels like to really love someone, she thought, and to be loved in return, and she could feel the tears beginning to form. She blinked, trying to will them back, but all at once, they were impossible to stop. She loved him and wanted him, but more than that, she wanted him to love the real her, with all her flaws and secrets. She wanted him to know the whole truth.

They kissed for a long time in the kitchen, their bodies pressed together, his hand moving over her back and in her hair. She shivered at the feel of the slight stubble on his cheeks. When he ran a finger over the skin of her arm, she felt a flood of liquid heat course through her body.

"I want to be with you but I can't," she finally whispered, hoping that he wouldn't be angry.

"It's okay," he whispered. "There's no way tonight could have been any more wonderful than it's already been."

"But you're disappointed."

He brushed a strand of hair from her face. "It's not possible for you to disappoint me," he said.

She swallowed, trying to rid herself of her fears.

"There's something you should know about me," she whispered.

"Whatever it is, I'm sure I can handle it."

She leaned into him again.

"I can't be with you tonight," she whispered, "for the same reason I could never marry you." She sighed. "I have a husband."

"I know," he whispered.

"It doesn't matter to you?"

"It's not perfect, but trust me, I'm not perfect, either, so maybe it's best if we take all of this one day at a time. And when you're ready, if you're ever ready, I'll be waiting." He brushed her cheek with his finger. "I love you, Katie. You might not be ready to say those words now, and maybe you'll never be able to say them, but that doesn't change how I feel about you."

"Alex . . ."

"You don't have to say it," he said.

"Can I explain?" she asked, finally pulling back.

He didn't bother to hide his curiosity.

"I want to tell you something," she said. "I want to tell you about me."

17

Three days before Katie left New England, a brisk early January wind made the snowflakes freeze, and she had to lower her head as she walked toward the salon. Her long blond hair blew in the wind and she could feel the pinpricks of ice as they tapped against her cheeks. She wore high-heeled pumps, not boots, and her feet were already freezing. Behind her, Kevin sat in the car watching her. Though she didn't turn, she could hear the car idling and could imagine the mouth that was set into a hard, straight line.

The crowds that had filled the strip mall during Christmas were gone. On either side of the salon was a Radio Shack and a pet store, both of them empty; no one wanted to be out on a day like today. When Katie pulled the door, it flew open in the wind and she struggled to close it. Chilled air followed her into the salon and the shoulders of her jacket were coated with a fine layer of white. She slipped off her gloves and jacket, turning around as she did so. She waved good-bye to Kevin and smiled. He liked it when she smiled at him.

Her appointment was at two with a woman named Rachel. Most of the stations were already filled and Katie was unsure where to go. It was her first time here and she was uncomfortable.

None of the stylists looked older than thirty and most had wild hair with red and blue tints. A moment later, she was approached by a girl in her mid-twenties, tanned and pierced with a tattoo on her neck.

"Are you my two o'clock? Color and trim?" she asked.

Katie nodded.

"I'm Rachel. Follow me."

Rachel glanced over her shoulder. "It's cold out there, huh?" Rachel said. "I almost died on my way to the door. They make us park on the far side of the lot. I hate that, but what can I do, right?"

"It is cold," Katie agreed.

Rachel led her to a station near the corner. The chair was purple vinyl and the floor was black tile. A place for younger people, Katie thought. Singles who wanted to stand out. Not married women with blond hair. Katie fidgeted as Rachel put a smock over her. She wiggled her toes, trying to warm her feet.

"Are you new in the area?" Rachel asked.

"I live in Dorchester," she said.

"That's kind of out of the way. Did someone give you a referral?"

Katie had passed by the salon two weeks earlier, when Kevin had taken her shopping, but she didn't say that. Instead, she simply shook her head.

"I guess I'm lucky I answered the phone then." Rachel smiled. "What sort of color do you want?"

Katie hated to stare at herself in the mirror but she didn't have a choice. She had to get this right. She *had* to. Tucked into the mirror in front of her was a photograph of Rachel with someone Katie assumed to be her boyfriend. He had more piercings than she did and he had a Mohawk. Beneath the smock, Katie squeezed her hands together.

"I want it to look natural, so maybe some lowlights for winter? And fix the roots, too, so they blend."

Rachel nodded into the mirror. "Do you want it about the same color? Or darker or lighter? Not the lowlights, I mean."

"About the same."

"Foil okay?"

"Yes," Katie answered.

"Easy as pie," Rachel said. "Just give me a couple of minutes to get things ready and I'll be back, okay?"

Katie nodded. Off to the side, she saw a woman leaning back at the sink, another stylist beside her. She could hear the water as it was turned on and the hum of conversation from the other stations. Music played faintly over the speakers.

Rachel returned with the foil and the color. Near the chair, she stirred the color, making sure the consistency was right.

"How long have you lived in Dorchester?"

"Four years."

"Where'd you grow up?"

"Pennsylvania," Katie said. "I lived in Atlantic City before I moved here."

"Was that your husband who dropped you off?"

"Yes."

"He's got a nice car. I saw it when you were waving. What is it? A Mustang?"

Katie nodded again but didn't answer. Rachel worked for a little while in silence, applying color and wrapping the foil.

"How long have you been married?" Rachel asked as she coated and wrapped a particularly tricky strand of hair.

"Four years."

"That's why you moved to Dorchester, huh?"

"Yes."

Rachel kept up her patter. "So what do you do?"

Katie stared straight ahead, trying not to see herself. Wishing that she were someone else. She could be here for an hour and a half before Kevin came back and she prayed he wouldn't arrive early.

"I don't have a job," Katie answered.

"I'd go crazy if I didn't work. Not that it's always easy. What did you do before you were married?"

"I was a cocktail waitress."

"In one of the casinos?"

Katie nodded.

"Is that where you met your husband?"

"Yes," Katie said.

"So what's he doing now? While you're getting your hair done?"

He's probably at a bar, Katie thought. "I don't know."

"Why didn't you drive, then? Like I said, it's kind of out of the way."

"I don't drive. My husband drives me when I need to go somewhere."

"I don't know what I'd do without a car. I mean, it's not much but it gets me to where I need to go. I'd hate to have to depend on someone else like that."

Katie could smell perfume in the air. The radiator below the counter had begun to click. "I never learned to drive."

Rachel shrugged as she worked another piece of foil into Katie's hair. "It's not hard. Practice a little, take the test, and you're good to go."

Katie stared at Rachel in the mirror. Rachel seemed to know what she was doing, but she was young and starting out and Katie still wished she were older and more experienced. Which was odd, because she was probably only a couple of years older than Rachel. Maybe less than that. But Katie felt old.

"Do you have kids?"

"No."

Perhaps the girl sensed that she'd said something wrong, because she worked in silence for the next few minutes, the foils making Katie look like she had alien antennae, before finally leading Katie to another seat. Rachel turned on a heat lamp.

"I'll be back to check in a few minutes, okay?"

Rachel wandered off, toward another stylist. They were talking but the chatter in the salon made it impossible to overhear them. Katie glanced at the clock. Kevin would be back in less than an hour. Time was going fast, too fast.

Rachel came back and checked on her hair. "A little while longer," she chirped, and resumed her conversation with her colleague, gesturing with her hands. Animated. Young and carefree. Happy.

More minutes passed. Then, a dozen. Katie tried not to stare at the clock. Finally, it was time, and Rachel removed the foil before leading Katie to the sink. Katie sat and leaned back, resting her neck against the towel. Rachel turned the water on and Katie felt a splash of cool water against her cheek. Rachel massaged the shampoo in her hair and scalp and rinsed, then added conditioner and rinsed again.

"Now let's trim you up, okay?"

Back at the station, Katie thought her hair looked okay, but it was hard to tell when it was wet. It had to be right or Kevin would notice. Rachel combed Katie's hair straight, getting out the tangles. There were forty minutes left.

Rachel stared into the mirror at Katie's reflection. "How much do you want taken off?"

"Not too much," Katie said. "Just enough to clean it up. My husband likes it long."

"How do you want it styled? I've got a book over there if you want something new."

"How I had it when I came in is fine."

"Will do," Rachel said.

Katie watched as Rachel used a comb, running her hair through her fingers, then snipped it with the scissors. First the back, then the sides. And finally the top. Somewhere, Rachel had found a piece of gum and she chewed, her jaw moving up and down as she worked.

"Okay so far?"

"Yes. I think that's enough."

Rachel reached for the hair dryer and a circular brush. She ran the brush slowly through Katie's hair, the noise of the dryer loud in her ear.

"How often do you get your hair done?" Rachel asked, making small talk.

"Once a month," Katie answered. "But sometimes I just get it cut."

"You have beautiful hair, by the way."

"Thank you."

Rachel continued to work. Katie asked for some light curls and Rachel brought out the curling iron. It took a couple of minutes to heat up. There were still twenty minutes left.

Rachel curled and brushed until she was finally satisfied and studied Katie in the mirror.

"How's that?"

Katie examined the color and the style. "That's perfect," she said.

"Let me show you the back," Rachael said. She spun Katie's chair around and handed her a mirror. Katie stared into the double reflection and nodded.

"Okay, that's it, then," Rachel said.

"How much is it?"

Rachel told her and Katie dug into her purse. She pulled out the money she needed, including the tip. "Could I have a receipt?"

"Sure," Rachel said. "Just come with me to the register."

The girl wrote it up. Kevin would check it and ask for the change when she got back in the car, so she made sure Rachel included the tip. She glanced at the clock. Twelve minutes.

Kevin had yet to return and her heart was beating fast as she slipped her jacket and gloves back on. She left the salon while Rachel was still talking to her. Next door, at Radio Shack, she asked the clerk for a disposable cell phone and a card that allowed her twenty hours of service. She felt faint as she said the words, knowing that after this, there was no turning back.

He pulled one out from under the counter and began to ring her up while he explained how it worked. She had extra money in her purse tucked into a tampon case because she knew Kevin would never look there. She pulled it out, laying the crumpled bills on the counter. The clock was continuing to tick and she looked out at the lot again. She was beginning to feel dizzy and her mouth had gone dry.

It took the clerk forever to ring her up. Though she was paying cash, he asked for her name, address, and zip code. Pointless. Ridiculous. She wanted to pay and get out of there. She counted to ten and the clerk still typed. On the road, the light had turned red. Cars were waiting. She wondered if Kevin was getting ready to turn into the lot. She wondered if he would see her leaving the store. It was hard for her to breathe again.

She tried to open the plastic packaging, but it was impossible—as strong as steel. Too big for her small handbag, too big for her pocket. She asked the clerk for a pair of scissors and it took him a precious minute to find one. She wanted to scream, to tell him to hurry because Kevin would be here any minute. She turned toward the window instead.

When the phone was free, she jammed it into her jacket pocket along with the prepaid card. The clerk asked if she wanted a bag but she was out the door without answering. The phone felt like lead, and the snow and ice made it hard to keep her balance.

She opened the door of the salon and went back inside. She slipped off her jacket and gloves and waited by the register. Thirty seconds later, she saw Kevin's car turn into the lot, angling toward the salon.

There was snow on her jacket and she quickly brushed at it as Rachel came toward her. Katie panicked at the thought that

Kevin might have noticed. She concentrated, urging herself to stay in control. To act natural.

"Did you forget something?" Rachel asked.

Katie exhaled. "I was going to wait outside but it's too cold," she explained. "And then I realized I didn't get your card."

Rachel's face lit up. "Oh, that's right. Hold on a second," she said. She walked toward her station and pulled a card from the drawer. Katie knew that Kevin was watching her from inside the car, but she pretended not to notice.

Rachel returned with her business card and handed it over. "I usually don't work on Sundays or Mondays," she said.

Katie nodded. "I'll give you a call."

Behind her, she heard the door open and Kevin was standing in the doorway. He usually didn't come inside and her heart pounded. She slipped her jacket back on, trying to control the trembling of her hands. Then, she turned and smiled.

18

The snow was falling harder as Kevin Tierney pulled the car into the driveway. There were bags of groceries in the backseat and Kevin grabbed three of them before walking toward the door. He'd said nothing on the drive from the salon, had said little to her in the grocery store. Instead, he'd walked beside her as she scanned the shelves looking for sales and trying not to think about the phone in her pocket. Money was tight and Kevin would be angry if she spent too much. Their mortgage took nearly half his salary, and credit card bills consumed another chunk. Most of the time, they had to eat in, but he liked restaurant-type meals, with a main course and two side dishes and sometimes a salad. He refused to eat leftovers and it was hard to make the budget stretch. She had to plan the menu carefully, and she cut coupons from the newspaper. When Kevin paid for the groceries, she handed him the change from the salon and the receipt. He counted the money, making sure everything was there.

At home, she rubbed her arms to stay warm. The house was old and frigid air wormed its way through the window seams and beneath the front door. The bathroom floor was cold enough to make her feet ache, but Kevin complained about the cost of heating oil and never let her adjust the thermostat. When he was at work, she wore a sweatshirt and slippers around the house, but when he was home, he wanted her to look sexy.

Kevin placed the bags of groceries on the kitchen table. She put her bags beside his as he moved to the refrigerator. Opening the freezer, he pulled out a bottle of vodka and a couple of ice cubes. He dropped the cubes into a glass and poured the vodka. The glass was nearly full by the time he stopped pouring. Leaving her alone, he went to the living room and she heard the television come on and the sounds of ESPN. The announcer was talking about the Patriots and the play-offs and the chances of winning another Super Bowl. Last year, Kevin had gone to a Patriots game; he'd been a fan since childhood.

Katie slipped her jacket off and reached into the pocket. She had, she suspected, a couple of minutes and she hoped it was enough. After peeking in the living room, she hurried to the sink. In the cupboard below, there was a box of SOS scrubbing pads. She placed the cell phone at the bottom of the box and put the pads over the top of it. She closed the cupboard quietly before grabbing her jacket, hoping her face wasn't flushed, praying he hadn't seen her. With a long breath to steel herself, she looped it over her arm, carrying it through the living room toward the foyer closet. The room seemed to stretch as she moved through it, like a room viewed through a fun-house mirror at a carnival, but she tried to ignore the sensation. She knew he'd be able to see through her, to read her mind and know what she'd done, but he never turned away from the television. Only when she was back in the kitchen did her breathing begin to slow.

She began to unpack the groceries, still feeling dazed but knowing she had to act normal. Kevin liked a tidy house, especially the kitchen and bathrooms. She put away the cheese and eggs in their separate compartments in the refrigerator. She pulled the old vegetables from the drawer and wiped it down before putting the new vegetables on the bottom. She kept out some green beans and found a dozen red potatoes in a basket on the pantry floor. She left a cucumber on the counter, along with iceberg lettuce and a tomato for a salad. The main course was marinated strip steaks.

She'd put the steaks in the marinade the day before: red wine, orange juice, grapefruit juice, salt, and pepper. The acidity of the juices made the meat tender and gave it extra flavor. It was in a casserole dish on the bottom shelf of the refrigerator.

She put the rest of the groceries away, rotating the older items to the front, then folded the bags and put them under the sink. From a drawer, she removed a knife; the cutting board was beneath the toaster and she set that near the burner. She cut the potatoes in half, only enough for the two of them. She oiled a baking pan, turned the oven on, and seasoned the potatoes with parsley, salt, pepper, and garlic. They would go in before the steaks and she would have to reheat them. The steaks needed to be broiled.

Kevin liked his salads finely diced, with blue cheese crumbles and croutons and Italian dressing. She cut the tomato in half and cut a quarter of the cucumber before wrapping the remainder in plastic wrap and putting it back in the refrigerator. As she opened the door, she noticed Kevin in the kitchen behind her, leaning against the doorjamb that led to the dining room. He took a long drink, finishing his vodka and continuing to watch her, his presence all-encompassing.

He didn't know she'd left the salon, she reminded herself. He didn't know she'd bought a cell phone. He would have said something. He would have done something.

"Steaks tonight?" he finally asked.

She closed the refrigerator door and kept moving, trying to appear busy, staying ahead of her fears. "Yes," she said. "I just turned on the oven, so it'll be a few minutes. I've got to put the potatoes in first."

Kevin stared at her. "Your hair looks good," he said.

"Thank you. She did a good job."

Katie went back to the cutting board. She began to cut the tomato, making a long slice.

"Not too big," he said, nodding in her direction.

"I know," she said. She smiled as he moved to the freezer again. Katie heard the clink of cubes in his glass.

"What did you talk about when you were getting your hair done?"

"Not much. Just the usual. You know how stylists are. They'll talk about anything."

He shook his glass. She could hear the cubes clink against the glass. "Did you talk about me?"

"No," she said.

She knew he wouldn't have liked that and he nodded. He pulled the bottle of vodka out again and set it beside his glass on the counter before moving behind her. He stood, watching over her shoulder as she diced the tomatoes. Small pieces, no larger than a pea. She could feel his breath on her neck and tried not to cringe as he placed his hands on her hips. Knowing what she had to do, she set the knife down and turned toward him, putting her arms around his neck. She kissed him with a little tongue knowing he wanted her to, and didn't see the slap coming until she felt the sting against her cheek. It burned, hot and red. Sharp. Bee stings.

"You made me waste my entire afternoon!" he shouted at her. He gripped her arms tight, squeezing hard. His mouth was contorted, his eyes already bloodshot. She could smell the booze on his breath, and spittle hit her face. "My only day off and you pick that day to get your damn hair done in the middle of the city! And then go grocery shopping!"

She wiggled, trying to back away, and he finally let her go. He shook his head, the muscle of his jaw pulsing. "Did you ever stop to think that I might have wanted to relax today? Just take it easy on my only day off?"

"I'm sorry," she said, holding her cheek. She didn't say that she'd checked with him twice earlier in the week if it would be okay, or that he was the one who made her switch salons because he didn't want her making friends. Didn't want anyone knowing their business.

"I'm sorry," he mimicked her. He stared at her before shaking his head again. "Christ almighty," he said. "Is it so hard for you to think about anyone other than yourself?"

He reached out, trying to grab her, and she turned, trying to run. He was ready for her and there was nowhere to go. He struck fast and hard, his fist a piston, firing at her lower back. She gasped, her vision going black in the corners, feeling as though she'd been pierced with a knife. She collapsed to the floor, her kidney on fire, the pain shooting through her legs and up her spine. The world was spinning, and when she tried to get up, the movement only made it worse.

"You're so damn selfish all the time!" he said, towering over her.

She said nothing. Couldn't say anything. Couldn't breathe. She bit her lip to keep from screaming and wondered if she would pee blood tomorrow. The pain was a razor, slashing at her nerves, but she wouldn't cry because that only made him angrier.

He continued to stand over her, then let out a disgusted sigh. He reached for his empty glass and grabbed the bottle of vodka on the way out of the kitchen.

It took her almost a minute to summon the strength to get up. When she started cutting again, her hands were shaking. The kitchen was cold and the pain was intense in her back, pulsing with every heartbeat. The week before, he'd hit her so hard in the stomach that she'd spent the rest of the night vomiting. She'd fallen to the floor and he'd grabbed her by the wrist to pull her up. The bruise on her wrist was shaped like fingers. Branches of hell.

Tears were on her cheeks and she had to keep shifting her

weight to keep the pain at bay as she finished dicing the to-mato. She diced the cucumber as well. Small pieces. Lettuce, too, diced and chopped. The way he wanted it. She wiped the tears away with the back of her hand and moved slowly toward the refrigerator. She pulled out a packet of blue cheese before finding the croutons in the cupboard.

In the living room, he'd turned the volume up again.

The oven was ready and she put the baking sheet in and set the timer. When the heat hit her face, she realized her skin was still stinging, but she doubted that he'd left a mark there. He knew exactly how hard to strike and she wondered where he'd learned that, whether it was something that all men knew, whether there were secret classes with instructors who special-ized in teaching such things. Or whether it was just Kevin.

The pain in her back had finally begun to lessen to a throb. She could breathe normally again. Wind blew through the seams in the window and the sky had turned a dark gray. Snow tapped gently on the glass. She peeked toward the living room, saw Kevin seated on the couch, and went to lean against the counter. She took off one pump and rubbed her toes, trying to get the blood flowing, trying to warm her feet. She did the same with the other foot before slipping her pumps back on.

She rinsed and cut the green beans and put some olive oil in the frying pan. She would start the beans when the steaks went in the broiler. She tried again not to think about the phone beneath the sink.

She was removing the baking sheet from the oven when Kevin came back in the kitchen. He was holding his glass and it was half empty. His eyes were already glassy. Four or five drinks so far. She couldn't tell. She put the sheet on the stove.

"Just a little bit longer," she said, her tone neutral, pretend-ing that nothing had happened. She'd learned that if she acted angry or hurt, it only enraged him. "I have to finish the steaks and then dinner will be ready."

"I'm sorry," he said. He swayed slightly.

She smiled. "I know. It's okay. It's been a hard few weeks. You've been working a lot."

"Are those new jeans?" The words came out slurry.

"No," she said. "I just haven't worn them for a while."

"They look good."

"Thank you," she said.

He took a step toward her. "You're so beautiful. You know I love you, right?"

"I know."

"I don't like hitting you. You just don't *think* sometimes."

She nodded, looking away, trying to think of something to do, needing to stay busy, then remembered she had to set the table. She moved to the cupboard near the sink.

He moved behind her as she was reaching for the plates and rotated her toward him, pulling her close. She inhaled before offering a contented sigh, because she knew he wanted her to make those kinds of sounds. "You're supposed to say that you love me, too," he whispered. He kissed her cheek and she put her arms around him. She could feel him pressed against her, knew what he wanted.

"I love you," she said.

His hand traveled to her breast. She waited for the squeeze, but it didn't come. Instead, he caressed it gently. Despite herself, her nipple began to harden and she hated it but she couldn't help it. His breath was hot. Boozy.

"God, you're beautiful. You've always been beautiful, from the first time I saw you." He pressed himself harder against her and she could feel him. "Let's hold off on putting the steaks in," he said. "Dinner can wait for a little while."

"I thought you were hungry." She made it sound like a tease.

"I'm hungry for something else right now," he whispered. He unbuttoned her shirt and pulled it open before moving to the snap on her jeans.

"Not here," she said, leaning her head back, letting him continue to kiss her. "In the bedroom, okay?"

"How about the table? Or on the counter instead?"

"Please, baby," she murmured, her head back as he kissed her neck. "That's not very romantic."

"But it's sexy," he said.

"What if someone sees us through the window?"

"You're no fun," he said.

"Please?" she said again. "For me? You know how hot you make me in bed."

He kissed her once more, his hands traveling to her bra. He unsnapped it from the front; he didn't like bras that snapped in the back. She felt the cold air of the kitchen on her breasts; saw the lust in his face as he stared at them. He licked his lips before leading her to the bedroom.

He was almost frenzied as soon as they got there, working her jeans down around her hips, then to her ankles. He squeezed her breasts and she bit her lip to keep from crying out before they fell onto the bed. She panted and moaned and called his name, knowing he wanted her to do those things, because she didn't want him to be angry, because she didn't want to be slapped or punched or kicked, because she didn't want him to know about the phone. Her kidney was still shooting pain and she changed her cries into moans, saying the things he wanted her to say, turning him on until his body started to spasm. When it was over, she got up from the bed, dressed, and kissed him, then she went back to the kitchen and finished making dinner.

Kevin went back to the living room and drank more vodka before going to the table. He told her about work and then went to watch television again while she cleaned the kitchen. Afterward, he wanted her to sit beside him and watch television so she did, until it was finally time to turn in.

In the bedroom, he was snoring within minutes, oblivious to Katie's silent tears, oblivious to her hatred of him, her hatred of herself. Oblivious to the money she'd been stashing away for almost a year or the hair dye she'd snuck into the grocery cart a month ago and hidden in the closet, oblivious to the cell phone hidden in the cupboard beneath the kitchen sink. Oblivious to the fact that in just a few days, if all went the way she hoped, he would never see or hit her ever again.

19

Katie sat beside Alex on the porch, the sky above them a black expanse dotted with light. For months, she'd tried to block out the specific memories, focusing only on the fear that had been left behind. She didn't want to remember Kevin, didn't want to think about him. She wanted to erase him entirely, to pretend he never existed. But he would always be there.

Alex had stayed silent throughout her story, his chair angled toward hers. She'd spoken through her tears, though he doubted she even knew she was crying. She'd told him without emotion, almost in a trance, as if the events had happened to someone else. He felt sick to his stomach by the time she'd trailed off.

She couldn't look at him as she told him. He'd heard versions of the same story before, but this time it was different. She wasn't simply a victim, she was his friend, the woman he'd come to love, and he tucked a loose strand of hair behind her ear.

At his touch, she flinched slightly before relaxing. He heard her sigh, tired now. Tired of talking. Tired of the past.

"You did the right thing by leaving," he said. His tone was soft. Understanding.

It took her a moment to respond. "I know," she said.

"It had nothing to do with you."

She stared into the darkness. "Yes," she said, "it did. I chose him, remember? I married him. I let it happen once and then again, and after that, it was too late. I still cooked for him and cleaned the house for him. I slept with him whenever he wanted, did whatever he wanted. I made him think I *loved* it."

"You did what you had to do to survive," he said, his voice steady.

She grew silent again. The crickets were chirping and locusts hummed from the trees. "I never thought something like this could happen, you know? My dad was a drunk, but he wasn't violent. I was just so . . . weak. I don't know why I let it happen."

His voice was soft. "Because at one time you loved him. Because you believed him when he promised it wouldn't happen again. Because he gradually grew more violent and controlling over time, slowly enough that you felt like he would change until you finally realized he wouldn't."

With his words, she inhaled sharply and lowered her head, her shoulders heaving up and down. The sound of her anguish made his throat clench with anger at the life she'd lived and sadness because she was still living it. He wanted to hold her, but knew that right now, at this moment, he was doing all she wanted. She was fragile, on edge. Vulnerable.

It took a few minutes before she was finally able to stop crying. Her eyes were red and puffy. "I'm sorry I told you all that," she said, her voice still choked up. "I shouldn't have."

"I'm glad you did."

"The only reason I did was because you already knew."

"I know."

"But you didn't need to know the details about the things I had to do."

"It's okay."

"I hate him," she said. "But I hate myself, too. I tried to tell you that I'm better off alone. I'm not who you thought I was. I'm not the woman you think you know."

She was on the verge of crying again and he finally stood. He tugged at her hand, willing her to stand. She did but wouldn't look at him. He suppressed his anger at her husband and kept his voice soft.

"Listen to me," he said. He used a finger to raise her chin. She resisted at first then gave in, finally looking at him. He went on. "There's nothing you can tell me that will change how I feel about you. Nothing. Because that isn't you. It's never been you. You're the woman I've come to know. The woman I love."

She studied him, wanting to believe him, knowing somehow he was telling the truth, and she felt something give way inside her. Still . . .

"But . . ."

"No buts," he said, "because there are none. You see yourself as someone who couldn't get away. I see the courageous woman who escaped. You see yourself as someone who should be ashamed or guilty because she let it happen. I see a kind, beautiful woman who should feel proud because she stopped it from happening ever again. Not many women have the strength to do what you did. That's what I see now, and that's what I've always seen when I look at you."

She smiled. "I think you need glasses."

"Don't let the gray hair fool you. My eyes are still perfect." He moved toward her, making sure it was okay before leaning in to kiss her. It was brief and soft. Caring. "I'm just sorry you had to go through it at all."

"I'm still going through it."

"Because you think he's looking for you?"

"I know he's looking for me. And he'll never stop." She paused. "There's something wrong with him. He's . . . insane."

Alex thought about that. "I know I shouldn't ask, but did you ever think of calling the police?"

Her shoulders dropped slightly. "Yes," she said. "I called once."

"And they didn't do anything?"

"They came to the house and talked to me. They convinced me not to press charges."

Alex considered it. "That doesn't make sense."

"It made perfect sense to me." She shrugged. "Kevin warned me that it wouldn't do any good to call the police."

"How would he know?"

She sighed, thinking she might as well tell him everything. "Because he is the police," she finally said. She looked up at him. "He's a detective with the Boston Police Department. And he didn't call me Katie. Her eyes telegraphed despair. "He called me Erin."

20

---❦---

On Memorial Day, hundreds of miles to the north, Kevin Tierney stood in the backyard of a house in Dorchester, wearing shorts and a Hawaiian-style shirt he'd bought when he and Erin had visited Oahu on their honeymoon.

"Erin's back in Manchester," he said.

Bill Robinson, his captain, flipped burgers on the grill. "Again?"

"I told you that her friend has cancer, right? She feels like she's got to be there for her friend."

"That cancer's bad stuff," Bill said. "How's Erin holding up?"

"Okay. I can tell she's tired, though. It's hard to keep going back and forth like she's been doing."

"I can imagine," Bill said. "Emily had to do something like that when her sister got lupus. Spent two months up in Burlington in the middle of winter cooped up in a tiny apartment, just the two of them. Drove them both crazy. In the end, the sister packed up Em's suitcases and set them outside the front door and said she was better off alone. Not that I could blame her, of course."

Kevin took a pull on his beer, and because it was expected of him, he smiled. Emily was Bill's wife and they'd been married almost thirty years. Bill liked to tell people they'd been the happiest six years of his life. Everyone at the precinct had heard the joke about fifty times in the past eight years, and a big chunk of those people were here now. Bill hosted a barbecue at his house every Memorial Day and pretty much everyone who wasn't on duty showed up, not only out of obligation, but because Bill's brother distributed beer for a living, a lot of which ended up here. Wives and husbands, girlfriends and boyfriends, and kids were clustered in groups, some in the kitchen, others on the patio. Four detectives were playing horseshoes and sand was flying around the stakes.

"Next time she's back in town," Bill added, "why don't you bring her by for dinner? Em's been asking about her. Unless, of course, you two would rather make up for lost time." He winked.

Kevin wondered if the offer was genuine. On days like these, Bill liked to pretend he was just one of the guys instead of the captain. But he was hard-edged. Cunning. More a politician than a cop. "I'll mention it to her."

"When did she take off?"

"Earlier this morning. She's already there."

The burgers were sizzling on the grill, the drippings making the flames jump and dance.

Bill pressed down on one of the patties, squeezing out the juice, drying it out. The man knew nothing about barbecuing, Kevin thought. Without the juice they would taste like rocks— dry, flavorless, and hard. Inedible. "Hey, about the Ashley Henderson case," Bill said, changing the subject. "I think we're finally going to be able to indict. You did good work, there."

"It's about time," Kevin said. "I thought they had enough a while ago."

"I did, too. But I'm not the DA." Bill pressed down on another patty, ruining it. "I also wanted to talk to you about Terry."

Terry Canton had been Kevin's partner for the last three

years, but he'd had a heart attack in December and had been out of work since. Kevin had been working alone since then.

"What about him?"

"He's not coming back. I just found out this morning. His doctors recommended that he retire and he decided they were right. He figures he's already put in his twenty and his pension is waiting for him."

"What does that mean for me?"

Bill shrugged. "We'll get you a new partner, but we can't right now with the city on a budget freeze. Maybe when the new budget passes."

"Maybe or probably?"

"You'll get a partner. But it probably won't be until July. I'm sorry about that. I know it means more work for you, but there's nothing I can do. I'll try my best to keep your load manageable."

"I appreciate that."

A group of kids ran across the patio, their faces dirty. Two women exited the house carrying bowls of chips, probably gossiping. Kevin hated gossips. Bill motioned with his spatula toward the railing on the deck. "Hand me that plate over there, would you? I think these are getting close to being done."

Kevin grabbed the serving platter. It was the same one that had been used to bring the hamburger patties out to the grill and he noted smears of grease and bits of raw hamburger. Disgusting. He knew that Erin would have brought a clean platter, one without bits of raw hamburger and grease. Kevin set the platter next to the grill.

"I need another beer," Kevin said, raising his bottle. "You want one?"

Bill shook his head and ruined another burger. "I'm still working on mine right there. But thanks."

Kevin headed toward the house, feeling the grease from the platter on his fingertips. Soaking in.

"Hey," Bill shouted from behind him. Kevin turned.

"Cooler's over there, remember?" Bill pointed to the corner of the deck.

"I know. But I want to wash my hands before dinner."

"Make it back quick then. Once I set the platter out, it's every man for himself."

Kevin paused at the back door to wipe his feet on the mat before heading inside. In the kitchen, he walked around a group of chattering wives and toward the sink. He washed his hands twice, using soap both times. Through the window, he saw Bill set the platter of hot dogs and burgers on the picnic table, near the buns, condiments, and bowls of chips. Almost immediately flies caught the scent and descended on the feast, buzzing over the food and landing on the burgers. People didn't seem to care as they formed a crazy line. Instead, they shooed the flies and loaded their plates, pretending that flies weren't swarming.

Ruined burgers and a cloud of flies.

He and Erin would have done it differently. He wouldn't have pressed the burgers with the spatula and Erin would have placed the condiments and chips and pickles in the kitchen so people could serve up there, where it was clean. Flies were disgusting and the burgers were as hard as rocks and he wasn't going to eat them because the thought made him nauseated.

He waited until the platter of burgers had been emptied before heading back outside. He wandered to the table, feigning disappointment.

"I warned you they'd go fast." Bill beamed. "But Emily's got another platter in the refrigerator, so it won't be long until round two. Grab me a beer, would you, while I go get it?"

"Sure," Kevin said.

When the next batch of burgers was done, Kevin loaded a plate of food and complimented Bill and told him it looked fantastic. Flies were swarming and the burgers were dry and when Bill turned away, Kevin tossed the food into the metal garbage can on the side of the house. He told Bill that the burger tasted fantastic.

He stayed at the barbecue for a couple of hours. He talked with Coffey and Ramirez. They were detectives like him, except they ate the burgers and didn't care that the flies were swarming. Kevin didn't want to be the first one to leave, or even the second one, because the captain wanted to pretend he was one of the guys and he didn't want to offend the captain. He didn't like Coffey or Ramirez. Sometimes, when Kevin was around, Coffey and Ramirez stopped talking, and Kevin knew they had been talking about him behind his back. Gossips.

But Kevin was a good detective and he knew it. Bill knew it, and so did Coffey and Ramirez. He worked homicide and knew how to talk to witnesses and suspects. He knew when to ask questions and when to listen; he knew when people were lying to him and he put murderers behind bars because the Bible says *Thou shalt not kill* and he believed in God and he was doing God's work by putting the guilty in jail.

Back at home, Kevin walked through the living room. He resisted the urge to call for Erin. If Erin had been here, the mantel would have been dusted and the magazines would have fanned out on the end table and there wouldn't have been an empty bottle of vodka on the couch. If Erin had been here, the drapes would have been opened, allowing the sunlight to stretch across the floorboards. If Erin had been here, the dishes would have been washed and put away and dinner would have been waiting on the table and she would have smiled at him and asked him how his day had gone. Later they would make love because he loved her and she loved him.

Upstairs in the bedroom, he stood at the closet door. He could still catch a whiff of the perfume she'd worn, the one he'd bought her for Christmas. He'd seen her lift a tab on an ad in one of her magazines and smile when she smelled the perfume sample. When she went to bed, he tore the page out of the magazine and tucked it into his wallet so he'd know exactly which perfume to buy. He remembered the tender way she'd dabbed a little behind each ear and on her wrists when he'd taken her out on New Year's Eve, and how pretty she'd looked in the black cocktail dress she was wearing. In the restaurant, Kevin had noticed the way other men, even those with dates, had glanced in her direction as she passed by them on the way to the table. Afterward, when they'd returned home, they made love as the New Year rolled in.

The dress was still there, hanging in the same place, bringing back those memories. A week ago, he remembered removing it from the hanger and holding it as he'd sat on the edge of the bed and cried.

Outside, he could hear the steady sound of crickets but it did nothing to soothe him. Though it was supposed to have been a relaxing day, he was tired. He hadn't wanted to go to the barbecue, hadn't wanted to answer questions about Erin, hadn't wanted to lie. Not because lying bothered him, but because it was hard to keep up the pretense that Erin hadn't left him. He'd invented a story and had been sticking to it for months: that Erin called every night, that she'd been home the last few days but had gone back to New Hampshire, that the friend was undergoing chemotherapy and needed Erin's help. He knew he couldn't keep that up forever, that soon the helping-a-friend excuse would begin to sound hollow and people would begin to wonder why they never saw Erin in church or at the store or even around the neighborhood or how long she would continue to help her friend. They'd talk about him behind his back and say things like, *Erin must have left him*, and *I guess their marriage wasn't as perfect as I thought it was*. The thought made his stomach clench, reminding him that he hadn't eaten.

There wasn't much in the refrigerator. Erin always had turkey and ham and Dijon mustard and fresh rye bread from the bakery, but his only choice now was whether to reheat the

Mongolian beef he'd picked up from the Chinese restaurant a couple of days earlier. On the bottom shelf, he saw food stains and he felt like crying again, because it made him think about Erin's screams and the way her head had sounded when it had hit the edge of the table after he'd thrown her across the kitchen. He'd been slapping and kicking her because there were food stains in the refrigerator and he wondered now why he'd become so angry about such a little thing.

Kevin went to the bed and lay down. Next thing he knew, it was midnight, and the neighborhood outside his window was still. Across the street, he saw a light on in the Feldmans' house. He didn't like the Feldmans. Unlike the other neighbors, Larry Feldman never waved at him if both of them happened to be in their yards, and if his wife, Gladys, happened to see him, she'd turn away and head back into the house. They were in their sixties, the kind of people who rushed outside to scold a kid who happened to walk across their grass to retrieve a Frisbee or baseball. And even though they were Jewish, they decorated their house with Christmas lights in addition to the menorah they put in the window at the holidays. They confounded him and he didn't think they were good neighbors.

He went back to bed but couldn't fall asleep. In the morning, with sunlight streaming in, he knew that nothing had changed for anyone else. Only his life was different. His brother, Michael, and his wife, Nadine, would be getting the kids ready for school before heading out to their jobs at Boston College, and his mom and dad were probably reading the *Globe* as they had their morning coffee. Crimes had been committed, and witnesses would be in the precinct. Coffey and Ramirez would be gossiping about him.

He showered and had vodka and toast for breakfast. At the precinct, he was called out to investigate a murder. A woman in her twenties, most likely a prostitute, had been found stabbed to death, her body tossed in a Dumpster. He spent the morning talking to bystanders while the evidence was collected. When he finished with the interviews, he went to the precinct to start the report while the information was fresh in his mind. He was a good detective.

The precinct was busy. End of a holiday weekend. The world gone crazy. Detectives were speaking into phones and writing at their desks and talking to witnesses and listening as victims told detectives about their victimization. Noisy. Active. People coming and going. Phones ringing. Kevin walked toward his desk, one of four in the middle of the room. Through the open door, Bill waved but stayed in his office. Ramirez and Coffey were at their desks, sitting across from him.

"You okay?" Coffey asked. Coffey was in his forties, overweight and balding. "You look like hell."

"I didn't sleep well," Kevin said.

"I don't sleep well without Janet, either. When's Erin coming back?"

Kevin kept his expression neutral.

"Next weekend. I've got a few days coming and we've decided to go to the Cape. We haven't been there in years."

"Yeah? My mom lives there. Where at the Cape?"

"Provincetown."

"So does she. You'll love it there. I go there all the time. Where are you staying?"

Kevin wondered why Coffey kept asking questions. "I'm not sure," he finally said. "Erin's making the arrangements."

Kevin walked toward the coffeepot and poured himself a cup, even though he didn't want any. He'd have to find the name of a bed-and-breakfast and a couple of restaurants, so if Coffey asked about it, he'd know what to say.

His days followed the same routine. He worked and talked to witnesses and finally went home. His work was stressful and he wanted to relax when he finished, but everything was different at home and the work stayed with him. He'd once believed that he would get used to the sight of murder victims, but their gray, lifeless faces were etched in his memory, and sometimes the victims visited him in his sleep.

He didn't like going home. When he finished his shift, there was no beautiful wife to greet him at the door. Erin had been gone since January. Now, his house was messy and dirty and he had to do his own laundry. He hadn't known how to work the washing machine, and the first time he ran it he added too much soap and the clothes came out looking dingy. There were no home-cooked meals or candles on the table. Instead, he grabbed food on the way home and ate on the couch. Sometimes, he put on the television. Erin liked to watch HGTV, the home and garden channel on cable, so he often watched that and when he did, the emptiness he felt inside was almost unbearable.

After work he no longer bothered to store his gun in the gun box he kept in his closet; in the box, he had a second Glock for his personal use. Erin had been afraid of guns, even before he'd placed the Glock to her head and threatened to kill her if she ever ran away again. She'd screamed and cried as he'd sworn that he'd kill any man she slept with, any man she cared about. She'd been so stupid and he'd been so angry with her for running away and he demanded the name of the man who had helped her so he could kill him. But Erin had screamed and cried and begged for her life and swore there wasn't a man and he believed her because she was his wife. They'd made their vows in front of God and family and the Bible says *Thou shalt not commit adultery*. Even then, he hadn't believed that Erin had been unfaithful. He'd never believed another man was involved. While they were married, he'd made sure of that. He made random calls to the house throughout the day and never let her go to the store or to the hair salon or to the library by herself. She didn't have a car or even a license and he swung by their house whenever he was in the area, just to make sure she was at home. She hadn't left because she wanted to commit adultery. She left because she was tired of getting kicked and punched and thrown down the cellar stairs and he knew he shouldn't have done those things and he always felt guilty and apologized but it still hadn't mattered.

She shouldn't have run away. It broke his heart because he loved her more than life and he'd always taken care of her. He bought her a house and a refrigerator and a washer and dryer and new furniture. The house had always been clean, but now the sink was full of dishes and his hamper was overflowing.

He knew he should clean the house but he didn't have the energy. Instead, he went to the kitchen and pulled a bottle of vodka from the freezer. There were four bottles left; a week ago, there'd been twelve. He knew he was drinking too much. He knew he should eat better and stop drinking but all he wanted to do was take the bottle and sit on the couch and drink. Vodka was good because it didn't make your breath smell, and in the mornings, no one would know he was nursing a hangover.

He poured a glass of vodka, finished it, and poured another before walking through the empty house. His heart ached because Erin wasn't here and if she suddenly showed up at the door, he knew he'd apologize for hitting her and they'd work things out and then they'd make love in the bedroom. He wanted to hold her and whisper how much he adored her, but he knew she wasn't coming back, and even though he loved her, she made him so angry sometimes. A wife didn't just leave. A wife didn't just walk away from a marriage. He wanted to hit and kick and slap her and pull her hair for being so stupid. For being so damn selfish. He wanted to show her it was pointless to run away.

He drank a third and fourth glass of vodka.

It was all so confusing. The house was a wreck. There was an empty pizza box on the floor of the living room and the casing around the bathroom door was splintered and cracked. The door would no longer close all the way. He'd kicked it in after she'd locked it, trying to get away from him. He'd been holding her by the hair as he punched her in the kitchen and she'd run to the bathroom and he'd chased her through the house and kicked the door in. But now he couldn't remember what they'd been fighting about.

He couldn't remember much about that night. He couldn't remember breaking two of her fingers, even though it was obvious that he had. But he wouldn't let her go to the hospital for a week, not until the bruises on her face could be covered by makeup, and she'd had to cook and clean one-handed. He bought her flowers and apologized and told her that he loved her and promised it would never happen again, and after she got the cast off, he'd taken her into Boston for a dinner at Petroni's. It was expensive and he'd smiled across the table at her. Afterward, they'd gone to a movie and on the way home he remembered thinking about how much he loved her and how lucky he was to have someone like her as his wife.

21

Alex had stayed with Katie until after midnight, listening as she'd told the story of her prior life. When she was too spent and exhausted to talk anymore, he put his arms around her and kissed her good night. On his drive home, he thought that he had never met anyone braver or stronger or more resourceful.

They spent much of the next couple of weeks together—or as much as they could, anyway. Between the hours he worked at the store and her shifts at Ivan's, it wasn't usually more than a few hours a day, but he anticipated his visits to her place with a sense of excitement he hadn't felt in years. Sometimes, Kristen and Josh went with him. Other times, Joyce would shoo him out the door with a wink, urging him to have himself a good time before he headed over.

They seldom spent time at his house and when they did, it was only for short periods. In his mind, he wanted to believe it was because of the kids, that he wanted to take things slowly, but part of him realized it also had to do with Carly. Though he knew he loved Katie—and he grew more certain with every passing day—he wasn't sure he was ready for that just yet. Katie seemed to understand his reluctance and didn't seem to mind, if only because it was easier to be alone at her place.

Even so, they'd yet to make love. Though he often found himself imagining how wonderful it would be, especially in those moments before sleep, he knew Katie wasn't ready for that. They both seemed to realize it would signal a change in their relationship, a hopeful permanence of sorts. For now, it was enough to kiss her, to feel her arms wrapped around him. He loved the scent of jasmine shampoo in her hair and the way her hand nestled so perfectly in his; the way their every touch was charged with delicious anticipation, as if they were somehow saving themselves for each other. He hadn't slept with anyone since his wife had died, and now he felt that in some way he had unknowingly been waiting for Katie.

He took pleasure in showing her around the area. They walked the waterfront and past the historic homes, examining the architecture, and one weekend he took her to the Orton Plantation Gardens, where they wandered among a thousand blooming rosebushes. Afterward, they went to lunch at a small oceanfront bistro at Caswell Beach, where they held hands across the table like teenagers.

Since their dinner at her house, she hadn't broached her past again, and he didn't bring it up. He knew she was still working things out in her mind: how much she'd told him already and how much there still was to tell, whether or not she could trust him, how much it mattered that she was still married, and what would happen if Kevin somehow found her here. When he sensed she was brooding over such things, he would remind her gently that no matter what happened, her secret would always be safe with him. He would never tell anyone.

Watching her, he would sometimes be overcome with an overwhelming rage at Kevin Tierney. Such men's instincts to victimize and torture were as foreign to him as the ability to breathe underwater or fly; more than anything, he wanted revenge. He wanted justice. He wanted Kevin to experience Katie's anguish and terror, the unending bouts of brutal physical pain. During his time in the army, he'd killed one man, a soldier strung out on methamphetamines who was threatening a hostage with a gun. The man was dangerous and out of control and when the opportunity arose, Alex had pulled the trigger without hesitation. The death had given his job a sobering new meaning, but in his heart he knew that there were moments in life when violence was necessary to save lives. He knew that if Kevin ever showed up, Alex would protect Katie, no matter what. In the army, he'd slowly come to the realization that there were people who added goodness to the world and people who lived to destroy it. In his mind, the decision to protect an innocent woman like Katie from a psychopath like Kevin was as clear as black and white—a simple choice.

On most days, the specter of Katie's past life didn't intrude, and they spent each day together in a state of relaxed and growing intimacy. The afternoons with the kids were particularly special for him. Katie was a natural with children— whether helping Kristen feed the ducks at the pond or playing catch with Josh, she always seemed to fall effortlessly into rhythm with them, by turns playful, comforting, rowdy, or quiet. In this way she was much like Carly, and he somehow felt certain that Katie was the kind of woman Carly had once spoken about.

In the final weeks of Carly's life, he had maintained a vigil beside her bed. Even though she slept most of the time, he was afraid of missing those times when she was conscious, no matter how short they might be. By then, the left side of her body was almost paralyzed, and speech was difficult for her. But one night, during a brief lucid period in the hour just before dawn, she'd reached for him.

"I want you to do something for me," she said with effort, licking her cracked lips. Her voice was hoarse from disuse.

"Anything."

"I want you to be . . . happy." At this, he saw the ghost of her

old smile, the confident, self-possessed smile that had capti-
vated him at their first meeting.

"I am happy."

She gave a faint shake of her head. "I'm talking about the
future." Her eyes gleamed with the intensity of hot coals in her
sunken face. "We both know what I'm talking about."

"I don't."

She ignored his response. "Marrying you . . . being with you
every day and having children with you . . . it's the best thing
I've ever done. You're the best man I've ever known."

His throat closed up. "Me, too," he said. "I feel the same
way."

"I know," she said. "And that's why this is so hard for me.
Because I know that I've failed—"

"You haven't failed," he broke in.

Her expression was sad. "I love you, Alex, and I love our
kids," she whispered. "And it would break my heart to think
that you'll never be completely happy again."

"Carly—"

"I want you to meet someone new." She struggled to take a
deep breath, her fragile rib cage heaving with the effort. "I want
her to be smart and kind . . . and I want you to fall in love with
her, because you shouldn't spend the rest of your life alone."

Alex couldn't speak, could barely see her through his tears.

"The kids need a mom." To his ears, it sounded almost like
a plea. "Someone who loves them as much as I do, someone
who thinks of them as her own children."

"Why are you talking about this?" he asked, his voice cracking.

"Because," she said, "I have to believe that it's possible." Her
bony fingers clutched at his arm with desperate intensity. "It's
the only thing I have left."

Now, as he saw Katie chasing after Josh and Kristen on the
grassy shoulder of the duck pond, he felt a bittersweet pang at
the thought that maybe Carly had gotten her last wish after all.

* * *

She liked him too much for her own good. Katie knew that she was walking a dangerous line. Telling him about her past had seemed like the right thing to do at the time, and speaking the words had freed her somehow from the crushing burden of her secrets. But the morning after their first dinner, she was paralyzed with anxiety by what she had done. Alex used to be an investigator, after all, which probably meant he could easily make a phone call or two, no matter what he'd said to her. He'd talk to someone and they'd talk to someone and eventually, Kevin would learn of it. She hadn't told him that Kevin had an almost eerie ability to connect seemingly random information; she hadn't mentioned that when a suspect was on the run, Kevin almost always knew where to find him. Simply thinking about what she'd done made her sick to her stomach.

But gradually, over the next couple of weeks, she felt her fears ebb. Instead of asking her more questions when they were alone, Alex acted as if her revelations had no bearing on their lives in Southport. The days passed with easy spontaneity, untroubled by shadows from her prior life. She couldn't help it: she trusted him. And when they kissed, which happened with surprising frequency, there were times when her knees went shaky and it was all she could do to stop from taking his hand and dragging him into the bedroom.

On Saturday, two weeks after their first date, they stood on her front porch, his arms wrapped around her, his lips against hers. Josh and Kristen were at an end-of-the-year swimming party hosted by a kid in Josh's class. Later, Alex and Katie planned to take them to the beach for an evening barbecue, but for the next few hours, they'd be alone.

When they finally separated, Katie sighed. "You really have to stop doing that."

"Doing what?"

"You know exactly what you're doing."

"I can't help it."

I know the feeling, Katie thought. "Do you know what I like about you?"

"My body?"

"Yes. That, too." She laughed. "But I also like that you make me feel special."

"You are special," he said.

"I'm serious," she said. "But it makes me wonder why you never found someone else. Since your wife passed away, I mean."

"I haven't been looking," he said. "But even if there was someone else, I would have dumped her so I could be with you instead."

"That's not nice." She poked him in the ribs.

"It's true, though. Believe it or not, I'm picky."

"Yeah," she said, "real picky. You only go out with emotionally scarred women."

"You're not emotionally scarred. You're tough. You're a survivor. It's actually kind of sexy."

"I think you're just trying to flatter me in the hopes I'll rip off your clothes."

"Is it working?"

"You're getting closer," she admitted, and the sound of his laughter reminded her again how much he loved her.

"I'm glad you ended up in Southport," he said.

"Uh-huh." For an instant she seemed to disappear inside herself.

"What?" He scrutinized her face, suddenly alert.

She shook her head. "It was so close . . ." She sighed, hugging her arms around herself at the memory. "I almost didn't make it."

22

Brittle snow coated the yards of Dorchester, forming a glittering shell over the world outside her window. The January sky, gray the day before, had given way to an icy blue and the temperature was below freezing.

It was Sunday morning, the day after she'd had her hair done. She peeked in the toilet for blood, sure she'd see some after she peed. Her kidney still throbbed, radiating pain from her shoulder blades to the backs of her legs. It had kept her up for hours as Kevin snored beside her, but thankfully, it wasn't as serious as it could have been. After closing the bedroom door behind her, she limped to the kitchen, reminding herself that in just a couple of days, it would be over. But she had to be careful not to arouse Kevin's suspicions, to play things exactly right. If she ignored the beating he had given her the night before, he would be suspicious. If she went too far, he would be suspicious. After four years of hell, she'd learned the rules.

Kevin had to go into work at noon, even though it was Sunday, and she knew he'd be up soon. The house was cold and she pulled on a sweatshirt over her pajamas; in the mornings, Kevin didn't mind, usually because he was too hung over to care. She started the coffee and put the milk and sugar on the table, along

with butter and jelly. She set his silverware out and placed a
cup of ice water beside the fork. After that, two pieces of toast
went in the toaster, though she couldn't toast them just yet.
She put three eggs on the counter, where she could reach them
quickly. When that was done, she placed half a dozen slices of
bacon in the frying pan. They were sizzling and popping when
Kevin finally wandered into the kitchen. He took a seat at the
empty table and drank his water as she brought him a cup of
coffee.

"I was dead to the world last night," he said. "What time did
we end up going to bed?"

"Maybe ten?" she answered. She put the coffee beside his
empty glass. "It wasn't late. You've been working hard and I
know you've been tired."

His eyes were bloodshot. "I'm sorry about last night. I didn't
mean it. I've just been under a lot of pressure lately. Since
Terry's heart attack, I've been having to do the work of two
people, and the Preston case starts this week."

"It's okay," she said. She could still smell the alcohol on his
breath. "Your breakfast will be ready in a few minutes."

At the stove, she turned the bacon with a fork and a splash
of grease scalded her arm, making her temporarily forget the
pain in her back.

When the bacon was crispy, she put four pieces on Kevin's
plate and two on hers. She drained the grease into a soup can,
wiped the frying pan with a paper towel, and oiled it again with
cooking spray. She had to move fast, so the bacon wouldn't get
cold. She started the toaster and cracked the eggs. He liked his
over medium, with the yolk intact, and she'd grown adept at the
process. The pan was still hot and the eggs cooked quickly. She
turned them once before sliding two onto his plate and one onto
hers. The toast came up and she placed both slices on his plate.

She sat across from him at the table because he liked them
to have breakfast together. He buttered his toast and added

grape jelly before using his fork to break the eggs. The yolk pooled like yellow blood and he used his toast to sop it up.

"What are you going to do today?" he asked. He used his fork to cut another piece of egg. Chewing.

"I was going to do the windows and the laundry," she said.

"The sheets probably need a wash, too, huh? After our fun last night?" he said, waggling his eyebrows. His hair was pointing in different directions and there was a piece of egg at the corner of his mouth.

She tried not to show her revulsion. Instead, she changed the subject.

"Do you think you'll get a conviction in the Preston case?" she asked.

He leaned back and rolled his shoulders before hunching over his plate again.

"That's up to the DA. Higgins is good, but you never know. Preston has a shyster lawyer and he's going to try to twist all the facts around."

"I'm sure you'll do fine. You're smarter than he is."

"We'll see. I just hate that it's in Marlborough. Higgins wants to prep me Tuesday night, after court finishes for the day."

Erin knew all of this already and she nodded. The Preston case had been widely publicized and the trial was due to start on Monday in Marlborough, not Boston. Lorraine Preston had supposedly hired a man to kill her husband. Not only was Douglass Preston a billionaire hedge-fund manager, but his wife was a scion of society, involved in charities ranging from art museums and the symphony to inner-city schools. The pretrial publicity had been staggering; a day hadn't gone by in weeks without one or two articles on the front page and a top story on the evening news. Megamoney, lurid sex, drugs, betrayal, infidelity, assassination, and an illegitimate child. Because of the endless publicity, the trial had been moved to Marlborough. Kevin had been one of several detectives assigned to the investigation and all were scheduled to testify Wednesday. Like everyone else, Erin had been following the news but she'd been asking Kevin questions every now and then about the case.

"You know what you need after you're finished in court?" she asked. "A night out. We should get dressed up and go out to dinner. You're off on Friday, right?"

"We just did that on New Year's," Kevin grumbled, sopping up more yolk on his plate. There were smears of jelly on his fingers.

"If you don't want to go out, I can make you something special here. Whatever you want. We can have wine and maybe start a fire and I could wear something sexy. It could be really romantic." He looked up from his plate and she went on. "The point is, I'm open to whatever," she purred, "and you need a break. I don't like it when you work so hard. It's like they expect you to solve every case out there."

He tapped his fork against his plate, studying her. "Why are you acting all lovey-dovey? What's going on?"

Telling herself to stick to the script, she pushed back from the table.

"Just forget it, okay?" She grabbed her plate and the fork clattered off it, hitting the table and then the floor. "I was trying to be supportive since you're going out of town, but if you don't like it, fine. I'll tell you what—you figure out what you want to do and let me know sometime, okay?"

She stormed over to the sink and turned the faucet on hard. She knew she'd surprised him, could feel him vacillating between anger and confusion. She ran her hands under the water then brought them to her face. She drew a series of rapid breaths, hiding her face, and made a choking sound. She let her shoulders heave a little.

"Are you crying?" he asked. She heard his chair slide back. "Why the hell are you crying?"

She choked out the words, doing her best to make them

sound broken. "I don't know what to do anymore. I don't know what you want. I know how big this case is and how important it is and how much pressure you're under . . ."

She choked off the final words, sensing his approach. When she felt him touch her, she shuddered.

"Hey, it's okay," he said grudgingly. "You don't have to cry."

She turned toward him, squeezing her eyes shut, putting her face against his chest. "I just want to make you happy," she stammered. She wiped her wet face on his shirt.

"We'll figure it out, okay? We'll have a nice weekend. I promise. To make up for last night."

She put her arms around him, pulling him close, sniffling. She drew another rasping inhale. "I'm really sorry. I know you didn't need that today. Me getting all blubbery for nothing. You've got so much on your plate already."

"I can handle it," he said. He tilted his head and she leaned up to kiss him, her eyes still shut. When she pulled back, she wiped her face with her fingers and pulled close to him again. As he pressed against her, she could feel him getting excited. She knew how her vulnerability turned him on.

"We've got a little time before I have to head into work," he said.

"I should clean the kitchen first."

"You can do it later," he said.

Minutes later, with Kevin moving atop her, she made the sounds he wanted while staring out the window of the bedroom and thinking of other things.

She had learned to hate winter, with the endless cold and a yard half-buried in snow, because she couldn't go outside. Kevin didn't like her to walk around the neighborhood but he let her garden in the backyard because of the privacy fence. In the spring, she always planted flowers in pots and vegetables in a small plot near the back of the garage, where the sun was full and strong, unshaded by the maple trees. In the fall, she would pull on a sweater and read books from the library as fallen leaves, brown and crinkly, drifted around the yard.

But winter made her life a prison, cold and gray and gloomy. Misery. Most days were spent without setting foot outside the door because she never knew when Kevin would show up unexpectedly. She knew the names of a single neighbor, the Feldmans, who lived across the street. In her first year of marriage, Kevin rarely hit her and sometimes she went for walks without him. The Feldmans, an older couple, liked to work in their garden, and in the first year she'd lived here, she'd often stopped to talk to them for a while. Kevin gradually tried to put an end to those friendly visits. Now she saw the Feldmans only when she knew Kevin was busy at work, when she knew he couldn't call. She would make sure no other neighbors were watching before darting across the street to their front door. She felt like a spy when she visited with them. They showed her photos of their daughters growing up. One had died and the other had moved away and she had the sense that they were as lonely as she was. In the summer, she made them blueberry pies and would spend the rest of the afternoon mopping up the flour in the kitchen so Kevin wouldn't know.

After Kevin went to work, she cleaned the windows and put fresh sheets on the bed. She vacuumed, dusted, and cleaned the kitchen. As she worked, she practiced lowering her voice so she could sound like a man. She tried not to think about the cell phone she had charged overnight and put under the sink. Even though she knew that she might never get a better chance, she was terrified because there was still so much that could go wrong.

She made Kevin breakfast on Monday morning, just as she always did. Four slices of bacon, eggs over medium, and two pieces of toast. He was grumpy and distracted and he read the paper without saying much to her. When he was about to leave, he put a coat on over his suit and she told him she was going to hop into the shower.

"Must be nice," he grunted, "to wake up every day knowing you can do whatever the hell you want to do whenever you want to do it."

"Is there anything special you want for dinner?" she asked, pretending not to have heard him.

He thought about it. "Lasagna and garlic bread. And a salad," he said.

When he left, she stood at the window watching as his car reached the corner. As soon as he turned, she walked to the phone, dizzy at the thought of what was to come next.

When she called the phone company, she was directed to customer service. Five minutes passed, then six. It would take Kevin twenty minutes to get to work, and no doubt he would call as soon as he arrived. She still had time. Finally, a rep got on the line and asked her name and the billing address and, for purposes of identification, Kevin's mother's maiden name. The account was in Kevin's name, and she spoke in a low voice as she recited the information, in the voice she'd been practicing. She didn't sound like Kevin, maybe not even masculine, but the representative was harried and didn't notice.

"Is it possible to get call forwarding on my line?" she asked.

"It's an extra charge, but with that, you also get call waiting and voice mail. It's only—"

"That's fine. But is it possible to have it turned on today?"

"Yes," the representative said. She heard him beginning to type. It was a long time before he spoke again. He told her the extra charge would show up on the next bill, which would be sent out next week, but that it would still reflect the full monthly amount, even though she activated the service today. She told him it was fine. He took some more information and then told her it was done and that she would be able to use the service right away. She hung up and glanced at the clock. The whole transaction had taken eighteen minutes.

Kevin called from the precinct three minutes later.

As soon as she got off the phone with Kevin, she called Super Shuttle, a van service that transported people to the airport and bus station. She made a reservation for the following day. Then, after retrieving the cell phone, she finally activated it. She called a local movie theater, one that had a recording, to make sure it worked. Next, she activated the landline's call-forwarding service, sending incoming calls to the number of the movie theater. As a test, she dialed the home number from her cell phone. Her heart was pounding as the landline rang. On the second ring, the ring cut off and she heard the recording from the movie theater. Something broke free inside her and her hands were shaking as she powered off the cell phone and replaced it in the box of SOS pads. She reset the landline.

Kevin called again forty minutes later.

She spent the rest of the afternoon in a daze, working steadily to keep from worrying. She ironed two of his shirts and brought the suit bag and suitcase in from the garage. She set out clean socks and she polished his other pair of black shoes. She ran the lint brush over his suit, the black one he wore to court, and laid out three ties. She scrubbed the bathroom until the floor was shiny, and scrubbed the baseboards with vinegar. She dusted every item in the china cabinet and then started preparing the lasagna. She boiled the pasta and made a meat sauce and layered all of it with cheese. She brushed four pieces of sourdough bread with butter, garlic, and oregano and diced everything she needed for the salad. She showered and dressed sexy, and at five o'clock, she put the lasagna in the oven.

When he got home, dinner was ready. He ate the lasagna and talked about his day. When he asked for a second serving, she rose from the table and brought it to him. After dinner, he drank vodka as they watched reruns of *Seinfeld* and *The King of Queens*. Afterward, the Celtics were playing the Timberwolves and she sat beside him, her head on his shoulder, watching the game. He fell asleep in front of the television and she wandered to the bedroom. She lay in bed, staring at the ceiling, until he finally woke and staggered in, flopping onto the mattress. He fell asleep immediately, one arm draped over her, and his snores sounded like a warning.

She made him breakfast on Tuesday morning. He packed his clothes and toiletries and was finally ready to head to Marlborough. He loaded his things into the car, then went back to the front door, where she was standing. He kissed her.

"I'll be home tomorrow night," he said.

"I'll miss you," she said, leaning into him, putting her arms around his neck.

"I should be home around eight."

"I'll make something that I can reheat when you get home," she said. "How about chili?"

"I'll probably eat on the way home."

"Are you sure? Do you really want to eat fast food? It's so bad for you."

"We'll see," he said.

"I'll make it anyway," she said. "Just in case."

He kissed her as she leaned into him. "I'll call you," he said, his hands drifting downward. Caressing her.

"I know," she answered.

In the bathroom, she took off her clothes and set them on the toilet, then rolled up the rug. She'd placed a garbage bag in the sink, and naked, she stared at herself in the mirror. She fingered the bruises on her ribs and on her wrist. All of her ribs stood out, and dark circles beneath her eyes gave her face a hollowed-out look. She was engulfed by a wave of fury mixed with sadness as she imagined the way he'd call for her when he walked through the house upon his return. He'd call her name and walk to the kitchen. He'd look for her in the bedroom. He'd check the garage and the back porch and the cellar. *Where are you?* he'd call out. *What's for dinner?*

With the scissors, she began to chop savagely at her hair. Four inches of blond hair fell onto the garbage bag. She seized another chunk, using her fingers to pull it tight, telling herself to measure, and snipped. Her chest felt constricted and tight.

"I hate you!" she hissed, her voice trembling. "Degraded me all the time!" She lopped off more hair, her eyes flooding with rage-fueled tears. "Hit me because I had to go shopping!" More hair gone. She tried to slow down, even out the ends. "Made me steal money from your wallet and kicked me because you were drunk!"

She was shaking now, her hands unsteady. Uneven lengths of hair collected at her feet. "Made me hide from you! Hit me so hard that I vomit!"

She snapped the scissors. "I loved you!" She sobbed. "You promised me you'd never hit me again and I believed you! I wanted to believe you!" She cut and cried, and when her hair was all the same length, she pulled out the hair dye from its hiding place behind the sink. Dark Brown. Then she got in the shower and wet her hair. She tilted the bottle and began massaging the dye into her hair. She stood at the mirror and sobbed uncontrollably while it set. When it was done, she climbed into the shower again and rinsed it out. She shampooed and conditioned and stood before the mirror. Carefully, she applied mascara to her eyebrows, darkening them. She added bronzer to her skin, darkening it. She dressed in jeans and a sweater and stared at herself.

A dark, short-haired stranger looked back at her.

She cleaned the bathroom scrupulously, making sure no hair remained in the shower or on the floor. Extra strands went into the garbage bag, along with the box of hair dye. She wiped the sink and counter down and tied up the garbage bag. Last, she put eyedrops in, trying to erase the evidence of her tears.

She had to hurry now. She packed her things in a duffel bag. Three pairs of jeans, two sweatshirts, shirts. Panties and bras. Socks. Toothbrush and toothpaste. A brush. Mascara for her eyebrows. The little jewelry she owned. Cheese and crackers and nuts and raisins. A fork and a knife. She went to the back porch and dug out the money from beneath the flowerpot. The cell phone from the kitchen. And finally, the identification she needed to start a new life, identification she'd stolen from people who trusted her. She'd hated herself for stealing and knew it was wrong, but she'd had no other choice and she'd prayed to God for forgiveness. It was too late to turn back now.

She had rehearsed the scenario in her head a thousand times, and she moved fast. Most of the neighbors were off at work: she'd watched them in the mornings and knew their routines. She didn't want anyone to see her leave, didn't want anyone to recognize her.

She threw on a hat and her jacket, along with a scarf and gloves. She rounded the duffel bag and stuffed it beneath her sweatshirt, kneading and working it until it was round. Until she looked pregnant. She put on her long coat, one that was roomy enough to cover the bump.

She stared at herself in the mirror. Short, dark hair. Skin the color of copper. Pregnant. She put on a pair of sunglasses, and on her way out the door, she turned on her cell phone and set the landline on call forwarding. She left the house through the gate at the side. She walked between her house and the neighbors', following the fence line, and deposited the garbage bag in their garbage can. She knew that both of them worked, that neither was at home. Same thing for the house behind hers. She walked through their yard and past the side of the house, finally emerging onto the icy sidewalk.

Snow had begun to fall again. By tomorrow, she knew, her footprints would be gone.

She had six blocks to go but she was going to make it. She kept her head down and walked, trying to ignore the biting wind, feeling dazed and free and terrified, all at the same time. Tomorrow night, she knew, Kevin would walk through the house, calling for her, and he wouldn't find her because she wasn't there. And tomorrow night, he would begin his hunt.

Snow flurries swirled as Katie stood at the intersection, just outside a diner. In the distance, she saw Super Shuttle's blue van round the corner and her heart pounded in her chest. Just then, she heard the cell phone ring.

She paled. Cars roared past her, their tires loud as they rolled through the slush. In the distance, the van changed lanes, angling toward her side of the road. She had to answer; there was no choice but to answer. But the van was coming and it was noisy on the street. If she answered now, he would know she was outside. He would know she'd left him.

Her phone rang a third time. The blue van stopped at a red light. One block away.

She turned around, walking into the diner, the sounds muffled but still noticeable—a symphony of plates clanking and people talking; directly ahead was the hostess stand, where a man was asking for a table. She felt sick to her stomach. She cupped the phone and faced the window, praying that he couldn't hear the commotion behind her. Her legs went wobbly as she pressed the button and answered.

"What took you so long to answer?" he demanded.

"I was in the shower," she said. "What's going on?"

"I'm about ten minutes out," he said. "How are you?"

"I'm okay," she said.

He hesitated. "You sound kind of funny," he said. "Is something wrong with the phone?"

Up the street, the signal light turned green. The Super Shuttle van's turn signal indicated that it was pulling over. She prayed that it would wait. Behind her, people in the diner had gone surprisingly quiet.

"I'm not sure. But you sound fine," she said. "It's probably bad service where you are. How's the drive?"

"Not too bad once I got out of the city. But it's still icy in places."

"That doesn't sound good. Be careful."

"I'm fine," he said.

"I know," she said. The van was pulling over to the curb, the driver craning his neck, looking for her. "I hate to do this, but can you call me in a few minutes? I still have conditioner in my hair and I want to rinse it out."

"Yeah," he grumbled. "Okay. I'll call you in a bit."

"I love you," she said.

"Love you, too."

She let him hang up before she pressed the button on her phone. Then she walked out of the diner and hurried to the van.

At the bus terminal, she bought a ticket to Philadelphia, hating the way the man who sold her the ticket kept trying to talk to her.

Rather than waiting at the terminal, she went across the street to have breakfast. Money for the shuttle and the bus ticket had taken more than half of the savings she'd collected during the year, but she was hungry and she ordered pancakes and sausage and milk. At the booth, someone had left a newspaper and she forced herself to read it. Kevin called her while she was eating and when he told her again that the phone sounded funny, she suggested that it was the storm.

Twenty minutes later, she got on the bus. An elderly woman motioned to her bulge as she moved down the aisle.

"How much longer?" the woman asked.

"Another month."

"First one?"

"Yes," she answered, but her mouth was so dry it was hard to keep talking. She started down the aisle again and took a seat toward the rear. People sat in the seats in front of and behind her. Across the aisle was a young couple. Teenagers, draped over each other, both of them listening to music. Their heads bobbed up and down.

She stared out the window as the bus pulled away from the station, feeling as if she were dreaming. On the highway, Boston began to recede into the distance, gray and cold. Her lower back ached as the bus rolled forward, miles from home. Snow continued to fall and cars whipped up slush as they passed the bus.

She wished she could talk to someone. She wanted to tell them that she was running away because her husband beat her and that she couldn't call the police because he was the police. She wanted to tell them that she didn't have much money and she could never use her real name again. If she did, he would find her and bring her home and beat her again, only this time he might not stop. She wanted to tell them that she was terrified because she didn't know where she was going to sleep tonight or how she was going to eat when the money ran out.

She could feel cold air against the window as towns drifted past. Traffic on the highway thinned and then the roads became crowded again. She didn't know what she was going to do. All her plans had stopped at the bus and there was no one to call for help. She was alone and had nothing but the things she carried with her.

An hour from Philadelphia, her cell phone rang again. She cupped the phone and talked to him. Before he hung up, he promised to call her before he went to bed.

She arrived in Philadelphia in the late afternoon. It was cold, but not snowy. Passengers got off the bus and she hung back, waiting for all of them to leave. In the restroom, she removed the duffel bag and then went into the waiting room and took a seat on a bench. Her stomach was growling and she sliced off a little cheese and ate it with crackers. She knew she had to make it last, though, so she put the rest of it away, even though she was still hungry. Finally, after buying a map of the city, she stepped outside.

The terminal wasn't located in a bad part of town; she saw the convention center and Trocadero Theater, which made her feel safe, but it also meant she could never afford a hotel room in the area. The map indicated that she was close to China-town, and for lack of a better plan she headed in that direction.

Three hours later, she'd finally found a place to sleep. It was dingy and reeked of smoke, and her room was barely large enough for the small bed that had been crammed inside. There was no lamp; instead, a single bulb protruded from the ceiling and the communal bathroom was down the hall. The walls were gray and water stained and the window had bars. From the rooms on ei-ther side of her, she could hear people talking in a language she couldn't understand. Still, it was all she could afford. She had enough money to stay three nights, four if she could somehow survive on the little food she'd brought from home.

She sat on the edge of the bed, trembling, afraid of this place, afraid of the future, her mind whirling. She had to pee but she didn't want to leave the room. She tried to tell herself that it was an adventure and everything would be okay. As crazy as it sounded, she found herself wondering if she'd made a mistake by leaving; she tried not to think about her kitchen and bed-room and all the things she'd left behind. She knew she could buy a ticket back to Boston and get home before Kevin even realized she was gone. But her hair was short and dark and there was no way she could explain that.

Outside, the sun was down but streetlights shone through the dirty window. She heard horns honking and she looked out. At the street level, all the signs were in Chinese and some businesses were still open. She could hear conversations rising in the darkness and there were plastic bags filled with garbage piled near the street. She was in an unfamiliar city, a city filled with strangers. She couldn't do this, she thought. She wasn't strong enough. In three days, she'd have no place to stay unless she could find a job. If she sold her jewelry, she might buy herself another day, but then what?

She was so tired and her back throbbed. She lay down on the bed and drifted off to sleep almost immediately. Kevin called later, the bleating of the cell phone waking her up. It took everything she had to keep her voice steady, to betray nothing, but she sounded as tired as she felt and she knew that Kevin believed that she was in their bed. When he hung up, she fell asleep again within minutes.

In the morning, she could hear people walking down the hall, heading for the bathroom. Two Chinese women stood at the sinks and there was green mold in the grout and wet toilet paper on the floor. The door to the stall wouldn't lock and she had to hold it closed with her hand.

In the room, she had cheese and crackers for breakfast. She wanted to shower but she realized she'd forgotten to pack shampoo and soap, so there wasn't much point. She changed her clothes and brushed her teeth and hair. She repacked the duffel bag, unwilling to leave it in the room while she wasn't there, and slung the strap over her shoulder and walked down the steps. The same clerk who'd given her the key was at the desk and she wondered whether he ever left this place. She paid for another night and asked him to hold her room.

Outside, the sky was blue and the streets were dry. She realized the pain in her back had all but vanished. It was cold but not as cold as Boston, and despite her fears she found herself smiling. She'd done it, she reminded herself. She'd escaped and Kevin was hundreds of miles away and didn't know where she was. Didn't even know she'd left yet. He would call a couple more times, then she'd throw away the cell phone and never speak with him again.

She stood straighter and breathed in the crisp air. The day felt almost new, with endless possibilities. Today, she told herself, she was going to find a job. Today, she decided, she was going to start living the rest of her life.

She had run away twice before and she wanted to think she'd learned from her mistakes. The first time was a little less than a year after she was married, after he'd beaten her while she was cowering in the corner of the bedroom. The bills had come in and he was angry with her because she'd turned up the thermostat to make the house warmer. When he'd finally stopped, he'd grabbed his keys and headed out to buy more liquor. Without thinking, she'd grabbed her jacket and left the house, limping down the road. Hours later, with sleet coming down and nowhere to go, she'd called him and he went to pick her up.

The next time she'd gotten as far as Atlantic City before he found her. She'd taken money from his wallet and purchased a ticket on the bus, but he'd found her within an hour of her arrival. He'd driven his car at breakneck speed, knowing she would run to the only place where she might still find friends. He'd handcuffed her in the backseat of the car on the drive back. He stopped once, pulling the car over to the side of a closed office building, and beat her; later that night, the gun came out.

After that, he'd made it harder to leave. He usually kept the money locked away and started tracking her whereabouts obsessively. She knew that he would go to extraordinary lengths to find her. As crazy as he was, he was persistent and diligent and his instincts were usually right. He would find out where she'd gone, she knew; he would come to Philadelphia to find her. She had a head start, that was all, but with no extra money to start over somewhere else, all she could do was watch for him over her shoulder for the time being. Her time in Philadelphia was limited.

She found a job as a cocktail waitress on her third day in town. She made up a name and social security number. Eventually, it would be checked, but she'd be long gone by then. She found another room to rent on the far side of Chinatown. She worked for two weeks, accumulated some tip money while searching for and finding another job, and quit without bothering to pick up her paycheck. There was no point; without identification, she wouldn't be able to cash it. She worked another three weeks at a small diner and eventually moved out of Chinatown to a run-down motel that rented by the week. Although it was in a seedier section of town, the room was more expensive, but she had her own shower and bathroom and it was worth it, if only to have some privacy and a place to leave her things. She'd saved a few hundred dollars, more than she had when she'd left Dorchester, but not enough to start over. Again, she left before picking up her paycheck, without even going back to quit. She found yet another job at yet another diner a few days later. In the new job, she told the manager her name was Erica.

The constant job changing and moves had kept her vigilant, and it was there, only four days after she started, that she'd rounded the corner on her way to work and saw a car that seemed somehow out of place. She stopped.

Even now, she wasn't sure how she'd realized it, other than the fact that it was shiny enough to reflect the early morning light. As she stared at the car, she noticed movement in the driver's seat. The engine wasn't running and it struck her as odd that someone would be sitting in an unheated car on a cold morning. The only people, she knew, who did that were those who were waiting for someone.

Or watching for someone.

Kevin.

She knew it was him, knew it with a certainty that surprised her, and she backed around the corner, the way she'd come, praying that he hadn't glanced in the rearview mirror. Praying he hadn't seen her. As soon as the car was out of sight, she began to run back toward the motel, her heart hammering. She hadn't run so fast in years, but all the walking she'd been doing had strengthened her legs and she moved quickly. One block. Two. Three. She looked constantly over her shoulder but Kevin didn't follow.

No matter. He knew she was here. He knew where she worked. He would know if she didn't show up. Within hours, he would find out where she was staying.

In her room, she threw her things into the duffel bag and was out the door within minutes. She started toward the bus station. It would take forever, though. An hour, maybe more, to walk there, and she didn't have the time. That would be the first place he went when he realized she wasn't there. Turning around, she went back into the motel and had the clerk call her a cab. It arrived ten minutes later. The longest ten minutes of her life.

At the bus station, she frantically searched the schedule and selected a bus to New York. It was scheduled to leave in half an hour. She hid in the women's restroom until it was time to board. When she got on the bus she lowered herself into a seat. It didn't take long to get to New York. Again, she scanned the schedules and bought a ticket that would take her as far as Omaha.

In the evening, she got off the bus somewhere in Ohio. She slept in the station, and the next morning she found her way to a truck stop. There she met a man who was delivering materials to Wilmington, North Carolina.

A few days later, after selling her jewelry, she wandered into Southport and found the cottage. After she paid the first month's rent, there was no money left to buy food.

23

⎯⎯ ❧ ⎯⎯

It was mid-June and Katie was leaving Ivan's after finishing up a busy dinner shift when she spotted a familiar figure standing near the exit.

"Hey there." Jo waved from beneath the lamppost where Katie had locked up her bike.

"What are you doing here?" Katie asked, leaning in to give her friend a hug. She'd never run into Jo in town before, and seeing her out of context felt strange for some reason.

"I came to see you. Where've you been, stranger?"

"I could ask you the same question."

"I've been around enough to know you've been seeing Alex for a few weeks." Jo winked. "But as a friend, I've never been one to impose. I figured you two needed some time alone."

Katie blushed despite herself. "How did you know I was here?"

"I didn't. But your lights weren't on at the house and I took a chance." Jo shrugged. She motioned over her shoulder. "Are you doing anything? Do you want to grab a drink before you head home?" When she saw Katie's hesitation, she went on. "I know it's late. One drink, I promise. Then I'll let you go to bed."

"One drink," Katie agreed.

A few minutes later, they stepped inside the pub, a local favorite paneled in dark wood scarred with decades of use, with a long mirror behind the bar. It was quiet tonight; only a few tables were occupied and the two women took a seat at a corner table in the back. Since there didn't seem to be table service, Katie ordered two glasses of wine at the bar and brought them back to the table.

"Thanks," Jo said, taking her glass. "Next time, it's on me." She leaned back. "So you and Alex, huh?"

"Is that really what you wanted to talk to me about?" Katie asked.

"Well, since my own love life is in the dumps, I have to live vicariously through you. It seems to be going well, though. He was over there . . . what? Two or three times last week? And the same thing the week before that?"

Actually more, Katie thought. "Something like that."

Jo twisted the stem of her wineglass. "Uh-oh."

"Uh-oh what?"

"If I didn't know better, I'd think it was getting serious." She raised an eyebrow.

"We're still getting to know each other," Katie offered, not sure where Jo was going with this line of questioning.

"That's how every relationship starts. He likes you, you like him. Then you both go from there."

"Is this why you came down?" Katie tried not to sound exasperated. "To hear all the details?"

"Not *all* of them. Just the juicy ones."

Katie rolled her eyes. "How about we talk about your love life instead?"

"Why? Are you in the mood to be depressed?"

"When was the last time you went on a date?"

"A good date? Or just a date-date?"

"A good date."

Jo hesitated. "I'd have to say that it's been at least a couple of years."

"What happened?"

Jo dipped a finger in her wine, then ran it around the rim of her glass, making it hum. Finally, she looked up. "A good man is hard to find," she said wistfully. "Not everyone is as lucky as you are."

Katie didn't know quite how to respond to that, so instead she touched Jo's hand. "What's really going on?" she asked gently. "Why did you want to talk to me?"

Jo looked around the empty bar as if trying to draw inspiration from her surroundings. "Do you ever sit back and wonder what it all means? Whether this is it or if there's something greater out there? Or if you were meant for something better?"

"I think everyone does," Katie answered, her curiosity growing.

"When I was a girl, I used to make believe that I was a princess. One of the good ones, I mean. Someone who always does the right thing and has the power to make people's lives better so that, in the end, they live happily ever after."

Katie nodded. She could remember doing the same thing, but she still wasn't sure where Jo was going so she stayed quiet.

"I think that's why I do what I do now. When I started, I just wanted to help. I'd see people who were struggling with the loss of someone they loved—a parent, a child, a friend—and my heart just overflowed with sympathy. I tried to do everything in my power to make things better for them. But as time passed, I came to realize that there was only so much I could do myself. That in the end, people who are grieving have to *want* to move on—that first step, that motivating spark, has to come from within them. And when it does, it opens the door to the unexpected."

Katie took a deep breath, trying to make sense of Jo's rambling. "I don't know what you're trying to tell me."

Jo swirled her wine, studying the little whirlpool in her glass.

For the first time, her tone became utterly serious. "I'm talking about you and Alex."

Katie couldn't hide her surprise. "Me and Alex?"

"Yes." She nodded. "He's told you about losing his wife, right? About how hard it was for him—for the whole family—to get past it?"

Katie stared across the table, suddenly uncomfortable. "Yes . . ." she began.

"Then be careful with them," Jo said, her tone serious. "All of them. Don't break their hearts."

In the awkward silence that followed, Katie found herself recalling their first conversation about Alex.

Did you two ever see each other? she remembered asking Jo.

Yes, but maybe not in the way you're thinking, Jo had answered. *And just so we're clear: it was a long time ago and everyone has moved on.*

At the time, she'd assumed that it meant that Jo and Alex had dated in the past, but now . . .

She was struck by the obviousness of the conclusion. The counselor Alex had mentioned, who had seen the kids and consulted with him in the aftermath of Carly's death—it must have been Jo. Katie sat up straight. "You worked with Alex and the kids, didn't you? After Carly died, I mean."

"I'd rather not say," Jo answered. Her tone was measured and calm. Just like a counselor's. "I can say that all of them . . . mean a lot to me. And if you're not serious about a possible future with them, I think you should end it now. Before it's too late."

Katie felt her cheeks flush; it seemed inappropriate—presumptuous, even—for Jo to be talking to her like this. "I'm not sure any of this is really your concern," she said, her voice tight.

Jo acknowledged her point with a reluctant nod. "You're right. It's not my concern—and I'm crossing some important boundaries here. But I really do think they've been through enough. And the last thing I want for them is to become attached to someone who has no intention of staying in Southport. Maybe I'm worried that the past is never really in the past and that you might decide to leave, no matter how much sadness you leave in your wake."

Katie was speechless. This conversation was so unexpected, so uncomfortable, and Jo's words had definitely thrown her emotions into turmoil.

If Jo sensed Katie's discomfort, she pressed on anyway.

"Love doesn't mean anything if you're not willing to make a commitment," she said, "and you have to think not only about what you want, but about what he wants. Not just now, but in the future." She continued to stare at Katie across the table, her brown eyes unwavering. "Are you ready to be a wife to Alex and a mother to his kids? Because that's what Alex wants. Maybe not right now, but he will in the future. And if you're not willing to make a commitment, if you're only going to toy with his feelings and those of his children, then you're not the person he needs in his life."

Before Katie could say anything, Jo got up from the table as she went on. "It might have been wrong of me to say all this, and maybe we won't be friends any longer, but I wouldn't feel right about myself if I didn't speak plainly. As I've said from the very beginning, he's a good man—a rare man. He loves deeply and never stops loving." She let those words sink in before her expression suddenly softened. "I think you're the same way, but I wanted to remind you that if you care about him, then you have to be willing to commit to him. No matter what the future might bring. No matter how scared you might be."

With that, she turned and left the bar, leaving Katie sitting at the table in stunned silence. It was only as she got up to leave that she noticed that Jo hadn't touched her wine.

24

Kevin Tierney didn't go to Provincetown on the weekend he'd told Coffey and Ramirez that he would. Instead, he stayed home with the curtains closed, brooding over how close he'd come to finding her in Philadelphia.

He wouldn't have succeeded in tracking her that far, except that she'd made a mistake in going to the bus station. He knew it was the only transportation choice she could have made. Tickets were cheap and identification wasn't necessary, and though he wasn't sure how much she'd stolen from him, he knew it couldn't have been much. From the first day they were married, he'd controlled the money. He always made her keep receipts and give him any change, but after she'd run away the second time, he'd also started locking his wallet in the gun box with his guns when he went to sleep. Sometimes, though, he fell asleep on the couch and he imagined her slipping the wallet from his pocket and stealing his money. He imagined the way she silently laughed at him as she did it, and how, in the morning, she would make him breakfast and pretend that she'd done nothing wrong. She would smile and kiss him, but inside she was laughing. Laughing at *him*. She'd stolen from him and he knew that was wrong because the Bible says *Thou shalt not steal.*

In the darkness, he chewed his lips, remembering his initial hope that she might come back. It was snowing and she couldn't get far; the first time she'd run away it had also been on a bitter cold night, and she'd called him within a few hours and asked him to pick her up because she had nowhere else to go. When she got home, she apologized for what she'd done and he made her a cup of hot cocoa as she sat shivering on the couch. He brought her a blanket and watched as she covered herself, trying to get warm. She smiled at him and he smiled at her, but once she stopped shivering, he crossed the room and slapped her until she cried. By the time he rose for work in the morning, she'd cleaned the spilled cocoa from the floor, though there was still a stain on the rug that she couldn't get out, and sometimes the sight of it made him angry.

On the night he realized she was missing last January, he drank two glasses of vodka while he waited for her to come back, but the phone didn't ring and the front door stayed closed. He knew she hadn't been gone long. He'd spoken to her less than an hour before and she'd told him she was making dinner. But there was no dinner on the stove. No sign of her in the house or in the cellar or in the garage. He stood on the porch and looked for footprints in the snow, but it was obvious that she hadn't left through the front door. But the snow in the backyard was equally pristine, so she hadn't left that way, either. It was as if she'd floated away or vanished into thin air. Which meant she had to be here . . . except that she wasn't.

Two more vodkas later and another half hour passed. By then, he was in a rage and he punched a hole in the bedroom door. He stormed from the house and banged on the neighbors' doors, asking if they'd noticed her leaving, but none of them could tell him anything. He hopped in his car and drove up and down the streets of the neighborhood, looking for traces of her, trying to figure out how she'd been able to leave the house without leaving any clues behind. By then, he figured she had a two-hour head start, but she was walking, and in this weather she couldn't have gotten far. Unless someone had come to pick her up. Someone she cared about. A man.

He pounded the wheel, his face contorted in fury. Six blocks away was the commercial district. He went to the businesses there, flashing a wallet-size photograph and asking if anyone had seen her. No one had. He told them she might have been with a man and still they shook their heads. The men he asked were adamant about it: *A pretty blond like that?* they said. *I would have noticed her, especially on a night like tonight.*

He drove each and every road within five miles of the house two or three times before finally going back home. It was three a.m. and the house was empty. After another vodka he cried himself to sleep.

In the morning, when he woke, he was enraged again, and with a hammer he smashed the flowerpots she kept in the backyard. Breathing hard, he went to the phone and called in sick, then went to the couch and tried to figure out how she'd gotten away. Someone had to have picked her up; someone must have driven her someplace. Someone she knew. A friend from Atlantic City? Altoona? Possible, he supposed, except that he checked the phone bills every month. She never placed long-distance phone calls. Someone local, then. But who? She never went anywhere, never talked to anyone. He made sure of that.

He went to the kitchen and was pouring himself another drink when he heard the phone ring. He lunged for it, hoping it was Erin. Strangely, however, the phone rang only once, and when he picked up he heard a dial tone. He stared at the receiver, trying to figure it out before hanging up the phone.

How had she gotten away? He was missing something. Even if someone local had picked her up, how had she gotten to the road without leaving footprints? He stared out the window, trying to piece together the sequence of events. Something seemed off, though he couldn't identify what it was. He turned away from the window and found himself focused on the telephone. It was then that the pieces suddenly came together and he pulled out his cell phone. He dialed his home number and listened as it rang once. The cell phone kept ringing. When he picked up the landline, he heard a dial tone and realized that she'd forwarded the calls to a cell phone. Which meant she hadn't been here when he'd called her last night. Which also explained the bad reception he'd noticed over the past two days. And, of course, the lack of footprints in the snow. She'd been gone, he now knew, since Tuesday morning.

At the bus station, she made a mistake, even if she couldn't really help it. She should have purchased her tickets from a woman, since Erin was pretty and men always remembered pretty women. It didn't matter whether their hair was long and blond or short and dark. Nor did it matter if she'd pretended she was pregnant.

He went to the bus station. He showed his badge and carried a larger photograph of her. The first two times he visited, none of the ticket sellers had recognized her. The third time, though, one of them hesitated and said that it might have been her, except that her hair was short and brown and that she was pregnant. He didn't, however, remember her destination. Back at home, Kevin found a photograph of her on the computer and used Photoshop to change her hair from blond to brown and then shortened it. He called in sick again on Friday. *That's her*, the ticket seller confirmed, and Kevin felt a surge of energy. She thought she was smarter than he was, but she was stupid and careless and she'd made a mistake. He took a couple of vacation days the following week and continued to hang around the bus station, showing the new photograph to drivers. He arrived in the morning and left late, since the drivers came and went all day long. There were two bottles in the car, and he poured the vodka into a Styrofoam cup and sipped it with a straw.

On Saturday, eleven days after she'd left him, he found the driver. The driver had taken her to Philadelphia. He remembered her, he said, because she was pretty and pregnant and she didn't have any luggage.

Philadelphia. She might have left again from there to parts unknown, but it was the only lead he had. Plus, he knew she didn't have much money.

He'd packed a bag and hopped in his car and drove to Philadelphia. He parked at the bus station and tried to think like her. He was a good detective and he knew that if he could think like her, he'd be able to find her. People, he'd learned, were predictable.

The bus had arrived a few minutes before four o'clock, and he stood in the bus station, looking from one direction to the next. She had stood here days earlier, he thought, and he wondered what she would do in a strange city with no money and no friends and no place to go. Quarters and dimes and dollar bills wouldn't go far, especially after purchasing a bus ticket.

It was cold, he remembered, and it would have been getting dark soon. She wouldn't want to walk far and she would need a place to stay. A place that took cash. But where? Not here, in this area. Too expensive. Where would she go? She wouldn't want to get lost or head in the wrong direction, which meant that she probably looked in the phone book. He went back inside the terminal and looked under hotels. Pages and pages, he realized. She might have picked one, but then what? She'd have to walk there. Which meant she'd need a map.

He went to the convenience store at the station and bought himself a map. He showed the clerk the photograph but he shook his head. He hadn't been working on Tuesday, he said. But it felt right to Kevin. This, he knew, was what she did. He unfolded the map and located the station. It bordered on Chinatown and he guessed she had headed in that direction.

He got back in his car and drove the streets of Chinatown, and again it felt right. He drank his vodka and walked the streets. He started at those businesses closest to the bus station and showed her picture around. No one knew anything but he had the sense that some of them were lying. He found cheap rooms, places he never would have taken her, dirty places with dirty sheets, managed by men who spoke little English and took only cash. He implied that she was in danger if he couldn't find her. He found the first place she'd stayed, but the owner didn't know where she'd gone after that. Kevin put a gun to the man's head, but even though he cried, he couldn't tell Kevin anything more.

Kevin had to go back to work on Monday, furious that she'd eluded him. But the following weekend, he was back in Philadelphia. And the weekend after that. He expanded his search, but the problem was that there were too many places and he was only one person and not everyone trusted an out-of-town cop.

But he was patient and diligent and he kept coming back and took more vacation days. Another weekend passed. He widened his search, knowing she would need cash. He stopped in bars and restaurants and diners. He would check every one in the city if he had to. Finally, a week after Valentine's Day, he met a waitress named Tracy who told him that Erin was working at a diner, except she was calling herself Erica. She was scheduled to work the following day. The waitress trusted him because he was a detective, and she'd even flirted with him, handing him her phone number before he left.

He rented a car and waited up the block from the diner the following morning, before the sun was up. Employees entered through a door in the alley. He sipped from his Styrofoam cup in the front seat, watching for her. Eventually, he saw the owner and Tracy and another woman head down the alley. But

Erin never showed, and she didn't show up the following day, either, and no one knew where she lived. She never came back to pick up her paycheck.

He found where she lived a few hours later. It was walking distance from the diner, a piece-of-crap hotel. The man, who accepted only cash, knew nothing except that Erin had left the day before and come back and left again in a hurry. Kevin searched her room but there was nothing inside, and when he finally raced to the bus station there were only women in the ticket booths and none of them remembered her. Buses in the last two hours were traveling north, south, east, and west, going everywhere.

She'd disappeared again, and in the car Kevin screamed and beat his fists against the wheel until they were bruised and swollen.

In the months that Erin had been gone, he felt the ache inside grow more poisonous and all-consuming, spreading like a cancer every day. He had returned to Philadelphia and questioned the drivers over the next few weeks, but it hadn't amounted to much. He eventually learned that she'd gone on to New York, but from there, the trail went cold. Too many buses, too many drivers, too many passengers; too many days had passed since then. Too many options. She could be anywhere, and the thought that she was gone tormented him. He flew into rages and broke things; he cried himself to sleep. He was filled with despair and sometimes felt like he was losing his mind.

It wasn't fair. He'd loved her since the first time they met in Atlantic City. And they'd been happy, hadn't they? Early on in the marriage, she used to sing to herself as she put on her makeup. He used to bring her to the library and she would check out eight or ten books. Sometimes she would read him passages and he would hear her voice and watch the way she leaned against the counter and think to himself that she was the most beautiful woman in the world.

He'd been a good husband. He bought her the house she wanted and the curtains she wanted and the furniture she wanted, even though he could barely afford it. After they were married, he often bought flowers from street vendors on the way home, and Erin would put them in a vase on the table along with candles, and the two of them would have romantic dinners. Sometimes, they ended up making love in the kitchen, her back pressed against the counter.

He never made her work, either, and she didn't know how good she had it. She didn't understand the sacrifices he made for her. She was spoiled and selfish and it used to make him so angry because she didn't understand how *easy* her life was. Clean the house and make a meal and she could spend the rest of her days reading stupid books she checked out from the library and watching television and taking naps and never having to worry about a utility bill or mortgage payment or people who talked about him behind his back. She never had to see the faces of people who had been murdered. He kept that from her because he loved her, but it had made no difference. He never told her about the children who'd been burned with irons or tossed from the roofs of buildings or women stabbed in the alley and thrown in Dumpsters. He never told her that sometimes he had to scrape the blood from his shoes before he got in the car, and when he looked into the eyes of murderers he knew he was coming face-to-face with evil because the Bible says *To kill a person is to kill a living being made in God's image.*

He loved her and she loved him and she had to come home because he couldn't find her. She could have her happy life again and he wouldn't hit or punch or slap or kick her if she walked in the door because he'd always been a good husband. He loved her and she loved him and he remembered that on the day he asked her to marry him, she reminded him of the night they'd met outside the casino when the men were following her. Dangerous men. He'd stopped them from hurting her that night, and in the morning they'd walked along the boardwalk and he took her for coffee. She told him that of course she would marry him. She loved him, she'd said. He made her feel safe.

Safe. That was the word she used. Safe.

25

The third week of June was a series of glorious high summer days. The temperature crept up over the course of the afternoon, bringing with it humidity heavy enough to thicken the air and blur the horizon. Heavy clouds would then form as if by magic, and violent thunderstorms would drop torrents of rain. The showers never lasted long, though, leaving behind only dripping leaves and a layer of ground mist.

Katie continued to work long evening shifts at the restaurant. She was tired when she rode home, and in the morning her legs and feet often ached. She put half the money she earned in tips in the coffee can, and it was almost filled to the brim. She had more money than she'd imagined she'd be able to save, more than enough to get away if she had to. For the first time, she wondered whether she needed to add more.

Lingering over her last few bites of breakfast, she stared out the window at Jo's house. She hadn't spoken with her since their encounter, and last night, after her shift, she'd seen lights burning in Jo's kitchen and living room. Earlier this morning, she'd heard her car start up and listened to the crunching of dirt and gravel as it pulled away. She didn't know what to say to Jo, or even whether she wanted to say anything at all. She couldn't even decide whether she was angry with her. Jo cared about Alex and the kids; she was worried about them and had expressed her concerns to Katie. It was hard to find malice in anything she'd done.

Alex, she knew, would be by later today. His visits had settled into something of a routine, and when they were together, she was constantly reminded of all the reasons she'd fallen for him in the first place. He accepted her occasional silences and varying moods, and he treated her with a gentleness that astonished and touched her. But since her conversation with Jo, she wondered if she was being unfair to him. What would happen, after all, if Kevin showed up? How would Alex and the kids react if she disappeared, never to return? Was she willing to leave all of them behind and never talk to them again?

She hated the questions Jo had raised, because she wasn't ready to face them. *You have no idea what I've been through*, she'd wanted to say afterward, once she had time to think about it. *You have no idea what my husband is like*. But even she knew that begged the question.

Leaving her breakfast dishes in the sink, she walked through the small cottage, thinking how much had changed in the last few months. She owned virtually nothing, but felt like she had more than ever. She felt loved for the first time in years. She'd never been a parent, but she found herself thinking and worrying about Kristen and Josh when she least expected it. She knew she couldn't predict the future, and yet she was struck with the sudden certainty that leaving this new existence behind was inconceivable.

What had Jo once said to her? *I just tell people what they already know but are afraid to admit to themselves*.

Reflecting on her words, she knew exactly what she had to do.

* * *

"Sure," Alex said to her, after she related her request. She could tell he was surprised, but he also seemed encouraged. "When do you want to start?"

"How about today?" she suggested. "If you have any time."

He looked around the store. There was only one person eating in the grill area, and Roger was leaning against the counter, chatting with him.

"Hey, Roger? Do you think you could watch the register for an hour?"

"No problem, boss," Roger said. He stayed where he was; Alex knew he wouldn't come up front unless necessary. But on a weekday morning, after the initial rush, he didn't expect many people in the store, so Alex didn't mind. He moved out from behind the register.

"You ready?"

"Not really." She hugged herself nervously. "But it's something I should know how to do."

They left the store, walking toward his jeep. Climbing in, she could feel his gaze on her.

"Why the sudden rush to learn how to drive?" he asked. "Is the bike not good enough?" he teased.

"The bike is all I need," she said. "But I want to get a driver's license."

He reached for the car keys before pausing. He turned back to her again, and as he stared at her, she caught a glimpse of the investigator he used to be. He was alert and she sensed his caution. "Learning how to drive is only part of it. To get a license, the state requires identification. Birth certificate, social security card, things like that."

"I know," she said.

He chose his words carefully. "Information like that can be tracked," he pointed out. "If you get a license, people might be able to find you."

"I'm already using a safe social security number," she said.

"If Kevin knew about it, he would have tracked me down already. And if I'm going to stay in Southport, it's something I need to do."

He shook his head. "Katie . . ."

She leaned over and kissed him on the cheek. "It's okay," she said. "My name's not Katie, remember?"

He traced the curve of her cheek with his finger. "To me, you'll always be Katie."

She smiled. "I have a secret," she said. "My hair isn't naturally brown. I'm really a blond."

He sat back, processing this new information. "Are you sure you want to be telling me this?"

"I figure you'll find out eventually, anyway. Who knows? Maybe I'll go back to being a blond one day."

"What's this all about? Wanting to learn how to drive, volunteering information?"

"You told me I could trust you." She shrugged. "I believe you."

"That's it?"

"Yes," she said. "I feel like I can tell you anything."

He studied their hands, locked together on the seat divider, before looking at her. "Then I'll cut to the chase. Are you sure your documents will hold up? They can't be copies. They have to be originals."

"I know," she said.

He knew better than to ask anything more. He reached for the keys but didn't start the engine.

"What is it?" she asked.

"Since you want to learn how to drive, we may as well start now." He opened the door and got out. "Let's get you behind the wheel."

They switched places. As soon as Katie was behind the wheel, Alex pointed out the basics: gas and brake pedals, how to put the car in gear, turn signals, lights and wipers, gauges on the dashboard. It was always best to start at the beginning.

"You ready?" he asked.

"I think so," she said, concentrating.

"Since it's not a manual transmission, you use only one foot. It's either on the accelerator or the brake, okay?"

"Okay," she said. She moved her left foot near the door.

"Now, push down on the brake and start the car. When you're ready, keep the brake on while you put the transmission in reverse. Don't use the accelerator, and slowly release the brake. Then turn the wheel to back out, keeping your foot lightly on the brake."

She did exactly as she was told and backed the car out gingerly before he guided her out of the parking lot. For the first time, she paused. "Are you sure I should drive onto the main road?"

"If there was a lot of traffic, I'd say no. If you were sixteen, I'd say no. But I think you can handle it, and I'm right here to help. You ready? What you're going to do is turn right, and we'll follow that until the next turn. Then we'll turn right again. I want you to get a feel for the car."

They spent the next hour driving along rural roads. Like most beginners, she had trouble with oversteering, she sometimes veered onto the shoulder, and parking took a little while to get used to, but other than that, she did better than probably either of them expected. As they were getting close to finishing, Alex had her park on one of the downtown streets.

"Where are we going?"

He pointed to a small coffee shop. "I figured you might want to celebrate. You did well."

"I don't know," she said. "I didn't feel like I knew what I was doing."

"That comes with practice," he said. "The more you drive, the more natural it feels."

"Can I drive tomorrow?" she asked.

"Of course," he said. "Can we do it in the morning, though?

Now that Josh is out of school, he and Kristen are at day camp for a couple of weeks. They get home around noon."

"Mornings are perfect," she said. "Do you really think I did okay?"

"You could probably pass the driving portion of the exam with a couple more days of practice. Of course, you have to pass the written test, too, but all that takes is some prep time."

She reached out and gave him a spontaneous hug. "Thanks for this, by the way."

He hugged her back. "I'm glad to help. Even if you don't have a car, it's something you should probably know how to do. Why didn't you . . . ?"

"Learn to drive when I was younger?" She shrugged. "Growing up, we had only one car and my dad was usually using it. Even if I got my license, I wouldn't have been able to drive, so it never struck me as all that important. After I moved out, I couldn't afford a car, so again, I didn't bother. And then, when I was married, Kevin didn't want me to have one." She turned. "And here I am. A twenty-seven-year-old bike rider."

"You're twenty-seven?"

"You knew that."

"Actually, I didn't."

"And?"

"You don't look a day over thirty."

She punched him lightly in the arm. "For that, I'm going to make you buy me a croissant, too."

"Fair enough. And since you're in the mood for full disclosure, I'd like to hear the story of how you finally got away."

She hesitated only briefly. "Okay," she said.

At a small table outside, Katie related the account of her escape—the forwarded phone calls, the trip to Philadelphia, the ever-changing jobs and miserable flophouses, the eventual trip to Southport. Unlike the first time, now she was able to describe her experiences calmly, as though talking about someone else. When she finished, he shook his head.

"What?"

"I was just trying to imagine how you must have felt after hanging up on that final call from Kevin. When he still thought you were at home. I'll bet you were relieved."

"I was. But I was also terrified. And at that point, I still didn't have a job and didn't know what I was going to do."

"But you made it."

"Yes," she said. "I did." Her gaze was focused on some distant point. "It's not the kind of life I ever imagined for myself."

Alex's tone was gentle. "I'm not sure anyone's life turns out exactly the way they imagine. All we can do is to try to make the best of it. Even when it seems impossible."

She knew he was talking as much about himself as he was about her, and for a long moment neither of them said anything.

"I love you," he finally whispered.

She leaned forward and touched his face. "I know. And I love you, too."

26

By late June, the flower gardens in Dorchester that had been ablaze with color in the spring were beginning to wilt, the blooms turning brown and curling inward. The humidity had begun to creep up and the alleys in downtown Boston began to smell of rotting food and urine and decay. Kevin told Coffey and Ramirez that he and Erin were going to spend the weekend at home, watching movies and doing a little gardening. Coffey had asked about Provincetown and Kevin had lied and told him about the bed-and-breakfast where they'd stayed and some of the restaurants they'd gone to. Coffey had said that he'd been to all of those places and asked if Kevin had ordered the crab cakes at one of them. Kevin said that he hadn't but would the next time.

Erin was gone, but Kevin still looked for her everywhere. He couldn't help it. As he drove the streets of Boston and saw the glint of gold brushing a woman's shoulders, he would feel his heart catch in his throat. He would watch for the delicate nose and green eyes and the graceful way she walked. Sometimes he would stand outside the bakery, pretending that he was waiting for her.

He should have been able to find her, even if she'd gotten

away in Philadelphia. People left trails. Paper left trails. In Philadelphia, she'd used a phony name and phony social security number, but that couldn't last forever unless she was willing to keep on living in cheap hotels and changing jobs every few weeks. To this point, though, she hadn't used her own social security number. An officer from another precinct who had connections checked for him, and that officer was the only one who knew that Erin was gone, but he'd keep his mouth shut because Kevin knew he was having an affair with his underage babysitter. Kevin felt dirty whenever he had to talk to him because the guy was a pervert and he belonged in prison, since the Bible says *Let there be no sexual immorality among you.* But right now, Kevin needed him so that he could find Erin and bring her home. Man and wife were supposed to stay together because they'd made their vows in front of God and family.

He'd known he would find her in March; he'd felt sure she would turn up in April. He was certain that her name would surface in May, but the house stayed empty. Now it was June and his thoughts were often scattered and sometimes it was all he could do to go through the motions. It was hard to concentrate and the vodka didn't seem to help and he had to lie to Coffey and Ramirez and walk away while they gossiped.

This he knew: she wasn't running any longer. She wouldn't move from place to place or job to job forever. It wasn't like her. She liked nice things and wanted to have them around her. Which meant she had to be using someone else's identity. Unless she was willing to live a life continually on the run, she needed a real birth certificate and a real social security number. These days, employers required identification, but where and how would she have assumed another's identity? He knew the most common way was to find someone of a similar age who'd recently died, and then to take on the identity of the deceased. The first part of that was conceivable, if only because of Erin's frequent visits to the library. He could imagine her scanning the obituaries on microfiche, looking for a name to steal. She schemed and planned in the library while pretending to peruse the bookshelves, and she'd done those things after he'd taken time out of his busy day to drive her there. He showed her kindness and she repaid him with treachery, and it infuriated him to think of the way she must have laughed while she did it. It made him so angry to imagine those things, and with a hammer he smashed the set of china they'd been given for their wedding. Having let off steam, he was able to focus on what he had to do. Throughout March and April, Kevin spent hours in the library just as she must have done, trying to find her new identity. But even if she had found a name, how had she retrieved the identification? Where was she now? And why hadn't she come home?

These were the questions that tormented him, and sometimes it was so confusing he couldn't stop crying because he missed her and wanted her to come home and he hated to be alone. But other times, the thought that she had left him made him dwell on how selfish she was and all he wanted to do was kill her.

July rolled in with the breath of dragons: hot and moist and horizons that shimmered like a mirage when seen from a distance. The holiday weekend passed and another week started. The air conditioner had broken in his home and Kevin hadn't called the repairman. He had a headache every morning when he went to work. Trial and error proved that vodka worked better than Tylenol, but the pain was always there, pounding in his temple. He'd stopped going to the library, and Coffey and Ramirez asked about his wife again and he said that she was fine but said nothing else about her and then he changed the subject. He got a new partner named Todd Vannerty, who'd just been promoted. He was happy to let Kevin do most of the questioning when they talked to witnesses and victims, and that was fine with Kevin.

Kevin told him that, almost always, the victim knew the murderer. But not always in an obvious way. At the end of their first week together, they were called out to an apartment less than three blocks from the precinct, where they found a ten-year-old boy who'd died of a bullet wound. The shooter was a recent emigrant from Greece who had been celebrating a Greek soccer victory when he'd fired his gun at the floor. The bullet passed through the ceiling of the apartment below him and killed the boy just as he was taking a bite of pizza. The bullet entered the top of his head and the boy fell face-first into his pizza. When they saw the boy, there was cheese and tomato sauce on the boy's forehead. His mother had screamed and cried for two hours and had tried to tackle the Greek as he was led down the stairs in handcuffs. She ended up tumbling down to the landing and they'd had to call an ambulance.

Kevin and Todd went to a bar after their shift ended and Todd tried to pretend he could forget what he'd seen, but he drank three beers in less than fifteen minutes. He told Kevin that he'd failed his detective exam once, before finally passing it. Kevin drank vodka, though because Todd was with him, he told the bartender to add a splash of cranberry juice.

It was a cop bar. Lots of cops, low prices, dim lights, and women who liked to hook up with cops. The bartender let people smoke, even though it was against the law, since most of the smokers were cops. Todd wasn't married and had been there often. Kevin had never been there before and wasn't sure he liked it, but he didn't want to go home, either.

Todd went to the bathroom and when he came back, he leaned closer to Kevin.

"I think those two at the end of the bar are checking us out."

Kevin turned. Like him, the women appeared to be around thirty. The brunette noticed him staring before she turned back to her redheaded friend.

"Too bad you're married, huh? They look pretty good."

They looked worn, Kevin thought. Not like Erin, who had clear skin and smelled of lemon and mint and the perfume he'd bought her for Christmas.

"Go ahead and talk to them if you want," Kevin said.

"I think I will," Todd said. Todd ordered another beer and walked to the end of the bar and smiled. He probably said something stupid, but it was enough to make the women laugh. Kevin ordered a double vodka, no cranberry juice, and saw their reflection in the mirror behind the bar. The brunette met his eyes in the mirror, and he didn't turn away. Ten minutes later, she sauntered over and took a seat on the stool that Todd had been occupying.

"Not feeling social tonight?" the brunette asked.

"I'm not good at small talk."

The brunette seemed to consider this. "I'm Amber," she said.

"Kevin," he replied, and again, he didn't know what to say. He took a drink, thinking it tasted almost like water.

The brunette leaned toward him. She smelled musky, not like lemon and mint. "Todd says that the two of you work homicide."

"We do."

"Is that hard?"

"Sometimes," he said. He finished his drink and raised the glass. The bartender brought another over. "What do you do?"

"I'm an office manager at my brother's bakery. He makes rolls and bread products for restaurants."

"That sounds interesting."

She gave a cynical smile. "No, it doesn't. And it's not, but it pays the bills." Her teeth flashed white in the gloom. "I haven't seen you here before."

"Todd brought me."

She nodded in Todd's direction. "Him, I've seen. He hits on anything in a skirt who's still breathing. And I think the breathing part is optional. My friend loves it here, but usually I can't stand the place. She makes me come with her."

Kevin nodded and shifted on his stool. He wondered if Coffey and Ramirez ever came here.

"Am I boring you?" she asked. "I can leave you alone if you'd like."

"You're not boring me."

She flipped her hair and Kevin thought she was prettier than he'd first realized. "Would you like to buy me a drink?" she suggested.

"What would you like?"

"Cosmopolitan," she said, and Kevin signaled to the bartender. The cosmopolitan arrived.

"I'm not very good at this," Kevin admitted.

"Not good at what?"

"This."

"We're just talking," she said. "And you're doing fine."

"I'm married."

She smiled. "I know. I saw your ring."

"Does that bother you?"

"Like I said, we're just talking."

She ran a finger along her glass and he could see the moisture collect on the tip.

"Does your wife know you're here?" she asked.

"My wife is out of town," he said. "Her friend is sick and she's helping her out."

"And so you thought you'd hit the bars? Meet some women?"

"I'm not like that," Kevin said tightly. "I love my wife."

"You should. Since you married her, I mean."

He wanted another double vodka but didn't want to order it in front of her, since he'd already done so. Instead, as if reading his mind, she signaled to the bartender and he brought over another one. Kevin took a large gulp, still thinking it tasted like water.

"Is it okay that I did that?" she asked.

"It's okay," he said.

She stared at him, her expression sultry. "I wouldn't tell your wife that you were here if I were you."

"Why not?" he asked.

"Because you're way too handsome for a place like this. You never know who would try to hit on you."

"Are you hitting on me?"

It took her a moment to answer. "Would you be offended if I said yes?"

He spun the glass slowly on the bar. "No," he said, "I wouldn't be offended."

After drinking and flirting for another two hours, they ended up at her place. Amber understood that he wanted to be discreet and gave him her address. After Amber and her friend left, Kevin stayed in the bar with Todd for another half hour before he told Todd that he had to get home so he could call Erin.

When he drove, the world blurred around the edge of his vision. His thoughts were jumbled and confusing and he knew he was swerving but he was a good detective. Even if he was stopped, he wouldn't be arrested because cops don't arrest other cops, and what were a few drinks?

Amber lived in an apartment a few blocks away from the bar. He knocked at the door, and when she opened it she was wearing nothing beneath the sheet she had wrapped around her. He kissed her and carried her to the bedroom and felt her fingers unbuttoning his shirt. He placed her on the bed and undressed and turned out the light because he didn't want to be reminded that he was cheating on his wife. Adultery was a sin and now that he was here he didn't want to have sex with her, but he'd been drinking and the world appeared smudged and she'd been wearing nothing except a sheet and it was all so confusing.

She wasn't like Erin. Her body was different, her shape was different, and her scent was different. She smelled spicy, animal-like almost, and her hands moved too much, and everything with Amber was new and he didn't like it but he couldn't stop, either. He heard her calling out his name and saying dirty things and he wanted to tell her to shut up so he could think about Erin, but it was hard to concentrate because everything was so confusing.

He squeezed her arms and heard her gasp and say, "Not so hard," and he loosened his grip, but then he squeezed her arms again because he wanted to. This time she said nothing. He thought about Erin and where she was and whether she was okay and thought again how much he missed her.

He shouldn't have hit Erin because she was sweet and kind and gentle and she didn't deserve to be punched or kicked. It was his fault she was gone. He'd driven her away, even though he loved her. He'd searched for her and hadn't been able to find her and he'd been to Philadelphia and now he was with a woman named Amber who didn't know what to do with her hands and made strange noises and it felt all wrong.

When they were done, he didn't want to stay. Instead, he got out of bed and started to get dressed. She turned on the lamp and sat up in bed. The sight of her reminded him that she wasn't Erin and he suddenly felt sick to his stomach. The Bible says *The man who commits adultery is an utter fool, for he destroys his own soul.*

He had to get away from Amber. He didn't know why he'd come, and as he stared at her, his stomach was in knots.

"Are you okay?" she asked.

"I shouldn't be here," he said. "I shouldn't have come."

"It's a little late now," she said.

"I have to go."

"Just like that?"

"I'm married," he said again.

"I know." She gave a weary smile. "And it's okay."

"No, it's not," he said, and after getting dressed, he left her apartment and raced down the steps and jumped in his car. He drove fast but didn't swerve because the guilt he felt was like a sharp tonic to his senses. He made it home and saw a light on at the Feldmans' and he knew they would peek out their window as he pulled in his driveway. The Feldmans were bad neighbors and never waved at him and told kids to stay off their lawn. They would know what he'd done because they were bad people and he had done a bad thing and birds of a feather flocked together.

When he went inside, he needed a drink but the thought of vodka made him sick and his mind was racing. He'd cheated on his wife and the Bible says *His shame will never be erased.* He'd broken a commandment of God and broken his vow to Erin and he knew the truth would come out. Amber knew and Todd knew and the Feldmans knew and they'd tell someone who'd tell someone else and Erin would learn what he had done. He paced the living room, his breaths coming fast because he knew he wouldn't be able to explain it to Erin in a way she would understand. She was his wife and she would never forgive him. She'd be angry and she'd tell him to sleep on the couch and in the morning she would look at him with disappointment because he was a sinner and she would never trust him again. He shivered, feeling nauseated. He slept with another woman and the Bible says *Have nothing to do with sexual sin, impurity, lust, and shameful desires.* It was all so confusing and he wanted to stop thinking but he couldn't. He wanted to drink but he couldn't and he had the feeling that Erin would suddenly appear at their doorstep.

The house was messy and dirty and Erin would know what he'd done, and even though his thoughts were jumbled, he knew those two things were linked. He paced the living room frantically. Dirty and cheating were linked because cheating was dirty and Erin would know that he'd cheated because the house was dirty, and the two of them went together. Suddenly, he stopped pacing and he strode to the kitchen and found a garbage bag beneath the sink. In the living room, he dropped to his knees and crawled around, filling it with empty takeout containers and magazines and plastic utensils and empty bottles of vodka and pizza boxes. It was well past midnight and he didn't have to work in the morning, so he stayed awake cleaning the house and doing the dishes and running the vacuum that he'd bought for Erin. He cleaned so she wouldn't know, because he knew that cheating and dirty went together. He put the dirty clothes in the washer and when they were done he dried them and folded them while other loads were washing and drying. The sun came up and he pulled the cushions from the sofa and vacuumed until all the crumbs were gone. As he worked, he glanced out the window, knowing Erin would be home any minute. He scrubbed the toilet and washed the food stains from the refrigerator and mopped the linoleum. Dawn turned to morning and then to late morning. He washed the sheets and opened the drapes and dusted the frame that held the photograph of their wedding day. He mowed the lawn and emptied the clippings in the garbage can and when he was done he went shopping and bought turkey and ham and Dijon mustard and fresh rye bread from the bakery. He bought flowers and set them on the table. He added candles. When he was finished he was breathing hard. He poured himself a tall, icy glass of vodka and sat at the kitchen table and waited for Erin. He was happy because he'd cleaned the house because it meant that Erin would never know what he'd done and they would have the kind of marriage he'd always wanted. They would trust each other and be happy and he would love her forever and never cheat on her again because why on earth would he ever do something as disgusting as that?

27

Katie got her driver's license in the second week of July. In the days leading up to her test, Alex had taken her driving regularly, and despite some pretest jitters, she'd passed with a nearly perfect score. The license arrived in the mail within a few days and when Katie opened the envelope, she felt almost dizzy. There was a photograph of her next to a name she'd never imagined having, but according to the state of North Carolina, she was as real as any other resident of the state.

That night, Alex took her to dinner in Wilmington. Afterward, they'd walked the downtown streets holding hands and browsing the shops. Every now and then, she saw Alex regarding her with amusement.

"What?" she finally demanded.

"I was just thinking that you don't look like an Erin. You look like a Katie."

"I should look like a Katie," she said. "That's my name and I've got a driver's license to prove it."

"I know you do," he said. "Now all you need is a car."

"Why do I need a car?" She shrugged. "It's a small town and I've got a bike. And when it's raining, there's this guy who's willing to drive me anywhere I need to go. It's almost like having a chauffeur."

"Really?"

"Uh-huh. And I'm pretty sure that if I asked, he'd even let me borrow his car. I have him wrapped around my little finger."

Alex cocked an eyebrow. "He doesn't sound like much of a man."

"He's all right," she teased. "He seemed a little desperate in the beginning, what with all the freebies he gave me, but I eventually got used to it."

"You have a heart of gold."

"Obviously," she said. "I'm pretty much one in a million."

He laughed. "I'm beginning to think that you're finally coming out of your shell and I'm beginning to glimpse the real you."

She walked a few steps in silence. "You know the real me," she said, stopping to peer up at him. "More than anyone else."

"I know," he said, pulling her toward him. "And that's why I think that somehow we were meant to find each other."

Though the store was as busy as ever, Alex took a vacation. It was his first in a while, and he spent most afternoons with Katie and the kids, relishing the lazy days of summer in a way he hadn't since childhood. He fished with Josh and built dollhouses with Kristen; he took Katie to a jazz festival in Myrtle Beach. When the fireflies were out in force, they caught dozens with nets and put them in a jar; later that night, they watched the eerie glow with a mixture of wonder and fascination before Alex finally opened the lid.

They rode their bikes and went to the movies, and when Katie wasn't working evenings, Alex liked to fire up the grill. The kids would eat and then swim in the creek until it was almost dark. After they'd showered and gone to bed, Alex would sit with Katie on the small dock out back, their legs dangling over the water, while the moon slowly traversed the sky. They sipped wine and talked about nothing important, but Alex grew to savor those quiet moments together.

Kristen particularly loved spending time with Katie. When the four of them were walking together, Kristen often reached for Katie's hand; when she fell down in the playground, she'd begun to run to Katie. While it warmed Alex's heart to see those things, he always felt a pang of sadness, too, because it reminded him that he could never be everything that his daughter needed, no matter how hard he tried. Still, when Kristen came running up to him and asked if Katie could take her shopping, Alex couldn't say no. Though Alex made a point to take her shopping once or twice a year, he tended to view it more as a parental duty than an opportunity for fun. By contrast, Katie seemed delighted by the idea. After giving Katie some money, Alex handed her the keys to the jeep and waved from the parking lot as they left.

As happy as Katie's presence had made Kristen, Josh's feelings weren't quite as obvious. The day before, Alex had picked him up from a friend's swimming party, and he hadn't said anything to either Katie or Alex the rest of the evening. Earlier, at the beach, he'd been subdued as well. Alex knew that something was bothering him and suggested that they get out their fishing poles, just as dusk was settling in. Shadows began to stretch across the blackened water and the creek was still, a darkened mirror reflecting the slowly drifting clouds.

They cast their lines for an hour while the sky turned violet, then indigo, the lures making circular ripples as they splashed into the water. Josh remained strangely quiet. At other times the tableau might have seemed peaceful, but now Alex had the nagging feeling that something was wrong. Just when he was about to ask Josh about it, however, his son half-swiveled in his direction.

"Hey, Dad?"

"Yeah?"

"Do you ever think about Mom?"

"All the time," he said.

Josh nodded. "I think about her, too."

"You should. She loved you very much. What do you think about?"

"I remember when she made us cookies. She let me put the frosting on."

"I remember that. You had pink frosting all over your face. She took your picture. It's still on the refrigerator."

"I think that's why I remember." He propped the rod in his lap. "Do you miss her?"

"Of course I do. I loved her very much," Alex said, holding Josh's gaze. "What's going on, Josh?"

"At the party yesterday . . ." Josh rubbed his nose, hesitating.

"What happened?"

"Most of the moms stayed the whole time. Talking and stuff."

"I would have stayed if you wanted me to."

Josh dropped his eyes, and in the silence, Alex suddenly knew what he hadn't said. "I was supposed to stay, too, wasn't I. Some parent-child thing." His tone was more a statement than a question. "But you didn't want to tell me because I would have been the only dad there, right?"

Josh nodded, looking guilty. "I don't want you to be mad at me."

Alex slipped an arm around his son. "I'm not mad," he said.

"Are you sure?"

"I'm positive. I couldn't be mad at you for that."

"Do you think Mom would have gone? If she was still here?"

"Of course she would have. She wouldn't have missed it."

On the far side of the creek, a mullet jumped and the tiny ripples began moving toward them.

"What do you do when you go out with Miss Katie?" he asked.

Alex shifted slightly. "It's kind of like what we did at the beach today. We eat and talk and maybe go for a walk."

"You've been spending a lot of time with her lately."

"Yes."

Josh considered that. "What do you talk about?"

"Just regular stuff." Alex tilted his head. "And we talk about you and your sister, too."

"What do you say?"

"We talk about how much fun it is to spend time with you two, and how well you did in school, or how good you are at keeping your room clean."

"Will you tell her that I didn't tell you that you were supposed to stay at the party?"

"Do you want me to?"

"No," he said.

"Then I won't say anything."

"Promise? Because I don't want her to be mad at me."

Alex raised his fingers. "Scout's honor. But just so you know, she wouldn't be mad at you even if I did. She thinks you're a great kid."

Josh sat up straighter and began reeling in his line. "Good," he said. "Because I think she's pretty great, too."

The conversation with Josh kept Alex awake that night. He found himself studying the portrait of Carly in his bedroom as he sipped his third beer of the evening.

Kristen and Katie had returned to the house, full of energy and excitement as they showed him the clothes they'd purchased. Surprisingly, Katie had returned nearly half the money, saying only that she was pretty good at finding things on sale. Alex sat on the couch as Kristen modeled an outfit for him, only to vanish back into her bedroom before returning wearing something completely different. Even Josh, who ordinarily wouldn't have cared in the slightest, set his Nintendo game aside, and when Kristen had left the room, he approached Katie.

"Could you take me shopping, too?" he asked, his voice

barely above a whisper. "Because I need some new shirts and stuff."

Afterward, Alex ordered Chinese food and they sat around the table, eating and laughing. At one point during dinner, Katie pulled a leather wristband from her purse and turned toward Josh. "I thought this was pretty cool-looking," she said, handing it to Josh. His surprise gave way to pleasure as he put it on, and Alex noticed how Josh's eyes continually flickered toward Katie for the rest of the evening.

Ironically, it was at times like tonight that he missed Carly most. Even though she'd never experienced nights like these as a family—the kids were too young when she died—he found it easy to imagine her being at the table.

Perhaps that was the reason he couldn't sleep, long after Katie went home and Kristen and Josh were asleep in their beds. Tossing back the covers, he went to the closet and opened the safe he'd installed a few years earlier. In it were important financial and insurance documents, stacked beside treasures from his marriage. They were items that Carly had collected: photos from their honeymoon, a four-leaf clover they'd found while vacationing in Vancouver, the bouquet of peonies and calla lilies she'd carried on her wedding day, ultrasound images of Josh and Kristen while each was still in her womb, along with the outfits that each had worn on the way home from the hospital. Photo negatives and camera disks, chronicling their years together. The articles were heavy with meaning and memories, and since Carly's death, Alex had added nothing to the safe, except for the letters that Carly had written. One had been addressed to him. The second had no name on it, however, and it remained unopened. He couldn't open it—a promise, after all, was a promise.

He pulled out the letter he'd read a hundred times, leaving the other in the safe. He'd known nothing about the letters until she'd handed the envelopes to him less than a week before she died. By that point, she was bedridden and could only sip liquids. When he carried her to the bathroom, she was light, as if somehow she'd been hollowed out. He spent her few waking hours sitting quietly beside her. Usually, she would fall asleep again within minutes, and Alex would stare at her, afraid to leave in case she needed him and afraid to stay in case he might rob her of rest. On the day she gave him the envelopes, he saw that they had been tucked into the blankets, appearing as if by magic. Only later would he learn that she'd written them two months earlier and her mom had been holding them.

Now, Alex opened the envelope and pulled out the much-handled letter. It was written on yellow legal paper. Bringing it to his nose, he was still able to discern the scent of the lotion she often wore. He remembered his surprise and the way her eyes pleaded with him for understanding.

"You want me to read this one first?" he remembered asking. He pointed to the one inscribed with his name and she nodded slightly. She relaxed as he pulled the letter out, her head sinking into the pillow.

My dearest Alex,

There are dreams that visit us and leave us fulfilled upon waking, there are dreams that make life worth living. You, my sweet husband, are that dream, and it saddens me to have to put into words the way I feel about you.

I'm writing this letter now, while I still can, and yet I'm not sure how to capture what I want to say. I'm not a writer, and words seem so inadequate right now. How can I describe how much I love you? Is it even possible to describe a love like that? I don't know, but as I sit here with pen in hand, I know that I have to try.

I know you like to tell the story of how I played hard to get, but when I think back on the night we first met, I think I realized even then that we were meant to be together. I remember that night clearly, just as I can recall the exact sensation of your hand in mine, and every detail of the cloudy afternoon at the beach when you dropped to one knee and asked me to become your wife. Until you came along, I never knew how much I'd been missing. I never knew that a touch could be so meaningful or an expression so eloquent; I never knew that a kiss could literally take my breath away. You are, and always have been, everything I've always wanted in a husband. You're kind and strong and caring and smart; you lift my spirits and you're a better father than you know. You have a knack with children, a way of making them trust you, and I can't express the joy it has brought me to see you holding them as they fall asleep on your shoulder.

My life is infinitely better for having you in it. And that's what makes all of this so hard; it's why I can't seem to find the words I need. It scares me to know that all of this will be ending soon. I'm not simply scared for me, though—I'm scared for you and our children, too. It breaks my heart to know that I'm going to cause you all such grief, but I don't know what I can do, other than to remind you of the reasons I fell in love with you in the first place and express my sorrow at hurting you and our beautiful children. It pains me to think that your love for me will also be the source of so much anguish.

But I truly believe that while love can hurt, love can also heal . . . and that's why I'm enclosing another letter.

Please don't read it. It's not meant for you, or our families, or even our friends. I highly doubt that either of us has met the woman to whom you will give this letter. You see, this one is meant for the woman who eventually heals you, the one who makes you whole again.

Right now, I know you can't imagine something like that. It might take months, it might take years, but someday, you'll give that letter to another woman. Trust your instincts, just as I did on the night you first walked up to me. You'll know when *and where to do that, just as you'll know which woman deserves it. And when you do, trust me when I say that somewhere, somehow, I'll be smiling down on both of you.*

Love,
Carly

After reading the letter again, Alex slipped it back into the envelope and returned it to the safe. Beyond the window, the sky was filled with moonlit clouds and it glowed with an eerie incandescence. He stared upward, thinking of Carly and of Katie. Carly had told him to trust his instincts; Carly had told him that he would know what to do with the letter.

And Carly, he suddenly realized, had been exactly right, about half of it, anyway. He knew he wanted to give the letter to Katie. He just wasn't sure whether she was ready to receive it.

28

―――― 🌱 ――――

Hey, Kevin." Bill gestured to him. "Can you come into my office for a minute?"

Kevin had almost reached his desk, and Coffey and Ramirez followed him with their eyes. His new partner, Todd, was already at his desk and offered a weak smile, but it faded quickly before Todd suddenly turned away.

His head was throbbing and he didn't want to talk to Bill first thing in the morning but Kevin wasn't worried. He was good with witnesses and victims and knew when criminals were lying and he made lots of arrests and the criminals were convicted.

Bill motioned for him to sit in the chair and though Kevin didn't want to sit, he took a seat and wondered why Bill wanted him to sit because usually he stood when the two of them were talking. The pain in his temple felt as if he were being stabbed with a pencil, and for a moment Bill simply stared. Bill finally got up and closed the door before propping himself on the edge of his desk.

"How are you doing, Kevin?"

"I'm fine," Kevin answered. He wanted to close his eyes to lessen the pain, but he could tell that Bill was studying him. "What's up?"

Bill crossed his arms. "I called you in here to let you know that we received a complaint about you."

"What kind of complaint?"

"This is serious, Kevin. Internal Affairs is involved, and as of now, you're being suspended pending an investigation."

The words sounded jumbled, making no sense at all, not at first, anyway, but as he concentrated, he could see Bill's expression and wished he hadn't woken with a headache and didn't need so much vodka.

"What are you talking about?"

Bill lifted a few pages from his desk. "The Gates murder," he said. "The little boy who was shot through the floor? Earlier this month?"

"I remember," Kevin said. "He had pizza sauce on his forehead."

"Excuse me?"

Kevin blinked. "The boy. That's how we found him. It was horrible. Todd was pretty shaken up."

Bill furrowed his brow. "An ambulance was called," he said.

Kevin breathed in and out. Concentrating.

"It came for the mom," Kevin said. "She was upset, obviously, and she went after the Greek who'd fired the bullet. They struggled and she fell down the stairs. We called it in immediately . . . as far as I know, she was taken to the hospital."

Bill continued to stare at him before finally setting the pages aside. "You talked to her beforehand, right?"

"I tried to . . . but she was pretty hysterical. I tried to calm her down, but she went crazy. What else is there to tell? It's all in the report."

Bill reached for the papers on his desk again. "I saw what you wrote. But the woman is claiming that you told her to push the perp down the stairs."

"What?"

Bill read from the pages. "She claims you were talking about

God and told her, quote, 'The man was a sinner and deserved to be punished because the Bible says *Thou shalt not kill*.' She says that you also told her that the guy was probably going to get probation, even though he killed her kid, so she should take matters into her own hands. Because wrongdoers deserve to be punished. Does any of this ring a bell?"

Kevin could feel the blood in his cheeks. "That's ridiculous," he said. "You know she's lying, right?"

He expected Bill to immediately agree with him, to say that he knew Internal Affairs would clear him. But Bill didn't. Instead, his boss leaned forward.

"What exactly did you tell her? Word for word."

"I didn't *tell* her anything. I asked her what happened and she told me and I saw the hole in the ceiling and went upstairs and I arrested the neighbor after he admitted to firing the gun. I cuffed him and started bringing him down the stairs; the next thing I know, she went after him."

Bill was silent, his gaze locked on Kevin. "You never talked to her about sin?"

"No."

He held up the paper he had been reading from. "You never said the words *Vengeance is mine, I will repay, says the Lord*."

"No."

"None of this sounds familiar at all?"

Kevin felt the anger rising but forced it back down. "Nothing. It's a lie. You know how people are. She probably wants to sue the city so she can get a big payday."

Bill's jaw muscle was flexing and it took a long time before he spoke.

"Had you been drinking before you talked to the woman?"

"I don't know where this is coming from. No. I don't do that. I wouldn't do that. You know my clear rate. I'm a good detective." Kevin held out his hands, almost blind from the throbbing pain in his head. "C'mon, Bill. We've worked together for years."

"That's why I'm talking to you instead of firing you. Because in the past few months, you haven't been yourself. And I've been hearing rumors."

"What rumors?"

"That you're drunk when you come into work."

"It's not true."

"So if I gave you a Breathalyzer, you'd blow a zero, right?"

Kevin could feel his heart hammering in his chest. He knew how to lie and he was good at it but he had to keep his voice steady. "Last night, I was up late with a buddy and we were drinking. There might still be some alcohol in my system, but I'm not drunk and I didn't drink before coming into work this morning. Or that day, either. Or any day, for that matter."

Bill stared at him. "Tell me what's going on with Erin," he said.

"I've already told you. She's helping a friend in Manchester. We went to the Cape just a few weeks ago."

"You told Coffey that you went to a restaurant in Province-town with Erin, but the restaurant closed six months ago and there was no record of you checking into the bed-and-breakfast you mentioned. And no one has seen or heard from Erin in months."

Kevin felt his head filling with blood, making the pounding worse. "You checked up on me?"

"You've been drinking on the job and you've been lying to me."

"I haven't—"

"Stop lying to me!" the captain suddenly shouted. "I can smell your breath from here!" His eyes flared anger. "And as of now, you're suspended from duty. You should call your union rep before you meet with Internal Affairs. Leave your gun and your badge on my desk and go home."

"How long?" Kevin managed to croak out.

"Right now, suspension is the least of your worries."

"Just so you know, I didn't say anything to that woman."

"They heard you!" Bill shouted. "Your partner, the medical examiner, the crime scene investigators, the boyfriend." He paused, visibly trying to regain his calm. "Everyone heard you," he said with finality, and all at once, Kevin felt as though he'd lost control of everything and he knew it was all Erin's fault.

29

August rolled in, and although Alex and Katie were enjoying the hot, slow summer days they spent together, the kids were beginning to get bored. Wanting to do something unusual, Alex took Katie and the kids to see the rodeo monkeys in Wilmington. Much to Katie's disbelief, it turned out to be exactly what it sounded like: monkeys, dressed in cowboy outfits, rode dogs and herded rams for almost an hour before a show of fireworks that rivaled the Fourth of July. On their way out, Katie turned toward him with a smile.

"That has to be the craziest thing I've ever seen," she said, shaking her head.

"And you probably thought we lacked culture in the South."

She laughed. "Where do people come up with these ideas?"

"I have no idea. But it's a good thing I heard about it. They're in town for only a couple of days." He scanned the parking lot for his car.

"Yes, it's hard to imagine how unfulfilling my life would have been had I never seen monkeys riding dogs."

"The kids liked it!" Alex protested.

"The kids loved it," Katie agreed. "But I can't figure out

whether the monkeys liked it. They didn't look all that happy to me."

Alex squinted at her. "I'm not sure I'd be able to tell whether a monkey was happy or not."

"My point exactly," she said.

"Hey, it's not my fault that there's still another month until school, and I'm just about out of new things for the kids to do."

"They don't need to do something special every day."

"I know. And they don't. But I don't want them watching television all the time, either."

"Your kids don't watch a lot of television."

"That's because I take them to see the rodeo monkeys."

"And next week?"

"That's easy. The carnival will be in town. One of those traveling things."

She smiled. "Those kinds of rides always made me sick to my stomach."

"And the kids love them, anyway. But that reminds me. Are you working next Saturday?"

"I'm not sure. Why?"

"Because I was hoping you'd come to the carnival with us."

"You want me to be sick to my stomach?"

"You don't have to go on the rides if you don't want to. But I would like to ask a favor."

"What's that?"

"I was hoping you'd watch the kids later that evening. Joyce's daughter is flying into Raleigh, and Joyce asked if I could drive her to the airport to pick her up. Joyce doesn't like to drive at night."

"I'd be glad to watch them."

"It'll have to be at my place, so they go to bed at a reasonable hour."

She looked at him. "Your place? I never get to spend time at your house."

"Yeah, well . . ."

He didn't seem to know what to say next and she smiled. "No problem," she said. "That sounds like fun. Maybe we'll watch a movie together and have some popcorn."

Alex walked in silence for a few steps before he asked, "Do you ever want to have kids?"

Katie hesitated. "I'm not sure," she finally said. "I haven't really thought about it."

"Ever?"

She shook her head. "In Atlantic City I was too young, with Kevin I couldn't bear the idea, and I've had my mind on other things the last few months."

"But if you did think about it?" he persisted.

"I still don't know. I guess it would depend on a lot of things."

"Like what?"

"Like whether I was married, for starters. And, as you know, I can't get married."

"Erin can't get married," he said. "But Katie probably could. She has a driver's license, remember."

Katie took a few steps in silence. "She might be able to, but she wouldn't do it unless she met the right guy."

He laughed and slipped his arm around her. "I know that working at Ivan's was just what you needed at the time you took the job, but did you ever think about doing something else?"

"Like what?"

"I don't know. Going back to college, getting a degree, finding a job that you really love."

"What makes you think I don't love waiting tables?"

"Nothing." He shrugged. "I was just curious as to what you might be interested in."

She thought about it. "Growing up, like every other girl I knew, I loved animals and I thought I'd be a veterinarian. But there's no way I'd be willing to go back to school for that now. It would take too long."

"There are other ways to work with animals. You could train rodeo monkeys, for instance."

"I don't think so. I still haven't decided whether the monkeys liked it."

"You've got a soft spot for those monkeys, don't you?"

"Who wouldn't? I mean, who on earth came up with that idea in the first place?"

"Correct me if I'm wrong, but I think I heard you laughing."

"I didn't want to make the rest of you feel bad."

He laughed again, pulling her even closer. Ahead of them, Josh and Kristen were already slumped against the jeep. She knew they would probably fall asleep before they got back to Southport.

"You never answered my question," Alex said. "About what you want to do with your life."

"Maybe my dreams aren't that complicated. Maybe I think that a job is just a job."

"What does that mean?"

"Maybe I don't want to be defined by what I do. Maybe I'd like to be defined by what I am."

He considered the response. "Okay," he said. "Then who do you want to be?"

"Do you really want to know?"

"I wouldn't have asked you otherwise."

She stopped and met his gaze. "I'd like to be a wife and mother," she finally said.

He frowned. "But I thought you said that you weren't sure whether you wanted to have children."

She cocked her head, looking as beautiful as he'd ever seen. "What does that have to do with anything?"

The kids fell asleep before they reached the highway. It wasn't a long trip back, maybe half an hour, but neither Alex nor Katie wanted to risk waking the kids with their conversation.

Instead, they were content to hold hands in silence as they made the drive back to Southport.

As Alex pulled to a stop in front of her house, Katie spotted Jo sitting on the steps of her porch, as if waiting for her. In the darkness, she wasn't sure whether Alex recognized her, but at that moment Kristen stirred and he turned around in his seat to make sure she hadn't woken up. Katie leaned over and kissed him.

"I should probably talk to her," Katie whispered.

"Who? Kristen?"

"My neighbor." Katie smiled, gesturing over her shoulder. "Or rather, she probably wants to talk to me."

"Oh." He nodded. "Okay." He glanced toward Jo's porch and back again. "I had a great time tonight."

"I did, too."

He kissed her before she opened the door, and when Alex pulled out of the driveway she started toward Jo's house. Jo smiled and waved, and Katie felt herself relax slightly. They hadn't talked since that night in the bar, and as she approached, Jo stood and came to the railing.

"First off, I want to apologize for the way I talked to you," she said without preamble. "I was out of line. I was wrong and it won't happen again."

Katie climbed the steps to her porch and sat down, waving Jo to a spot next to her on the top step. "It's okay," she said. "I wasn't mad."

"I still feel terrible about it," Jo said, her remorse obvious. "I don't know what got into me."

"I do," Katie said. "It's obvious. You care about them. And you want to watch out for them."

"I still shouldn't have talked to you the way I did. That's why I haven't been around. It embarrassed me and I knew you'd never forgive me."

Katie touched her arm. "I appreciate the apology, but it's not necessary. You actually made me realize some important things about myself."

"Yeah?"

Katie nodded. "And just so you know, I think I'm going to stay in Southport for a while."

"I saw you driving the other day."

"Hard to believe, isn't it? I still don't feel comfortable behind the wheel."

"You will," she said. "And it's better than the bike."

"I still ride my bike every day," she said. "I can't afford a car."

"I'd say you could use mine, but it's back in the shop again. Thing's always breaking down. I'd probably be better off with a bike."

"Be careful what you wish for."

"Now you sound like me again." Jo nodded toward the road. "I'm happy for you and Alex. And the kids. You're good for them, you know."

"How can you be so sure?"

"Because I can see the way he looks at you. And the way you look at all of them."

"We've spent a lot of time together," Katie hedged.

Jo shook her head. "It's more than that. The two of you look like you're in love." She squirmed a bit under Katie's blushing gaze. "Okay, I'll admit it. Even if you haven't seen me, let's just say that I've seen the way the two of you kiss when you say good-bye."

"You spy on us?" Katie pretended to be outraged.

"Of course." Jo snorted. "How else am I supposed to occupy myself? It's not like anything else interesting ever happens around here." She paused. "You do love him, don't you?"

Katie nodded. "And I love the kids, too."

"I'm so glad." Jo clasped her hands together, prayer-style.

Katie paused. "Did you know his wife?"

"Yes," Jo said.

Katie stared down the road. "What was she like? I mean, Alex's talked about her and I can sort of picture in my mind what she was like—"

Jo didn't let her finish. "Based on what I've seen, she was a lot like you. And I mean that in a good way. She loved Alex and she loved the kids. They were the most important things in her life. That's really all you have to know about her."

"Do you think she would have liked me?"

"Yes," Jo said. "I'm sure she would have loved you."

30

August, and Boston was sweltering.

Kevin vaguely remembered seeing the ambulance outside the Feldmans' home, but he hadn't thought much about it because the Feldmans were bad neighbors and he didn't care about them. Only now did he realize that Gladys Feldman had died and cars were parked along both sides of the street. Kevin had been suspended for two weeks and he didn't like cars parked in front of his house, but people were in town for the funeral and he lacked the energy to ask any of them to move.

He'd showered infrequently since he'd been suspended, and he sat on the porch, drinking straight from the bottle, watching people walk in and out of the Feldmans' house. He knew the funeral was later in the afternoon and people were at the Feldmans' house because they would be going to the funeral as a group. People clustered like flocks of geese whenever there was a funeral.

He hadn't talked to Bill or Coffey or Ramirez or Todd or Amber or even his parents. There were no pizza boxes on the living room floor and no leftover Chinese in the refrigerator because he hadn't been hungry. Vodka was enough and he drank until the Feldmans' house was a blur. Across the street, he saw a woman walk out of their house to smoke a cigarette. She was wearing a black dress and Kevin wondered if she knew the Feldmans yelled at neighborhood kids.

He watched the woman because he didn't want to watch the home and garden channel on the television. Erin used to watch that channel but she ran away to Philadelphia and called herself Erica and then she disappeared and he'd been suspended from his job but before that he'd been a good detective.

The woman in black finished her cigarette and dropped it in the grass and stepped on it. She scanned the street and noticed him sitting on the porch. She hesitated before crossing the street toward him. He didn't know her; had never seen her before.

He didn't know what she wanted but he put the bottle down and climbed down the porch steps. She stopped on the sidewalk out front.

"Are you Kevin Tierney?" the woman asked.

"Yes," he said, and his voice sounded strange because he hadn't spoken in days.

"I'm Karen Feldman," she said. "My parents live across the street. Larry and Gladys Feldman?" She paused but Kevin said nothing and she went on. "I was just wondering if Erin was planning to attend the funeral."

He stared at her.

"Erin?" he finally said.

"Yes. My mom and dad used to love it when she came by to visit. She used to make them pies and sometimes she helped them clean up, especially once my mom started getting sick. Lung cancer. It was awful." She shook her head. "Is Erin around? I've been hoping to meet her. The funeral starts at two."

"No, she's not. She's helping a sick friend in Manchester," he said.

"Oh . . . well, okay then. That's too bad. I'm sorry to have bothered you."

His mind began to clear and he noticed that she was about to leave. "I'm sorry for your loss, by the way. I told Erin and she's upset that she can't be here. Did you get the flowers?"

"Oh, probably. I haven't checked. The funeral home is full of them."

"No big deal. I just wish Erin could have been here."

"Me, too. I've always wanted to meet her. My mom told me that she reminded her of Katie."

"Katie?"

"My younger sister. She passed away six years ago."

"I'm sorry to hear that."

"Me, too. We all miss her—my mom did especially. That's why she got along so well with Erin. They even looked alike. Same age and everything." If Karen noticed Kevin's blank expression, she gave no sign. "My mom used to show Erin the scrapbook she'd put together about Katie . . . She was always so patient with my mom. She's a sweet woman. You're a lucky man."

Kevin forced himself to smile. "Yes, I know."

He'd been a good detective but in truth sometimes the answers came down to luck. New evidence surfacing, an unknown witness stepping forward, a street camera catching a license plate. In this case the lead came from a woman in black named Karen Feldman, who crossed the street on a morning he'd been drinking and told him about her dead sister.

Even though his head still ached, he poured the vodka down the drain and thought about Erin and the Feldmans. Erin knew them and visited them, even though she'd never mentioned going to their house. He'd called her and dropped by unexpectedly and she'd always been home, but somehow, he'd never found out. She'd never told him and when he'd complained that they were bad neighbors, she'd never said a word.

Erin had a secret.

His mind was clearer than it had been in a long time and he got in the shower and washed and put on a black suit. He made a ham-and-turkey sandwich with Dijon mustard and ate it, then made another and ate it as well. The street was filled with cars and he watched people walking in and out of the house. Karen came outside and smoked another cigarette. While he waited, he tucked a small pad of paper and a pen in his pocket.

In the afternoon, people started filing toward their cars. He heard the engines start up and one by one they began to pull away. It was past one o'clock and they were going to the service. It took fifteen minutes for everyone to leave and he saw Larry Feldman being helped to the car by Karen. Karen got in the driver's seat and drove off, and finally there were no more cars on the street or in the driveway.

He waited ten more minutes, making sure everyone had left before finally walking out his front door. He crossed his lawn and paused at the street and headed for the Feldmans' house. He didn't hurry and didn't try to hide. He'd noticed that a lot of the neighbors had gone to the funeral and those who hadn't would simply remember a mourner wearing a black suit. He went to the front door and it was locked, but there'd been a lot of people in the house so he walked around the side and headed to the back. There, he found another door and it was unlocked and he stepped into the house.

It was quiet. He paused, listening for the sound of voices or footsteps but heard nothing. There were plastic cups on the countertop and platters of food on the table. He walked through the house. He had time, but he didn't know how much time, and he decided to start in the living room. He opened cabinet doors and closed them, leaving everything the way it had been before. He searched in the kitchen and the bedroom and finally went to the study. There were books on the shelves and a recliner and a television. In the corner, he spotted a small file cabinet.

He went to the file cabinet and opened it. Quickly, he scanned the tabs. He found a file labeled KATIE and pulled it out, opened it, and examined what was inside. There was a newspaper article—it turns out that she'd drowned after breaking through the ice of a local pond—and there were pictures of her that had been taken at school. In her graduation photo, she looked re-markably like Erin. In the back of the file, he found an envelope. He opened it and found an old report card. On the front of the envelope was a social security number, and he took the pad of paper and his pen and wrote it down. He didn't find the social security card, but he had the number. The birth certificate was a copy, though it was wrinkled and worn, as if someone had crumpled it up and then tried to flatten it again.

He had what he needed and he left the house. As soon as he reached home he called the officer from the other precinct, the one who was sleeping with the babysitter. The following day, he received a call in return.

Katie Feldman had recently been issued a driver's license, with an address listed in Southport, North Carolina.

Kevin hung up the phone without another word, knowing he'd found her.

Erin.

31

Remnants of a tropical storm blew through Southport, rain falling most of the afternoon and into the evening. Katie worked the lunch shift, but the weather kept the restaurant only half full and Ivan let her leave early. She had borrowed the jeep and after spending an hour at the library, she'd dropped it off at the store. When Alex drove her home, she'd invited him to come by later with the kids for dinner.

She'd been on edge the rest of the afternoon. She wanted to believe it had something to do with the weather, but as she stood at her kitchen window, watching the branches bend in the wind and rain falling in sheets, she knew it had more to do with the uneasy feeling that everything in her life these days seemed almost too perfect. Her relationship with Alex and the afternoons she spent with the kids filled a void she hadn't known existed, but she'd learned long ago that nothing wonderful lasted forever. Joy was as fleeting as a shooting star that crossed the evening sky, ready to blink out at any moment.

Earlier that day, at the library, she'd perused the *Boston Globe* online at one of the computers and had come across Gladys Feldman's obituary. She'd known Gladys was ill, had known about her terminal diagnosis of cancer before she left. Even though she'd been checking the Boston obituaries regularly, the sparse description of her life and survivors struck her with un-expected force.

She hadn't wanted to take the identification from the Feld-mans' files, hadn't even considered the possibility until Gladys had pulled out the file to show her Katie's graduation photo. She'd seen the birth certificate and the social security card next to the photo and recognized the opportunity they presented. The next time she'd gone to the house, she'd excused herself to go to the bathroom and had gone to the file cabinet instead. Later, as she ate blueberry pie with them in the kitchen, the documents felt like they were burning in her pockets. A week later, after making a copy of the birth certificate at the library and folding and wrinkling it to make it appear dated, she put the document in the file. She would have done the same with the social security card, but she couldn't make a good enough copy and she hoped that if they noticed it was missing, they would believe it had been lost or misplaced.

She reminded herself that Kevin would never know what she'd done. He didn't like the Feldmans and the feeling was mutual. She suspected that they knew he beat her. She could see it in their eyes as they watched her dart across the road to visit them, in the way they pretended never to notice the bruises on her arms, in the way their faces tightened whenever she mentioned Kevin. She wanted to think that they would have been okay with what she'd done, that they would have wanted her to take the identification, because they knew she needed it and wanted her to escape.

They were the only people she missed from Dorchester and she wondered how Larry was doing. They were her friends when she had no one else, and she wanted to tell Larry that she was sorry for his loss. She wanted to cry with him and talk about Gladys and to tell him that because of them, her life was better now. She wanted to tell him that she'd met a man who loved her, that she was happy for the first time in years.

But she would do none of those things. Instead, she simply stepped out onto the porch and, through eyes that were blurry with tears, watched the storm tear leaves from the trees.

"You've been quiet tonight," Alex said. "Is everything okay?"

She'd made tuna casserole for dinner and Alex was helping her with the dishes. The kids were in the living room, both of them playing handheld computer games; she could hear the beeps and buzzes over the sound of the faucet.

"A friend of mine passed away," she said. She handed him a plate to dry. "I knew it was coming, but it's still sad."

"It's always sad," he agreed. "I'm sorry." He knew enough not to ask for further details. Instead, he waited on the chance she wanted to say more, but she washed another glass and changed the subject.

"How long do you think the storm is going to last?" she asked.

"Not long. Why?"

"I was just wondering whether the carnival tomorrow is going to be canceled. Or whether the flight is going to be canceled."

Alex glanced out the window. "It should be fine. It's already blowing through. I'm pretty sure we're on the tail end of it now."

"Just in time," Katie remarked.

"Of course. The elements wouldn't dare mess with the well-laid plans of the carnival committee. Or Joyce for that matter."

She smiled. "How long is it going to take you to pick up Joyce's daughter?"

"Probably four or five hours. Raleigh's not exactly convenient to this place."

"Why didn't she fly into Wilmington? Or just rent a car?"

"I don't know. I didn't ask, but if I had to guess I'd say she wanted to save some money."

"You're doing a good thing, you know. Helping Joyce like that."

He gave a nonchalant shrug, indicating that it wasn't a big deal. "You'll have fun tomorrow."

"At the carnival or with the kids?"

"Both. And if you ask me nice, I'll treat you to some deep-fried ice cream."

"Fried ice cream? It sounds disgusting."

"It's actually tasty."

"Is everything fried down here?"

"If it can be fried, believe me, someone will find a way. Last year, there was a place serving deep-fried butter."

She almost gagged. "You're kidding."

"Nope. It sounded terrible, but people were lining up to buy it. They might as well have been lining up for heart attacks."

She washed and rinsed the last of the cups, then passed it to him. "Do you think the kids liked the dinner I made? Kristen didn't eat very much."

"Kristen never eats much. And more important, I liked it. I thought it was delicious."

She shook her head. "Who cares about the kids, right? As long as you're happy?"

"I'm sorry. I'm a narcissist at heart."

She ran the soapy sponge over a plate and rinsed it. "I'm looking forward to spending some time at your house."

"Why?"

"Because we're always here, not there. Don't get me wrong— I understand it was the right thing to do because of the kids." *And because of Carly*, she also thought, but she didn't mention that part. "It'll give me the chance to see how you live."

Alex took the plate. "You've been there before."

"Yes, but not for more than a few minutes, and then only in the kitchen or living room. It's not like I've had the chance to check out your bedroom or peek in your medicine cabinet."

"You wouldn't do that." Alex feigned outrage.

"Maybe if I had the chance, I might."

He dried the plate and put it in the cupboard. "Feel free to spend as much time in my bedroom as you like."

She laughed. "You're such a man."

"I'm just saying that I wouldn't mind. And feel free to peek in the medicine cabinet, too. I have no secrets."

"So you say," she teased. "You're talking to someone who only has secrets."

"Not from me."

"No," she agreed, her face serious. "Not from you."

She washed two more plates and handed them to him, feeling a wave of contentment wash over her as she watched him dry and put them away.

He cleared his throat.

"Can I ask you something?" he said. "I don't want you to take it the wrong way, but I've been curious."

"Go ahead."

He used the towel on his arms, dabbing at stray droplets, buying time. "I was wondering if you'd given more thought to what I said last weekend. In the parking lot, after seeing the rodeo monkeys?"

"You said a lot of things," she said cautiously.

"Don't you remember? You told me that Erin couldn't get married, but I said that Katie probably could?"

Katie felt herself stiffen, less at the memory than at the serious tone he was using. She knew exactly where this was leading. "I remember," she said with forced lightness. "I think I said I would have to meet the right guy."

At her words, his lips tightened, as if he were debating whether to continue. "I just wanted to know if you thought about it. Us eventually getting married, I mean."

The water was still warm as she started on the silverware. "You'd have to ask first."

"But if I did?"

She found a fork and scrubbed it. "I suppose I'd tell you that I love you."

"Would you say yes?"

She paused. "I don't want to get married again."

"You don't want to, or you don't think you can?"

"What's the difference?" Her expression remained stubborn, closed. "You know I'm still married. Bigamy is illegal."

"You're not Erin anymore. You're Katie. As you pointed out, your driver's license proves it."

"But I'm not Katie, either!" she snapped before turning toward him. "Don't you get that? I stole that name from people I cared about! People who trusted me." She stared at him, feeling the surge of tension from earlier in the day, recalling with fresh intensity Gladys's kindness and pity, her escape, and the nightmarish years with Kevin. "Why can't you just be happy with the way things are? Why do you have to push so hard for me to be the person you want me to be rather than the person that I am?"

He flinched. "I love the person that you are."

"But you're making it conditional!"

"I'm not!"

"But you are!" she insisted. She knew she was raising her voice but she couldn't seem to stop it. "You have this idea of what you want in life and you're trying to make me fit into it!"

"I don't," Alex protested. "I simply asked you a question."

"But you wanted a specific answer! You wanted the *right* answer, and if you didn't get it, you were going to try to convince me otherwise. That I should do what you want! That I should do everything you want!"

For the first time ever, Alex narrowed his eyes at her. "Don't do this," he said.

"Do what? Tell the truth? Tell you how I feel? Why? What are you going to do? Hit me? Go ahead."

He physically recoiled as though she'd slapped him. She knew her words had hit their mark, but instead of getting angry, Alex set the dish towel on the counter and took a step backward. "I don't know what's going on, but I'm sorry that I even brought it up. I didn't mean to put you on the spot or try to convince you of anything. I was just trying to have a conversation."

He paused, waiting for her to say something, but she stayed silent. Shaking his head, he started to leave the kitchen before coming to a stop. "Thank you for dinner," he whispered.

In the living room, she heard him tell the kids it was getting late, heard the front door open with a squeak. He closed the door softly behind him and the house was suddenly quiet, leaving her alone with her thoughts.

32

Kevin was having trouble staying between the lines on the highway. He'd wanted to keep his mind sharp, but his head had begun to pound and he'd been sick to his stomach, so he'd stopped at a liquor store and bought a bottle of vodka. It numbed the pain, and as he sipped it through a straw, all he could think about was Erin and how she'd changed her name to Katie.

The interstate was a blur. Headlights, double pinpricks of white, rose in intensity as they approached from the opposite direction and then vanished when they passed him. One after another. Thousands. People going places, doing things. Kevin driving to North Carolina, heading south to find his wife. Leaving Massachusetts, driving through Rhode Island and Connecticut. New York and New Jersey. The moon rose, orange and angry before turning white, and crossed the blackened sky above him. Stars overhead.

Hot wind blew through the open window and Kevin held the wheel steady, his thoughts a jigsaw of mismatched pieces. The bitch had left him. She'd abandoned the marriage and left him to rot and believed she was smarter than he was. But he'd found her. Karen Feldman had crossed the street and he'd learned that Erin had a secret. But not anymore. He knew where Erin lived, he knew where she was hiding. Her address was scribbled on a piece of paper on the seat beside him, held in place by the Glock he'd brought from home. On the backseat was a duffel bag filled with clothes and handcuffs and duct tape. On his way out of town, he stopped at an ATM and withdrew a few hundred dollars. He wanted to smash Erin's face with his fists as soon as he found her, bloody it to an ugly pulp. He wanted to kiss her and hold her and beg her to come home. He filled the tank near Philadelphia and remembered how he'd tracked her there.

She'd made a fool of him, carrying on a secret life he hadn't even known about. Visiting the Feldmans, cooking and cleaning for them while she plotted and schemed and lied. What else, he wondered, had she lied about? A man? Maybe not then, but there had to be a man by now. Kissing her. Caressing her. Taking her clothes off. Laughing at him. They were probably in bed together right now. Her and the man. Both of them laughing at him behind his back. *I showed him, didn't I?* she was saying as she laughed. *Kevin didn't even see it coming.*

It made him crazy to think about. Furious. He'd been on the road for hours already, but Kevin kept driving. He sipped his vodka and blinked rapidly to clear his vision. He didn't speed, didn't want to get pulled over. Not with a gun on the seat beside him. She was afraid of guns and always asked him to lock his up when he finished his shift, which he did.

But it wasn't enough. He could buy her a house, furniture, and pretty clothes and take her to the library and the hair salon and it still wasn't enough. Who could understand it? Was it so hard to clean the house and cook dinner? He never wanted to hit her, only did it when he had no other choice. When she was stupid or careless or selfish. She brought it on herself.

The engine droned, the noise steady in his ears. She had a driver's license now and she was a waitress at a restaurant called

Ivan's. Before he left, he'd spent some time on the Internet and had made some calls. It hadn't been hard to track her down because the town was small. It took him less than twenty minutes to find out where she worked. All he had to do was dial the number and ask if Katie was there. On the fourth call, someone said yes. He hung up without a word. She thought she could hide forever, but he was a good detective and he'd found her. *I'm coming*, he thought to himself. *I know where you live and where you work and you won't get away again.*

He passed billboards and exit ramps, and in Delaware the rain started to fall. He rolled up the window and felt the wind begin to push the car sideways. A truck ahead of him was swerving, the trailer wheels riding the lines. He turned on the wipers and the windshield cleared. But the rain began to fall even harder and he leaned over the wheel, squinting into the fuzzy orbs of oncoming headlights. His breath began to fog the glass and he turned on the defroster. He would drive all night and find Erin tomorrow. He'd bring her home and they'd start over again. Man and wife, living together, the way it was supposed to be. Happy.

They used to be happy. Used to do fun things together. Early on in the marriage, he remembered, he and Erin would visit open houses on the weekends. She was excited about buying a house and he would listen as she talked to the Realtors, her voice trilling like music in the empty homes. She liked to take her time as she walked through the rooms, and he knew she was imagining where to put furniture. When they found the house in Dorchester, he'd known she wanted it by the way her eyes were sparkling. That night, lying in bed, she traced small circles on his chest as she pleaded with him to make an offer and he could remember thinking that he would do anything she wanted because he loved her.

Except have children. She'd told him that she wanted kids, wanted to start a family. In the first year of marriage, she'd talked about it all the time. He tried to ignore her, didn't want to tell her that he didn't want her to get fat and puffy, that pregnant women were ugly, that he didn't want to hear her whining about how tired she was or how her feet were swollen. He didn't want to hear a baby fussing and crying when he got home from work, didn't want toys scattered around the house. He didn't want her to get frumpy and saggy or hear her ask him whether he thought her butt was getting fat. He married her because he wanted a wife, not a mother. But she kept bringing it up, kept harping day after day until he finally slapped her and told her to shut up. After that, she never talked about it again, but now he wondered whether he should have given her what she wanted. She wouldn't have left if she had a child, wouldn't have been able to run away in the first place. By the same token, she could never run away again.

They would have a child, he decided, and the three of them would live in Dorchester and he would work as a detective. In the evenings, he'd come home to his pretty wife and when people saw them in the grocery store, they would marvel and say, *They look like the all-American family*.

He wondered whether her hair was blond again. Hoped it was long and blond and that he could run his fingers through it. She liked when he did that, always whispering to him, saying the words he liked, turning him on. But it hadn't been real, not if she'd been planning to leave him, not if she hadn't come back. She'd lied to him, been lying all along. For weeks. Months, even. Stealing from the Feldmans, the cell phone, taking money from his wallet. Scheming and plotting and he'd had no idea at all and now another man was sharing her bed. Running his fingers through her hair, listening to her moans, feeling her hands on him. Kevin bit his lip and tasted blood, hating her, wanting to kick and punch her, wanting to throw her down the stairs. He took another sip from the bottle next to him, rinsing the metallic taste from his mouth.

She'd fooled him because she was beautiful. Everything about her was pretty. Her breasts, her lips, even the small of her back. At the casino, in Atlantic City, when he'd first met her, he'd thought she was the prettiest woman he'd ever seen, and in their four years of marriage, nothing had changed. She knew he desired her, and she used it to her advantage. Dressing sexy. Getting her hair done. Wearing lacy underwear. It made him lower his guard, made him think she loved him.

But she didn't love him. She didn't even care about him. She didn't care about the broken flowerpots and smashed-up china, didn't care that he'd been suspended from his job, didn't care that he'd cried himself to sleep for months. Didn't care that his life was falling apart. All that mattered was what she wanted, but she'd always been selfish and now she was laughing at him. Laughing for months and thinking only about herself. He loved her and hated her and he couldn't make sense of it. He felt tears beginning to form and he blinked them back.

Delaware. Maryland. The outskirts of Washington DC. Virginia. Hours lost to the never-ending night. Raining hard at first, then gradually the rain dissipated. He stopped near Richmond at dawn and ate breakfast. Two eggs, four pieces of bacon, wheat toast. He drank three cups of coffee. He put more gas in the car and went back to the interstate. He crossed into North Carolina under blue skies. Bugs were cemented against the windshield and his back had begun to ache. He had to wear sunglasses to keep from squinting and his whiskers had begun to itch.

I'm coming, Erin, he thought. *I'll be there soon.*

33

Katie awoke exhausted. She had tossed and turned for hours during the night, replaying the horrible things she'd said to Alex. She didn't know what had come over her. Yes, she was upset about the Feldmans, but for the life of her, she couldn't remember how the argument had started in the first place. Or rather, she did remember, but it didn't make sense. She'd known he hadn't been pressuring her or trying to force her to do anything she wasn't ready for. She knew he wasn't remotely like Kevin, but what had she said to him?

What are you going to do? Hit me? Go ahead.

Why would she have said something like that?

She eventually dozed off sometime after two a.m., when the wind and rain were beginning to taper off. By dawn, the sky was clear and birdsong was drifting from the trees. From the porch, she noticed the effects of the storm: broken branches strewn out front, a carpet of pinecones littered across the yard and drive. The air was already thick with humidity. It was going to be a scorcher, maybe the hottest day of the summer yet. She made a note to herself to remind Alex not to keep the kids out in the sun too long before she realized that he might not want her with them. That maybe he was still mad at her.

Not maybe, she corrected herself. He was almost certainly mad at her. And hurt as well. He hadn't even let the kids say good-bye last night.

She took a seat on the steps and turned toward Jo's, wondering if she was up and about. It was early, probably too early to knock on her door. She didn't know what she would say to her or what good it would do. She wouldn't tell her what she'd said to Alex—that was a memory she'd rather erase in its entirety—but maybe Jo could help her understand the anxiety she'd been feeling. Even after Alex left, she noted the tension in her shoulders, and last night, for the first time in weeks, she'd wanted the light on.

Her intuition told her that something was wrong but she couldn't pinpoint what it was, other than that her thoughts kept returning to the Feldmans. To Gladys. To the inevitable changes in the house. What would happen if someone realized Katie's information was missing? Simply imagining it made her sick to her stomach.

"It's going to be okay," she suddenly heard. Whirling around, she saw Jo standing off to the side in her running shoes, cheeks flushed and perspiration staining her shirt.

"Where did you come from?"

"I went for a jog," Jo said. "I was trying to beat the heat, but obviously, it didn't work. It's so steamy I could barely breathe and I thought I was going to die of heatstroke. Even so, I think I'm doing better than you. You seem downright glum." She motioned to the steps and Katie scooted over. Jo took a seat beside her.

"Alex and I had a fight last night."

"And?"

"I said something terrible to him."

"Did you apologize?"

"No," Katie answered. "He left before I could. I should have, but I didn't. And now . . . ."

"What? You think it's too late?" She squeezed Katie's knee.

"It's never too late to do the right thing. Go over there and talk to him."

Katie hesitated, her anxiety plain. "What if he won't forgive me?"

"Then he's not who you thought he was."

Katie drew her knees up, propping her chin on them. Jo peeled her shirt away from her skin, trying to fan herself before going on. "He'll forgive you, though. You know that, right? He might be angry and you might have hurt his feelings, but he's a good man." She smiled. "Besides, every couple needs to argue now and then. Just to prove that the relationship is strong enough to survive it."

"That sounds like the counselor talking."

"It is, but it's also true. Long-term relationships—the ones that matter—are all about weathering the peaks and the valleys. And you *are* still thinking long-term, right?"

"Yes." Katie nodded. "I am. And you're right. Thanks."

Jo patted Katie's leg and winked as she unfolded herself from the steps and stood. "What are friends for, right?"

Katie squinted up. "Do you want some coffee? I was going to start a pot."

"Not this morning. Too hot. What I need is a glass of ice water and a cool shower. I feel like I'm melting."

"Are you going to the carnival today?"

"Maybe. I haven't decided yet. But if I do, I'll try to find you," she promised. "Now head on over there before you change your mind."

Katie sat on the steps a few minutes longer before retreating into the house. She showered and made herself a cup of coffee—but Jo was right, it was too hot to drink it. Instead, she changed into shorts and sandals before walking around to the back of the house and getting on her bicycle.

Despite the recent downpour, the gravel road was already

drying and she was able to pedal without exerting much energy. Good thing. She had no idea how Jo had been able to jog in this heat, even first thing in the morning. Everything, it seemed, was trying to escape the heat. Normally, there were squirrels or birds, but as she turned onto the main road, she saw no movement at all.

On the road, traffic was light. A couple of cars zipped past, leaving fumes in their wake. Katie pedaled onward and as she rounded a bend, the store came into view. Already, there were half a dozen cars parked out front. Regulars who came to eat biscuits.

Talking to Jo had helped, she thought. A little, anyway. She was still anxious, but it had less to do with the Feldmans or other troubling memories than what she was going to say to Alex. Or rather, what he was going to say to her in return.

She pulled to a stop out front. A couple of older men were fanning themselves on the benches and she walked past them toward the door. Behind the register, Joyce was ringing up a customer and she smiled.

"Good morning, Katie," she said.

Katie quickly scanned the store. "Is Alex around?"

"He's upstairs with the kids. You know the way, right? The stairs out back?"

Katie left the store and went around the side, toward the rear of the building. At the dock, a line of boats queued, waiting to fill up.

She hesitated at the door before finally knocking. Inside, she could hear footfalls approaching. When the door swung open, Alex stood before her.

She offered a tentative smile. "Hi," she said.

He nodded, his expression unreadable. Katie cleared her throat.

"I wanted to tell you that I'm sorry about what I said. I was wrong."

His expression remained neutral. "Okay," he said. "I appreciate the apology."

For a moment, neither of them said anything, and Katie suddenly wished she hadn't come. "I can go. I just need to know whether you still need me to watch the kids tonight."

Again, he said nothing, and in the silence Katie shook her head. When she turned to leave, she heard him take a step toward her. "Katie . . . wait," he said. He peeked over his shoulder at the kids before closing the door behind him.

"What you said last night . . ." he began. He trailed off, uncertain.

"I didn't mean it," she said, her voice soft. "I don't know what got into me. I was upset about something else and I took it out on you."

"I admit it—it bothered me. Not so much that you said it, but that you imagined me capable of . . . that."

"I don't think that," Katie said. "I would never think that about you."

He seemed to take that in, but she knew he had more to say.

"I want you to know that I value what we have right now, and more than anything, I want you to be comfortable. Whatever that means. I'm sorry for making you feel like I was putting you on the spot. That wasn't what I was trying to do."

"Yes, you were." She gave him a knowing smile. "A little, anyway. But it's okay. I mean, who knows what the future might bring, right? Like tonight, for instance."

"Why? What happens tonight?"

She leaned against the doorjamb. "Well, once the kids are asleep and depending when you get back, it might be too late for me to ride back to my house. You might just find me in your bed . . ."

When he realized she wasn't kidding, he brought a hand to his chin in mock contemplation. "That is a dilemma."

"Then again, traffic might be light and you'll get home early enough to bring me home."

"I'm generally a pretty safe driver. As a rule, I don't like to speed."

She leaned into him and breathed into his ear. "That's very conscientious of you."

"I try," he whispered, before their lips met. When he pulled back, he noticed half a dozen boaters watching them. He didn't care. "How long did it take you to rehearse that speech?"

"I didn't. It just sort of . . . came to me."

He could still feel the remnants of their kiss. "Have you had breakfast yet?" he whispered.

"No."

"Would you like to have cereal with me and the kids? Before we head off to the carnival?"

"Cereal sounds delicious."

34

North Carolina was ugly, a strip of road sandwiched between monotonous strands of pine trees and rolling hills. Along the highway, there were clusters of mobile homes and farmhouses and rotting barns overgrown with weeds. He left one interstate and got on another, turning toward Wilmington, and drank some more out of sheer boredom.

As he passed through the unchanging landscape, he thought about Erin. Thought about what he was going to do when he found her. He hoped she would be at home when he arrived, but even if she was at work, it would only be a matter of time before she came home.

The interstate wove past uninteresting towns with forgettable names. He was in Wilmington by ten. He drove through the city and turned onto a small, rural highway. Heading south, with the sun coming hard through the driver's-side window. He put the gun in his lap and then back on the seat again and kept on going.

And finally, he was there, in the town where she was living. Southport.

* * *

He drove slowly through town, detouring around a street fair, occasionally consulting the directions he'd printed out on the computer before he left. He pulled a shirt from the duffel bag and placed it over the gun to conceal it.

It was a small town with neat, well-kept houses. Some were typically Southern, with wide porches and magnolia trees and American flags waving from poles, others reminded him of homes in New England. There were mansions on the waterfront. Sunlight dappled the water in the spaces between them and it was hot as hell. Like a steam bath.

Minutes later, he found the road where she lived. On the left, up ahead, was a general store and he pulled in to buy some gas and a can of Red Bull. He stood behind a man buying charcoal and lighter fluid. At the register, he paid the old woman. She smiled and thanked him for coming, and commented in that nosy way that old women have that she hadn't seen him around before. He told her he was in town for the fair.

As he turned back onto the road, his pulse raced at the knowledge that it wasn't far now. He rounded a bend and slowed the car. In the distance, a gravel road came into view. The directions indicated that he was supposed to turn but he didn't stop the car. If Erin was home, she would recognize his car immediately, and he didn't want that. Not until he had everything ready.

He turned the car around, searching for an out-of-the-way place to park. There wasn't much. The store parking lot, maybe, but wouldn't someone notice if he parked it there? He passed the store again, scanning the area. The trees on either side of the road might provide cover . . . or they might not. He didn't want to take the chance that someone would grow suspicious of an abandoned car in the trees.

The caffeine was making him jittery and he switched to vodka to settle his nerves. For the life of him, he couldn't find a place to stash the car. What the hell kind of a place was this? He turned around again, getting angry now. It shouldn't have been this hard and he should have rented a car but he hadn't and now he couldn't find a way to get close enough to her without her noticing.

The store was the only option and he pulled back into the lot, stopping along the side of the building. It was at least a mile to the house from here but he didn't know what else to do. He brooded before turning off the engine. When he opened the door, the heat enveloped him. He emptied the duffel bag, tossing his clothes on the backseat. Into the duffel bag went the gun, the ropes, the handcuffs, and the duct tape—and a spare bottle of vodka. Tossing the bag over his shoulder, he glanced around. No one was watching. He figured he could keep his car here for maybe an hour or two before someone got suspicious.

He left the lot, and as he walked down the shoulder of the road he could feel the pain starting in his head. The heat was ridiculous. Like something alive. He walked the road, staring at the drivers in passing cars. He didn't see Erin, even a brown-haired one.

He reached the gravel road and turned. The road, dusty and potholed, seemed to lead nowhere until he finally spotted a pair of small cottages a half mile down. He felt his heart speed up. Erin lived in one of them. He moved to the side of the road, hugging the trees, staying out of sight as much as possible. He was hoping for shade but the sun was high and the heat remained constant. His shirt was drenched, sweat dripped down his cheeks and plastered his hair to his skull. His head pounded and he stopped for a drink, straight from the bottle.

From a distance, neither of the cottages appeared occupied. Hell, neither one looked habitable. It was nothing like their house in Dorchester, with its shutters and corbels and red front door. On the cottage closest to him, the paint was peeling and the planks were rotting in the corners. Moving forward, he watched the windows, looking for signs of movement. There was nothing.

He didn't know which cottage was hers. He stopped to study them closely. Both were bad, but one looked practically abandoned. He moved toward the better one, angling away from the window.

It had taken thirty minutes to get here from the store. Once he surprised Erin, he knew she'd try to get away. She wouldn't want to go with him. She would try to get away, might even try to fight, and he would tie her up and tape her mouth shut and then go get the car. Once he returned with the car, he would put her in the trunk until they were far away from this town.

He reached the side of the house and flattened himself against it, staying away from the window. He listened for movement, the sound of opening doors or water running or dishes clattering, but heard nothing.

His head still hurt and he was thirsty. The heat poured down and his shirt was wet. He was breathing too fast but he was so close to Erin now and he thought again how she'd left him and hadn't cared that he'd cried. She'd laughed behind his back. Her and the man, whoever he was. He knew there had to be a man. She couldn't make it on her own.

He peeked around the back of the house and saw nothing. He crept forward, watching. Ahead, there was a small window and he took a chance and looked in. No lights on, but it was clean and tidy, with a dish towel draped over the kitchen sink. Just like Erin used to do. He silently approached the door and turned the knob. Unlocked.

Holding his breath, he opened the door and stepped inside, pausing again to listen and hearing nothing. He crossed the kitchen and entered the living room—then the bedroom and bathroom. He cursed aloud, knowing she wasn't home.

Assuming he was in the right home, of course. In the bedroom, he spied the chest of drawers and pulled the top one open. Finding a stack of her panties, he sifted through them, rubbed them between his thumb and forefinger, but it had been so long, he wasn't sure he could remember if they were the ones she had back home. The other clothes he didn't recognize, but they were her size.

He recognized the shampoo and conditioner, he recognized the brand of toothpaste. In the kitchen, he rifled through the drawers, opening them one by one until he found a utility bill. It was listed in the name of Katie Feldman, and now he leaned against the cupboard, staring at the name and feeling a sense of completion.

The only problem was that she wasn't here, and he didn't know when she would return. He knew he couldn't leave his car at the store indefinitely, but all at once, he was just so tired. He wanted to sleep, needed to sleep. He'd driven all night and his head was pounding. Instinctively, he wandered back to her bedroom. She'd made the bed, and when he peeled back the cover, he could smell her scent in the sheets. He crawled into the bed, breathing deeply, breathing her in. He felt the tears flood his eyes as he realized how much he missed her and loved her and that they could have been happy if she hadn't been so selfish.

He couldn't stay awake and he told himself that he would sleep for just a little while. Not long. Just enough so that when he came back later in the evening, his mind would be sharp and he wouldn't make mistakes and he and Erin could be husband and wife once more.

35

———— ✿ ————

Alex, Katie, and the kids rode their bikes to the carnival because parking downtown was almost impossible. Trying to get home, once cars started pulling out, would be even worse.

Booths displaying arts and crafts lined either side of the street, and the air was thick with the scent of hot dogs and burgers, popcorn and cotton candy. On the main stage, a local band was playing "Little Deuce Coupe" by the Beach Boys. There were sack races and a banner promising a watermelon-eating contest later in the afternoon. Games of chance, too—throwing darts at balloons, tossing rings around bottles, sinking three shots with a basketball to win a stuffed animal. The Ferris wheel at the far end of the park towered above all of it, drawing families like a beacon.

Alex stood in line to buy tickets while Katie followed behind with the kids, heading toward the bumper cars and tilt-a-whirl. Long lines were everywhere. Mothers and fathers clung to the hands of children, and teens clustered in groups. The air sounded with the roar of generators and clacking noises as the rides went round and round.

The world's tallest horse could be viewed for a dollar. Another dollar bought admission to the tent next door, which

housed the smallest horse. Ponies, walking in circles and teth-
ered to a wheel, were hot and tired, their heads hanging low.

The kids were antsy and wanted to ride everything, so Alex
purchased a small fortune in tickets. The tickets went fast,
because most of the rides required three or four. The cumula-
tive cost was ridiculous, and Alex tried to make them last by
insisting they do other things as well.

They watched a man juggle bowling pins and cheered for a
dog that could walk across a tightrope. They had pizza for lunch
at one of the local restaurants, eating inside to escape the heat,
and listened to a country-western band play a number of songs.
Afterward, they watched people racing jet skis in the Cape Fear
River before heading back to the rides. Kristen wanted cotton
candy and Josh got a press-on tattoo.

And so the hours passed, in a blur of heat and noise and
small-town pleasures.

Kevin woke two hours later, his body slick with sweat, his stomach knotted with cramps. His heat-induced dreams had been
vivid and colorful, and it was hard to remember where he was.
His head felt like it was splitting in two. He staggered from the
bedroom and into the kitchen, slaking his thirst directly from
the tap. He was dizzy and weak and felt more tired than when
he lay down in the first place.

But he couldn't linger. He shouldn't have slept at all, and he
went to the bedroom and remade the bed so that she wouldn't
know he'd been there. He was about to leave when he remembered the tuna casserole he'd spied in her refrigerator earlier,
when he'd searched her kitchen. He was ravenous, and he remembered that she hadn't cooked him dinner in months.

It had to be close to a hundred degrees in this airless shack,
and when he opened the refrigerator, he stood for a long minute
in the cool air as it spilled out. He grabbed the tuna casserole
and rummaged through the drawers until he found a fork. After

peeling back the plastic wrap, he took a bite and then a second one. Eating did nothing for the pain in his head but his stomach felt better and the cramps began to subside. He could have eaten all of the casserole, but he forced himself to take just one more bite before putting it back in the refrigerator. She couldn't know that he'd been here.

He rinsed the fork, dried it, and put it back in the drawer. He straightened the towel and checked the bed again, making sure it looked the way it had when he entered.

Satisfied, he left the house and headed up the gravel road, toward the store.

The roof of the car was scalding to the touch and when he opened the door, it felt like a furnace. No one was in the parking lot. Too hot to be outside. Sweltering, without a cloud or hint of breeze. Who in God's name would want to live in a place like this?

In the store, he grabbed a bottle of water and drank it while standing near the coolers. He paid for the empty container and the old woman threw it out. She asked him if he enjoyed the carnival. He told the nosy old woman that he had.

Back in the car, he drank more vodka, not caring that it was now the temperature of a cup of coffee. As long as it made the pain go away. It was too hot to think and he could have been on his way back to Dorchester if Erin had been home. Maybe when he brought Erin back and Bill realized how happy they were together, he would give him his job back. He was a good detective and Bill needed him.

As he drank, the throbbing in his temples began to recede, but he started to see two of everything when he knew there should be only one. He needed to keep his mind sharp, but the pain and the heat were making him sick and he didn't know what to do.

He started the car and turned onto the main road, heading back to downtown Southport. Many streets were closed off and he made countless detours before he found a spot to park. No shade for miles, just sun and endless, stifling heat. He felt like he might vomit.

He thought about Erin and where she might be. Ivan's? At the carnival? He should have called to ask whether she was working today, should have stopped at a hotel last night. No reason to rush, because she wasn't at home, but he hadn't known that then, and it made him angry to think she was probably laughing about that, too. Laughing and laughing at poor Kevin Tierney while she cheated on him with another man.

He changed his shirt and tucked the gun into the waistband of his jeans and started toward the waterfront. He knew that's where he'd find Ivan's, because he'd searched for the location on the computer. He knew he was taking a risk if he went there and he turned around twice, but he had to find her, had to make sure she was still real. He'd been in her house and inhaled her scent but it wasn't enough.

Crowds of people were everywhere. The streets reminded him of a county fair, without the pigs and horses and cows. He bought a hot dog and tried to eat it, but his stomach rebelled and he threw most of it away. Weaving among the people, he spotted the waterfront in the distance, and then Ivan's. His progress through the throngs was excruciatingly slow. His mouth was dry by the time he reached the door of the restaurant.

Ivan's was packed, people waiting outside the entrance for tables. He should have brought a hat and sunglasses, but he hadn't been thinking. He knew she would recognize him instantly, but he worked his way to the door anyway and stepped inside.

He spotted a waitress, but she wasn't Erin. Saw another, but she wasn't Erin, either. The hostess was young and harried and trying to figure out where to put the next group of customers. It was loud—people talking, forks clanking against plates, glasses sloshing in the bus tubs. Loud and confusing and the damn pounding in his head wouldn't go away. His stomach burned.

"Is Erin working today?" he called out to the hostess, raising his voice above the noise.

She blinked at him in confusion. "Who?"

"Katie," he said. "I meant Katie. Katie Feldman."

"No," the hostess shouted back. "She's off. She's working tomorrow, though." She nodded toward the windows. "She's probably out there somewhere, along with everyone else. I thought I saw her walk past here earlier."

Kevin turned and left, bumping into people as he went. Ignoring it. Outside, he paused at a sidewalk vendor. He bought a baseball hat and a pair of inexpensive sunglasses. And then he began to walk.

The Ferris wheel went round and round, Alex and Josh in one seat and Kristen and Katie in another, hot wind in their faces. Katie had her arm draped over Kristen's shoulders, knowing that despite Kristen's smile, she was nervous about the height. As the seat rotated to its peak, unveiling a panorama of the town, Katie realized that while she wasn't exactly thrilled with the height, either, she was more concerned with the Ferris wheel itself. The thing looked like it was held together with bobby pins and chicken wire, even if it had supposedly passed inspection earlier that morning.

She wondered if Alex had been telling the truth about the inspection, or if he'd heard her saying aloud whether it might be dangerous. It was too late to worry about it now, she supposed, so instead she occupied herself by staring at the throngs of people below. The carnival had become even more crowded as the afternoon wore on, but aside from boating, there wasn't a lot to do in Southport. It was a sleepy little town, and she surmised that an event like this was probably the highlight of the year.

The Ferris wheel slowed and stopped, stranding them as the first of the passengers got out and others crawled on. It rotated a bit, and she found herself scrutinizing the crowd more closely. Kristen seemed more relaxed and was doing the same.

She recognized a couple of people eating snow cones as regulars at Ivan's, and she wondered how many others were out there. Her eyes began to travel from group to group, and for some reason she remembered that she used to do the same thing when she first started working at Ivan's. Back when she was watching for Kevin.

Kevin walked past the booths that lined either side of the street, just wandering and trying to think like Erin. He should have asked the hostess if she'd seen Erin with a man because he knew she wouldn't be at the carnival alone. It was hard to keep reminding himself that she might have short brown hair because she'd cut and dyed it. He should have had the pedophile at the other precinct get a copy of the driver's license photo, but he hadn't been thinking at the time, and it didn't matter now because he knew where she lived and he would go back.

He could feel the gun in his waistband, pressing against his skin. It felt uncomfortable, pinching his flesh, and it was hot under the ball hat, especially since it was pulled low and tight. His head felt like it would explode.

He moved around groups of people, lines that formed. Arts and crafts. Decorated pinecones, stained glass in frames, wind chimes. Old-fashioned toys carved from wood. People were stuffing their faces with food: pretzels and ice cream, nachos, cinnamon rolls. He saw babies in strollers and remembered again that Erin wanted to have a baby. He decided he would give her one. A girl or a boy, it didn't matter, but he preferred a boy because girls were selfish and wouldn't appreciate the life he gave them. Girls were like that.

People talked and whispered all around him and he thought some of them were staring at him, like Coffey and Ramirez used to do. He ignored them, focused on his search. Families. Teens with their arms around one another. A guy in a sombrero. A couple of the carnival workers stood near a streetlight, smoking. Thin and tattooed, with bad teeth. Probably drug users, with long records. They gave him a bad feeling. He was a good detective and knew how to read people and he didn't trust them but they did nothing as he brushed past them.

He veered left and right, working his way steadily through the crowd, studying people's faces. He paused while an overweight couple waddled past him, eating corn dogs, their faces red and blotchy. He hated fat people, thought they were weak and had no discipline, people who complained about their blood pressure and diabetes and heart problems and whined about the cost of medicine, but couldn't summon the strength to put the fork down. Erin was always thin but her breasts were big and now she was here with another man who fondled them at night and the thought made him burn inside. He hated her. But he wanted her, too. Loved her. It was hard to keep it straight in his head. He'd been drinking too much and it was just so damn hot. Why had she moved to a place as hellish as this?

He wandered among the carnival rides and noticed the Ferris wheel up ahead. He moved closer, bumping into a man in a tank top, ignoring his muttered outrage. He checked the seats on the ride, his gaze flashing on every face. Erin wasn't there, or in the line, either.

He moved on, walking in the heat among the fat people, looking for skinny Erin and the man who touched her breasts at night. With every step, he thought about the Glock.

The swings, spinning clockwise, were a big hit with the kids. They'd ridden them twice in the morning, and after the Ferris wheel Kristen and Josh begged to ride them once more. There were only a few tickets left and Alex agreed, explaining that after this last ride they would have to go home. He wanted to have time to shower and eat and maybe relax before he had to drive to Raleigh.

Despite his best efforts, he couldn't stop thinking about Katie's earlier suggestive remark. She seemed to sense the direction of his thoughts, because he'd caught her staring at him a number of times, a provocative smile playing at the corner of her lips.

Now she stood beside him, smiling up at the kids. He scooted closer, slipping his arm around her, and felt her lean into him. He said nothing, for there was no need for words, and she said nothing, either. Instead, she tilted her head, resting it against his shoulder, and Alex was struck by the notion that there was nothing better in the world.

Erin wasn't at the tilt-a-whirl or the maze of mirrors or the haunted house. He watched from the ticket line, trying to blend in, wanting to see her before she spotted him. He had the advantage because he knew she was here and she didn't know about him, but sometimes people got lucky and strange things happened. He flashed on the memory of Karen Feldman and the day she revealed Erin's secret.

He wished he hadn't left his vodka in the car. There didn't seem to be anywhere to buy more, not a bar in sight. He hadn't even seen a booth selling beer, which he didn't like but would have bought if he had no other choice. The smell of food made him nauseated and hungry at the same time and he could feel the sweat plastering his shirt to his back and armpits.

He walked by the games of chance, run by con artists. Waste of money because the games were rigged, but morons packed around them. He searched faces. No Erin.

He wandered toward the other rides. There were kids in bumper cars, people fidgeting in the line. Beyond that were the swings, and he started in that direction. He circumvented a cluster of people, straining for a better view.

* * *

The swings had begun to slow, but Kristen and Josh were still grinning with excitement. Alex was right about needing to call it a day; the heat had drained Katie and it would be nice to be able to cool off for a while. If there was one bad thing about the cottage—well, there was actually more than one bad thing, she supposed—it was that it didn't have air-conditioning. She'd gotten used to keeping the windows open at night, but it didn't help much.

The ride came to a stop and Josh unhooked the chain and jumped down. It took Kristen a little longer before she could manage it, but a moment later, the two children were scrambling back toward Katie and their dad.

Kevin saw the swings come to a stop and a bunch of kids jump down from their seats, but that wasn't where he focused his attention. Instead, he concentrated on the adults who were crowding the perimeter of the ride.

He kept walking, his eyes moving from one woman to the next. Blond or brunette, it didn't matter. He watched for Erin's lean figure. From his angle, he couldn't see the faces of the people directly in front of him, so he changed directions. In a few seconds, once the kids reached the exit, everyone would scatter again.

He walked quickly. A family stood in front of him, holding tickets, debating where to go next, arguing in confusion. Idiots. He skirted them, straining to see faces near the swings.

No skinny women, except for one. A short-haired brunette, standing next to a man with gray hair, his arm around her waist.

She was unmistakable. Same long legs, same face, same sinewy arms.

Erin.

36

─────── ❧ ───────

Alex and Katie held hands as they walked toward Ivan's with the kids. They'd stored their bicycles near the back door, Katie's regular spot. On the way out, Alex bought some water for Josh and Kristen before they started toward home.

"Good day, guys?" Alex asked, bending over to unlock the bikes.

"Great day, Daddy," Kristen answered, her face red with the heat.

Josh wiped his mouth on his arm. "Can we come back tomorrow?"

"Maybe," Alex fudged.

"Please? I want to ride the swing again."

Finished with the locks, Alex slung the chains over his shoulder. "We'll see," he said.

An overhang in the back of the restaurant provided some shade, but it was still warm. After seeing how crowded it had been as she'd walked past the windows, Katie was glad she'd taken the day off, even if she had to work a double shift tomorrow and Monday. It was worth it. It had been a good day, and she'd get to relax and watch a movie with the kids while Alex was away tonight. And then later, when he got back . . .

"What?" Alex said.

"Nothing."

"You were staring at me like you were going to eat me up."

"Just drifting off there for a second," she said with a wink. "I think the heat kind of got to me."

"Uh-huh." He nodded. "If I didn't know better . . ."

"I'd like to remind you that there are some young ears tuning in right now, so I'd watch what you say." She kissed him before patting him lightly on the chest.

Neither of them noticed the man in the baseball hat and sunglasses watching them from the deck of the neighboring restaurant.

Kevin felt dizzy as he watched Erin and the gray-haired man kiss, seeing the way Erin flirted with him. He saw her lean down and smile at the little girl. Watched as she tousled the hair of the little boy. Noticed the gray-haired man pat her on her butt when the children's attention was elsewhere. And Erin—his wife—was playing along. Liking it. Encouraging it. Cheating on him with her new family, as if Kevin and their marriage had never existed at all.

They got on their bikes and started pedaling, heading around the side of the building, away from Kevin. Erin rode beside the gray-haired man. She was wearing shorts and sandals, showing skin, looking sexy for someone else.

Kevin followed them. Her hair was blond and long and flowing . . . but then he blinked, and it was short and brown again. Pretending she wasn't Erin and riding bikes with her new family and kissing another man and smiling and smiling, without a care in the world. It wasn't real, he told himself. It was nothing but a dream. A nightmare. Docked boats wobbled in their slips as they passed.

He rounded the corner. They were riding and he was on foot, but they were moving slowly to allow the little girl to keep up. He was closing the distance and he was near enough to hear

Erin laugh, sounding happy. He reached for the Glock in his waistband and pulled it out, then slid it beneath his shirt, keeping it pressed against his skin. He took off the baseball hat and used it to hide the gun from the people around him.

His thoughts ricocheted like pachinko balls, bouncing fast, left and right, downward, downward. Erin lying and cheating and plotting and scheming. Running away to find a lover. Talking and laughing behind his back. Whispering to the gray-haired man, saying dirty things, the man's hands on her breasts, her breaths coming hard. Pretending she wasn't married, ignoring all he'd done for her and the sacrifices he'd made and that he had to scrape the blood from his shoes and that Coffey and Ramirez were always gossiping about him and there were flies buzzing on the burgers because she'd run away and he'd had to go to the barbecue alone and she couldn't tell Bill the captain that he wasn't just one of the guys.

And there she was, pedaling easily, her hair short and dyed, as pretty as ever, never thinking about her husband at all. Never caring about him. Forgetting him and the marriage so she could have a life with the gray-haired man and pat his chest and kiss him with a dreamy expression on her face. Happy and serene, without a concern in the world. Going to carnivals, riding bikes. She probably sang to herself in the shower while he'd been crying and remembering the perfume he'd bought her for Christmas, and none of it mattered because she was selfish and thought she could throw a marriage away, like an empty pizza box.

He unconsciously picked up his pace. The crowds were slowing them down, and he knew that he could raise the gun and kill her right now. His finger moved to the trigger and he slipped the safety off because the Bible says *Let marriage be held in honor among all, and let the bed be undefiled*, but he realized that it meant he had to kill the gray-haired man as well. He could kill him in front of her. All he had to do was pull the trigger, but then hitting moving targets from a distance was almost impossible with a Glock, and there were people everywhere. They would see the gun and scream and shout and the shot was almost impossible, so he removed his finger from the trigger.

"Quit veering toward your sister!" the gray-haired man said, up ahead, his voice almost lost in the distance. But his words were real and Kevin imagined the dirty things he whispered to Erin. He could feel the rage building inside him. Then, all at once, the kids turned the corner and they were followed by Erin and the gray-haired man.

Kevin stopped, panting and feeling ill. As she'd rounded the corner, her profile had flashed in the bright light and he thought again that she was beautiful. She'd always reminded him of a delicate flower, so pretty and refined, and he remembered that he'd saved her from being raped by thugs after she left the casino and how she used to tell him that he made her feel safe but even that hadn't been enough to keep her from leaving him.

Gradually, he began to hear the voices of people walking on either side of him as they passed by. Chattering about nothing, going nowhere, but it jolted him into action. He started to jog, trying to reach the spot where they'd turned, feeling like he was going to vomit with every footfall under the blazing sun. His palm felt slick and sweaty around the gun. He reached the corner and peered up the street.

No one in sight, but two blocks up, there were barricades blocking the road for the street fair. They must have turned on the street before it. No other choice. He figured they had turned right, the only way to leave the downtown area.

He had a choice. Chase them on foot and risk being spotted or run back to the car and try to follow them that way. He tried to think like Erin and figured they would go to the house where the gray-haired man lived. Erin's house was too small, too hot for the four of them, and Erin would want to go to a pretty house with expensive furniture, because she believed she deserved a life like that, instead of appreciating the life she had.

Pick and choose. Follow on foot or in the car. He stood, blinking and trying to think, but it was hot and confusing and his head pounded and all he could think was that Erin was sleeping with a gray-haired man and the realization made him sick to his stomach.

She probably dressed in lace and danced for him, whispered words that made him hot. Begged him to let her please him, so she could live in his house with fancy things. She'd become a prostitute, selling her soul for luxuries. Selling herself for pearls and caviar. Probably slept in a mansion now, after the gray-haired man took her out for fancy dinners.

He felt sick, imagining it. Hurt and betrayed. The fury helped his thoughts clear and he realized that he was standing in place as they were getting farther and farther away. His car was blocks away, but he turned and started to run. At the carnival, he pushed through people wildly, ignoring their shouts and protests. "Move, move!" he shouted, and some people moved and others were shoved aside. He reached a spot clear of the throngs of people, but he was breathing hard and he had to stop to vomit near a fire hydrant. A couple of teenage boys laughed at him and he felt like shooting them right then and there, but after wiping his mouth, he simply pulled the gun and pointed it at them and they shut up fast enough.

He stumbled forward, feeling the ice pick chip away at his head. Stab and pain, stab and pain. Every damn step it was stab and pain and Erin was probably telling the gray-haired man about the sexy things they would do in bed. Telling the gray-haired man about Kevin and laughing, whispering, *Kevin could never please me the way you do*, even though it wasn't true.

It took forever to get to his car. When he reached it, the sun was baking it like a loaf of bread. Heat spilled out in clouds, and the steering wheel was scalding to the touch. Hellhole. Erin had chosen to live in a hellhole. He started the car and opened the windows, making a U-turn back toward the carnival and honking at people in the street.

Detours again. Barricades. He wanted to blow through them, to blast them into pieces, but even here, there were cops and they would arrest him. Stupid cops, fat and lazy cops. Barney Fife cops. Idiots. None of them were good detectives but they had guns and badges. Kevin drove the side streets, trying to zero in on where Erin was heading. Erin and her lover. Both of them adulterers, and the Bible says *Whoever gazes at a woman with lust has committed adultery in his heart.*

People everywhere. Crossing the street haphazardly. Making him stop. He leaned over the steering wheel, straining to see through the windshield, and caught sight of them, tiny figures in the distance. They were just beyond another barricade, heading toward the road that led to her house. A cop was standing at the corner, another Barney Fife.

He surged forward, only to be stopped when a man suddenly appeared at the front of his car, banging on the hood. A redneck with a mullet, skulls on his shirt, tattoos. Fat wife and greasy-looking kids. Losers, all of them.

"Watch where you're going!" the redneck shouted.

Kevin mentally shot all of them, *bang-bang-bang-bang*, but forced himself not to react because the cop at the corner was eyeballing him. *Bang*, Kevin thought again.

He turned, speeding up, heading through the neighborhood. Turned left and sped up again. Turned left again. More barricades up ahead. Kevin made another U-turn, went right, and turned left at the next block.

More barricades. He was stuck in a maze, like a rodent undergoing an experiment. The town conspiring against him while Erin got away. He slammed the car into reverse and backed up. He found the road again and turned, then raced straight to the next intersection. It had to be close now and he turned left again, saw a line of traffic ahead, moving in the direction he wanted. He turned, muscling his car between a couple of trucks.

He wanted to accelerate but couldn't. Cars and trucks stretched before him, some with Confederate flags on the bumper stickers, others with gun racks on the roof. Rednecks. People in the road made it impossible for the cars to move forward, walking as if they weren't aware that any of the cars existed. People sauntered past, moving faster than he was. Fat people, still eating. Probably eating all day long and slowing the traffic while Erin got farther and farther away.

His car went forward one length and stopped again. Went forward and stopped. Over and over. He felt like screaming, wanted to pound the wheel, but people were everywhere. If he wasn't careful someone would say something and Barney Fife would investigate and remember his out-of-state plates and probably arrest him on the spot, simply because he wasn't a local.

Forward and stopping, over and over, movement measured in inches until he reached the corner. The traffic had to ease up now, he thought, but it didn't, and up ahead, Erin and the gray-haired man were gone. There was only a long line of cars and trucks ahead of him on a road that led nowhere and everywhere at exactly the same time.

37

A dozen cars were parked in front of the store as Katie trailed the kids up the stairs to the house. Josh and Kristen had whined most of the ride home about how tired their legs were, but Alex ignored it, reminding them periodically that they were getting closer. When that didn't work, he simply commented that he was getting tired, too, and didn't want to hear any more about it.

The complaining ended when they got to the store. Alex let them grab Popsicles and Gatorade before they went upstairs, and the burst of cool air as they opened the door was ridiculously refreshing. Alex led Katie to the kitchen and she watched as he drenched his face and neck at the kitchen sink. In the living room, the kids were already sprawled on the couch, the television on.

"Sorry," he said. "I thought I was about to die about ten minutes ago."

"You didn't say anything."

"That's because I'm tough," he said, pretending to puff out his chest. He retrieved two glasses from the cupboard and added ice cubes before pouring water from a pitcher he kept in the refrigerator.

"You're a trouper," he added, handing her a glass. "It's like a sauna out there."

"I can't believe how many people are still at the carnival," she said, taking a drink.

"I've always wondered why they don't move up the date to either May or October, but then again, the crowds seem to come no matter what."

She glanced at the clock on the wall. "What time do you have to leave?"

"In an hour or so. But I should be back before eleven."

Five hours, she thought. "Do you want me to make the kids anything special for dinner?"

"They like pasta. Kristen likes hers with butter, Josh likes his with marinara, and I've got a bottle of that in the refrigerator. They've been snacking all day, though, so they might not eat much."

"What time do they go to bed?"

"Whenever. It's always before ten, but sometimes it's as early as eight. You'll have to use your best judgment."

She held the cool glass of water against her cheek and glanced around the kitchen. She hadn't spent much time in their home, and now that she was here she noticed remnants of a woman's touch. Little things—red stitching on the curtains, china prominently displayed in a cabinet, Bible verses on painted ceramic tiles near the stove. The house was filled with evidence of his life with another woman, but to her surprise, it didn't bother her.

"I'm going to go hop into the shower," Alex said. "Will you be okay for a few minutes?"

"Of course," she said. "I can snoop around your kitchen and think about dinner."

"The pasta's in the cupboard over there," he said, pointing. "But listen, when I get out, if you want me to drive you over to your place so you can shower and change, I'd be glad to do it. Or you can shower here. Whatever you want."

She struck a sultry pose. "Is that an invitation?"

His eyes widened and then flashed to the kids.

"I was kidding." She laughed. "I'll shower after you're gone."

"Do you want to pick up a change of clothes first? If not, you can borrow sweats and a T-shirt . . . the sweats will be too big for you, but you can adjust the drawstring."

Somehow the idea of wearing his clothes sounded extremely sexy to her. "That's fine," she assured him. "I'm not picky. I'm just watching movies with the kids, remember?"

Alex drained his glass before putting it in the sink. He leaned forward and kissed her, then headed toward the bedroom.

Once he was gone, Katie turned toward the kitchen window. She watched the road outside, feeling a nameless anxiety come over her. She'd felt the same way earlier in the morning and assumed it was an aftershock of the argument she'd had with Alex, but now she found herself thinking of the Feldmans again. And about Kevin.

She'd thought of him when she was on the Ferris wheel. As she'd scanned the crowd, she knew she hadn't been searching for people from the restaurant. Not really. She'd been looking for Kevin. Believing for some inexplicable reason that he might be in the crowd. Thinking he was there.

But that was just her paranoia surfacing again. There was no way he could know where she was, no way to know her identity. It was impossible, she reminded herself. He never would have connected her to the Feldmans' daughter; he never even spoke to them. But why, then, had she felt all day like someone was following her, even as they left the carnival?

She wasn't psychic and didn't believe in such things. But she did believe in the power of the subconscious mind to put together pieces that the conscious mind might miss. Standing in Alex's kitchen, however, the pieces were still scrambled, without shape or order of any kind, and after watching a dozen cars pass by on the road out front, she finally turned away. It was probably just her old fears raising their ugly head again.

She shook her head and thought of Alex in the shower. The thought of joining him made her flush hot with anticipation. And yet . . . it wasn't quite that simple, even if the kids hadn't been around. Even if Alex thought of her as Katie, Erin was still married to Kevin. She wished that she were another woman, a woman who could simply move into her lover's arms without hesitation. After all, it was Kevin who had broken all the rules of marriage when he first raised his fists against her. When God looked into her heart, she was pretty sure that He would agree that what she was doing wasn't a sin. Wouldn't He?

She sighed. Alex . . . he was all she could think about. *Later* was all she could think about. He loved her and wanted her and she wanted, more than anything, to show him that she felt the same way. She wanted to feel his body against hers, wanted all of him for as long as he wanted her. Forever.

Katie forced herself to stop picturing herself with Alex, to stop dreaming about what was to come. She shook her head to clear it and went to the living room, where she took a seat on the couch next to Josh. They were watching a Disney Channel television show she didn't recognize. After a while she looked up at the clock, and noticed that only ten minutes had gone by. It felt like an hour.

Once he finished with his shower, Alex made a sandwich and sat beside her on the couch as he ate. He smelled clean and his hair was still wet at the ends, clinging to his skin in a way that made her want to trace the line of dampness with her lips. The kids, glued to the screen, ignored them, even after he put the plate on the end table and began to run his finger slowly up and down her thigh.

"You look beautiful," he whispered into her ear.

"I look terrible," she countered, trying to ignore the line of fire burning its way up her thigh. "I haven't showered yet."

When it was time for him to leave, he kissed the kids in the living room. She followed him to the door and when he kissed her good-bye, he let his hand wander lower, past her waist, his lips soft against hers. Obviously in love with her, obviously wanting her, making sure she knew it. He was driving her crazy, and he seemed to be enjoying it.

"See you in a bit," he said, pulling back.

"Drive safely," she whispered. "The kids will be fine."

When she heard his footsteps descending the steps outside, she leaned against the door for a long, slow breath. Good Lord, she thought. Good Lord. Vows or not, guilt or not, she decided that even if *he* wasn't in the mood, she definitely was.

She peeked up at the clock again, certain that this would be the longest five hours of her life.

38

Damn!" Kevin kept saying. "Damn!" He'd been driving for hours. He'd stopped to buy four bottles of vodka at the ABC store. One of them was half gone, and as he drove he saw two of everything unless he squinted, keeping one eye closed.

He was searching for bicycles. Four of them, including one with baskets. He might as well have been looking for a specific piece of plankton in the ocean. Up one road and down the next, as the afternoon wound down and dusk settled in. He looked from left to right and back again. He knew where she lived, knew he would eventually find her at home. But in the meantime the gray-haired man was out there with Erin, laughing at him, saying, *I'm so much better than Kevin, baby.*

He screamed curses in the car, pounding on the steering wheel. He flipped the safety on the Glock from the off to the on position and back again, imagining Erin kissing him, his arm around her waist. Remembering how happy she'd looked, thinking she had tricked her husband. Cheated on him. Moaned and murmured beneath her lover while he panted atop her.

He could barely see, fighting the blurriness with one eye. A car came up behind him on the neighborhood streets, tailgating for a while, then flashing his lights. Kevin slowed the car and pulled over, fingering the gun. He hated rude people, people who thought they owned the road. *Bang.*

Dusk turned the streets into shadowy mazes, making it difficult to see the spindly outlines of bicycles. When he drove past the gravel road for the second time, he decided on impulse to turn around and visit her house again, just in case. He stopped just out of sight of the cottage and got out. A hawk circled overhead, and he heard cicadas humming, but otherwise the place seemed deserted. He started toward the house but could see already from a distance that there was no bicycle parked out front. No lights on, either, but it wasn't dark yet, so he crept to the back door. Unlocked, just like before.

She wasn't home, and he didn't think she'd been home since he'd been here earlier. The house was sweltering, all the windows shut tight. She would have opened the windows, he felt sure, would have had a glass of water, might have taken a shower. Nothing. He left through the back door, staring at the neighboring house. A dump. Probably deserted. Good. But the fact that Erin wasn't home meant she was with the gray-haired man, had gone to his house. Cheating, pretending she wasn't married. Forgetting the home that Kevin had bought for her.

His head throbbed in time with his heartbeats, a knife going in and out. Stab. Stab. Stab. It was hard to focus as he pulled the door closed behind him. Mercy of all mercies, it was cooler outside. She lived in a sweatbox, sweated with a gray-haired man. They were sweating together now, somewhere, writhing in sheets, bodies intertwined. Coffey and Ramirez were laughing about that, slapping their thighs, having a good old time at his expense. *I wonder if I could do her, too,* Coffey was saying to Ramirez. *Don't you know?* Ramirez answered back. *She let half the precinct do her while Kevin was working. Everyone knows about it.* Bill waving from his office, holding suspension papers. *I did her, too, every Tuesday for a year. She's wild in bed. Says the dirtiest things.*

He stumbled back to his car, his finger on the gun. Bastards, all of them. Hated them, imagined walking into the precinct and unloading the Glock, emptying the clip, showing them. Showing all of them. Erin, too.

He stopped and bent over, vomiting onto the side of the road. Stomach cramping, a clawing in his gut like a rodent was trapped inside him. Puked again, and then dry heaves and the world spun when he tried to stand. The car was close and he staggered to it. Grabbed the vodka and drank and tried to think like Erin, but then he was at the barbecue holding a burger covered in flies and everyone was pointing and laughing at him.

Back to the car. Bitch had to be somewhere. She'd watch gray-hair die. Watch them all die. Burn in hell. Burn and burn, all of them. Carefully, he climbed in and started the car. He backed into a tree as he was trying to turn around, and then, cursing, tore out on the gravel, spinning rocks.

Night would soon be falling. She came in this direction, had to be down this way. Little kids couldn't ride far. Three or four miles, maybe five. He'd been down every road this way, looked at every house. No bicycles. They could be in the garage, could be parked in fenced yards. He'd wait and she'd come home sometime. Tonight. Tomorrow. Tomorrow night. He'd stick the gun in her mouth, aim it at her breasts. *Tell me who he is*, he'd say. *I just want to talk to him*. He'd find gray-hair and show him what happened to men who slept with other men's wives.

He felt like he had been weeks without sleep, weeks without food. He couldn't understand why it was dark and he wondered when that happened. Couldn't remember when he got here exactly. He remembered seeing Erin, remembered trying to follow her and driving, but wasn't even sure where he was.

A store loomed on the right, looking like a house with a porch out front. GAS FOOD, the sign said. He remembered that from earlier, but how long ago he couldn't say. He slowed the car involuntarily. He needed food, needed to sleep. Had to find a place to stay the night. His stomach lurched. He grabbed the bottle and tilted the bottom up, feeling the burn in his throat, soothing him. But as soon as he lowered the bottle, his stomach heaved again.

He pulled into the lot, fighting to keep the liquor down, his mouth watering. Running out of time. He skidded to a stop alongside the store and jumped out. Ran to the front of his car and heaved into the darkness. His body shivered, his legs wobbled. His stomach coming up. His liver. All of it. Somehow, he was still holding the bottle, hadn't put it down. He breathed hard in and out and drank, using it to rinse his mouth, swallowing it. Finishing another bottle.

And there, like an image from a dream, in the darkened shadows behind the house, he saw four bicycles parked side by side.

39

———— ❦ ————

Katie had the kids take a bath before getting them into their pajamas. Afterward, she showered, lingering under the spray and enjoying the luxurious feeling of shampoo and soap rinsing the salt from her body after a day in the sun.

She made the kids their pasta, and after dinner they sorted through the collection of DVDs, trying to find one that both kids wanted to watch, until they finally agreed on *Finding Nemo*. She sat between Josh and Kristen on the couch, a bowl of popcorn in her lap, their little hands reaching in automatically from either direction. She wore a comfy pair of sweats that Alex had laid out and a worn Carolina Panthers jersey, tucking her legs up under her as they watched the movie, utterly at ease for the first time that day.

Outside, the heavens bloomed like fireworks, displaying vibrant rainbow colors that faded to pastel washes before finally giving way to bluish-gray and then indigo skies. Stars began to flicker as the last shimmering waves of heat rose from the earth.

Kristen had begun to yawn as the movie progressed, but every time Dory appeared on-screen, she managed to chirp, "She's my favorite, but I can't remember why!" On the other side of her, Josh was struggling to stay awake.

When the movie ended and Katie leaned forward to turn it off, Josh raised his head and let it fall to the couch. He was too big for her to carry, so she nudged his shoulder, telling him it was time for bed. He grunted and whined before sitting up. He yawned and rose to his feet and, with Katie by his side, staggered to the bedroom. He crawled into bed without complaint and she kissed him good night. Unsure whether he needed a night-light, she kept the light in the hallway on but closed the door partway.

Kristen was next. She asked Katie to lie beside her for a few minutes, and Katie did, staring at the ceiling, feeling the heat of the day beginning to take its toll. Kristen fell asleep within minutes, and Katie had to force herself to stay awake before tiptoeing out of the room.

Afterward, she cleaned up the remnants of their dinner and emptied the bowl of popcorn. As she glanced around the living room, she noticed evidence of the kids everywhere: a stack of puzzles on a bookshelf, a basket of toys in the corner, comfortable leather couches that were gloriously spill-proof. She studied the knickknacks scattered about: an old-fashioned clock that had to be wound daily, an ancient set of encyclopedias on a shelf near the recliner, a crystal vase on the table near the windowsill. On the walls hung framed black-and-white architectural photographs of decaying tobacco barns. They were quintessentially Southern, and she remembered seeing many of these rustic scenes on her journey through North Carolina.

There were also signs of the chaotic life Alex led: a red stain on the runner in front of the couch, gouges in the wood floor, dust on the baseboards. But as she surveyed the house, she couldn't help smiling, because those things, too, seemed to reflect who Alex was. He was a widowed father, doing his best to raise two kids and keep a tidy, if imperfect, house. The house was a snapshot of his life, and she liked its easy, comfortable feel.

She turned out the lights and collapsed on the couch. She picked up the remote and surfed TV channels, trying to find something interesting but not too demanding. It was coming up on ten o'clock, she noted. An hour to go. She lay back on the couch and started watching a show on the Discovery Channel, something about volcanoes. She noticed a glare on the screen and stretched to turn off the lamp on the end table, darkening the room. She leaned back again. Better.

She watched for a few minutes, barely aware that every time she blinked, her eyes stayed closed a fraction longer. Her breath slowed and she began to melt into the cushions. Images began to float through her mind, disjointed at first, thoughts of the carnival rides, the view from the Ferris wheel. People standing in random clusters, young and old, teens and couples. Families. And somewhere in the distance, a man in a baseball hat and sunglasses, weaving among the crowd, moving with purpose before she lost sight of him again. Something she'd recognized: the walk, the jut of his jaw, the way he swung his arms.

She was drifting now, relaxing and remembering, the images beginning to blur, the sound of the television fading. The room growing darker, quieter. She drifted further, her mind flashing back again and again to the view from the Ferris wheel. And, of course, to the man she'd seen, a man who'd been moving like a hunter through the brush, in search of game.

40

—— ❧ ——

Kevin stared up at the windows, nursing his half-empty bottle of vodka, his third of the night. No one gave him a second glance. He was standing on the dock at the rear of the house; he'd changed into a black long-sleeved shirt and dark jeans. Only his face was visible, but he stood in the shade of a cypress tree, hidden behind the trunk. Watching the windows. Watching the lights, watching for Erin.

Nothing happened for a long while. He drank, working on finishing the bottle. People came through the store every few minutes, often using their credit cards to buy gas at the pump. Busy, busy, even out here, in the middle of nowhere. He moved around to the side of the store, gazing up at the windows. He recognized the flickering blue glow of a television. The four of them, watching TV, acting like a happy family. Or maybe the kids were already in bed, tired from the carnival, tired from the bike ride. Maybe it was just Erin and the gray-haired man snuggling on the couch, kissing and touching each other while Meg Ryan or Julia Roberts fell in love on the screen.

Everything hurt and he was tired and his stomach kept churning. He could have walked up the stairs and kicked the door in, could have killed them half a dozen times already, and he wanted to get it over with, but there were people in the store. Cars in the lot. He'd pushed his own car forward with the engine off to a spot beneath a tree at the rear of the store, out of sight from passing cars. He wanted to aim the Glock and pull the trigger, wanted to watch them die, but he also wanted to lie down and go to sleep because he'd never been more tired in his life and when he woke up he wanted to find Erin beside him and think to himself that she had never left him.

Later, he spotted her profile at the window, saw her smiling as she turned away and knew she was thinking about the gray-haired man. Thinking about sex and the Bible says *Those who gave themselves over to fornication and strange flesh are set forth for an example and suffering the vengeance of eternal fire.*

He was an angel of the Lord. Erin had sinned and the Bible says *She shall be tormented with fire and brimstone in the presence of holy angels.*

In the Bible there was always fire because it purified and condemned, and he understood that. Fire was powerful, the weapon of angels. He finished the bottle of vodka and kicked it under the bushes. A car pulled up to the gasoline pumps and a man stepped out. He slid his credit card in and began to pump gas. The sign near the pump informed people it was illegal to smoke, because gasoline was flammable. Inside the store, there was lighter fluid for use with charcoal. He remembered the man in line ahead of him earlier, holding a can of it.

Fire.

Alex shifted and adjusted his hands on the wheel, trying to get comfortable. Joyce and her daughter were in the backseat and hadn't stopped talking from the moment they'd gotten in the car.

The clock on the dashboard showed it was getting late. The kids were either in bed or soon would be, which sounded good right now. On the drive back, he'd had a bottle of water, but he was still thirsty and debated whether to stop again. He was sure that neither Joyce nor her daughter would mind, but he didn't want to stop. He just wanted to get home.

As he drove, he felt his mind drifting. He thought about Josh and Kristen, about Katie, and he sifted through memories of Carly. He tried to imagine what Carly would say about Katie and whether Carly would have wanted him to give the letter to her. He remembered the day he'd seen Katie helping Kristen with her doll, and recalled how beautiful she had looked on the night she'd made him dinner. The knowledge that she was at his house waiting for him made him want to floor the accelerator.

On the other side of the highway, distant pinpricks of light appeared at the horizon, slowly separating and growing larger, forming headlamps of oncoming cars. They grew brighter until they flashed past. In the rearview mirror, red lights receded into the distance.

Heat lightning crackled to the south, making the sky blink like a slide show. Off to the right was a farmhouse, lights on downstairs. He passed a truck with Virginia plates and rolled his shoulders, trying to shake off the fatigue he felt. He passed the sign indicating the number of miles to Wilmington and sighed. He still had a ways to go.

Katie's eyelids fluttered as she dreamed, her subconscious working overtime. Bits and pieces, fragments, trying to connect with each other.

The dream ended, and a few minutes later she tucked her knees up and shifted onto her side, almost waking. Her breathing began to slow again.

At ten o'clock the lot was nearly empty. It was just before closing time, and Kevin walked around to the front of the store, squinting at the light coming through the front door. He pushed the door open and heard a bell jingle. At the register was a man in an apron. Kevin vaguely recognized him, but couldn't place him. He was wearing a white apron, the name ROGER stenciled on the right.

Kevin walked past the register, trying not to slur his words. "I ran out of gas up the road."

"Gas cans are along the far wall," Roger answered without looking up. When he finally did, he blinked. "You okay?"

"Just tired," Kevin said from the aisle, trying not to draw attention to himself but knowing the man was watching. The Glock was in his waistband and all Roger had to do was mind his own business. At the far wall, Kevin saw three five-gallon plastic cans and reached for two of them. He brought them to the register and put money on the counter.

"I'll pay after I fill 'em," he said.

Outside, he pumped the gas into the can, watching the numbers roll past. He filled the second and went back inside. Roger was staring at him, hesitating to make change.

"That's a lot of gas to carry."

"Erin needs it."

"Who's Erin?"

Kevin blinked. "Can I buy the damn gas or not?"

"You sure you're okay to drive?"

"I've been sick," Kevin muttered. "Puking all day."

He wasn't sure whether Roger believed him, but after a moment, Roger took the money and made change. Kevin had left the cans near the gas pumps and went to pick them up. It was like lifting cans of lead. He strained, his stomach churning, pulsating pain between his ears. He started up the road, leaving behind the lights of the store.

In the darkness, he set the cans down in the tall grass just off the road. After that, he circled back behind the store. Waiting for Roger to close up, waiting for the lights to go out. Waiting for everyone to fall asleep upstairs. He retrieved another bottle of vodka from the car and took a sip.

In Wilmington, Alex began to perk up, knowing he was getting close. It wouldn't be long now, maybe half an hour before he reached Southport. It would take another few minutes to drop off Joyce and her daughter, but then he would be home.

He wondered if he would find Katie waiting up for him in the living room or whether, as she'd teased, he would find her in his bed.

It was the kind of thing that Carly used to say. They might have been talking about the business or whether her parents were enjoying Florida, when out of the blue, she'd announce that she was bored and ask him whether he wanted to go to the bedroom and fool around.

He stared at the clock. A quarter after ten and Katie was waiting. On the side of the road, Alex saw half a dozen deer frozen on the grass, their eyes reflecting the headlights, glowing like something unnatural. Haunted.

Kevin watched the fluorescent lights above the gas pumps flicker off. Lights in the store went out next. From his hidden vantage point, he watched Roger locking the door. He tugged on it, making sure it was secure, before turning away. He walked to a brown pickup truck parked on the far side of the gravel lot and got in.

The engine started with a whine and squeak. A loose fan belt. Roger revved the engine, turned on the headlights, then put the truck in gear. He turned onto the main road, heading toward downtown.

Kevin waited five minutes, making sure Roger wouldn't turn around and come back. The road in front of the store was quiet now, no cars or trucks coming from either direction. He jogged over to the bushes, where he'd hidden the cans. Checked the road again, and then carried one of them to the back of the store. He did the same with the second can, setting them next to a couple of metal garbage cans filled with rotting food. The stench was overwhelming.

Upstairs, the TV continued to bathe one of the windows in blue light. There were no other lights and he knew they were naked. He felt the rage well up inside him. Now, he thought. It was time. When he reached for the gas cans, he saw four of them. He closed one eye and it was back to two. He stumbled as he took a step and jerked forward, off balance, swaying as he tried to grab the corner of the wall to keep from falling. He missed and fell, landing hard, his head hitting the gravel. Sparks and stars, shooting pains. It was hard to breathe. Tried to stand up and fell again. He rolled over onto his back, staring up at the stars.

He wasn't drunk because he never got drunk, but something was wrong. Twinkling lights were whirling round and round, caught in an accelerating tornado. He squeezed his eyes shut, but the spinning got worse. He rolled to his side and vomited onto the gravel. Someone must have slipped him drugs because he'd barely had anything to drink all day and he'd never been sick like this.

He reached out blindly for the garbage can. He grabbed the lid and tried to use it for balance, but he pulled too hard. The lid clattered off and a bag of garbage spilled out, making an unholy racket.

Upstairs, Katie flinched at the sound of something crashing. She was lost in her dream, and it took a moment for her eyes to flutter open. Groggy, she listened but wasn't sure why, wasn't sure whether she'd dreamed the sound or not. But there was nothing.

She leaned back, giving way to sleep again, and the dream picked up from where it left off. She was at the carnival, on the Ferris wheel, but it was no longer Kristen sitting beside her.

It was Jo.

Kevin was finally able to struggle to his feet and stay upright. He couldn't figure out what was happening to him, why he couldn't keep his balance. He concentrated on catching his breath, in and out, in and out. He spotted the cans of gas and stepped toward them, almost falling again.

But he didn't fall. He lifted a can, then staggered toward the stairs at the back of the house. He reached out for the railing and missed it, then tried again. Got it. He lugged the can of gas up the stairs, toward the door, a Sherpa in the Himalayas. He finally reached the landing at the top, panting, and bent over to remove the cap. His head filled with blood, making him swoon, but he used the gas can to keep from falling. It took awhile before he could get the cap off because it kept slipping between his fingers.

Once open, he picked up the can and doused the landing, splashing its contents against the door. With every heave, the can got lighter, gas spilling out in arcs, drenching the wall. Getting easier now. He splashed left and right, trying to coat either side of the building. He started back down the stairs, splashing left and right. The fumes made him sick but he kept going.

There wasn't much gas left in the can when he reached the bottom and he rested at ground level. He was breathing hard and the fumes were making him feel sick again but he began moving again, with purpose now. Determination. He tossed the empty can aside and reached for the other. He couldn't douse the upper reaches of the walls, but he did what he could. He splashed one side and then circled around the back to the other side. Above him, the window still flickered with light from the television but all was quiet.

He drained the can on the other side of the building and had nothing left for the front. He scanned the road; no cars were coming from either direction. Upstairs, Erin and the gray-haired man were naked and laughing at him and Erin ran away and he almost found her in Philadelphia but back then she was calling herself Erica, not Erin, and now she pretended her name was Katie.

He stood in front of the store, thinking about the windows. Maybe they were alarmed and maybe not. He didn't care. He needed lighter fluid, motor oil, turpentine, anything that would burn. But once he broke the window, he wouldn't have much time.

He shattered the window with his elbow but heard no alarm. Pulling out pieces of glass, he barely felt his fingers getting cut and beginning to bleed. More chunks, the window coming apart in sections. He thought the opening was big enough for him to climb inside, but his arm caught on a jagged shard, deep. He pulled, tearing flesh. But he couldn't stop now. Blood flowed from his arm, dripping and mingling with the cuts on his fingers.

The coolers along the back wall were still illuminated and he walked the aisles, wondering idly if Cheerios would burn, if Twinkies would burn. DVDs. He located the charcoal and the lighter fluid—only two cans, not much. Not enough. He blinked, looking around for something else. He spotted the grill in the rear of the store.

Natural gas. Propane.

He approached the grill area, lifted the divider, and stood facing the grill itself. He turned a burner on, then another. There had to be a valve somewhere, but he didn't know where to find it and he didn't have time because someone might be coming and Coffey and Ramirez were talking about him, laughing and asking whether he'd had the crab cakes in Provincetown.

Roger's apron hung on a rack and he tossed it onto the flame. He opened the can of lighter fluid he was holding and sprayed it on the walls of the grill. The can was slippery with blood and he wondered where the blood had come from. He hopped up onto the counter and squirted some lighter fluid on the ceiling and got down again. He ran a trail of fluid along the front of the store, noticing that the apron had begun to burn in earnest. He emptied the can and tossed it aside. Opening the second can, he squirted more fluid at the ceiling. The flames from the apron began leaping toward the walls and the ceiling. He went to the register and searched for a lighter and found a bunch of them in a plastic bin, near the cigarettes. He squirted lighter fluid on the register and on the little table behind him. The can was empty now, too, and he stumbled toward the window he'd broken earlier. He climbed out, stepping on broken glass, hearing it crack and pop. Standing by the side of the house, he flicked the lighter and held it against the gas-soaked wall, watching as the wood caught fire. At the back of the house, he touched the flame to the stairs and the flames rose quickly, shooting up to the door and spreading to the roof. Next came the far side.

Fire blossomed everywhere, the exterior rippling with flame, and Erin was a sinner and her lover was a sinner and the Bible says *They will suffer the punishment of eternal destruction.*

He stood back, watching the fire start to consume the building, wiping his face, leaving trails of blood. In the glowing orange light, he looked like a monster.

In her dream, Jo wasn't smiling as she sat beside Katie on the Ferris wheel. She seemed to be searching the crowd below, a frown of concentration on her face.

There, she said, pointing. *Over there. Do you see him?*

What are you doing here? Where's Kristen?

She's sleeping. But you have to remember, now.

Katie looked but there were so many people, so much movement. *Where?* she asked. *I don't see anything.*

He's here, Jo said.

Who?

You know.

In her dream, the Ferris wheel lurched to a stop. The sound was loud, like the shattering of glass, and it seemed to signal a change. The carnival's colors began to fade, the scene below dissolving into cloud banks that hadn't been there a moment before. As if the world were slowly being erased, and then everything suddenly dimmed. She was surrounded by impenetrable darkness, broken only by an odd flickering at the periphery of her vision, and the sound of someone talking.

Katie heard Jo's voice again, almost a whisper.

Can you smell it?

Katie sniffed, still lost in the haze. Her eyes fluttered open, stinging for some reason as she tried to clear her sight. The television was still on and she realized she must have fallen asleep. The dream was already fading away but she heard Jo's words clearly in her head.

Can you smell it?

Katie took a deep breath as she pushed herself to a sitting position and immediately started coughing. It took only an instant to realize that the room was filled with smoke. She bolted off the couch.

Smoke meant fire, and now she could see the flames outside the window, dancing and twisting orange. The door was on fire, smoke billowing from the kitchen in thick clouds. She heard roaring, a sound like a train, heard cracks and pops and splintering, her mind taking it in at once.

Oh, my God. The kids.

She ran toward the hallway, panicked at the sight of heavy smoke billowing from both rooms. Josh's room was closest and she rushed in, waving her arms against the stinging black fog.

She reached the bed and grabbed Josh's arm, dragging him up. "Josh! Get up! The house is on fire! We've got to get out!"

He was about to whine, but she pulled him up, cutting him

off. "C'mon!" she screamed. He immediately began to cough, doubled over as she dragged him out. The hallway was an impenetrable wall of smoke, but she rushed forward nonetheless, pulling Josh behind her. Groping, she found the doorjamb to Kristen's room across the hall.

It wasn't as bad as Josh's room, but she could feel the enormous heat building behind them. Josh continued to cough and wail, struggling to keep up, and she knew better than to let go. She raced to Kristen's bedside and shook her, pulling her out of bed with her other hand.

The roaring of the fire was so loud, she could barely hear the sound of her own voice. Half-carrying, half-dragging the kids back out into the hallway, she saw an orange glow, barely visible through the smoke, where the entrance to the hallway was. The wall crawled with fire, flames on the ceiling, moving toward them. She didn't have time to think, only had time to react. She turned and pushed the kids back down the hallway toward the master bedroom, where the smoke was less thick.

She rushed into the room, flicking on the light. Still working. Alex's bed stood against one wall, a chest of drawers against another. Straight ahead was a rocking chair and windows, thankfully untouched as yet by fire. She slammed the door behind her.

Racked by coughing spasms, she stumbled forward, dragging Josh and Kristen. Both of them were wailing between hoarse bouts of coughing. She tried to free herself to raise the bedroom window, but Kristen and Josh clung to her.

"I need to open the window!" she screamed, shaking herself free. "This is the only way out!" In their panic, they didn't understand, but Katie didn't have time to explain. Frantically, she tore at the old-fashioned window lock and tried to heave the heavy pane up. It wouldn't budge. Peering closer, Katie realized that the frame had been painted shut, probably years ago. She didn't know what to do, but the sight of the two children staring at her in terror cleared her head. She looked around, frantic, finally seizing the rocking chair.

It was heavy, but somehow she lifted it above her shoulder and heaved it at the window with all her might. It cracked but didn't break. She tried again, sobbing through a last burst of adrenaline and fear, and this time the rocking chair went flying out, crashing onto the overhang below. Moving fast, Katie raced to the bed and tore off the comforter. She bundled it around Josh and Kristen and began pushing them toward the window.

There was a loud splintering sound behind her as part of the wall burst into flame, tendrils licking the ceiling. Katie turned in panic, pausing long enough to notice the portrait that hung on the wall. She stared at it, already knowing it was of Alex's wife, because there was no one else it could be. She blinked, thinking it was an illusion, a distortion created by the smoke and fear. She took an involuntary step toward the eerily familiar face when she heard a roar above her as the ceiling started to give way.

Whirling around, she pushed through the window, holding the kids in the circle of her arms and praying that the comforter would protect them from glass shards. They seemed to hang in the air for an eternity, Katie twisting as they fell so that the kids would land on top of her. She hit the overhang on her back with a whump. It wasn't far, maybe four or five feet, but the impact left her breathless before pain rolled over her in waves.

Josh and Kristen were hiccuping in fear, wailing and coughing. But they were alive. She blinked, trying not to pass out, sure she'd broken her back. But she hadn't; she moved one leg, then the other. She shook her head to clear her vision. Josh and Kristen were struggling on top of her, trying to get free of the comforter. Above her, tongues of flame began to flare from the broken bedroom window. Flames were everywhere now, all over the house, and she knew they had only seconds to live unless she somehow summoned the strength to move.

On his way back from Joyce's house, Alex noticed the sky glowing orange just above the blackened tree line on the outskirts of town. He hadn't seen that as they drove into town and navigated the streets to Joyce's home. Now, however, he frowned as he turned in that direction. Something in his gut told him that danger lay ahead, and he debated only an instant before pressing down on the accelerator.

Josh and Kristen were already sitting up as Katie rolled over. The ground was perhaps a ten-foot drop from the overhang, but she had to risk it. They were running out of time. Josh continued to sob but didn't protest as Katie quickly explained what was going to happen next. She seized his arms, trying to keep her voice steady.

"I'm going to lower you as far as I can, but then you're going to have to jump."

He nodded, seemingly in shock, and she quickly scooted toward the edge, dragging Josh with her. He moved to the edge and she grabbed his hand. The overhang was shaking now, fire climbing up both support columns. Josh climbed over, legs first, holding on, Katie sliding on her belly toward the edge. Lowering him . . . God, the agony in her arms . . . four feet, no more, she told herself. He wouldn't fall far and he would land on his feet.

She let go as the roof shuddered. Kristen crawled toward her, trembling.

"Okay, baby, your turn," Katie urged. "Give me your hand."

She did the same thing with Kristen, holding her breath as she let go. A moment later, both of them were on their feet, staring up at her. They were waiting for her.

"Run!" she screamed. "Move back!"

Her words were swallowed by another coughing spasm, and she knew she had to move. She grabbed the edge of the overhang and swung one leg off, then the other. She dangled for only an instant before her grip weakened.

She hit the ground and felt her knees buckle before she rolled to a stop in front of the store entrance. Her legs screamed with pain, but she had to get the kids to safety. She scrambled toward them, seizing their hands and beginning to drag them away.

Fire was dancing, leaping, spurting toward the sky. Nearby trees caught fire, their upper branches sparking like firecrackers. There was a sharp clap, loud enough to make her ears ring. She chanced a peek over her shoulder, just in time to see the walls of the building collapse inward. Then there was the deafening sound of an explosion, and Katie and the kids were knocked over in the scorching blast of air.

By the time the three of them caught their breath and turned to look, the store was nothing but a gigantic cone of fire.

But they'd made it. She pulled both Josh and Kristen toward her. They were whimpering as she put her arms around them and she kissed the tops of their heads. "You're okay," she murmured. "You're safe now."

It was only when a shadow appeared before her that she realized she was wrong.

It was him, looming over them, a gun at his side.

Kevin.

In the jeep, Alex kept his foot clamped down on the gas pedal, growing more worried with every passing second. Though the fire was still too far away to pinpoint the location with accuracy, his stomach began to seize up. There weren't too many structures in that direction, mostly a few isolated farmhouses. And, of course, the store.

He leaned over the steering wheel, as if to urge the car forward. *Faster*.

Katie had trouble processing what she was seeing.

"Where is he?" Kevin rasped out. The words came out slurred, but she recognized the voice, even with his face partly in shadow. The inferno blazed behind him and his face was covered in soot and blood. There were smears of what she thought was blood on his shirt as well. In his hand the Glock shone, like it had been dipped in a barrel of oil.

He's here, Jo had said in Katie's dream.

Who?

You know.

Kevin raised the gun, pointing it at her. "I just want to talk to him, Erin."

Katie got to her feet. Kristen and Josh clung to her, fear etched on their faces. Kevin's eyes were feral, his movements jerky. He took a step toward them, almost losing his balance. The gun swung back and forth. Unsteady.

He was ready to kill them all, Katie realized. He'd already tried to kill them with the fire. But drunk, very drunk. Worse than she'd ever seen him. He was out of control, beyond reason.

She had to get the kids away, had to give them a chance to run.

"Hi, Kevin," she purred. She forced herself to smile. "Why are you holding that gun? Did you come to get me? Are you all right, baby?"

Kevin blinked. The voice, soft and sultry, sweet. He liked it when she sounded like that, and he thought it was a dream. But he wasn't dreaming and Erin was standing in front of him. She smiled as she took a step forward. "I love you, Kevin, and I always knew you'd come."

He stared. There were two of her now and then only one. He had told people she was in New Hampshire taking care of a sick friend, but there weren't any footprints in the snow and his calls were forwarded and a little boy had been shot and there was pizza sauce on his forehead and now Erin was here, telling him that she loved him.

Closer, Katie thought. *Almost there.* She took another step forward, pushing the kids behind her.

"Can you bring me home?" Her voice pleaded with him, begged like Erin used to, but her hair was short and brown and she was moving closer and he wondered why she wasn't scared and he wanted to pull the trigger but he loved her. If only he could stop the hammering inside his head—

Suddenly, Katie lunged forward, pushing the gun away. It fired, the sound like a vicious slap, but she kept moving forward, clinging to his wrist, not letting go. Kristen started to scream.

"RUN!" Katie shouted over her shoulder. "Josh, take Kristen and run! He's got a gun! Get as far away as you can and hide!"

The panic in Katie's voice seemed to galvanize Josh and he grabbed Kristen's hand and took off running. They headed toward the road, racing for Katie's house. Fleeing for their lives.

"Bitch!" Kevin screamed, trying to free his arm. Katie lowered her mouth and bit down as hard as she could and Kevin let out a ferocious cry. Trying to pull the arm free, he slammed his other fist into her temple. Instantly, she saw flashes of white light. She bit down again, finding his thumb this time, and he screamed, letting go of the gun. It clattered to the ground and he punched her again, catching her on her cheekbone, knocking her to the ground.

He kicked her in the back and she arched with pain. But she kept moving, in panic now, fueled by the certainty that he meant to kill her and the kids. She had to give them time to get away. She rose to all fours and started crawling, moving fast, gaining speed. Finally, she surged to her feet, a sprinter coming out of the blocks.

She ran as fast as she could, forcing herself forward, but she felt his body slam into her from behind and she lay breathless on the ground again. He grabbed her by the hair and hit her again. He seized an arm and twisted it, trying to work it behind her back, but he was off balance and she was slippery enough to turn onto her back. Reaching up, she clawed at his eyes, catching one in the corner, tearing hard.

Fighting for her life, adrenaline flooding her limbs. Fighting now, for all the times she hadn't. Fighting to give the kids time to run away and hide. Screaming curses at him, hating him, refusing to let him beat her again.

He snatched at her fingers, tottering off balance, and she used the opportunity to wiggle away. She felt him clawing at her legs, but his grip wasn't good enough and she pulled one leg free. Pulling her knee up toward her chin, she kicked him with all her force, stunning him as she connected with his chin. She did it again, watching this time as he toppled sideways, his arms grabbing at nothing.

She scrambled to her feet and started to run again, but Kevin was up just as quickly. A few feet away, she saw the gun and she lunged for it.

Alex was driving recklessly now, praying for the safety of Kristen and Josh and Katie, whispering their names in panic.

He passed the gravel road and rounded the bend, his stomach dropping as his premonition proved right. Before him the entire tableau spread out beyond his windshield, like a portrait of hell.

He noticed movement on the side of the road, up ahead. Two small figures, dressed in white pajamas. Josh and Kristen. He slammed on the brakes.

He was out of the car and rushing toward them almost before the jeep came to a halt. They cried out for him as they ran, and he bent down to scoop them into his arms.

"You're okay," he murmured over and over, holding them in the tight circle of his arms. "You're okay, you're okay."

Kristen and Josh were both sobbing and hiccuping and at first he didn't understand what they were saying because they weren't talking about the fire. They were crying about a man with a gun, that Miss Katie was fighting him, and then he suddenly knew with chilling clarity what had happened.

He pushed them into the jeep and wheeled it around, racing toward Katie's house as his fingers punched the speed dial on his cell phone. He reached a startled Joyce on the second ring and told her to have her daughter drive her to Katie's house now, that it was an emergency, that she should call the police immediately. Then he hung up.

Gravel sprayed as he came to a skidding halt in front of Katie's house.

He dropped the kids off and told them to run inside, that he would be back for them as quick as he could. He counted off the seconds as he turned around and gunned the engine for the store, praying that he wasn't too late.

Praying that Katie was still alive.

Kevin saw the gun in the same instant she did and dove for it, reaching it first. He snatched it up and pointed it at her, enraged. He grabbed her by the hair and put the gun to her head as he began dragging her across the lot.

"Leave me? You can't leave me!"

Behind the store, beneath a tree, she saw his car, with its Massachusetts plates. The heat from the fire scorched her face, singeing the hair on her arms. Kevin was raging at her, his voice slurred and raw.

"You're my wife!"

In the distance, she could faintly make out sirens, but they seemed so far away.

When they reached the car, she tried to fight again but Kevin slammed her head onto the roof and she almost passed out. He opened the trunk and tried to force her in. Somehow she turned and managed to drive her knee into his groin. She heard him gasp and felt his grip loosen momentarily.

She pushed blindly, tearing out of his grasp, and started running for her life. She knew the bullet was coming, that she was about to die.

He couldn't understand why she was fighting, could barely breathe through the pain. She'd never fought him before, had never scratched at his eyes or kicked or bitten him. She wasn't acting like his wife and her hair was brown but she sounded like Erin . . . He started staggering after her, raising the gun, aiming, but there were two Erins and both were running.

He pulled the trigger.

Katie gasped as she heard the shot, waiting for the flash of pain, but it didn't come. She kept running and suddenly it occurred to her that he'd missed. She veered left and then right, still in the lot, desperate for some kind of shelter. But there was nothing.

Kevin staggered after her, his hands slippery with blood, slipping on the trigger. He felt like he was about to vomit again. She was getting farther away, moving from side to side, and he couldn't keep her in sight. She was trying to get away but she wouldn't because she was his wife. He would bring her home because he loved her, and then he would shoot her dead because he hated her.

Katie saw the headlights of a car on the road, moving as fast as a race car. She wanted to get to the road, to flag the car down, but she knew she wouldn't reach the road in time. Surprising her, the car suddenly began to slow, and all at once, she recognized the jeep as it careened into the lot, recognized Alex behind the wheel.

Roaring past her, toward Kevin.

The sirens were getting closer now. People were coming and she felt a surge of hope.

Kevin saw the jeep coming and raised the gun. He began firing, but the jeep kept coming toward him. He leapt out of the way as the jeep roared past, but it clipped his hand, breaking all the bones and knocking the gun somewhere into the darkness.

Kevin screamed in agony, instinctively cradling his hand as the jeep careened forward, past the burning wreckage of the store, skidding on the gravel and crashing headlong into the storage shed.

There were sirens in the distance. He wanted to chase Erin but he would get arrested if he stayed. The fear took over and Kevin began to limp and jog to his car, knowing that he had to get out of there and wondering how everything had gone so wrong.

Katie watched Kevin tear out of the lot, gravel spinning, onto the main road. Turning around, she saw that Alex's jeep was half buried in the storage shed, its engine still spewing exhaust, and she raced toward it. The fire cast its flickering light on the rear of the car and she felt panic rising inside her, as she prayed for Alex to show himself.

She was closing in on the car when her foot hit something hard, making her stumble. Spotting the gun she'd tripped on, she picked it up and started toward the car again.

Ahead, the door of the car pushed open slightly, but it was blocked by debris on either side. She felt a surge of relief that Alex was alive at the same instant she remembered that Josh and Kristen were missing.

"Alex!" she cried. She reached the back of the jeep and started to pound on it. "You have to get out! The kids are out there—need to find them!"

The door was still jammed but he was able to roll down the window. When he leaned out, she saw he was bleeding from his forehead and his voice was weak. "They're okay . . . I brought them to your house . . ."

Ice flooded her veins. "Oh, my God," she croaked out, thinking, *No, no, no . . .* "Hurry up!" She pounded the rear of the car. "Get out! Kevin just left!" She could hear the raw fear in her own voice. "That's the direction he went!"

The pain in his hand was beyond anything he'd ever experienced, and he felt dizzy from blood loss. Nothing was making any sense, and his hand was useless now. He heard the sirens coming but he would wait for Erin at her house, because he knew she would be home tonight or tomorrow.

He parked behind the other, deserted cottage. Strangely, he saw Amber standing behind a tree, asking if he wanted to buy her a drink, but then her image vanished. He remembered that he had cleaned the house and mowed the lawn but he had never learned how to do laundry and now Erin was calling herself Katie.

There was nothing to drink and he was getting so tired. Blood stained his pants and he realized that his fingers and arm were bleeding, too, but he couldn't remember how that had happened. He wanted so much to sleep. He needed to rest for a while because the police would be searching for him and he needed to be fresh if they got close.

The world around him was growing faint and distant, as if viewed through the far end of a telescope. He heard the trees swaying back and forth, but instead a breeze, all he felt was the hot summer air. He began to shiver, but he was sweating, too. So much blood, and it drained out of his hands and arm, wouldn't seem to stop. He needed to rest, couldn't stay awake, and his eyes began to close.

Alex slammed the jeep into reverse and revved the engine, listening to the wheels spinning, but the jeep was going nowhere. His mind raced frantically with the knowledge that Josh and Kristen were in danger.

He lifted his foot off the gas, engaged the four-wheel drive, and tried again. This time the jeep began to move, the side mirrors ripping off, debris scraping and bending its body. The jeep came free with a final lurch. Katie pulled futilely at the passenger door until Alex rotated in his seat and kicked at it, flinging it open. Katie jumped in.

Alex turned the jeep around and accelerated hard, gaining the road as the fire trucks pulled in. Neither said a word as he slammed the pedal to the floor. Alex had never been more frightened in his life.

Around the bend, the gravel road. Alex turned sharply, the car skidding out. The rear fishtailed and he accelerated again. Up ahead, he spotted the cottages, lights glowing in the windows of Katie's. No sign of Kevin's car, and he exhaled before he even realized he'd been holding his breath.

Kevin heard the sound of an engine coming down the gravel road and he jerked awake.

The police, he thought, and he automatically reached for his gun using his crippled hand. He screamed in pain and confusion as he realized that the gun wasn't there. It had been on the front seat but it wasn't there now and none of this made sense.

He got out of the car and looked up the road. The jeep pulled into view, the one from the store parking lot, the one that had almost killed him. It came to a stop and Erin leapt out. At first he couldn't believe his good fortune, but then he remembered that she lived here and it was the reason he'd come.

His good hand was shaking hard as he opened the trunk and removed the crowbar. He saw Erin and her lover racing to the porch. He staggered and limped toward the house, unwilling and unable to stop, because Erin was his wife and he loved her and the gray-haired man had to die.

* * *

Alex skidded to a stop in front of the house and both of them jumped out simultaneously, running for the door, calling the kids' names. Katie still held the gun. They reached the door just as Josh opened it, and as soon as he saw his son, Alex swept him up in his arms. Kristen came out from behind the couch and rushed toward them. Alex opened his arms to her as well, catching her easily as she jumped.

Katie stood just inside the doorway, watching with tears of relief in her eyes. Kristen reached out for her, too, and Katie moved closer, accepting Kristen's hug with a blind rush of happiness.

Lost in the tidal wave of emotion, none of them noticed Kevin appear in the doorway, crowbar raised high. He swung hard, sending Alex crashing to the floor and the kids stumbling and falling backward in horror and shock.

Kevin heard the satisfying thud of the crowbar, felt the vibration up his arm. The gray-haired man lay crumpled on the floor and Erin screamed.

In that instant, Alex and the kids were all that mattered to her, and Katie instinctively rushed toward Kevin, driving him back out the door. There were only two porch steps, but it was enough, and Kevin toppled backward into the dirt.

Katie spun around. "Lock the door!" she screamed, and this time it was Kristen who moved first, even as she screamed.

The crowbar had fallen to the side and Kevin struggled to roll over and stand. Katie raised the gun, pointing it as Kevin finally made it to his feet. He swayed, almost losing his balance, his face a skeletal white. He seemed unable to focus and Katie could feel the tears in her eyes.

"I used to love you," she said. "I married you because I loved you."

He thought it was Erin, but her hair was short and dark, and Erin was a blond. A foot lurched forward as he almost fell again. Why was she telling him this?

"Why did you start to hit me?" she cried. "I never knew why you couldn't stop even when you promised." Her hand was shaking and the gun felt so, so heavy. "You hit me on our honeymoon because I left my sunglasses by the pool . . ."

The voice was Erin's and he wondered if he was dreaming.

"I love you," he mumbled. "I've always loved you. I don't know why you left me."

She could feel the sobs building in her chest, choking her. Her words flooded out in a torrent, unstoppable and nonsensical, years' worth of sorrow. "You wouldn't let me drive or have any friends and you kept the money and made me beg you for it. I want to know why you thought you could do that to me. I was your wife and I loved you!"

Kevin could barely stay upright. Blood dripped from his fingers and arm to the ground, slippery and distracting. He wanted to talk to Erin, wanted to find her, but this wasn't real. He was sleeping, Erin was beside him in bed, and they were in Dorchester. Then his thoughts leapfrogged, and he was standing in a dingy apartment and a woman was crying.

"There was pizza sauce on his forehead," he muttered, stumbling forward. "On the boy who was shot, but the mom fell down the stairs and we arrested the Greek."

She couldn't make sense of what he was saying, couldn't understand what he wanted from her. She hated him with a rage that had been building up for years. "I cooked for you and cleaned for you and none of it mattered! All you did was drink and hit me!"

Kevin was swaying, like he was about to fall. His words were slurred, unintelligible. "There were no footprints in the snow. But the flowerpots are broken."

"You should have let me go! You shouldn't have followed

me! You shouldn't have come here! Why couldn't you just let me go? You never loved me!"

Kevin lurched toward her, but this time he reached for the gun, trying to knock it away. He was weak now, though, and she managed to hold on. He tried to grab her, but he screamed in agony when his damaged hand connected with her arm. Acting on instinct, he threw his shoulder into her, driving her against the side of the house. He needed to take the gun away from her and press it into her temple. He stared at her with wide, hate-filled eyes, pulling her close, reaching for the gun with his good hand, using his weight against her.

He felt the barrel graze his fingertips and instinctively scrambled for the trigger. He tried to push the gun toward her, but it was moving in the wrong direction, pointing down now.

"I loved you!" she sobbed, fighting him with every ounce of rage and strength left in her, and he felt something give way, momentary clarity returning.

"Then you never should have left me," he whispered, his breath heavy with alcohol. He pulled the trigger and the gun sounded with a loud crack and then he knew it was almost over. She was going to die because he'd told her that he'd find her and kill her if she ever ran away again. He would kill any man who loved her.

But strangely, Erin didn't fall, didn't even flinch. Instead, she stared at him with fierce green eyes, holding his gaze without blinking.

He felt something then, burning in his stomach, fire. His left leg gave way and he tried to stay upright, but his body was no longer his own. He collapsed on the porch, reaching for his stomach.

"Come back with me," he whispered. "Please."

Blood pulsed through the wound, passing between his fingers. Above him, Erin was going in and out of focus. Blond hair and then brown again. He saw her on their honeymoon, wearing a bikini, before she'd forgotten her sunglasses, and she was so beautiful that he couldn't understand why she'd wanted to marry him.

Beautiful. She was always so beautiful, he thought, and then he was tired again. His breaths became ragged and then he started to feel cold, so cold, and he began to shake. He exhaled once more, the sound like air being released from a tire. His chest stopped moving. His eyes were wide open, uncomprehending.

Katie stood over him, shaking as she stared down at him. *No,* she thought. *I'll never go with you. I never wanted to go back.*

But Kevin didn't know what she was thinking, because Kevin was gone, and she realized then that it was finally, truly, over.

41

The hospital kept Katie under observation for most of the night before finally releasing her. Afterward, Katie remained in the hospital waiting room, unwilling to leave until she knew Alex would be okay.

Kevin's blow had nearly cracked Alex's skull, and he was still unconscious. Morning light illuminated the narrow rectangular windows of the waiting room. Nurses and doctors changed shifts, and the room began to fill with people: a child with a fever, a man having trouble breathing. A pregnant woman and her panicked husband pushed through the swinging doors. Every time she heard a doctor's voice, she looked up, hoping she would be allowed to see Alex.

Bruises mottled her face and arms, and her knee was swollen to almost twice its usual size, but after the requisite X-rays and exams, the doctor on call had merely given her ice packs for her bruises and Tylenol for the pain. He was the same doctor who was treating Alex, but he couldn't tell her when Alex would wake and said that the CAT scans were inconclusive. "Head wounds can be serious," he'd told her. "Hopefully, we'll know more in a few hours."

She couldn't think, couldn't eat, couldn't sleep, couldn't stop worrying. Joyce had taken the kids home from the hospital and Katie hoped they hadn't had nightmares. Hoped they wouldn't have nightmares forever. Hoped Alex was going to recover fully. Prayed for that.

She was afraid to close her eyes because every time she did, Kevin reappeared. She saw the smears of blood on his face and shirt, his wild eyes. Somehow, he'd tracked her down; somehow, he'd found her. He'd come to Southport to take her home or kill her, and he'd almost succeeded. In one night, he had destroyed the fragile illusion of security she had managed to construct since she'd arrived in town.

The terrifying visions of Kevin kept coming back, recurring endlessly with variations, sometimes changing entirely; there were moments she saw herself bleeding and dying on the porch, staring up at the man she hated. When that happened, she instinctively groped at her stomach, searching for wounds that didn't exist, but then she was back in the hospital, sitting and waiting under fluorescent lights.

She worried about Kristen and Josh. They'd be here soon; Joyce would bring them in to see their father. She wondered if they would hate her because of everything that happened, and the thought made tears sting her eyes. She covered her face with her hands, wishing she could burrow into a hole so deep that no one would ever find her. So that Kevin would never find her, she thought, and then remembered again that she'd watched him die on the porch. The words *He's dead* echoed like a mantra she couldn't escape.

"Katie?"

She looked up and saw the doctor who was now treating Alex.

"I can bring you back now," he said. "He woke up about ten minutes ago. He's still in ICU, so you can't stay long, but he wants to see you."

"Is he okay?"

"Right now, he's about as good as can be expected. He took a nasty blow."

Limping slightly, she followed the doctor as they made their way to Alex's room. She took a deep breath and straightened her posture before she entered, telling herself that she wasn't going to cry.

The ICU was filled with machines and blinking lights. Alex was in a bed in the corner, a bandage wrapped around his head. He turned toward her, his eyes only half open. A monitor beeped steadily beside him. She moved to his bedside and reached for his hand.

"How are the kids?" he whispered. The words came out slowly. Labored.

"They're fine. They're with Joyce. She took them home."

A faint, almost imperceptible smile crossed his lips.

"You?"

"I'm okay." She nodded.

"Love you," he said.

It was all she could do not to break down again. "I love you, too, Alex."

His eyelids drooped, his gaze unfocused. "What happened?"

She gave him an abbreviated account of the past twelve hours, but midstory she saw his eyes close. When he woke again later that morning, he'd forgotten parts of what she had recounted, so she told him again, trying to sound calm and matter-of-fact.

Joyce brought Josh and Kristen by, and though children weren't ordinarily allowed in the ICU, the doctor let them visit with their dad for a couple of minutes. Kristen had drawn him a picture of a man lying in a hospital bed, complete with a crayon-scrawled GET WELL, DADDY; Josh gave him a fishing magazine.

As the day wore on, Alex became more coherent. By the afternoon, he was no longer nodding in and out, and although he complained of a monstrous headache, his memory had more or less returned. His voice was stronger and when he told the nurse he was hungry, Katie gave a smile of relief, finally sure that he was going to be okay.

Alex was released the next day, and the sheriff visited them at Joyce's to get their formal statements. He told them that the alcohol content in Kevin's blood was so high that he'd effectively poisoned himself. Combined with the blood loss he'd suffered, it was a wonder he had been conscious, much less coherent to any degree. Katie said nothing, but all she could think was that they didn't know Kevin or understand the demons that drove him.

After the sheriff left, Katie went outside and stood in the sunlight, trying to make sense of her feelings. Though she'd told the sheriff about the events of that night, she hadn't told him everything. Nor had she told Alex everything—how could she, when it barely made sense to her? She didn't tell them that in the moments after Kevin had died and she'd rushed to Alex's side, she'd wept for them both. It seemed impossible that even as she relived the terror of those last hours with Kevin, she also remembered their rare happy moments together—how they'd laughed at private jokes or lounged peacefully on the couch together.

She didn't know how to reconcile these conflicting pieces of her past and the horror of what she'd just lived through. But there was something more, too, something else she didn't understand: she'd stayed at Joyce's because she was afraid to go back home.

Later that day, Alex and Katie stood in the parking lot, staring at the charred remains of what had once been the store. Here and there she could see items she recognized: the couch, half burned, tilted on the rubble; a shelf that once housed groceries; a bathtub scorched black.

A couple of firemen were rooting through the remains. Alex

had asked them to look for the safe he'd kept in his closet. He'd removed the bandage and Katie could see the spot where they'd shaved his head to apply stitches, the area black and blue and swollen.

"I'm sorry," Katie murmured. "For everything."

Alex shook his head. "It's not your fault. You didn't do it."

"But Kevin came for me . . ."

"I know," he said. He was quiet for a moment. "Kristen and Josh told me how you helped them get out of the house. Josh said that after you grabbed Kevin, you told them to run. He said you distracted him. I just wanted to say thank you."

Katie closed her eyes. "You can't thank me for that. If anything had happened to them, I don't know that I could have lived with myself."

He nodded but couldn't seem to look at her. Katie kicked at a small pile of ash that had blown into the parking lot. "What are you going to do? About the store?"

"Rebuild, I guess."

"Where will you live?"

"I don't know yet. We'll stay at Joyce's for a bit, but I'll try to find someplace quiet, someplace with a view. Since I can't work, I might as well try to enjoy the free time."

She felt sick to her stomach. "I can't even imagine how you feel right now."

"Numb. Sad for the kids. Shocked."

"And angry?"

"No," he said. "I'm not angry."

"But you lost everything."

"Not everything," he said. "Not the important things. My kids are safe. You're safe. That's all I really care about. This"— he said motioning—"is just stuff. Most of it can be replaced. It just takes time." When he finished, he squinted at something in the rubble. "Hold on for a second," he said.

He walked toward a pile of charred debris and pulled out a

fishing pole that had been wedged between blackened planks of wood. It was grimy, but otherwise looked undamaged. For the first time since they'd arrived, he smiled.

"Josh will be happy about this," he said. "I just wish I could find one of Kristen's dolls."

Katie crossed her arms over her stomach, feeling tears in her eyes. "I'll buy her a new one."

"You don't have to. I'm insured."

"But I want to. None of this would have happened if it hadn't been for me."

He looked at her. "I knew what I was getting into when I first asked you out."

"But you couldn't have expected this."

"No," he admitted. "Not this. But it's going to be okay."

"How can you say that?"

"Because it's true. We survived and that's all that matters." He reached for her hand and she felt his fingers intertwine with hers. "I haven't had a chance to say that I'm sorry."

"Why would you be sorry?"

"For your loss."

She knew he was talking about Kevin and she wasn't sure what to say. He seemed to understand that she'd both loved and hated her husband. "I never wanted him to die," she began. "I just wanted to be left alone."

"I know."

She turned tentatively toward him. "Are we going to be okay? I mean, after all this?"

"I suppose that depends on you."

"Me?"

"My feelings haven't changed. I still love you, but you need to figure out whether your feelings have changed."

"They haven't."

"Then we'll find a way to work through all this together because I know I want to spend the rest of my life with you."

Before she could respond, one of the firemen called out to them and they turned in his direction. He was working to free something, and when he stood he was holding a small safe.

"Do you think it was damaged?" Katie said.

"It shouldn't be," Alex answered. "It's fireproof. That's why I bought it."

"What's in it?"

"Mainly records, but I'm going to need them. Some photo disks and negatives. Things I wanted to protect."

"I'm glad they found it."

"So am I," he said. He paused. "Because there's something in there for you, too."

42

After dropping Alex off at Joyce's, Katie finally drove back home, not wanting to return but knowing she couldn't put off the inevitable forever. Even if she didn't intend to stay there, she needed to pack up some of her belongings.

Dust rose from the gravel and she bounced through the potholes before pulling to a stop out front. She sat in the jeep—dented and scraped, but still running fine—and stared at the door, remembering how Kevin had bled to death on her porch, his gaze fixed on her face.

She didn't want to see the bloodstains. She was afraid that opening the door would remind her of the way Alex had looked after Kevin struck him. She could practically hear the sounds of Kristen and Josh crying hysterically as they clung to their father. She wasn't prepared to relive all of that.

Instead, she started toward Jo's. In her hand was the letter that Alex had given her. When she'd asked him why he'd written to her, he'd shaken his head. "It's not from me," he'd said. She'd stared at him, confused. "You'll understand once you read it," he'd told her.

As she approached Jo's, she felt the trace of a memory stir to life. Something that happened on the night of the fire. Something she'd seen but she couldn't quite place. Just as she felt her mind closing in on it, the memory slipped away. She slowed as she drew nearer to Jo's house, a frown of confusion creasing her face.

There were cobwebs on the window, and a shutter had fallen to the ground where it lay shattered in the grass. The porch railing was broken and she could see weeds sprouting between the planks. Her eyes took in everything, but she was unable to process the scene before her: a rusted doorknob, half dangling from the door, grime on the windows as if they hadn't been cleaned in years.

No curtains . . .

No entry mat . . .

No wind chime . . .

She hesitated, trying to make sense of what she was seeing. She felt odd and curiously weightless, as if she were in a waking dream. The closer she got, the more the house seemed to decay before her.

She blinked and noticed that the door was cracked down the middle with a two-by-four hammered across it, bracing it to the crumbling casing.

She blinked again and saw that part of the wall, up in the corner, had rotted away, leaving a jagged hole.

She blinked a third time and realized that the lower half of the window was cracked and broken; pieces of glass littered the porch.

Katie climbed onto the porch, unable to stop herself. Leaning in, she peered through the windows into the darkened cottage.

Dust and dirt, broken furniture, piles of garbage. Nothing painted, nothing cleaned. All at once, Katie stepped back on the porch, almost stumbling off the broken step. *No.* It wasn't possible, it just wasn't. What had happened to Jo, and what about all the improvements she'd made on the small cottage? Katie had seen Jo hang the wind chime. Jo had been over to her house, complaining about having to paint and clean. They'd had coffee and wine and cheese and Jo had teased Katie about the bicycle. Jo had met her after work and they'd gone to a bar. The waitress had seen them both. Katie had ordered both of them wine . . .

But Jo's glass had been untouched, she recalled.

Katie massaged her temples, her mind racing, searching for answers. She remembered that Jo had been sitting on the steps when Alex dropped her off. Even Alex had seen her . . .

Or had he?

Katie backed away from the decaying home. Jo was real. There was no way she'd been a figment of her imagination. She hadn't made her up.

But Jo liked everything you did: she drank her coffee the same way, she liked the clothes you bought, her thoughts about the employees at Ivan's mirrored your own.

A dozen random details suddenly began crowding her mind and voices dueled in her head . . .

She lived here!

But why is it such a dump?

We looked at the stars together!

You looked at the stars alone, which is why you still don't know their names.

We drank wine at my house!

You drank the bottle by yourself, which was why you were so dizzy.

She told me about Alex! She wanted us to be together!

She never mentioned his name until you already knew it, and you were interested in him all along.

She was the kids' counselor!

Which was the excuse you used as a reason to never tell Alex about her.

But . . .

      But . . .

          But . . .

One by one, the answers came as quickly as she could think of them: the reason she'd never learned Jo's last name or saw her drive a car . . . the reason Jo never invited her over or accepted her offer to help her paint . . . how Jo had been able to magically appear at Katie's side in jogging clothes . . .

Katie felt something give way inside her as everything clicked into place.

Jo, she suddenly realized, had never been there at all.

43

Still feeling as if she were in a dream, Katie stumbled back to her house. She took a seat in the rocker and stared at Jo's house, wondering if she'd gone utterly mad.

She knew that the creation of imaginary friends was common among children, but she wasn't a child. And yes, she'd been under a great deal of stress when she arrived in Southport. Alone and friendless, on the run and looking over her shoulder, terrified that Kevin was closing in—who wouldn't be anxious? But was that enough to have prompted the creation of an alter ego? Maybe some psychiatrists would say yes, but she wasn't so sure.

The problem was that she didn't want to believe it. She couldn't believe it because it had felt so . . . *real*. She remembered those conversations, could still see Jo's expressions, still hear the sound of her laughter. Her memories of Jo felt as real as her memories of Alex did. Of course, he probably wasn't real, either. Probably made him up, too. And Kristen and Josh. She was probably strapped to a bed in an asylum somewhere, lost in an entire world of her own creation. She shook her head, frustrated and confused and yet . . .

There was something else nagging at her, though, something

she couldn't quite put her finger on. She was forgetting about something. Something important.

As much as she tried, she couldn't seem to place it. The events of the past few days had left her feeling drained and jittery. She looked up. Dusk was beginning to spread across the sky and the temperature was falling. Near the trees, a mist was starting to roll in.

Looking away from Jo's house—which was how she'd always refer to it, regardless of the state of mind it implied—Katie reached for the letter and examined it. The outer envelope was blank.

There was something frightening about the unopened letter, even though she wasn't sure why. It might have been Alex's expression as he'd handed it over . . . somehow she knew it was not only serious, but also important to him, and she wondered why he hadn't told her anything about it.

She didn't know, but it would be getting dark soon and she knew she was running out of time. Turning the envelope over, she lifted the seal. In the waning light, she ran her finger over the yellow legal paper before unfolding the pages. Finally, she began to read.

To the woman my husband loves,

If it seems odd for you to read these words, please believe me when I tell you that it feels just as odd to write them. Then again, nothing about this letter feels normal. There's so much I want to say, so much I want to tell you, and when I first put pen to paper, everything was clear in my mind. Now, however, I find myself struggling and I'm not sure where to begin.

I can start by saying this: I've come to believe that in everyone's life, there's one undeniable moment of change, a set of circumstances that suddenly alters everything. For me, that moment was meeting Alex. Though I don't know when or where you're reading this, I know it means he loves you. It also

means he wants to share his life with you, and if nothing else,
we will always have that in common.

My name, as you probably know, is Carly, but for most of
my life, my friends called me Jo . . .

Katie stopped reading and looked at the letter in her hands, unable to absorb its words. Taking a deep breath, she reread those words: *for most of my life, my friends called me Jo . . .*

She gripped the pages, feeling the memory she'd been struggling to retrieve come into focus at last. Suddenly, she was back in the master bedroom on the night of the fire. She felt the strain in her arms and back as she heaved the rocking chair through the window, felt the surge of panic as she wrapped Josh and Kristen in the comforter, only to hear the loud splintering sound behind her. With sudden clarity, she remembered whirling around and seeing the portrait hanging on the wall, the portrait of Alex's wife. At the time, she'd been confused, her nerves short-circuiting in the hell of smoke and fear.

But she'd seen the face. Yes, she'd even taken a step closer to get a better look.

That looks a lot like Jo, she remembered thinking, even if her mind hadn't been able to process it. But now, as she sat on the porch beneath a slowly darkening sky, she knew with certainty that she was wrong. Wrong about everything. She raised her eyes to gaze at Jo's cottage again.

It looked like Jo, she suddenly realized, because it *was* Jo. Unbidden, she felt another memory float free, from the first morning that Jo had come over.

My friends call me Jo, she had said by way of introduction.

Oh, my God.

Katie paled.

. . . Jo . . .

She hadn't imagined Jo, she suddenly knew. She hadn't made her up.

Jo *had* been here, and she felt her throat begin to tighten. Not because she didn't believe it, but because she suddenly understood that her friend Jo—her only real friend, her wise adviser, her supporter and confidante—would never come back.

They would never have coffee, they would never share another bottle of wine, they would never visit on the porch out front. She'd never hear the sound of Jo's laughter or watch the way she arched her eyebrow. She would never hear Jo complain about having to do manual labor, and she began to cry, mourning the wonderful friend she'd never had the chance to meet in life.

She wasn't sure how much time passed before she was able to begin reading again. It was getting dark, and with a sigh, she stood and unlocked the front door. Inside, she took a seat at the kitchen table. Jo, she remembered, had once sat in the opposite chair, and for a reason she couldn't explain, Katie felt herself begin to relax.

Okay, she thought to herself. I'm ready to hear what you have to say.

> . . . *but for most of my life, my friends called me Jo. Please feel free to call me either, and just so you know, I already consider you a friend. I hope by the end of this letter, you'll feel the same about me.*
>
> *Dying is a strange business, and I'm not going to bore you with the details. I might have weeks or I might have months and though it's a cliché, it's true that so many of the things I once believed to be important no longer are. I don't read the newspaper anymore, or care about the stock market, or worry whether it's going to rain while I'm on vacation. Instead, I find myself reflecting on the essential moments of my life. I think about Alex and how handsome he looked on the day we were married. I remember my exhausted elation when I first held*

Josh and Kristen in my arms. They were wonderful babies, and I used to lay them in my lap and stare at them while they slept. I could do that for hours, trying to figure out whether they had my nose or Alex's, his eyes or mine. Sometimes, while they were dreaming, their little fists would curl around my finger, and I can remember thinking that I'd never experienced a purer form of joy.

It wasn't until I had children that I really understood what love meant. Don't get me wrong. I love Alex deeply, but it's different from the love I feel for Josh and Kristen. I don't know how to explain it and I don't know that I need to. All I know is that despite my illness, I nonetheless feel blessed, because I've been able to experience both. I've lived a full, happy life and experienced the kind of love that many people will never know.

But my prognosis scares me. I try to be brave around Alex, and the kids are still too young to understand what's really happening, but in quiet moments when I'm alone, the tears come readily, and sometimes I wonder if they're ever going to stop. Though I know I shouldn't, I'll find myself dwelling on the fact that I'm never going to walk my children to school or that I'll never get another chance to witness their excitement on Christmas morning. I'll never help Kristen shop for a prom dress or watch Josh play baseball. There is so much I will never see and do with them, and sometimes I despair that I'll be nothing but a distant memory by the time they get married.

How can I tell them that I love them if I'm no longer there?

And Alex. He's my dream and my companion, my lover and my friend. He's a devoted father, but more than that, he's my ideal husband. I can't describe the comfort I feel when he takes me in his arms, or how I look forward to lying down beside him at night. There's an unshakable humanity about him, a faith in the goodness of life, and it breaks my heart to imagine him alone. That's why I've asked him to give you this letter; I thought of it as a way of making him keep his promise that he would find someone special again—someone who loves him, and someone he could love. He needs that.

I was blessed to be married to him for five years and I've mothered my children for less time than that. Now, my life is almost over and you are going to take my place. You'll become the wife who grows old with Alex, and you'll become the only mother my children will ever know. You can't imagine how terrible it is to lie in bed, staring at my family and knowing these things, and realizing there's nothing I can do to change them. Sometimes, I dream that I'll find a way to come back, that I can find a way to ensure they're going to be all right. I like to believe that I'll watch over them from heaven, or that I can visit them in their dreams. I want to pretend that my journey isn't over and I pray that the boundless love I feel for them will somehow make it possible.

This is where you come in. I want you to do something for me.

If you love Alex now, then love him forever. Make him laugh again, and cherish the time you spend together. Take walks and ride your bikes, curl up on the couch and watch movies beneath a blanket. Make him breakfast, but don't spoil him. Let him make breakfast for you as well, so he can show you he thinks you're special. Kiss him and make love to him, and consider yourself lucky for having met him, for he's the kind of man who'll prove you right.

I also want you to love my children in the same way I do. Help them with their homework and kiss their scraped elbows and knees when they fall. Run your hand through their hair and assure them they can do anything they put their mind to. Tuck them in at night and help them say their prayers. Make their lunches; support them in their friendships. Adore them, laugh with them, help them grow into kind, independent adults. What you give them in love, they'll return tenfold in time, if only because Alex is their father.

Please. I beg you, do these things for me. After all, they are your family now, not mine.

I'm not jealous or angry that I've been replaced by you; as I mentioned already, I consider you a friend. You've made my husband and children happy, and I wish I were around to be able to thank you in person. Instead, all I can do is assure you that you have my everlasting gratitude.

If Alex has chosen you, then I want you to believe that I have chosen you as well.

Your friend in spirit,
Carly Jo

When Katie finished reading the letter, she wiped her tears and ran her finger over the pages before slipping them back into the envelope. She sat quietly, thinking about the words that Jo had written, already knowing she would do exactly as Jo had asked.

Not because of the letter, she thought, but because she knew that in some inexplicable way, Jo was the one who'd gently urged her to give Alex a chance in the first place.

She smiled. "Thank you for trusting me," she whispered, and she knew that Jo had been right all along. She'd fallen in love with Alex and she'd fallen in love with the children and she already knew that she couldn't imagine a future without them. It was time to go home, she thought, it was time to see her family.

Outside, the moon was a brilliant white disk that guided her as she made her way toward the jeep. But before climbing in, she glanced over her shoulder in the direction of Jo's.

The lights were on and the windows of the cottage were glowing yellow. In the painted kitchen, she saw Jo standing near the window. Though she was too far away to make out much more than that, Katie had the sense she was smiling. Jo raised a hand in a friendly farewell, and Katie was reminded again that love can sometimes achieve the impossible.

When Katie blinked, however, the cottage was dark again. No lights were on and Jo had vanished, but she thought she could hear the words in the letter being carried on the gentle breeze.

If Alex has chosen you, then I want you to believe that I have chosen you as well.

Katie smiled and turned away, knowing it wasn't an illusion or a figment of her imagination. She knew what she saw.

She knew what she believed.

Reading Group Guide

Discussion Questions

1. When Alex first meets Katie, he senses that she is in trouble. How does he figure out what has happened to her?

2. What is the nature of Jo and Katie's relationship? How does Jo's profession play into their friendship? How does Jo help Katie adjust to her life in Southport?

3. What role do Alex's children play in the development of his relationship with Katie?

4. Katie and Alex fall in love very quickly. What draws them together? Have you ever fallen in love so quickly? If not, do you think it's possible?

5. On their first date, Alex says to Katie, "Everyone has a past, but that's just it—it's in the past. You can learn from it, but you can't change it." Do you agree with him? Is it possible to truly put the past behind you?

6. Alex is a widower who has had to raise two children on his own. How has he dealt with his grief in the years since his wife passed away? How has his need to respond to his young children's grief affected this? Have you experienced grief of this magnitude in your own life? How did you handle it?

7. When Katie tells Alex about Kevin, she says, "I hate him, but I hate myself, too." Why does she feel this way? How does Katie change as she spends more and more time in Southport? How is she different by the end of the book?

8. Despite his violent behavior and his incessant drinking, Kevin quotes the Bible constantly and takes the Ten Commandments seriously. How do you understand his behavior?

9. Katie's past puts Alex and his family in potential danger. Do you think it was irresponsible of Alex to involve himself with a woman he knew could endanger him and his children?

10. Why do you think the author chose to write a portion of the book from Kevin's perspective? Do you have any sympathy for Kevin? Why or why not?

11. Did reading this book give you a new or better understanding of domestic abuse?

12. At the end of the novel, Alex tells Katie he is sorry for her loss. What does he mean by this? How does Katie react?

13. What do you make of Katie's discovery at the end of the novel? Do you find the book's ending believable?

14. This novel is in large part about safety and trust and how we often take these two things for granted. Did this book make you think differently about your own life and the things you value?

THE WINDOWS™
INTERFACE

An Application Design Guide

Microsoft
P R E S S

PUBLISHED BY
Microsoft Press
A Division of Microsoft Corporation
One Microsoft Way
Redmond, Washington 98052-6399

Library of Congress Cataloging-in-Publication Data
Microsoft Corporation.
    The Windows Interface, an application design guide
    / Microsoft Corporation.
        p.   cm.
    Includes index.
    ISBN 1-55615-384-8
    1. Microsoft Windows (Computer programs) 2. User interfaces
(Computer systems)
QA76.76.W56M523   1991
005.4'3--dc20   91-27590
                                                            CIP

Printed and bound in the United States of America.

1 2 3 4 5 6 7 8 9 AGAG 7 6 5 4 3 2

Distributed to the book trade in Canada by Macmillan of Canada, a division
of Canada Publishing Corporation.

Distributed to the book trade outside the United States and Canada by Penguin Books Ltd.

Penguin Books Ltd., Harmondsworth, Middlesex, England
Penguin Books Australia Ltd., Ringwood, Victoria, Australia
Penguin Books N.Z. Ltd., 182–190 Wairau Road, Auckland 10, New Zealand

British Cataloging-in-Publication Data available.

U.S. Patent No. 4974159

Document No. PC28921-0692

Contents

Introduction

This design guide provides guidelines for developing user interfaces for applications that run in the Microsoft® Windows™ graphical environment. It describes the components of the Windows user interface and explains design principles for software developers and designers of Windows-based applications.

Purpose

The purpose of this design guide is to promote visual and functional consistency within and across Windows-based applications. This has several advantages: When the interface for applications is consistent, users can move from one application to another with ease and speed. Consistency facilitates the learning process and minimizes the need for training when new applications are introduced into the workplace, resulting in increased productivity. Consistency also alleviates the confusion introduced by applications with divergent interfaces and eliminates the associated costs in efficiency and training. It gives users a sense of stability, which increases their confidence in the reliability of an application and in all applications with the same interface.

Scope

Most of the elements and techniques described in this guide are incorporated in the Windows operating system, version 3.1; some of these may not be available in earlier versions of the Windows environment. See your Microsoft Windows Software Development Kit (SDK) documentation for specific information on what is supported.

Because of the evolving nature of applications, this guide cannot provide specific recommendations for every possible interface issue. If an application requires elements or techniques not discussed in this guide, designers or developers may extend the existing guidelines in accordance with the principles in Chapter 1. They should review these guidelines as the minimum requirements for consistency with other Windows-based applications, and should evaluate their applications accordingly.

This guide focuses on recommendations that are specific to the development of Windows-based applications. These guidelines were developed to be generally compatible with guidelines that may be appropriately applied from the IBM® Common User Access (CUA) version 2.0 definition, published in *IBM Common User Access: Advanced Interface Design Guide* (Boca Raton, FL: IBM, 1989); but they are not intended to describe user interface requirements for CUA compliance.

The guidelines include recommendations that are generally applicable to a variety of Windows version 3.0 applications, as well as recommendations relating to new Windows version 3.1 features.

The information in this guide is tailored to applications developed for English-speaking countries. However, many of the guidelines are generally applicable to applications developed for non-English-speaking countries as well.

Implementation

The Microsoft Windows Software Development Kit (SDK) contains code samples for implementing many of the features described in this guide. See the SDK documentation for more information.

Support for Input Methods

This guide describes techniques for the mouse and keyboard, and includes a discussion of the pen which is gaining increasing acceptance as an input device. While a mouse is the preferred means of interaction in many cases, applications should also provide keyboard access to the interface for users who have systems without a mouse or who prefer using the keyboard. For applications that rely on the keyboard for entering data (for example, database, word-processing, or spread-sheet programs), keyboard access might be the preferred method of interaction for many users who do not wish to remove their hands from the keys. On the other hand, you may find that keyboard access to many features in graphics applications (such as drawing or painting programs) is a hindrance rather than a help. For this reason, you may wish to avoid keyboard access wherever its use is cumbersome.

Recommendation Levels

As stated earlier, the purpose of this design guide is to promote visual and functional consistency within and across Windows-based applications. The information presented is provided as a tool for those who would like to use it. Developers may choose to adopt any number of the guidelines in their own user interface designs. There is no conformance requirement, expressed or implied, in this set of guidelines.

The following definitions are provided to give designers an idea of the importance of specific guidelines:

- Guidelines that are labeled "recommended" represent the common way specific features, functions, operations, or behaviors should be implemented for the greatest degree of consistency. All recommended items need not be included in an application; however, if the items exist, the guidelines describe the preferred means of implementation. For example, although F6 is the recommended key for switching between panes, all applications need not include panes. Some of the recommended guidelines may be defined by the system (for example, ALT+ESC); others may be defined by the application (for example, F1).

- Guidelines that are labeled "optional" are common extensions that an application may implement. If these features or operations are implemented, the stated guidelines are the preferred means of implementation. The File and View menus illustrate the difference between recommended and optional guidelines: The File menu is recommended for all applications that provide access to data through files. The View menu is optional, but its contents follow preferred implementation guidelines.

- Guidelines that are labeled "suggested" state a particular direction that applications should follow, to the extent that the guidelines apply and do not conflict with other uses in the application.

Notation for Keys and Key Combinations

- Key names appear in small capitals; for example, CTRL or SHIFT.

- Simultaneous key combinations are linked by plus signs; for example, CTRL+B or CTRL+SHIFT+B. This notation indicates that the user should hold down the CTRL key while pressing the B key; or hold down the CTRL and SHIFT keys while pressing the B key.

- Sequential key combinations are linked by commas; for example: ALT,F. This notation indicates that the user should press and release the ALT key, and then press and release the F key.

Table 2.1   Mouse Input

Operation	Definition	Common Usage (Using Button 1)
Point	Move pointer ("hot spot*") to desired screen location.	Navigates; prepares for selection or for operation of control.
Press	Press and hold the button.	Identifies object to be selected.
Click	Press and release button without moving mouse.	Selects insertion point or item; operates control; activates inactive window or control.
Double-click**	Press and release button twice within specified interval, without moving mouse.	Shortcut for common operations, for example, activates icon, opens file, selects word.
Drag	Press button and hold while moving mouse.	Identifies range of objects; moves or resizes items.
Double-drag	Press button twice and hold while moving mouse.	Identifies selection by larger unit (for example, words).

* The hot spot is the position in the mouse pointer that marks the exact screen location that will be affected by a mouse action.

** There are no recommended assignments for triple-clicking or additional multi-clicking operations. Applications may define their own assignments, but remember that these operations are often difficult for users to master.

A mouse action is proposed when the mouse button is pressed down, and confirmed when the mouse button is released. For example, if the pointer is over a menu item, the item is highlighted when the button is pressed down and initiated when the button is released. Similarly, during drag operations the user gets visual feedback (for example, highlighting) while the button is down, but the operations are not accepted until the button is released. While this is the general rule, there may be occasional exceptions. For example, scrolling is initiated as soon as the user presses the mouse button over a scroll arrow; the action auto-repeats as long as the mouse button is down.

2.1.2 Guidelines for Using Mouse Operations

Mouse operations should not require extraordinary hand-eye coordination from the user. For example:

- If an object is so small or thin that pointing or clicking to select it would require extremely precise mouse positioning, provide a "hot zone" around the object to increase the area where clicking will select the object.

- The rapid button-pressing required by double-clicks and double-drags is difficult for some users; never use these input techniques as the only means of carrying out essential operations such as opening files.

Recommendation Levels

As stated earlier, the purpose of this design guide is to promote visual and functional consistency within and across Windows-based applications. The information presented is provided as a tool for those who would like to use it. Developers may choose to adopt any number of the guidelines in their own user interface designs. There is no conformance requirement, expressed or implied, in this set of guidelines.

The following definitions are provided to give designers an idea of the importance of specific guidelines:

- Guidelines that are labeled "recommended" represent the common way specific features, functions, operations, or behaviors should be implemented for the greatest degree of consistency. All recommended items need not be included in an application; however, if the items exist, the guidelines describe the preferred means of implementation. For example, although F6 is the recommended key for switching between panes, all applications need not include panes. Some of the recommended guidelines may be defined by the system (for example, ALT+ESC); others may be defined by the application (for example, F1).

- Guidelines that are labeled "optional" are common extensions that an application may implement. If these features or operations are implemented, the stated guidelines are the preferred means of implementation. The File and View menus illustrate the difference between recommended and optional guidelines: The File menu is recommended for all applications that provide access to data through files. The View menu is optional, but its contents follow preferred implementation guidelines.

- Guidelines that are labeled "suggested" state a particular direction that applications should follow, to the extent that the guidelines apply and do not conflict with other uses in the application.

Notation for Keys and Key Combinations

- Key names appear in small capitals; for example, CTRL or SHIFT.

- Simultaneous key combinations are linked by plus signs; for example, CTRL+B or CTRL+SHIFT+B. This notation indicates that the user should hold down the CTRL key while pressing the B key; or hold down the CTRL and SHIFT keys while pressing the B key.

- Sequential key combinations are linked by commas; for example: ALT,F. This notation indicates that the user should press and release the ALT key, and then press and release the F key.

Principles and Methodology

1.1 Principles of User Interface Design

Because applications continually evolve, it is impossible to provide specific recommendations that cover every possible interface issue. Applications should follow the general principles in this section, even when they include elements and techniques not covered in this guide.

1.1.1 User Control

One of the most important principles of user interface design is that the user should always be in control of the application, not vice versa. This principle has several implications.

First, applications should always be as interactive as possible. The user should not have to wait a long time for processing to be completed. In general, applications should avoid modes that severely restrict the interactions available to the user at any given time. If modes must be used, they should be visually obvious (for example, the pointer can change shape), easy to learn, and easy to get out of.

A second implication of the principle of user control concerns customization. Because users' abilities and preferences vary, users should be able to customize aspects of the interface (including aesthetic qualities, like color and function) such as the content and structure of menus. However, designers should provide good defaults and should not depend on the user customizing these settings. (Customization methods are discussed in Chapter 11, section 11.2.)

Finally, the interface should facilitate the user's tasks rather than calling attention to itself. The best interface is often the one that is hardly noticed. Users want to accomplish tasks, not to use computers; they want to write letters, calculate profits, manage projects, and prepare presentations—not to slide scroll boxes, open dropdown lists, pull down menus, and navigate among dialog boxes.

1.1.2 Directness

The interface should give users direct and intuitive ways to accomplish their tasks. The object-action paradigm supports this principle. The user performs tasks by selecting an object (such as an icon, a window, or some text), then selecting an action (such as move, close, or underline) for that object.

Manipulating objects directly, although not appropriate in all situations, is often easier than typing complex commands. For example, it is much easier to move a window by dragging it with the mouse than by visually estimating new coordinates and then typing them into a dialog box.

1.1.3 Consistency

Two broad categories of consistency are particularly important: consistency with the real world, and consistency within and among applications. First, applications should build on the user's real-world experience by exploiting concrete metaphors and natural mapping relationships. The use of familiar concepts and metaphors reduces the amount of new material that users must learn and thereby makes applications easier to use. Second, each application should be conceptually, linguistically, visually, and functionally consistent within itself and with other applications. Such consistency benefits users. It also benefits designers and developers, who can produce well-designed applications more quickly by reusing standard interface elements.

Occasionally the goals of cross-platform consistency and within-platform consistency may conflict. For example, two platforms may provide different interfaces for accomplishing the same function. In such cases, within-platform consistency should be given priority, because most users only work within one platform.

1.1.4 Clarity

An application interface should be visually, conceptually, and linguistically clear. Visual elements should be immediately comprehensible, ideally because they relate to real-world analogues, and should be arranged so that their functions are comprehensible. Conceptual metaphors should be simple and realistic. Interface text should be clear, unambiguous, and free of jargon.

1.1.5 Aesthetics

Both aesthetic appeal and visual clarity can be substantially enhanced by attention to basic graphic design principles concerning spatial grouping, contrast, and three-dimensional representation. The best interfaces combine powerful yet accessible functionality with a pleasing appearance.

1.1.6 Feedback

The user should receive immediate and tangible feedback for actions within an application. For example, when a person picks up a pencil, tactile and visual sensations provide feedback that the pencil has been touched. Similarly, if the user of an application selects a data object with the mouse, the application should provide visual feedback that the object has been selected. Graphical feedback is particularly effective, but textual and auditory feedback are also useful (see Chapter 3, section 3.6).

1.1.7 Forgiveness

Users like to explore an application and learn by trial and error. Such self-motivated learning can be extremely effective, but users may not always be aware of potential dangers. Even with the best-designed interface, users make mistakes—both physical mistakes (accidentally pointing to the wrong command or data) and mental mistakes (making a wrong decision about which command or data to select). The interface should accommodate user exploration and mistakes without pain or penalty, should minimize the opportunities for errors, and should handle errors gracefully. Error messages should not imply that the user is at fault; instead, they should state the problem objectively and offer possible solutions (see Chapter 3, section 3.6.1.2).

1.1.8 Awareness of Human Strengths and Limitations

By the age of five, we are wonderfully adept at many linguistic and visual tasks that stymie even the most advanced computer systems. Nevertheless, we also have unavoidable limitations in perception, memory, and reasoning. Applications should respect these limitations rather than forcing the user to overcome them. For example, the user should not be required to calculate information (such as the day of the week corresponding to a certain date) that can be provided by the application. Similarly, the user should not be required to recall complex sets of options or commands. Instead, the available choices should be presented explicitly; recognizing items is much easier than recalling them.

1.2 Design Methodology

For maximum effectiveness, design principles must be used in conjunction with a design methodology that puts the user at the heart of the design process, encompasses the broad context within which the application will be used, and leaves room for iterative testing and redesign of the interface.

Even the most creative and experienced designers cannot always produce the right interface design on the first try. Indeed, sometimes experience in user interface design can be a barrier to finding the right solution; to the extent that designers are intimately familiar with an interface, they are removed from the viewpoint of the new or casual user. It is essential to test new designs on real users—not only on colleagues from down the hall. Schedules should include time to redesign the interface in light of usability test results. Time spent in usability testing is time well spent; it is far better to uncover interface problems early in the design stage rather than after a product has been launched.

In designing and testing an interface, it is crucial to keep in mind the larger context within which the application will be used. For example, will it run on a stand-alone computer or as part of a network? Will it be used alone or with other applications? In the increasingly networked and multitasking computer environment of the 1990s, applications that allow for easy exchange of data with other users and other applications will have an enormous advantage over traditional stand-alone applications. The interface should reflect and facilitate this new integration by providing data exchange techniques that are consistent from one application to another.

1.3 Selected Bibliography

Chew, Jane Carrasco, and John Whiteside, eds. *Empowering People: CHI '90 Conference Proceedings*. New York, NY: ACM Press, 1990.

Helander, Martin, ed. *Handbook of Human-Computer Interaction*. Amsterdam: North-Holland, 1988.

IBM Corporation. *Common User Access: Advanced Interface Design Guide*. Boca Raton, FL: IBM, 1989.

Laurel, Brenda, ed. *The Art of Human-Computer Interface Design*. Reading, MA: Addison-Wesley, 1990.

Nielsen, Jakob, ed. *Coordinating User Interfaces for Consistency*. Boston: Academic Press, 1989.

Norman, Donald A. *The Design of Everyday Things*. New York: Basic Books, 1988.

Robertson, S.P., G.M. Olson, and J.S. Olson, eds. *Reaching Through Technology: CHI '91 Conference Proceedings*. Reading, MA: Addison-Wesley, 1991.

Shneiderman, Ben. *Designing the User Interface: Strategies for Effective Human-Computer Interaction*. Reading, MA: Addison-Wesley, 1987.

Tufte, Edward R. *Envisioning Information*. Cheshire, CT: Graphics Press, 1990.

In addition, ACM/SIGCHI publishes proceedings on computer-human interactions on a regular basis.

Fundamental Input Elements

The user interface is grounded in a relatively small set of fundamental input elements that define the user's interaction with the computer. The two basic elements are the mouse and the keyboard.

2.1 Mouse Input

The most important mouse operations are pointing, clicking, and dragging. These operations may be combined with modifier keys (SHIFT, CTRL, and ALT).

2.1.1 Basic Operations

- **Button 1.** This is the selection button. Most mouse actions rely on mouse button 1.[1]

- **Button 2.** This button is used to bring up context-specific actions and options. Assigning alternate operations to button 2 may confuse the user.

Additional mouse buttons may be supported but are typically not available. Therefore, a third (or additional) button should be assigned to operations or functions already in the interface. For example, a third mouse button (the middle button) can be used as an additional way to distinguish selection from direct (drag) manipulation.[2]

Table 2.1 lists the basic mouse input elements and gives examples of their use. For information on using modifier keys in conjunction with the mouse, see Chapter 3, section 3.1.2.

---

[1] By default, button 1 is the left button, but the Microsoft Windows Control Panel allows the user to switch the left/right mapping.

[2] A third mouse button can be simulated with a two-button device by using both buttons or the ALT key+ button 2 combination.

Table 2.1   Mouse Input

Operation	Definition	Common Usage (Using Button 1)
Point	Move pointer ("hot spot*") to desired screen location.	Navigates; prepares for selection or for operation of control.
Press	Press and hold the button.	Identifies object to be selected.
Click	Press and release button without moving mouse.	Selects insertion point or item; operates control; activates inactive window or control.
Double-click**	Press and release button twice within specified interval, without moving mouse.	Shortcut for common operations, for example, activates icon, opens file, selects word.
Drag	Press button and hold while moving mouse.	Identifies range of objects; moves or resizes items.
Double-drag	Press button twice and hold while moving mouse.	Identifies selection by larger unit (for example, words).

* The hot spot is the position in the mouse pointer that marks the exact screen location that will be affected by a mouse action.

** There are no recommended assignments for triple-clicking or additional multi-clicking operations. Applications may define their own assignments, but remember that these operations are often difficult for users to master.

A mouse action is proposed when the mouse button is pressed down, and confirmed when the mouse button is released. For example, if the pointer is over a menu item, the item is highlighted when the button is pressed down and initiated when the button is released. Similarly, during drag operations the user gets visual feedback (for example, highlighting) while the button is down, but the operations are not accepted until the button is released. While this is the general rule, there may be occasional exceptions. For example, scrolling is initiated as soon as the user presses the mouse button over a scroll arrow; the action auto-repeats as long as the mouse button is down.

2.1.2 Guidelines for Using Mouse Operations

Mouse operations should not require extraordinary hand-eye coordination from the user. For example:

- If an object is so small or thin that pointing or clicking to select it would require extremely precise mouse positioning, provide a "hot zone" around the object to increase the area where clicking will select the object.

- The rapid button-pressing required by double-clicks and double-drags is difficult for some users; never use these input techniques as the only means of carrying out essential operations such as opening files.

- Do not require the user to point at a moving target, except in games.

2.2 Keyboard Input

Keyboard input involves pressing types of keys: text keys, editing keys, mode keys, navigation keys, and shortcut (function) keys.

2.2.1 Text Keys

Text keys can be defined as the alphanumeric (a-z, 0-9), punctuation, symbol, TAB, and ENTER keys, and the SPACEBAR. In applications that have text-entry modes, pressing a text key in text mode causes the corresponding character to appear on the screen. (TAB and ENTER may not be visible except in certain views.) In non-text-entry modes, these keys can be used as shortcuts for other operations, such as choosing tools from a toolbox or selecting an item with a matching first letter from a list. In addition, TAB is used for navigation (see section 2.2.4), ENTER is used to press the default button in dialog boxes, and the SPACEBAR is used as the default Select key for explicit keyboard selection (see Chapter 3, section 3.1.3).

PC keyboards include two keys labeled ENTER: the normal ENTER and the keypad ENTER. These keys have the same label, so their default functions should be the same.

2.2.2 Editing Keys

Table 2.2 lists the editing keys and their functions. Unless otherwise indicated, these functions apply to text editing.

Table 2.2   Editing Keys

Key	Recommended Function
DEL	- If there is a selection: Deletes entire selection. - If there is an insertion point and no selection: Deletes character to *right* of insertion point.
BACKSPACE*	- If there is a selection: Deletes entire selection. - If there is an insertion point and no selection: Deletes character to *left* of insertion point.
INS	Toggles between Insert mode (new text characters push old ones to right) and Overtype mode (new text characters overwrite old ones).

* Characters deleted by the DEL and BACKSPACE keys are not placed on the clipboard. For additional information, see Chapter 3, section 3.7.

2.2.3 Mode Keys

Mode keys change the actions of the other keys. The two kinds of mode keys are toggle keys and modifier keys.

2.2.3.1 Toggle Keys

A toggle key turns a particular mode on or off each time it is pressed and released. For example, the INS key toggles between Insert mode (in which new text characters push old ones to the right) and Overtype mode (in which new characters overwrite old ones).

Table 2.3 lists the principal toggle keys. Function keys may also be used to toggle modes.

Table 2.3   Toggle Keys[3]

Key	Function
INS	Toggles between Insert mode (new text characters push old one to right) and Overtype mode (new text characters overwrite old ones).
CAPS LOCK	Pressing alphabetic key yields uppercase.
NUM LOCK	Numeric keypad keys yield numbers rather than direction.
SCROLL LOCK	Navigation keys scroll data without moving cursor; existing selections are preserved.
F8	Toggles Extend mode. In this mode, selection behaves as if the SHIFT key is locked down for all direction keys and mouse actions (see Chapter 3, section 3.1.1.5).
SHIFT+F8	Toggles Add mode, which allows disjoint selection through the keyboard. In Add mode, navigation keys move the focus without affecting existing selections, and pressing the SPACEBAR toggles the selection state of an item (see Chapter 3, section 3.1.3.2).

---

[3] Although these are the recommended assignments, applications need not support all of these keys.

2.2.3.2 Modifier Keys

The modifier keys are SHIFT, CTRL, and ALT. Like toggle keys, modifier keys also change the actions of other keys. Unlike toggle keys, however, the mode established by a modifier key remains in effect only while the key is pressed down; in other words, the mode is "spring-loaded," and the user must actively maintain it. Spring-loaded modes are preferable to self-maintaining modes, because the active maintenance required for a spring-loaded mode prevents the user from forgetting that a mode is in effect. Accordingly, if you need to switch modes from the keyboard, modifier keys are preferable to toggle keys, as long as the required actions within the mode can be quickly and easily accomplished while one hand is occupied by holding down the modifier key.

Table 2.4 lists the most common functions of the modifier keys. For more detailed descriptions, see the sections in Chapter 3 covering the functions mentioned in the table. Typically, the modifier key is pressed at the beginning of the operation and held down during the operation if its release cancels or changes the operation.

Table 2.4   Modifier Keys

Key	Typical Functions
SHIFT	▪ With alphanumeric keys, yields uppercase or the character inscribed on the top half of the key.*
	▪ With mouse click or navigation keys, extends or shrinks the contiguous selection range.
	▪ With function keys, alters meaning of action (for example, F1 brings up the Help application window, pressing SHIFT+F1 enters Help mode).
CTRL	▪ With mouse click, selects or deselects an item without affecting previous selections.
	▪ With alphabetic keys, yields shortcuts.
	▪ With navigation keys, typically moves cursor by a larger unit than the unmodified key.
ALT	With alphabetic key, navigates to the menu or control marked with that key as a mnemonic.

* With CAPS LOCK on, yields lowercase characters.

2.2.4 Navigation Keys

The navigation keys are HOME, END, PAGE UP, PAGE DOWN, the four arrow keys (LEFT, RIGHT, UP, and DOWN), and TAB. Table 2.5 lists the functions of these keys, singly and in combination with various modifier keys. The CTRL+key combination is generally used to move by a larger increment than the unmodified key. Navigation operations may also be assigned to keys in addition to those listed here (for example, to function keys).

Table 2.5   Navigation Keys

Key	Unmodified Key Moves Cursor To...	CTRL+Key Moves Cursor To...
HOME	Beginning of line. (Leftmost position in current line.)	Beginning of data. (Top left position in current field or document.*)
END	End of line. (Rightmost position occupied by data in current line.)	End of data. (Bottom right position occupied by data in current field or document.**)
PAGE UP	Screen up. (Previous screen, same horizontal position.)	Screen left/beginning. (Top of window; or, moves left one screen.)
PAGE DOWN	Screen down. (Next screen, same horizontal position.)	Screen right/end. (Bottom of window; or, moves right one screen.)
LEFT ARROW	Left one unit.§	Left one (larger) unit.§§
RIGHT ARROW	Right one unit.§	Right one (larger) unit.§§
UP ARROW	Up one unit/line.#	Up one (larger) unit.##
DOWN ARROW	Down one unit/line.#	Down one (larger) unit.##
TAB	Dialogs: Next field; may move left to right or top to bottom at designer's discretion; after last field, wraps to first. (SHIFT+TAB moves in the reverse order.)	(Not defined.)

* If there is no left dimension, the key combination may also be used to move to the top position.

** If there is no right dimension, the key combination may also be used to move to the bottom position.

§ For text, this moves between characters.

§§ For text, this is generally used to move between words (to the beginning of the next or previous word). Other usage may also be appropriate, as long as applications follow the general principle that CTRL+navigation key moves by a larger unit than the unmodified key.

\# Generally maintaining the same position.

\#\# For text, this is generally used to move between paragraphs. Other usage may also be appropriate, as long as applications follow the general principle that CTRL+navigation key moves by a larger unit than the unmodified key.

2.2.5 Shortcut Keys

Shortcut keys or key combinations can be used to provide more rapid access to frequently performed operations. Function keys and CTRL+letter combinations are often used as shortcuts. You may also use ALT+function key combinations, with the exceptions noted in section 2.2.5.3. Note that ALT+letter combinations are not recommended as shortcut keys because they provide standard keyboard access to menus and controls.

2.2.5.1 Function Key Shortcuts

Table 2.6 lists recommended PC function key assignments. Function keys that do not have recommended assignments are available for use by applications.

Table 2.6   Recommended PC Function Key Assignments

	(No modifier)	SHIFT	CTRL	ALT
F1	Help (Chapter 11, section 11.3.1).	Enter Help mode (Chapter 11, section 11.3.1).	(No recommended assignment.)	(No recommended assignment.)
F2, F3	(No recommended assignment.)	(No recommended assignment.)	(No recommended assignment.)	(No recommended assignment.)
F4	(No recommended assignment.)	(No recommended assignment.)	Close document window (Chapter 5, section 5.4.1).	Close application window (Chapter 5, section 5.4.1).
F5	(No recommended assignment.)	(No recommended assignment.)	(No recommended assignment.)	(No recommended assignment.)
F6*	Move clockwise to next pane of active window (Chapter 4, section 4.3.5.2.2).	Move counterclockwise to next pane of active window (Chapter 4, section 4.3.5.2.2).	Move to next document window; top window moves to bottom of stack (Chapter 4, section 4.3.5.2.3). (Adding SHIFT reverses action: previous window moves to top.)	Move to application's next open non-document window (Chapter 4, section 4.3.5.2.3). (Adding SHIFT reverses order of movement.)
F7	(No recommended assignment.)	(No recommended assignment.)	(No recommended assignment.)	(No recommended assignment.)
F8	Toggle Extend mode, if supported (Chapter 3, section 3.1.1.5).	Toggle Add mode, if supported (Chapter 3, section 3.1.3.2).	(No recommended assignment.)	(No recommended assignment.)
F9	(No recommended assignment.)	(No recommended assignment.)	(No recommended assignment.)	(No recommended assignment.)
F10	Toggle menu bar activation. (Supported for CUA 2.0 compatibility.)	(No recommended assignment.)	(No recommended assignment.)	(No recommended assignment.)
F11, F12	(No recommended assignment.)	(No recommended assignment.)	(No recommended assignment.)	(No recommended assignment.)

* In addition to the keys discussed here, applications may define their own specialized navigation keys.

If some target users of an application are unlikely to have keyboards that provide function keys, the application should avoid using function keys as the only means of performing essential operations.

2.2.5.2 Control Key Shortcuts

CTRL+letter combinations may also be used as keyboard shortcuts. Table 2.7 lists recommended CTRL+letter shortcuts that are equivalent to Edit menu commands. If an application does not provide the function corresponding to a particular recommended key combination, the application should avoid assigning that key combination to any other function.

Table 2.7   Recommended CTRL+Letter Shortcuts[4]

Key	Function
CTRL+Z	Undo
CTRL+X	Cut
CTRL+C	Copy
CTRL+V	Paste

Table 2.8 lists additional suggested shortcuts.

Table 2.8   Suggested CTRL+Letter Shortcuts

Key	Function
CTRL+N	New
CTRL+O	Open
CTRL+P	Print
CTRL+S	Save
CTRL+B	Bold*
CTRL+I	Italic*
CTRL+U	Underline*

* These shortcuts are suggested for text-formatting applications, in the context for which they make sense. Applications may use other modifiers for these operations.

---

[4] The shortcuts for Undo, Cut, Copy, and Paste are new in Windows version 3.1. For backward compatibility, we recommend that applications designed to run under Windows version 3.0 also support the old shortcuts: Undo = ALT+BACKSPACE, Cut = SHIFT+DEL, Copy = CTRL+INS, and Paste = SHIFT+INS. However, the old shortcuts should not be documented in user manuals or listed on the Edit menu.

2.2.5.3 Guidelines for Assigning Shortcut Keys

When selecting function keys or key combinations as shortcuts for actions in an application, designers should observe the following guidelines:

- Assign single keys for frequently performed, small-scale tasks. For example, if the application contains a command to split a window, a single function key (such as F6) can be used to move from one pane to another.

- Assign SHIFT+key combinations for actions that extend or are complementary to the actions of the key or key combination used without the SHIFT key. For example, if F6 moves from one pane to another in a clockwise direction, SHIFT+F6 moves through the panes in a counterclockwise direction.

- Assign CTRL+key combinations for infrequent actions, or for tasks that represent larger-scale versions of the tasks assigned to the unmodified key. For example, in text, LEFT ARROW moves left by one character, whereas CTRL+LEFT ARROW moves left to the beginning of the current word (see Table 2.5). Similarly, F6 moves clockwise from one window pane to the next, whereas CTRL+F6 moves clockwise from one document window to the next (see Table 2.6). Following the guideline for SHIFT listed above, SHIFT+CTRL+F6 moves counterclockwise through the document windows.

- Avoid assigning ALT+letter combinations; they are used as mnemonic access characters for menus and dialog box controls. You may use ALT+function key combinations, except for ALT+F4 and ALT+F6, which have the recommended assignments listed in Table 2.6. In addition, the ALT+TAB, ALT+ESC, and ALT+SPACEBAR assignments are reserved for system use.

- Function keys should not be the first choice for shortcuts. When deciding between a function key shortcut (with or without a modifier key) and a modifier+letter shortcut, remember that function key shortcuts are easier to localize but may be harder to remember because they are mapped to functions arbitrarily. Modifier+letter shortcuts offer more mnemonic possibilities and are easier to reach on the keyboard. Applications should use function key shortcuts in addition to modifier+letter shortcuts, or for operations that do not have good mnemonics.

2.2.6 Escape Key

The ESC key is generally used to terminate a function in process or to cancel a direct manipulation operation. It is also used to press the Cancel button in a dialog box. Thus, ESC is in some sense the opposite of ENTER, which presses the default button.[5] Applications may also allow the user to press ESC to cancel or to interrupt lengthy operations, such as printing.

---

[5] If Cancel is the default button (has a bold border), the ENTER key is used to press it.

General Techniques

Just as the visual components of the interface should be consistent from application to application, the techniques employed by the user to interact with interface components should also remain consistent. If visual consistency is reinforced with procedural consistency, users can develop habits that transfer from one application to another.

In general, mouse and keyboard access to an application should be parallel. However, techniques should be optimized for the input device. Well-tailored techniques should prevail over strict parallelism between mouse and keyboard techniques.

3.1 Selection

For the object-action paradigm (see Chapter 1, section 1.1.2) to work properly, the user must be able to select the object to which an action will apply. Applications therefore need to provide a means for the user to select data.

3.1.1 Concepts of Selection

Many selection concepts—highlighting, types of selection, adjusting selections, deselection, and selection modes—apply to both mouse and keyboard selection.

3.1.1.1 Indicating Selections: Highlighting

When data is selected, it appears highlighted. The appearance of highlighted text depends on the abilities of the system and the display. On monochrome displays, reverse video (XOR) should be used to indicate selected data (see Figure 3.1). On gray-scale displays, the selection should be marked with a shade of gray. On color displays, a highlight color should be used. Graphics may be highlighted in these same ways or by the addition of rectangles with resizing handles; these two methods may also be combined.

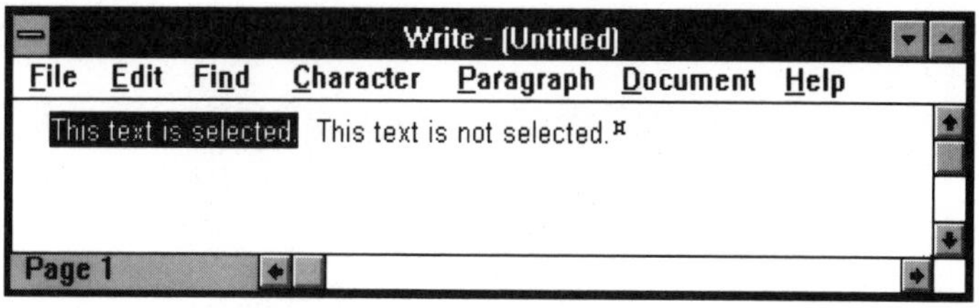

Figure 3.1   Indicating Selection by Reverse Video

Text in dialog boxes should be highlighted with the same methods used in data windows. For toolboxes and other collections of 3-D buttons, the depressed-button graphic should be used to indicate selection. For value set controls that do not contain 3-D buttons, an outline frame in the highlight color should surround the chosen value.

As a general guideline, selection highlighting should be visible only while the window is active. Leaving the selection highlighted in an inactive window is acceptable in special cases, when it is useful to the user. For example, if the user chooses a command with a dialog box that affects the selection, the selection can remain highlighted while the dialog box is open.

3.1.1.2 Types of Selection

Selections may be classified as single (involving only one item) or multiple (involving several items). Multiple selections may be further classified as contiguous or disjoint, depending on their spatial ordering. These selection types are illustrated in Figures 3.2, 3.3, and 3.4.

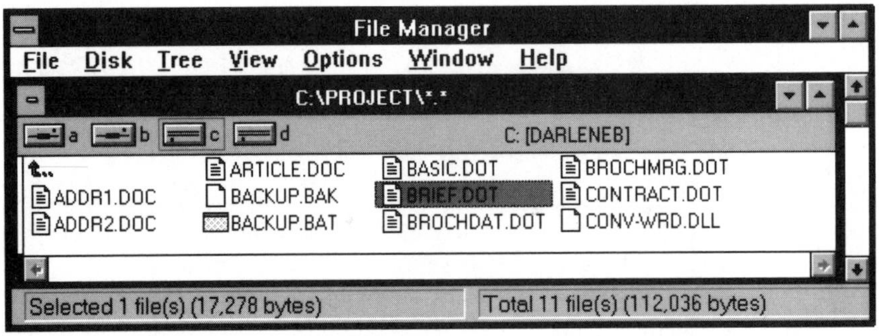

Figure 3.2   Single Selection

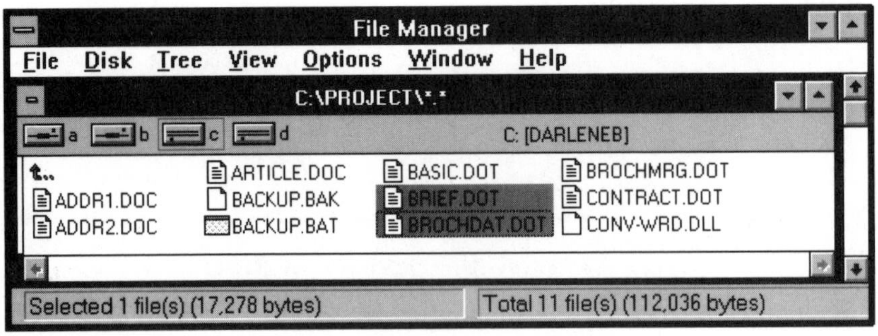

Figure 3.3   Contiguous Multiple Selection

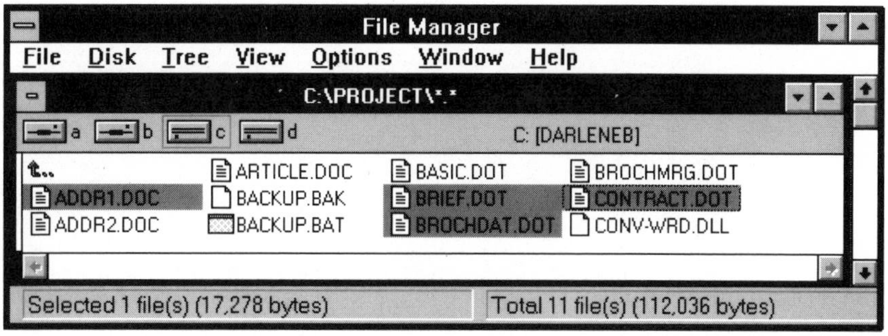

Figure 3.4   Disjoint Multiple Selection

Multiple selections may also be classified as homogeneous or heterogeneous, depending on the properties of the selected items. For example, if a text selection contains both plain and bold text, the selection is heterogeneous with respect to character attributes (see Figure 3.5). The user makes homogeneous and heterogeneous selections in the same way. In some cases, however, controls that indicate property settings for a selection should reflect the difference between the two types (see Chapter 6, sections 6.1.2 and 6.2).

Mouse and keyboard techniques for single and multiple selection are explained in sections 3.1.2 and 3.1.3.

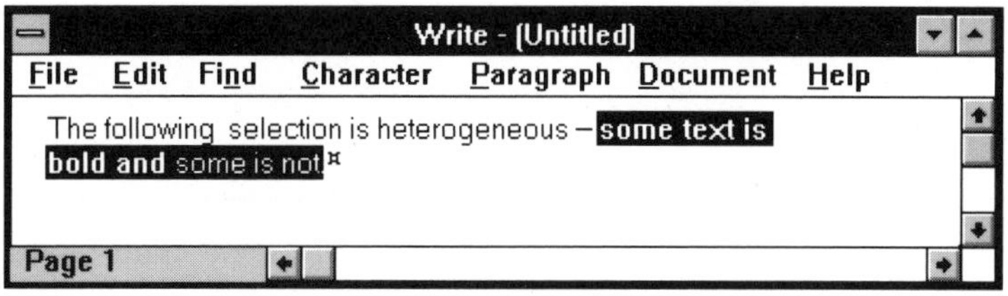

Figure 3.5   Heterogeneous Selection

3.1.1.3 Adjusting Selections

Adjusting a selection means changing its size relative to its original starting point, or anchor point. The opposite end of the selection is the active end of the selection. To extend the selection, the user moves the active end away from the anchor point. To shorten the selection, the user moves the active end toward the anchor point. When the active end reaches the anchor point, the selection is an insertion point. From the insertion point, the user can extend the selection in either direction, but not in both directions at the same time.

3.1.1.4 Deselection

To deselect data, the user generally clicks to make a new selection. Deselecting does not delete the data. Deselection is overridden when the user applies disjoint selection techniques. Multiple-selection list boxes (see Chapter 6, section 6.3.2) also override this default deselection behavior.

In multiple (contiguous or disjoint) selections, items can be deselected individually or as a group. To deselect a single item with the mouse, the user uses CTRL+click.[1] This combination toggles the selection state of the clicked item while preserving the selection state of all other items. For example, if an item is selected, CTRL+click deselects it without affecting other items. If the item is not selected, CTRL+click selects it. To deselect all currently selected items, the user clicks to make a new selection.

3.1.1.5 Selection Modes

Selection techniques that set a special selection mode are generally not recommended, except in special contexts. A selection mode should only supplement standard selection techniques. If selection modes are used, a visual cue should indicate that the mode is active. For example, if the mode affects a data window, a mode indicator should be displayed in the status bar (if there is one).

Extend mode is an example of a selection mode. In Extend mode, selection behaves as if the SHIFT key is locked down for all direction keys and mouse actions. The key for toggling Extend mode is F8.

3.1.2 Mouse Selection

Mouse selection relies on the basic techniques of clicking and dragging. In general, clicking selects a single item or location, and dragging selects a range consisting of all items between the button-down and button-up locations. If dragging is already used by the application for item movement, outline selection (see section 3.1.2.4) may be used to select a range of items.

---

[1] See section 3.1.3 for keyboard deselection techniques.

3.1.2.1 Mouse Selection Techniques for Item-Oriented Applications

In most item-oriented applications, selections made with the mouse can be contiguous (range selection) or disjoint (selected items are separated by nonselected items). The user clicks mouse button 1 without a modifier to make contiguous selections. Disjoint selection requires the use of the CTRL key with mouse button 1. Selections can be adjusted by using the SHIFT key with mouse button 1.[2]

Table 3.1 describes how these techniques work.

Table 3.1 Mouse Selection

Action	Clicked Item Is...	Resulting Selection =	Focus Moves To...	Anchor Moves To...
Click	Selected	Clicked item	Clicked item	Clicked item (anchor = focus)
SHIFT+click	Set to selection state of anchor item (which currently may or may not be selected)	Extend anchor item's selection state to clicked item (and all items in between). (If the anchor was not selected, SHIFT+click selects only the current item.)	Clicked item	No movement (anchor remains where it was)
CTRL+click	Toggled	Existing selection +/- clicked item	Clicked item	Clicked item (anchor = focus)
SHIFT+CTRL +click	(Same as SHIFT+click)	Existing selection +/- new range, as defined for SHIFT+click	Clicked item	(Same as SHIFT+click)

---

[2] Graphic objects in drawing applications have no well-defined ordering, so selection adjustment is not defined for such objects. In these applications, SHIFT+click may be defined as equivalent to CTRL+click (= disjoint selection).

3.1.2.2 Mouse Selection Techniques for Text-Oriented Applications

Table 3.2 shows the recommended techniques for contiguous text selection with the mouse.

Table 3.2 Mouse Selection in Text

Action	Resulting Selection=	Focus Moves To...	Anchor Moves To...
Click or drag	All text from button-down to button-up (for a click, this is just an insertion point)	Beginning of selection	Button-down
SHIFT+click or SHIFT+drag	All text between anchor and button-up location*	Beginning of selection	No movement
CTRL+click or CTRL+drag	Entire sentences from button-down to button-up	Beginning of first selected sentence	Beginning of selection**
Double-click or Double-drag	Entire words from button-down to button-up	Beginning of first selected word	Beginning of selection**

* Optional enhancement: If the original selection unit was a word (selected by double-click or double-drag) or sentence (selected by CTRL+click or CTRL+drag), the selection can be extended beyond the button-up location to the end of the unit.

** In some applications, the anchor point encompasses the entire selection; a subsequent SHIFT+click extends the selection from the most distant end. The Windows Write program puts the anchor point at the beginning of the selection.

3.1.2.3 Margin Selection in Text and Arrays

Margin selection is a convenient way to select large sections of data with a single click. In text, margin selection is used to select lines, paragraphs, or entire documents; in data arrays, it is used to select rows and columns. The margin selection area can be the row and column labels of a data array or the left margin area between the left window frame and the left edge of text.

Table 3.3 shows the actions that should be assigned to the mouse for margin selection in text and in data arrays.

Table 3.3 Margin Selection in Text and in Data Arrays*

Action in Margin	Resulting Selection=	Focus Moves To...	Anchor Moves To...
Click or drag	Entire lines, rows, or columns next to pointer from button-down to button-up	Beginning of selection	Beginning of selection
SHIFT+click or SHIFT+drag	Entire lines, rows, or columns between anchor and button-up location	Beginning of selection	No movement
CTRL+click or CTRL+drag			
in text documents	Entire document	Beginning of document	Encompasses entire document
in data arrays	Previous selections + entire rows or columns next to pointer from button-down to button-up	Beginning of new selection	Beginning of new selection
Double-click or Double-drag			
in text documents	Entire paragraphs from button-down to button-up	Beginning of first selected paragraph	Beginning of first selected paragraph**
in data arrays	(Same as click or drag)	(Same as click or drag)	(Same as click or drag)

* In this table, for text documents, the beginning of a selection is defined as the part nearest the beginning of the document. For data arrays, the beginning of a selection is defined as the cell nearest the button-down point.

** In some applications, the anchor point encompasses the entire first selected paragraph; a subsequent SHIFT+click extends the selection from the most distant end of that paragraph. Windows Write puts the anchor point at the beginning of the first selected paragraph.

3.1.2.4 Outline Selection of Graphical Objects

Outline selection is an extended form of drag selection that is particularly useful for graphical objects when normal drag selection conflicts with moving objects with the mouse. This technique allows the user to drag an outline frame (rectangular or free-form) around an object, a set of objects, or a portion of an object. When the mouse button is released, existing selections are removed, and all objects falling completely within the frame (including the frame itself) are selected. When outline selection is used with bitmaps rather than with graphical objects, only the bits falling within the frame are selected.

3.1.3 Keyboard Selection

Keyboard selection uses a selection cursor (such as a dotted outline box or an insertion point) and a form of selection emphasis (see section 3.1.1.1) to indicate the data that will be affected by any action the user initiates. There are two types of keyboard selection techniques: implicit and explicit.

- In implicit selection, the item under the selection cursor becomes selected automatically when the selection cursor moves; thus, the selection cursor and emphasis travel together. In general, implicit selection is associated with contiguous selection.

- In explicit selection, the selection cursor moves independently of the selection emphasis. That is, the item under the selection cursor is selected and given the selection emphasis only when the user explicitly selects it with the Select key.[3]

The Select key may also be used to deselect selected items; in other words, it toggles selection states. In general, explicit selection/deselection is associated with disjoint selection, in which selected data can be separated by nonselected items, and a new selection can be added to existing selections at any point in the data.

3.1.3.1 Keyboard Techniques for Contiguous Selection

In text-oriented applications, the user can select a single insertion point with the keyboard by simply navigating to the desired location. The anchor point is set at the new location. A range of characters is selected by using the SHIFT key in conjunction with navigation keys. While holding down the SHIFT key, the user can press any navigation key (or any combination of keys defined for navigation, such as CTRL+END; see section 3.3 for details). The cursor then moves to the location implied by the navigation key, and all characters between the anchor point and the destination are selected. The anchor point does not move.

The SHIFT+navigation technique works similarly for item-based applications, with one difference: Whereas in text, all characters between the anchor point and the destination are selected, in item-based applications, the fate of the items between the anchor and the destination depends on the selection state of the anchor item. If the anchor item is currently selected, all items in the range become selected; if the anchor item is not currently selected, all items in the range become deselected.

---

[3] By default, the Select key is the SPACEBAR, unless this assignment conflicts with the needs of an application in a specific context.

3.1.3.2 Keyboard Techniques for Disjoint Selection

The keyboard technique for making disjoint selections relies on using SHIFT+F8 to enter Add mode. In this mode navigation keys move the focus without affecting existing selections or the current anchor point. Pressing the SPACEBAR toggles the selection state of the item at the new location and sets a new anchor point there. SHIFT+navigation (while still in Add mode) can then be used in the usual way to extend the selection from the new anchor point, without disturbing previous selections. Pressing SHIFT+F8 again toggles the application out of Add mode.

Disjoint selection may also be permitted in list boxes, to let the user select multiple items from the list (see Chapter 6, section 6.3.2).

3.2 Focus

The "focus" represents the part of the interface that will receive the next piece of input if no navigation occurs before the input is generated. For mouse input, the focus always coincides with the pointer (button down) location. For keyboard input, the focus depends on the context:

- In text, the focus is shown by an insertion point, which indicates where newly typed characters will be inserted.

- In spreadsheets, the focus is shown by a highlighted cell border, which marks the cell that will receive typed input and that will be affected by commands.

- In menus and dialog box controls, the focus is shown by an active control indicator (described below), which identifies the control that will be affected by the Select key or by typing.

The active control indicator can be an insertion point, highlighting, or a dotted box:

- The insertion point is used for text boxes.

- Text highlighting is used in conjunction with the insertion point when the text box is initially activated (for example, with ALT+mnemonic). If the user then clicks the mouse over the text, the highlighting disappears, and the insertion point is placed at the click location.

- The dotted box is used for option buttons, check boxes, and command buttons; the box should enclose the label of the control (see Figure 3.6). The dotted box is also used for list boxes. In single-selection lists, the box should enclose the list item that is currently selected or that will be selected if the user presses the Select key. In multiple-selection lists, the box should enclose the item whose selection state will be toggled by pressing the Select key. In extended-selection lists, the box should enclose the most recently selected item, unless the list is in Add mode. In Add mode, the box should enclose the item whose selection state will be toggled by pressing the Select key. (For further information on these types of list boxes, see Chapter 6, section 6.3.)

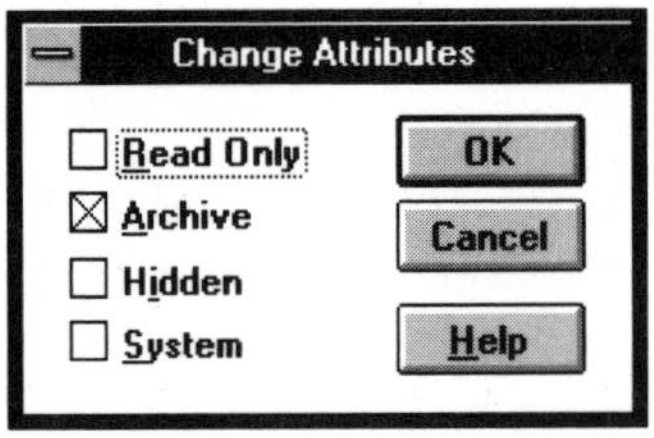

Figure 3.6   Use of Dotted Box to Indicate Active Control

When a window is reactivated, the focus and the selection should be displayed in the same locations as when the window was last active.

3.3 Navigation

The user can move the input focus by navigating on the screen.

3.3.1 Mouse Navigation

Navigation with the mouse is simple: When the mouse is moved left or right on the user's desktop, the pointer moves left or right on the screen; when the mouse is moved away from or toward the user, the pointer moves up or down. By moving the mouse, the user can move the pointer to any location on the screen. Mouse navigation typically does not affect existing selections.

3.3.2 Keyboard Navigation

Keyboard navigation is more complicated than mouse navigation. Several keys, such as HOME, END, and the arrow keys, are dedicated to keyboard navigation with respect to data items, as discussed in Chapter 2, section 2.2.4. Unlike mouse navigation, keyboard navigation changes the selection, unless Scroll Lock mode is in effect (see Chapter 2, section 2.2.3).

Keyboard navigation to controls relies primarily on mnemonic access characters and on the TAB, ENTER, and ESC keys. With mnemonic access, when the user presses ALT plus the mnemonic letter in a control label, the focus moves to the control, and the control is selected or operated. For example, "F" is the mnemonic assigned to the File menu, so ALT+F[4] selects and opens that menu.

---

[4] ALT,mnemonic (for example, ALT,F) is also supported.

The ALT+mnemonic method can also be used to navigate among controls in dialog boxes. If the control that currently has the focus does not capture character input (that is, if the control is not a text box, spin box, list box, or combo box[5]), mnemonics can be used without ALT. For example, the user can select the Ṉo command button in a dialog box by pressing ALT+N or just N. If the user presses the mnemonic for a dimmed control, the focus remains unchanged, and no action is taken on the control.

When the ALT+mnemonic method is used to reach and operate a control, the focus usually remains on the control after the operation (unless the operation closes the dialog). However, if the focus is on a list box and the user uses ALT+mnemonic to reach and operate a button associated with the list, the focus should return to the list after the button is pressed. For example, if the user adds or deletes individual items from a list box by selecting an item, then pressing the Add or Delete command button, the focus should return to the list after each Add or Delete operation so the user can select another item.

Dialog boxes also permit the use of the TAB, ENTER, and ESC keys for navigation:

- TAB moves the active control indicator among the available controls without operating them (the SPACEBAR can then be used to operate the control that currently has the focus).
- The ENTER key chooses the default command button.[6]
- The ESC key chooses the Cancel or Close command button if the dialog contains one of these buttons.

Table 3.4 lists recommended keyboard navigation techniques.

---

[5] See Chapter 6 for descriptions of these dialog box controls.

[6] The OK command button is typically the default, but a different button may be assigned instead if it is a more likely choice for the dialog. Users can also change the default button through keyboard navigation.

Table 3.4   Keyboard Access to Controls

Key	Action
ALT+mnemonic	Navigates to and selects or operates control. The mnemonic letter can be pressed without ALT if the current focus does not capture character input.
TAB	Moves focus to next control. The order of movement is generally from left to right and from top to bottom.*
SHIFT+TAB	Moves focus to preceding control. The order of movement is generally from right to left and from bottom to top (that is, the reverse of TAB).*
SPACEBAR	▪ Selects or operates a command button, option button, or check box that has the focus (equivalent to a mouse click on the control). ▪ In text box, combo box, or spin box, inserts a space character.
Arrow keys	▪ In text box, moves insertion point left and right. ▪ In group of option buttons, selects next button, wraps around at top and bottom of group. ▪ In group of check boxes, moves to next box without changing its state, wraps around at top and bottom of group. ▪ In list box, selects next item; stops at top and bottom of list. ▪ In spin box, increases or decreases value; wraps around at highest and lowest values.
DOWN ARROW	Opens a closed drop-down list box or drop-down combo box that currently has the focus.** If the drop-down control is already open, DOWN ARROW navigates within the list (see Chapter 6, section 6.3.1.3).
ALT+DOWN ARROW	Toggles state (collapsed or expanded) of active drop-down list box or drop-down combo box.***
ALT+UP ARROW	Toggles state (collapsed or expanded) of active drop-down list box or drop-down combo box.***
Alphanumeric keys	▪ As a mnemonic, see "ALT+mnemonic" at the beginning of this table. ▪ In list box, selects next item beginning with the character. ▪ If typed as the first character in the text field of a combo box, scrolls list to the first item beginning with the character.
ENTER	Presses default command button, if one is implemented. Otherwise, presses selected command button.
ESC	Presses the Cancel or Close button, if one is implemented.

* Unless there is a more logical order defined within the context of the operation.

** This is a new recommendation. Windows version 3.1 includes a style bit to enable the new behavior.

*** The use of F4 to open and close drop-down controls is no longer recommended.

3.3.3 Keyboard Access to Control Bars

ALT+mnemonic access can also be used in control bars (for example, ribbons and rulers; see Chapter 4, section 4.2.8), for labeled non-button controls, and for textual buttons (that is, buttons labeled with ordinary text rather than graphics).

- Purely graphical buttons (for example, for drawing tools) do not require mnemonic access. Keyboard access to these buttons is defined by the application.

- If the button label contains an underlined letter, the ALT+mnemonic method must be implemented. (In addition, applications may define CTRL+letter shortcuts.)

- Formatting buttons in ribbons and rulers often contain graphical text and thus are neither purely textual nor purely graphical. These buttons usually represent commands that are available through shortcuts, even when the control bar is not visible. These shortcuts typically use CTRL+letter (see Chapter 2, section 2.2.5.2). If the control bar happens to be visible, the command invoked by the shortcut also depresses the button. In a sense, then, the button is accessed by CTRL+letter. This behavior is acceptable; it is not necessary to add ALT+mnemonic as an additional access method.

Toolboxes are primarily a mouse-oriented feature, so keyboard access to toolboxes is not crucial and need not be implemented. For advanced users, however, keyboard access can be useful. Experienced graphics designers use a two-handed mouse/keyboard technique for operating the tools without interruption: the left hand presses keys to switch between tools while the right hand remains on the mouse to use the current tool. For example, the right hand draws a rectangle with the rectangle tool, the left hand presses a key to switch to the paint bucket tool, and the right hand fills the rectangle. Keyboard access to toolboxes can also be used to facilitate automated software testing.

The following methods are recommended for applications that choose to implement keyboard access to toolboxes:

- If the user will not typically access tools when the focus is in a text field, assign single-letter mnemonics to tools (for example, T for a text tool, R for a rectangle tool). Pressing the letter chooses the corresponding tool and depresses its button. The focus need not be in the toolbox when the letter is pressed. This method provides the most rapid access.

- If the user will need to access tools when the focus is in a text field, use CTRL+letter mnemonics instead of unmodified letters.

- The preceding methods provide rapid, direct access to tools, but they are somewhat obscure, because the mnemonic letters are not visible anywhere and so must be memorized. The following method provides a more standard way of accessing tools through the keyboard; it requires knowledge of standard Windows techniques for switching between non-document windows or between panes:

  - If the toolbox is a separate palette window, use the standard method of switching between non-document windows (ALT+F6) to activate the window.

  - If the toolbox is a pane (or a fixed child window) within the main application window (for example, as in Windows Paintbrush), use the standard method of switching between panes (F6 or SHIFT+F6) to move the focus to the pane. (TAB may also be used, as in the File Manager.)

  - Once the toolbox is active, use the arrow keys to choose a tool. When the arrow keys are used to move from one tool button to another, the new button is depressed and the old button returns to the up position.

3.4 Transfer Interface

The current interface for transferring objects and data from one location to another relies on a combination of techniques, such as direct manipulation (see the next section) and Edit menu commands (for example, Cut, Copy, Paste, and Paste Link; see Chapter 5, section 5.4.3, and Chapter 9, section 9.3.2).

3.5 Direct Manipulation

Direct manipulation is frequently used for moving an object from one location to another: The object is dragged with the mouse and dropped into the new location. For example, some file management programs use drag-and-drop to move files between directories on the same disk. Similarly, many word-processing applications use drag-and-drop to move tab stops on rulers.

Drag-and-drop can also be interpreted as a Copy or Link operation, if the context makes those operations more appropriate than a Move. For example, in the File Manager, dragging a file icon to a directory on a different disk causes the file to be copied rather than moved. Dropping a file icon from the File Manager into the Program Manager creates a link in the Program Manager. When more than one interpretation of drag-and-drop is possible for a given context, the application should provide a way to override the default interpretation by using modifier keys in conjunction with dragging.

In some cases, drag-and-drop is interpreted as "use the drop target to process (for example, open or print) the thing that was dropped." For example, dropping a document icon on the minimized Print Manager means "print the document."[7] In the File Manager, dropping a document icon on the associated application icon means "open the document for editing within the application." Dropping a document icon onto any non-document area of an open application window—for example, onto the title bar, menu bar, status bar, application workspace in a multiple-document interface (MDI) application, and so on—has the same meaning. Suppose, however, that the document icon is dropped into the document area of an open application window (for example, the text area of a mail memo or the drawing area of a paint program); in other words, the document icon is dropped into an open document. In this case, if the open document supports object embedding (see Chapter 9), the dropped document is copied (embedded) into the open document and displayed as an icon.[8]

Direct manipulation is particularly useful in pen-based systems, because manipulation of objects with the pen is even more direct than manipulation with the mouse. For a discussion of direct manipulation in pen applications, see Chapter 10, section 10.2.1.2.

---

[7] This feature is new in Windows version 3.1.

[8] What actually happens is that the file represented by the document is encapsulated in a "package"; this package is then embedded into the open document. To the user, however, the iconic document simply appears to have been embedded into the open document. For more information on packages, see Chapter 9.

Table 3.5 summarizes current recommendations for drag-and-drop operations with unmodified mouse button 1, originating in Windows version 3.1 File Manager.

Table 3.5   Unmodified Button 1 Drag/Drop Operations Originating in the File Manager

Dragged Object	Drop Target	Result
Document icon (representing, for example, a text document, spreadsheet, or drawing)	Open document	If target document supports embedding, embed dropped document and display it as an icon. Otherwise do nothing.
	Non-document area of open application window (for example, title bar, menu bar, status bar, MDI application workspace)	If dropped document is readable by application, open document within application window.
	Print Manager	Print document: 1. Launch associated application and bring window to top. 2. Load file. 3. Display dialog if Print command within application would normally lead to dialog; user can change settings if necessary. 4. If user presses Cancel, close application immediately without printing; if user presses OK, print file and then close application.
Any file icon (representing, for example, a document or application)	Application icon in File Manager	Start application, using dropped document as initial file. For example, if text document is dropped on word-processing application, open document for editing.
	Program Manager group window (open or closed)	Create program item in Program Manager that points to the file.

3.5.1 Differentiating Selection from Direct Manipulation

There are a variety of techniques for differentiating selection of an object from direct (drag) manipulation. It is difficult to come up with universal conventions that can be applied to all types of selected objects. In addition, it is common practice to use the left mouse button (button 1) to do this. This means that selection and drag manipulation may overlap. To distinguish these operations, it is recommended that a drag handle appropriate to the object be displayed when the object is selected. This can be a frame around the object or on the object. In many cases, it can simply be the object itself (for example, in icons). Some form of visual feedback (that is, a change in the pointer or in the object) should be provided on the button-down transition as a clue to the user that the operation will not result in selection, but instead in some form of direct manipulation. This visual feedback should be maintained during the operation, until the button-up (release) transition.[9]

Objects are not limited to displaying their drag manipulation handles when selected; it depends on the object. For example, window title bars and size borders act as manipulation handles that are always present. However, for many objects in context, the drag handle should only be displayed when the object is selected to avoid visual clutter.

3.6 Providing Feedback

Applications should keep the user informed about the current state of the application by providing feedback. Feedback can inform the user that a particular mode has been entered, acknowledge a command, point out an error, track the progress of an operation, and so on. Visual (either graphical or textual) feedback is the most common, but auditory feedback is also useful.

3.6.1 Visual Feedback

The user interface is primarily visual, therefore visual feedback is particularly effective. This type of feedback can consist of graphics, text, or both.

3.6.1.1 Graphical Feedback

Many of the interface techniques discussed previously in this chapter involve graphical feedback. Text selection, for example, is confirmed by the appearance of a highlight color; shifts of the focus are shown by movements of a dotted box, selection highlight, or insertion point. Another useful type of graphical feedback involves changing the pointer to reflect the current state of the application.

---

[9] This does not preclude changing the pointer further during the operation, if the nature of the destination or pressing a modifier key might change the operation while the button is down.

3.6.1.1.1 Pointers   The mouse is linked with a graphic on the screen called the pointer. By positioning the pointer and clicking the buttons on the mouse, the user selects data, icons, commands, and controls to initiate and complete actions. The shape of the pointer changes according to the current action or the current pointer position on the screen. Applications should use only as many pointer shapes as needed to inform the user about current status and position; too many shapes can confuse users.

Tables 3.6 through 3.9 list the suggested pointer shapes and their uses. Applications may supplement these pointers with modifier keys or add visual effects, such as animation. Animation is an effective technique for drawing the user's attention and conveying information, but should be used with caution. Remember that the main function of a pointer is to communicate information, so the movement of the pointer should not be distracting.

Table 3.6   Suggested Selection Pointers

Shape	Screen Location	Selects...
⬉	Over items or controls	Items and controls*
⬉	Left margin of document or cell	Lines, rows, cells
I (I-beam)	Text	Insertion point or characters
↓	Top of table column	Column

* Also used for resizing and moving objects; see Tables 3.7 and 3.8.

Table 3.7   Suggested Pointers for Resizing

Shape	Screen Location	Resizes...
⬉	On resize handles	Graphics*
↔	Along column gridlines	Column width
↕	Along row headings	Row height
⬍	Top or bottom window border	Window vertically
⬌	Left or right window border	Window horizontally
⬈	Lower left or upper right window border	Window diagonally
⬊	Upper left or lower right window border	Window diagonally

* Also used for selecting and moving objects; see Tables 3.6 and 3.8.

Table 3.8   Suggested Movement Pointers

Shape	Screen Location	Movement
▷	On item	Unconstrained*
↕	On item	Vertical
↔	On item	Horizontal
✥	On item	Vertical or horizontal

* Also used for selecting and resizing objects; see Tables 3.6 and 3.7.

Table 3.9   Other Suggested Pointers

Shape	Screen Location	Use
⧖	Anywhere	Indicates that a lengthy operation is in progress
▷?	Any region or control	Click activates associated help
⧂	Inside window	Zooms
✥	Inside window	Indicates that direction keys will move or resize window
⊘	An object that can't have other objects dropped on it	Indicates that dropping is not allowed*
⫶	Split box in vertical scroll bar	Splits window horizontally
⊣⊢	Split box in horizontal scroll bar	Splits window vertically

* Typically, the pointer does not change over valid drop targets (unless the nature of the operation changes). For additional information, see section 3.6.1.1.2.

3.6.1.1.2 Feedback for Drag-and-Drop Operations   For drag-and-drop operations, applications should provide the following types of visual feedback:

- As the pointer moves, the object, its outline, or some reasonable representation should move along with the pointer.

- The user should get feedback, if possible, over the target area. For example, possible destination locations can be highlighted or otherwise emphasized as the object is dragged over them.

- The pointer should change to the shape shown in Table 3.9 over invalid drop targets.

- As an optional but recommended extension, the pointer can be changed during the drag operation to reflect the operation (for example, Move, Copy, or Link) that will result if the object is dropped in the current location.

3.6.1.1.3 Progress Indicators When an operation that takes more than two or three seconds is in progress and the user cannot continue working in that application until the operation finishes, the application should display the hourglass pointer over the inaccessible window to indicate that the user must wait. If the user moves the mouse pointer to a second, accessible window, the normal pointer for that window should appear. If possible, the first application should let the user access the system or work in another application.

If an operation takes longer than five seconds and prevents access to the window during that time, the application should display a progress indicator in addition to the hourglass pointer.[10] Progress indicators reassure the user that the program is working on the task and indicate how much of the job has been completed. A progress indicator must be dynamic (applications should not use static messages or pictures) and the feedback from the progress indicator must be unmistakable and obvious.

The best progress indicators are graphical. For example, progress can be represented by a long rectangular bar that is initially empty but is gradually filled with color from left to right as the operation proceeds (see Figure 3.7). Animated cursors can also be used as graphical progress indicators.

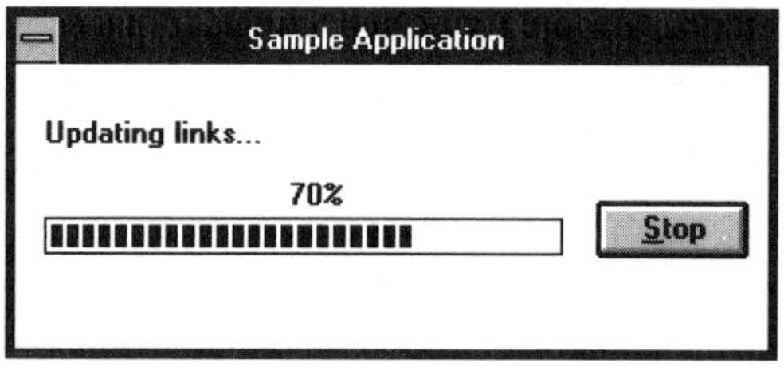

Figure 3.7   Graphical Progress Indicator

If graphical indicators take too long to update, percentage-complete messages can be used as a supplement or replacement. If the extent of the task is not known in advance, or a particular stage in the task takes a long time to complete (thereby freezing the percentage), an elapsed-time message can be used instead of the percentage-complete message. If the task is very long, applications may consider breaking it down into subtasks and using progress indicators for each subtask.

---

[10]Unless posting and updating the progress indicator takes longer than the process itself.

When possible, progress indicators should include a way of pausing and resuming lengthy operations, in case the performance of the rest of the system is adversely affected. The recommended way to provide pause/resume capability is through a command button whose label alternates between Pause and Resume. If the nature of a particular operation does not permit pause/resume functionality but does allow an irreversible interruption of the operation, the progress indicator should contain a command button labeled Cancel or Stop. The Cancel button interrupts the operation and returns the application and data to its state before the operation was invoked. If a return to that state is not possible, Stop should be used instead of Cancel. The Stop button interrupts the operation but does not reverse any changes that the operation has already caused.

3.6.1.1.4 Flashing for Attention

An application can flash for attention when it is inactive but needs to display a message dialog. If the application is a window, it flashes its title bar. If it is minimized, it flashes its icon. When the user activates the application, the message dialog is displayed. The flash rate should be based on the cursor blink rate (which can be adjusted by the user through the Control Panel).

The flashing technique has two advantages. First, it preserves the user's control over the work flow by allowing the response to the message to be postponed. Second, by preventing the sudden display of the message dialog while the user is typing, this technique ensures that the dialog is not accidentally closed by keypresses stored in the type-ahead buffer.

As an additional warning mechanism, the flash is accompanied by one or two beeps.[11] This audible warning also allows applications to attract the user's attention when their title bars or icons are not visible.

3.6.1.2 Textual Feedback

Graphical feedback can be highly effective and can enhance the visual appeal of applications, but sometimes it is not precise enough to convey details. In such cases applications should provide textual feedback in the form of brief messages. Such messages are usually provided in the message bar or status bar at the bottom of the screen (if provided; see Chapter 4, sections 4.2.6 and 4.2.7) or in modal dialog boxes called message dialogs (see Chapter 7, section 7.1.4).

Application designers should observe the following guidelines when writing message text:

- State the information, problem, or error clearly. Avoid technical descriptions or explanations, and use straightforward, easily understood terminology.
- Limit the message to two or three lines. Status bar messages should not exceed one line.

---

[11]Note that the warning beep can be turned off by the user.

- If possible, suggest a remedy for error situations. For example, if the user enters a measurement that is too large, the error message should not only say "Measurement is too large" but should also ask the user to enter a number within a specified range (for example, "Please enter a number between 1 and 10").

- Avoid phrasing that blames the user or implies user error. For example, use "Cannot find *<file name>*" instead of "File name error." Avoid the word "error" altogether.

- Use "Cannot" instead of "Can not" or "Can't."

- Use "Not enough _____ to _____" (for example, "Not enough space on drive C: to save file SAMPLE.TXT") instead of messages such as "Disk is full, save not completed," "Insufficient memory," or "Low on memory."

- Do not use colons in a message. For example, use "Cannot read *<file name>*" instead of "Cannot read: *<file name>*."

- If a message is accompanied by a message number, place the number at the end of the message text.

- Left-align multiple-line messages.

3.6.2 Auditory Feedback

The most common auditory feedback is the system beep, which can alert the user to minor and obvious errors (for example, invalid keypresses or mouse clicks). For example, if the user scrolls to the top of the data and clicks the up scroll arrow or presses the UP ARROW key, the system can beep instead of displaying a message. The beep can also be used with other forms of notification, such as flashing (discussed in section 3.6.1.1.4) or message dialogs.

System beeps should be used sparingly for the following reasons. First, many users (as well as non-users within hearing distance of the computer) find beeps annoying. Second, frequent use of the system beep jades the user to its sound. Third, beeps are ephemeral messages that leave no trace. If the user is momentarily away from the computer or if working conditions prevent the user from hearing the beep when it occurs, the beep will fail to convey its message. Finally, the user can turn the warning beep off, so it is not a reliable source of feedback.

3.7 Editing Text

Applications should implement the following text-editing actions to let users edit text in windows and dialog boxes:

- When text is being inserted with only an insertion point, the insertion point moves one character to the right for each character the user types, and new characters appear to the left of the insertion point.

- With any selection, inserting text (by typing or by using the Paste command) removes the selected text and reduces the selection to an insertion point. The insertion point then acts as described above. The deleted text does not go into the clipboard.

- With any selection, deleting text (by means of BACKSPACE, DEL, or Cut) removes the selected text. The Cut command and its shortcut (CTRL+X) put the deleted text on the clipboard; the BACKSPACE and DEL keys do not.

- When the selection is only an insertion point, BACKSPACE deletes the character to the left and moves the insertion point to the left. The deleted character does not go onto the clipboard.

- When the selection is only an insertion point, DEL deletes the character to the right of the insertion point, which does not move. The text to the right of the insertion point moves to the left to fill the place of the deleted character. The deleted character does not go onto the clipboard.

- Whenever text is deleted, close the gap. (This operation is sometimes called "auto-joining.")

- The following behavior is suggested when the user selects one or more words by double-clicking or double-dragging: If there is a space after the last word in the selection, the space is also selected. If the user then deletes the selection, the fate of this trailing space depends on how the selection was deleted.

  - If the user deleted the selection by using BACKSPACE, DEL, or Cut, the trailing space is also deleted. As a result, the words before and after the deleted selection are separated by one space instead of two. In most cases, this result is precisely what the user wants.

  - If the user deleted the selection by typing one or more new words, the trailing space is not deleted. Instead, it is retained to separate the last new word from the first word following the selection. Otherwise, the user would have to reinsert the space so that the two words do not run together.

- As an acceptable extension to the basic text-editing model, applications can implement a user-selectable mode that provides nondestructive typing and backspacing when text is selected.

3.8 Moving Objects

Objects are moved by clicking and dragging either within their filled area or on their border with mouse button 1. Users should not be required to click on other regions (for example, special borders or handles) to move objects.

3.9 Text Frames

Text frames are sizable fields into which the user can type text (see Figure 3.8).[12] They are generally rectangular, but other shapes may also be used. When the user resizes the text frame, the text is rewrapped to fit within the new borders of the frame.

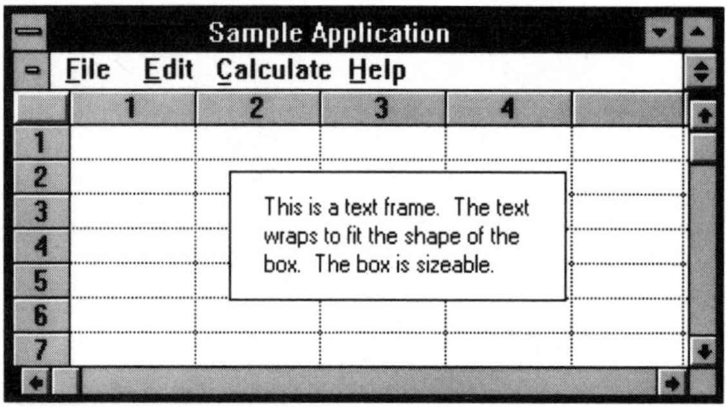

Figure 3.8   Text Frame

The pointer appears as an arrow over an unselected text frame; the user can click to select the frame. A selected frame has resize handles. While the frame is selected, the pointer changes to an I-beam over the text, to an arrow over the border, and to a resize pointer over a resize handle. These selection rules follow the general principle for hierarchical selection of objects and their contents: The first click selects the container, and the second click selects its contents.

When the pointer is an I-beam, the user can follow standard text selection techniques to select the text within the frame. Formatting commands apply whenever the text frame or the text within it is selected. If the user selects text from the frame, then moves the pointer over the border of the frame, the pointer changes back to an arrow to allow the frame to be selected.

---

[12]A text frame is a dynamic form of an edit field and should not be confused with the text box discussed in Chapter 6, section 6.4.

The user can move a text frame by dragging its border. If the frame is not currently selected, the user can also move the frame by clicking and dragging within it.

The Cut command, the Copy command, and the DEL key apply to the text frame as a whole if the frame is selected but does not contain a selection or an insertion point. If text is selected within the frame, the commands apply to the text. If there is no selection but there is an insertion point, Cut and Copy are dimmed, and DEL deletes the character after the insertion point.

When a text frame contains selected text or an insertion point, its resize handles are not displayed. Clicking in the empty space below the text places an insertion point at the end of the text.

Windows

Windows are the fundamental interface objects through which data, commands, and controls are organized and presented to the user.

4.1 Screen Window Types

There are three types of screen windows: application windows, document windows, and dialog boxes.[1]

4.1.1 Application Windows

Application windows are movable and sizable, and they constitute the fundamental visual framework for data and commands in an application. Virtually all activity in an application takes place within the application window, with three exceptions:

- If the application window has been resized so that one of its dialogs or menu drop-downs will not fit inside it, the dialog or menu drop-down may appear partially outside the window.

- Movable dialogs may be moved outside the application window.

- The Help window is actually an independent application window and may be moved outside the primary application window.

Figure 4.1 shows an example of an application window. Application windows should always include a sizable frame and a title bar that contains at least the title of the application, a Control-menu box, and Minimize and Restore (or Maximize) buttons. Application windows may also include some or all of the other components discussed in section 4.2.

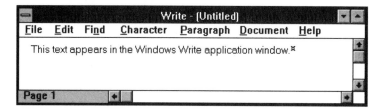

Figure 4.1 Application Window

[1] Dialog boxes are different in many ways from other types of windows and will be discussed separately in Chapter 7. Toolboxes and palettes are examples of control bars and may appear in any type of window. These are discussed in section 4.2.8.

If an application that works with documents operates only on a single view of a single document at any given time, the document is displayed in the application window, and the document title is displayed in the title bar after the application title, separated from it by a hyphen (for example, "Write - REPORT.WRI"). Applications that allow users to open multiple views or multiple documents simultaneously can display the different views or documents in document windows, using the multiple document interface (MDI) instead of the single document interface (SDI).

4.1.2 Document Windows (MDI)

The multiple document interface (MDI) allows an application to manage multiple documents, or multiple views of the same document, within the main application window (also known as the "workspace"). These views or documents are displayed in separate windows called "document windows." Document windows may also be referred to by names that describe the contents of the windows more specifically, such as "group windows" (in the Windows Program Manager), "directory windows" (in the Windows File Manager), or "worksheet windows," "chart windows," and "macro windows." Figure 4.2 illustrates an MDI application, the Windows Program Manager, in which two group windows, Main and Accessories, are open.

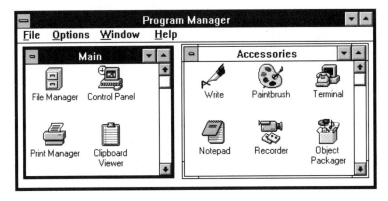

Figure 4.2   MDI: Windows Program Manager with Two Group Windows Open

4.1.2.1 Characteristics of Document Windows

A document window can be manipulated in the same way as the application window. Because document windows are movable and sizable, they have a title bar and a sizable window frame. All document windows must appear within the borders of the application window. If the user reduces the size of the application window so that it is smaller than a document window, the document window should be clipped.

A document window title bar should contain a caption that displays the name of the document in the window, a Control-menu box, and a Maximize button. Optionally, applications can allow document windows to be minimized; in this case, a Minimize button should appear on the title bar of the document window, to the left of the Maximize button (see Figure 4.2). Minimized windows are represented as icons. Applications should define a particular space within the application window (typically at the bottom) where the icons are placed by default, even if the user is allowed to move the icons elsewhere within the application window.

The Control menu for a document window parallels the Control menu for the application window. The document window Control menu can be accessed from the keyboard by typing ALT,HYPHEN (or ALT+HYPHEN). The document's Control menu can also be accessed through arrow keys, like other menus. Control menus are discussed further in Chapter 5, section 5.4.1.

If an MDI application has a menu bar, it should appear within the application window, along with any application controls (such as ribbons or toolboxes) that apply to all document windows. Placing these controls in the application window makes them available to all document windows. Scroll bars, however, are not shared among document windows; each document window should have its own scroll bar. The application window has a scroll bar if icons representing minimized document windows are hidden below the bottom of the application window, or if the application window contains a maximized document window that requires scrolling. The title bar of the application window should identify the application name but not the current document name, unless that document window is maximized.

4.1.2.2 Maximizing Document Windows

The multiple document interface allows the user to maximize the current document window to increase the amount of data that can be viewed. Maximization has the following effects, which are illustrated in Figure 4.3:

- The data from the document window is displayed in the application window.

- The document window and all associated controls disappear, except for the document window Control-menu box, which is displayed to the left of the first menu in the application window menu bar.

- The document title is placed in the application window title bar after the application name, separated from it by a hyphen (exactly as in an SDI application).
- A Restore button for the document window is added at the extreme right of the menu bar.

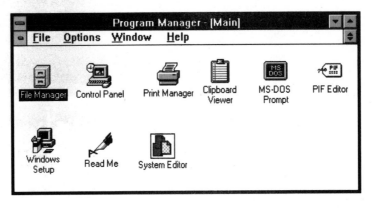

Figure 4.3   MDI: Windows Program Manager with Maximized Group Window

If the user maximizes one document window and then switches to another, the second window should also be maximized. Similarly, restoring one document window should restore the others to their pre-maximized sizes and locations.

4.1.2.3 Saving Window Configurations

If the user switches from an MDI application to another application (leaving the first application running) and then switches back, the arrangement of all document windows should be preserved, and the window that was active before the switch should be reactivated. If the user restarts an MDI application after exiting it, the application should provide a way to restore the workspace to its previous configuration, with all document windows arranged exactly as before. If the application cannot automatically preserve the information for restoring the previous configuration, a "Save Workspace" command may be added to the File menu. (This command generally follows the conventions of the Save command.) The user opens this file after restarting the application to restore the previous configuration. If the user opens other document windows before restoring the configuration, the new windows should be left open when the configuration is restored.

4.1.3 Launching Files Associated with MDI Applications

Suppose that one instance of an MDI application is running, and the user opens a file associated with the application by one of the following methods: by double-clicking an icon in the File Manager or Program Manager; by using the File Open command in the File Manager or Program Manager; or by dragging the file icon onto the application icon in the File Manager. In these cases, should a new instance of the MDI application be started, or should the file be loaded into a new document window within the existing instance?

Plausible scenarios favor each alternative. For example, if the user double-clicks on one file and then on another one immediately afterward, it is likely that he or she wants to load both files into the same MDI window. On the other hand, suppose that the user left the MDI application running earlier in the day with several files loaded into it. If the user later double-clicks on another file associated with the same application, it is not at all clear that he or she wants the new file loaded into the old instance; the new file may be part of a completely unrelated task.

Worse yet, suppose that the MDI application is a spreadsheet and that the newly opened file is an autoexecute macro that will operate on any other files that happen to be in the same MDI workspace. If the newly opened macro file were loaded into a spreadsheet window left over from some previous unrelated task, the results could be disastrous. Workspace configuration files are another type of file that the user almost certainly would not want to open inside an existing MDI window.

The cases mentioned so far—leftover unrelated instances, autoexecute files, and workspace configuration files—all argue that files opened from the Program Manager or the File Manager should be opened within new rather than existing instances of the application. An additional argument for the new-instance behavior is that all SDI applications already behave that way because they have no other alternative. Furthermore, the new-instance behavior is more consistent with the probable future movement away from an application-oriented window grouping model and toward a task-oriented model. Finally, the user who wants to open multiple files within the same MDI window can always do so by using the File Open command within the MDI window (rather than within the File Manager or the Program Manager). Because this method is available from the MDI application, it is not as important to provide same-instance functionality from the File Manager or from the Program Manager.

For these reasons, it is suggested that files opened from the File Manager or the Program Manager start a new instance of the associated application, except in the following cases:[2]

- File already open: If the file is already open, its window should be surfaced. If the file is already open inside an MDI application that contains several open document windows, its window should be brought to the front.

- Memory problems: If the file is associated with an MDI application that does not use memory efficiently when multiple instances are running, the application should make an intelligent decision about what to do. For example, the application could check available memory to see whether running one more instance would be likely to cause problems. If so, the application could display a warning and, if possible, offer the user a choice between starting a new instance or loading the file into an existing instance.

4.1.4 "Always on Top" Windows

Windows version 3.1 includes support for creating windows that remain on top of other windows.[3] This feature is useful for keeping control bar (palette) windows or modeless dialogs on top of the windows that they modify. However, the facility must be used carefully because these windows also sit on top of other application windows. Therefore, an application that uses this feature should change this attribute or hide supplemental windows when the main application window is inactive (or minimized).

It is suggested that windows that always exist on top of others be given a gray shadow (along the right and bottom edges) to visually distinguish them from other windows.

If the "always on top" feature is used on the main window of an application, the user should be allowed to change the attribute so that the window will not always float on top of other application windows. It is recommended that such applications include an "Always on Top" entry in the window's Control menu. Selecting this option should place a check mark next to the menu item and should set the attribute for the window. Selecting it again should remove the check mark and reset the window to overlap with other windows.

---

[2] One additional case will not be supported in Windows version 3.1, but is likely to be supported in future releases: Suppose that the file is part of a multiple selection in the File Manager. Any files in the selection that are associated with the same MDI application should be opened within the same MDI window, with each file in a separate document window. This behavior will provide a quick way to open a group of related files within the same window, without using the File Open command inside the MDI application.

[3] This feature should be used carefully because it is not explicity supported in Windows versions prior to 3.1.

4.2 Screen Window Components

All windows should include a frame, a title bar[4], and a control-menu box. In addition, windows may include some or all of the following components: menu bar, scroll bar, message bar, status bar, and control bars. Some of these components are illustrated in Figure 4.4.

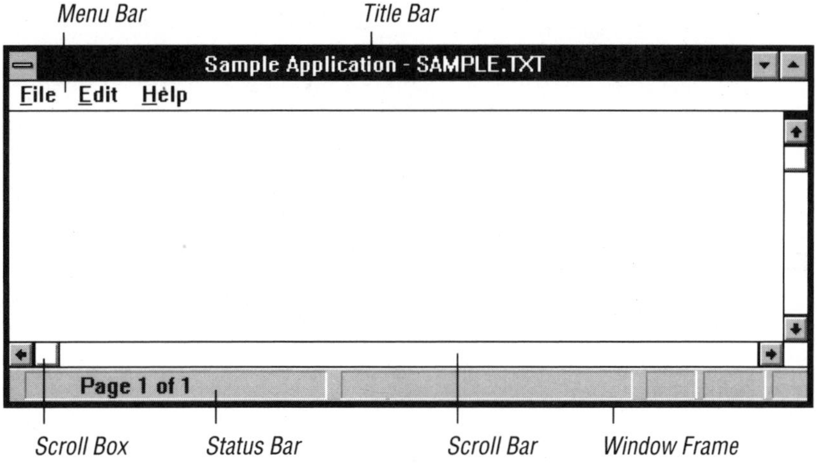

Figure 4.4   Screen Window Components

4.2.1 Window Frame

All windows have frames, except when they are maximized and fill the entire screen.[5] The frame defines the window boundary and distinguishes each window from others that it overlaps.

The frames of dialog windows are not sizable. The frame of a modal dialog is a one-pixel-thick line (default color black), inside which is a thicker border that shares the color of the title bar (default color blue). The frame of a modeless dialog is a single-pixel black line without an inner border. This difference in frames provides a visual cue for determining whether a dialog box is modal or

---

[4] Modal dialog windows in many current applications do not include title bars, but it is recommended that title bars be added to all dialogs. The title bar serves two purposes. First, it clarifies the purpose of the dialog by including the name of the command that invoked the dialog. Second, the title bar allows the user to move the dialog to reveal data obscured by the dialog. Adding a title bar to a dialog requires only trivial changes to program code.

[5] When the window is maximized to fill the entire screen, its frame is coextensive with the screen edge.

modeless; the distinction was previously provided by the presence or absence of a title bar (see footnote 4). For more information on types of dialog boxes, see Chapter 7, section 7.1.

Most other windows have sizable frames that consist of parallel one-pixel-thick lines inside of which is a thicker border. (Colors and border thickness are based on the settings in the Windows Control Panel.) When the pointer is moved over the border, it changes into the appropriate resizing pointer (see Chapter 3, Table 3.7). The user can then drag the frame with the mouse to resize the window. During the drag operation, a gray "ghost" frame moves under the pointer; when the mouse button is released, the window is redrawn at the new size. Dragging on the corners resizes the window horizontally and vertically at the same time; dragging on the horizontal parts of the frame resizes the window vertically, and dragging on the vertical parts of the frame resizes the window horizontally.

4.2.2 Title Bar

As shown in Figure 4.4, a title bar can contain a title, a Control-menu box (also known as a System-menu box), a Minimize button, and a Maximize button (if the window is not maximized) or a Restore button (if the window is currently maximized) . If the window is not maximized, the user can drag the title bar with the mouse to move the window to a new position. During the drag operation, a gray "ghost" window frame moves under the pointer; after the mouse button is released, the window is redrawn at the new location.

4.2.2.1 Title

The title is a unique label that identifies the application window. This identification is especially important when the user is working with multiple applications. At a minimum, the title should contain the name of the application with the first letter capitalized (for example, "Write"). The title may also contain additional text. For example, if the application operates on data files, the application name should be followed by a hyphen and the current file name (in uppercase letters and including any extension). The storage place for the file should not be included, because it may be long and it can intimidate inexperienced users who have no use for the information.[6] If no file is currently active, the title should contain a placeholder document name, such as (Untitled), Document$n$, Sheet$n$, Chart$n$, and so on, where n indicates a number (as in "Document1"). The placeholder should be in mixed case to provide a visual cue that it is not an official file name.

---

[6] Users can obtain this information from the Save As dialog box.

If a dialog box is displayed as the direct result of a command, its title should match the command name, unless the command name does not contain enough information. For example, in the Windows Write program, the dialog box produced by the File menu Open command is entitled Open, but the File menu Repaginate command is entitled Repaginate Document. If an intermediary message dialog is displayed before the dialog box (for example, to warn the user to save changes before executing the command), the application identifies itself in the title of the message dialog.

4.2.2.2 Control Menu

The Control menu contains commands for manipulating—changing the size, changing the position, and closing—the main window. These commands are described in Chapter 5, section 5.4.1. The Control menu is primarily an aid for keyboard users; the mouse has direct access to the actions the commands perform, but can also be used to select the commands from the Control menu. For example, the mouse user can double-click the Control menu to close the application window, instead of choosing the Close command from the Control menu.

4.2.2.3 Minimize, Maximize, and Restore Buttons

The Minimize, Maximize, and Restore buttons are graphical equivalents of the corresponding commands on the Control menu. Clicking the Minimize button reduces the main window to its minimum size (usually an icon) and hides all associated windows, including floating palettes or toolboxes. Clicking the Maximize button enlarges the main window to its maximum size; on many screens, the maximized main window fills the entire screen. When the user clicks the Maximize button or chooses the Maximize command from the Control menu, the Restore button replaces the Maximize button. When the user clicks the Restore button or chooses the Restore command, the Maximize button replaces the Restore button. Fixed-size windows do not have Maximize buttons.

4.2.3 Menu Bar

When a menu bar is used to provide access to commands in an application, it should be placed directly under the title bar of the application window. Document windows and dialogs do not generally have menu bars. The menu bar in the application window contains the titles of the menus provided by the application. The menus themselves contain items representing commands. Applications that support more than one document type may replace one menu bar with another according to the type of document displayed in the active window. (For additional information on menus, see Chapter 5, section 5.2.)

4.2.4 Scroll Bars

Applications should provide scroll bars for all windows in which the size of the data may exceed the size of the window. Scroll bars allow the user to move data through a window with the mouse, thereby revealing previously hidden portions of the data. A window can have vertical scroll bars, horizontal scroll bars, or both. If the user would never scroll in either direction, the associated scroll bar can be omitted. If a window with a scroll bar becomes inactive, the scroll bar should be left intact.

Inactive scroll bars in lists are discussed in Chapter 6, section 6.3.1.1.

4.2.4.1 Scroll Arrows

Scroll arrows appear at each end of the scroll bar, pointing in opposite directions away from the center of the scroll bar. The scroll arrows point in the direction that the window "moves" over the data, as if the data is fixed. When the user clicks a scroll arrow, the data in the window appears to move in the opposite direction of the arrow by an appropriate amount (for example, one line for text applications and one row or column for spreadsheets). When the window cannot be scrolled any farther in one direction or the other, the associated scroll arrow should be dimmed.

4.2.4.2 Scroll Box

The scroll box (also called the elevator, thumb, or slider) moves along the scroll bar to represent how far the current view of the document is from the top (for vertical scroll bars) or from the left edge (for horizontal scroll bars). For example, if the current view is at the middle of the document, the scroll box in the vertical scroll bar is in the middle of the scroll bar.[7] This behavior of the scroll box makes it a useful indicator for keyboard users as well as mouse users. The user can also drag the scroll box along the scroll bar to move to a different view of the document. If possible, the view should be updated continuously as the scroll box is dragged. However, if the view cannot be updated continuously with sufficient speed, it can be updated in a single jump at the end of the drag operation.

If documents in a particular application (for example, a spreadsheet) by default have substantial but mostly unused length and width, the behavior of the scroll box can be modified as follows: When the scroll box is dragged to the bottom of a vertical scroll bar or to the right of a horizontal scroll bar, the document scrolls to the end of the currently used portion of the document (that is, the portion containing data) rather than to the actual limit of the document. Pressing the scroll arrow next to the scroll box continues the scrolling into the unused portion of the document.

---

[7] As an optional extension to this model, applications may implement a proportional scroll box whose size indicates what portion of the document is visible in the window.

4.2.4.3 Scroll Bar Shaft

Clicking inside a vertical scroll bar shaft scrolls the data forward by the height of
the window (if the click location is below the scroll box) or backward by the
height of the window (if the click location is above the scroll box). To help users
keep their place within a document, the new screen should preserve at least one
line of data from the old screen. In other words, if the data is scrolled forward, the
top line on the new screen should be the line that was at the bottom of the old
screen; if the data is scrolled backward, the bottom line on the new screen should
be the line that was at the top of the old screen. Similar recommendations apply to
horizontal scroll bars.

4.2.5 Split Box and Split Bar

Applications can allow the user to split the application window into two or more
separate viewing areas, called panes, as shown in Figure 4.5. For example, a user
can split a window and then examine two parts of a spreadsheet at the same time.
A split window can also display different views of the same data (for example,
text view and outline view). Applications can let the user split the window into as
many panes as is useful and practical. All panes, however, should be kept within
the window.

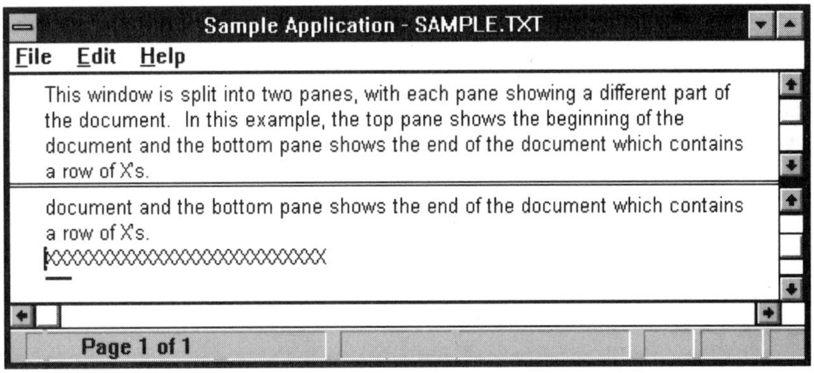

Figure 4.5   Application Window Split into Panes

For all splittable windows, applications should provide a split box. (For example,
this could be implemented as a solid box located at the top of the vertical scroll bar
and at the left end of the horizontal scroll bar beyond the tip of the scroll arrow.)
The user can drag the split box with the mouse to split the window into two separate panes at the desired split position. Double-clicking on the split box is an optional shortcut for splitting a window in the middle. Keyboard techniques for
splitting windows are discussed in section 4.3.4.

Splitting the window sets up a split bar between the panes. The split bar is a double line with a blank pixel between the lines. If the application allows only one split in a single direction, the split box appears only at the end of the split bar when the window is split. If the application allows multiple splits in a single direction, the split box appears at its original position, as well as at the end of each split bar.

When the pointer is positioned over the split bar or the split box, it changes to the split pointer (see Chapter 3, Table 3.9). After the window is split, the user can drag anywhere on the split bar or the split box with the mouse to adjust the sizes of the two panes proportionally. If the window is split both horizontally and vertically, the user can adjust multiple panes at once by dragging the intersection of the split bars. Dragging the split bar or box to either end of the workspace closes the pane in the direction of the drag. For example, if the user drags the split bar or box to the top of the window, the upper pane closes. Double-clicking on the split bar or box is an optional shortcut for closing the pane.

Applications should establish a minimum height and width for each pane. For example, the minimum height might be the amount needed to display the three parts of a scroll bar—two scroll arrows and a scroll box. The minimum width might be the amount needed to display the title bar controls and the shortest recognizable part of the title.

When the user splits a window, the application should display scroll bars to scroll each pane perpendicular to the direction of the split. For example, if the user splits a window horizontally (one pane above the other), each pane should have its own vertical scroll bar. The user can operate these scroll bars independently of each other, in the same way as for a window that is not split. The panes should share a single scroll bar in the direction parallel to the split border, unless users are likely to require independent scrolling of the panes in this direction. For example, if the split is horizontal, both panes should share one horizontal scroll bar (if any) that appears at the bottom of the lower pane.

For additional information about scrolling in panes, see section 4.3.6.

4.2.6 Message Bar

The message bar is an optional component at the bottom of an active window that lets an application request information from the user or display status information about a selection, a command, or a process. The message bar is also a convenient place to explain menu and control bar items as the user highlights each item (see Figure 4.6) and to display help information. Messages longer than the message bar should be displayed in message dialogs (see Chapter 7, section 7.1.4).

The standard placement of the message bar is at the bottom of the window, but applications may allow users to select another location. The application may also provide an option for suppressing the message bar, so this area should not be used to present essential information or messages that require acknowledgment by the user.[8]

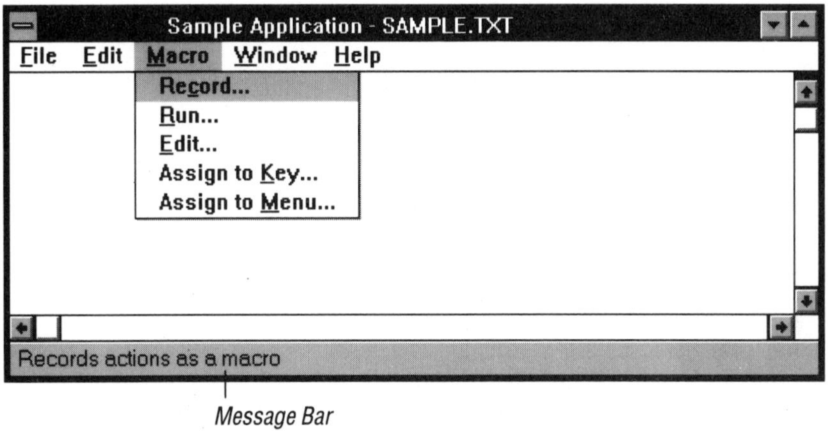

Message Bar

Figure 4.6   Message Bar

4.2.7 Status Bar

A more elaborate form of the message bar is the status bar (see Figure 4.7), an optional window component that displays information about the current state of the application.

In addition to brief messages, the status bar may include information such as the current cursor location and any current keyboard-initiated modes for selection (for example, Extend mode) and typing (for example, Overtype and Caps Lock). The "normal" modes, such as Insert or non-Caps-Lock mode, are indicated in the status bar by the absence of the indicator for the opposite mode.

---

[8] These message bar options, if provided, should be available from the dialog or menu used for other viewing options.

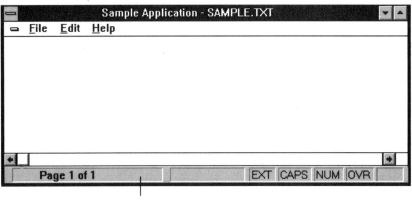

Status Bar

Figure 4.7   Status Bar

Table 4.1 lists the mode indicators that can optionally be used on the status bar. Applications can spell these out if there is enough room on the status bar. Additional keyboard modes can be indicated at the right end of the status bar, after the spaces reserved for the more common modes.

Table 4.1   Suggested Mode Indicators for Use in Status Bars[9]

Mode	Indicator
Extend Selection	EXT
Caps Lock	CAPS
Num Lock	NUM
Scroll Lock	SCRL
Overtype	OVR
Recording Macro	REC

Note: The mode indicators are listed in the order in which they should appear (from left to right) on the status bar.

Because the status bar takes up space that could be used to display data, applications should always provide a way for the user to control whether the status bar is displayed. Applications that contain a View menu should include a Status Bar toggle item on that menu.[10]

---

[9] Indicators that are not supported by the application can be omitted.

[10] The application should remember the display state for status bars, message bars, and control bars and restore them the next time the application is invoked.

4.2.8 Control Bars: Ribbons, Rulers, Toolboxes, and Palettes

Applications may implement control bars to provide quick and convenient access to frequently used choices and commands. In word-processing applications, ribbons and rulers are examples of control bars. In painting programs, toolboxes and color/pattern palettes are sometimes implemented as control bars, although they often appear as independent movable windows. Figures 4.8 and 4.9 show examples of control bars.

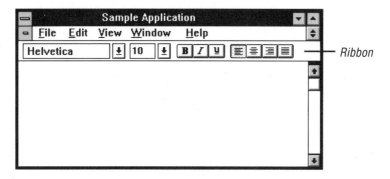

Figure 4.8   Control Bars Ribbon

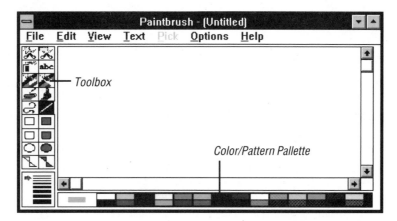

Figure 4.9   Control Bars: Toolbox and Color/Pattern Palette in Paintbrush

Control bars may occupy a fixed position within the application window, or they may be placed in a supplemental window or a dialog box and thus become movable. A movable control bar is always in front of the window to which it applies (see section 4.1.4). Thus, a control bar is never hidden by its associated parent window, although it may be hidden by one of its peers.

Movable control bars should include a miniature title bar and a Control-menu box. The title bar need not contain a title; its main purpose is to allow the mouse user to drag the control bar to a new location. The Control menu should contain the Move command to allow keyboard users to move the control bar. In addition, the Control menu may also include the Close command. Control menus for control bars typically do not include the other commands (for example, Maximize) that are found on Control menus for application or document windows (see Chapter 5, section 5.4.1).[11]

Like status bars, control bars take up space that could otherwise be used to display data, so applications should provide commands to specify which control bars are displayed. Commands for movable control bars should appear on the Window menu; commands for fixed-position control bars that are part of the main application window should appear on the View menu.

Mnemonic access to controls on control bars is discussed in Chapter 3, section 3.3.3.

4.3 Window Operations

Basic window operations include moving, resizing, and closing windows; splitting windows into panes; switching between windows or panes; and scrolling data in windows and panes. Mouse techniques for many of these operations rely on the window components described previously and have already been discussed in the sections devoted to those components. Keyboard techniques for many of these operations rely on Control menu commands and are discussed in Chapter 5, section 5.4.1. This section briefly summarizes all the major window techniques, but focuses on those not covered elsewhere—namely mouse techniques that do not involve specific window components and keyboard techniques that do not rely on Control menu commands.

4.3.1 Moving Windows

To move a window with the mouse, the user drags the title bar of the window. To move a window with the keyboard, the user chooses the Move command from the Control menu. This causes a gray "ghost" window frame to appear on top of the regular frame. The pointer changes to the window movement pointer (the last pointer shown in Chapter 3, Table 3.8). The arrow keys can be used to move the ghost frame to the desired location. Pressing ENTER completes the command and redraws the window at the new location.

---

[11]Size can be included if the window is sizable.

4.3.2 Resizing Windows

Mouse techniques for resizing windows rely on direct manipulation of window components (the window frame and the Minimize, Maximize, and Restore buttons) and have already been discussed in sections 4.2.1 and 4.2.2.3. Keyboard techniques rely on the Control menu resizing commands: Minimize, Maximize, Restore, and Size (see Chapter 5, section 5.4.1). These commands can also be accessed with the mouse.[12]

4.3.3 Closing Windows

To close a window with the mouse, the user can double-click on the Control-menu box. Windows can also be closed by selecting the Close command from the Control menu (see Chapter 5, section 5.4.1); this command can be selected with the mouse or with the keyboard.

4.3.4 Splitting Windows into Panes

The mouse user can split a window into panes by dragging the split bar to the desired location, as described previously in section 4.2.5. The keyboard user can split a window into panes by choosing the Split command from the View menu.[13] This results in a split bar being placed across the middle of the window, with a split box at the right end, inside the scroll bar. Pressing arrow keys moves the split bar up or down; pressing ENTER sets the split at the current position of the split bar.

4.3.5 Switching Windows and Panes

Either the mouse or the keyboard can be used to switch from one application window to another, from one child window to another child window within the same application, or from one pane to another pane within the same window. The reactivation of a window or pane does not affect any pre-existing selection there; the selection and focus are restored to the state that existed when the window or pane was last active.

---

[12]Some applications let users size windows by dragging the area at the intersection of the vertical and horizontal scroll bars. This behavior is a carryover from Windows version 1.0 and is neither encouraged nor supported in Windows version 3.1, particularly because this area is likely to be used for different purposes in the future.

[13]For MDI applications, the Split command can also be placed on the document window's Control menu or on the Window menu.

4.3.5.1 Mouse Techniques

- To switch from one window or pane to another, the user simply clicks on the desired window or pane.

- To switch to an application window that has been minimized, the user double-clicks on the icon; this reactivates the window and restores it to its previous size.

- To switch to an application window that is completely obscured by other windows, the user can double-click on the screen background (outside any application windows) to obtain a dialog that contains a list of running applications. (The same dialog is available from the Switch To command on the Control menu.) The user can activate the desired application by first clicking on its name to select it, and then pressing a confirmation button in the dialog. Double-clicking on the name of the application immediately activates the application without requiring confirmation.

4.3.5.2 Keyboard Techniques

Users can also switch between application windows, window panes, and document windows with the keyboard.

4.3.5.2.1 Switching Application Windows with the Keyboard Several keyboard techniques are available for switching between application windows (or between icons that represent minimized application windows):

- CTRL+ESC (equivalent to the Switch To command on the Control menu) invokes an explicit list of available applications.

- ALT+ESC and ALT+TAB (with or without SHIFT) treat the application windows as a stack of cards. The visible window is at the top and is called the active window. When a window becomes "active," it moves to the front of the stack. The keyboard user can manipulate the windows in the following ways:

  - Move the front window to the back of the stack (ALT+ESC) or the back window to the front (ALT+SHIFT+ESC).

  - Shuffle through the windows from front to back (ALT+successive TABS), or from back to front (ALT+SHIFT+successive TABS), and pick one to put at the front of the stack.

Table 4.2 describes these window-switching techniques in detail.

Table 4.2 Keyboard Techniques for Switching Application Windows

Key	Action
ALT+ESC	Moves top (active) application to bottom of stack, thereby deactivating the application. The application that was second in the stack is now on top. If its window was open, it is automatically activated; if it was minimized, it can be opened and activated by pressing ALT+SPACEBAR to display the Control menu and choosing Restore.
ALT+SHIFT+ESC	Opposite of ALT+ESC: Moves *bottom* application to *top* of stack. The application that was on top is now second and is deactivated.
ALT+TAB	Shuffles one step from front to back through stack of windows, displaying next application's name. Releasing ALT places named window on top of the stack, thereby activating it; if the window was minimized, it is restored to its previous size. All other windows remain in their previous relative stack positions.
ALT+SHIFT+TAB	Opposite of ALT+TAB: Shuffles one step from *back to front* through stack of windows, displaying next application's name. Releasing ALT activates named window. All other windows remain in their previous relative stack positions.
CTRL+ESC	Invokes a dialog that allows the user to switch to any application in a list of currently running applications.

4.3.5.2.2 Switching Window Panes with the Keyboard
Switching between panes follows either a clockwise or a counterclockwise rotation. Table 4.3 lists the relevant techniques.

Table 4.3 Keyboard Techniques for Switching Panes

Key	Action
F6	Moves clockwise to next pane of active window.
SHIFT+F6	Moves counterclockwise to next pane of active window.

4.3.5.2.3 Switching Windows within an Application with the Keyboard

Switching between windows within an application is conceptually similar to switching between panes. Consequently, the keyboard assignments for switching windows are extensions of the keys that switch panes. Table 4.4 lists these key assignments. Users can also choose a window from the numbered list provided in the Windows menu (see Chapter 5, section 5.5.2.1) through standard keyboard techniques.

Table 4.4   Keyboard Techniques for Switching Windows Within an Application

Key	Action
ALT+F6	Moves to the application's next open non-document window, such as a modeless dialog box or movable control bar.
ALT+SHIFT+F6	Same as ALT+F6, but moves through the non-document windows in the reverse order.
CTRL+F6*	Moves top document window to bottom of stack, thereby activating the formerly second document window. (Analogous to ALT+ESC for application windows.)
CTRL+SHIFT+F6*	Reverse of CTRL+F6; moves *bottom* document window to *top* of stack. (Analogous to ALT+SHIFT+ESC for application windows.)

* MDI applications only.

4.3.6 Scrolling Data in Windows and Panes

When a window or pane is too small to display all the available data, the user must be able to scroll the data to bring previously hidden portions into view.

4.3.6.1 Mouse Scrolling

The mouse can scroll data either explicitly or automatically.

4.3.6.1.1 Explicit Scrolling   Mouse techniques for explicit scrolling rely on scroll bars and have already been discussed in section 4.2.4. Table 4.5 lists these techniques. Note that explicit scrolling with the mouse does not move the cursor or change the selection.

Table 4.5   Mouse Techniques for Scrolling

Mouse Action	Effect
Click vertical scroll arrow	View moves over data in direction of arrow by height of one data unit (for example, line of text or spreadsheet cell).*
Click horizontal scroll arrow	View moves over data in direction of arrow by width of one data unit (for example, character or spreadsheet cell).*
Click scroll bar shaft between scroll arrow and scroll box	View moves over data in direction of arrow by size of window. To help user maintain context orientation, make old and new window contents overlap by at least one data unit (for example, for forward scrolling, display last line of old contents at top of new contents).
Drag scroll box to new position in shaft	Move view to the location analogous to the location of the scroll box within the shaft (for example, middle of shaft represents middle of document). If performance permits, view should be updated continuously as box is dragged; otherwise, view can be changed in a single jump after drag is complete.

* If the data unit is very small (for example, a pixel in a graphics program), applications may choose to
  move the view by more than one unit, to make scrolling less tedious.

4.3.6.1.2 Automatic Scrolling   The mouse scrolling techniques summarized in Table 4.5 all have scrolling as their explicit goal. Users may also scroll data as a secondary result of employing mouse techniques for object selection or object movement. This type of scrolling is called automatic scrolling. For example, in word-processing applications, if the user moves the pointer to the bottom boundary of the window during text selection, the data is scrolled upward (or equivalently, the view is moved downward) to allow the selection to be extended downward. Similarly, in graphics applications, if the user drags an object to the boundary of a window, the graphics document is automatically scrolled to let the user place the object in a part of the document that was not previously visible.

4.3.6.2 Keyboard Scrolling

The keyboard can also be used to scroll data through windows. An application can provide three types of keyboard scrolling:

- Normal scrolling moves data through the window and also moves the cursor.

- Automatic scrolling moves data or text when the user presses a cursor key with the cursor at the "boundary" of the visible data. (This type of scrolling is similar to the automatic mouse scrolling described previously; the only difference is that the cursor plays the role of the pointer.)

- Scroll Lock scrolling moves the data through the window without moving the cursor.

4.3.6.2.1 Normal Scrolling   For normal scrolling with the keyboard, the user presses one of the navigation keys. These keys move the data through the window and reposition the cursor within the visible data. The application is responsible for establishing a new position for the cursor in the data when scrolling moves the current cursor position outside the view of the data. If scrolling leaves the current cursor position in view, the position need not change. The navigation keys are listed in Chapter 2, Table 2.5.

4.3.6.2.2 Automatic Scrolling   When the cursor reaches the "boundary" of the visible data, pressing the arrow key that moves the cursor toward that boundary scrolls the data by some reasonable amount—typically, the height or width of one data unit. For example, if the user presses the down arrow key when the cursor is in the last line of the window, the window scrolls by one line. If a data unit is very small (for example, a single character in a line of text that is being scrolled horizontally), the application may scroll the data by a larger amount.

Mouse and keyboard techniques for automatic scrolling can also be used for lists and for text in text boxes.

4.3.6.2.3 Scroll Lock Scrolling   Applications can also (optionally) implement scrolling that is modified by the SCROLL LOCK key. When the user presses SCROLL LOCK and then uses a navigation key, the data scrolls as described previously, but the position of the cursor does not change and existing selections are preserved. In Scroll Lock mode, scrolling with the keyboard is the equivalent of scrolling with the mouse, which also does not change the cursor position and preserves existing selections.

4.3.6.3 Linked Scrolling in Panes

In most cases, scrolling data in panes is the same as scrolling data in windows. If two panes have separate scroll bars for scrolling in a particular direction, scrolling one pane has no effect on the other. If two panes share a scroll bar for a particular direction, scrolling one pane scrolls the other by the same amount. In a few cases, however, it is useful to provide special scrolling linkages between panes.

Suppose that the user splits a window into two panes and displays a different view of the data in each pane. Scrolling the data in one pane should move the data in the other by the same amount, but because different views result in different spacing arrangements, this movement may not result in the same data being displayed in the two panes. Instead, scrolling should move the data in different amounts, if necessary, so that both panes display the same information. For example, in a word-processing program with an outlining facility, suppose the user splits the window into two panes and turns on outline view in the top pane. Scrolling the outline view to the fifteenth outline heading in the document would also scroll the text view to the fifteenth heading. The outline view would only need to scroll by a small amount (through the headings) to reach the fifteenth heading, whereas the text view would have to scroll through a larger amount (through the headings and the text) to reach the fifteenth heading.

Grid-oriented applications, such as spreadsheets and databases, may provide a special type of linked scrolling with a Freeze Panes command. Suppose that the user has a large table of data with row and column headings. If the row headings are placed in a pane at the left and the column headings are placed in a pane at the top, the Freeze Panes command links the panes so that the headings are always kept in view when the user scrolls the data within the table. For example, if the user scrolls the data pane downward, the column headings do not move (that is, they remain in view), but the row headings scroll down with the data. Similarly, if the user scrolls the data pane to the right, the row headings do not move, but the column headings scroll right with the data. Thus, the relevant row and column headings for any part of the data always remain in view. The command also prevents the data pane from being scrolled into the area shown in the heading panes. When selected, the Freeze Panes menu item changes to Unfreeze Panes to allow the command to be reversed.

Menus

A menu is a list of items from which the user can choose; each item represents a command, either explicitly (for example, Cut) or implicitly (for example, Bold—that is, "apply bold formatting"). All applications that have commands should provide menus to give the user access to the commands.

5.1 Types of Menus

An application can implement three types of menus:

- Drop-down (also known as pull-down) menus on a menu bar.
- Pop-up (also known as contextual) menus.
- Cascading (also known as hierarchical) menus.

5.1.1 Drop-Down Menus

A drop-down menu is represented by a menu title (for example, File, Edit, Help) that appears in the menu bar of an application window (see Figure 5.1).

Figure 5.1 Closed Drop-Down Menus in Menu Bar

To display the menu, the user can either click on the menu title, or press ALT followed by the underlined mnemonic access character in the menu title.[1] Figure 5.2 shows an open drop-down menu. Drop-down menus are by far the most common type of menus in current applications, but applications may also use pop-up menus and cascading menus, as discussed in sections 5.1.2 and 5.1.3.

---

[1] ALT + underlined mnemonic access character is also supported.

Figure 5.2 Open Drop-Down Menu

5.1.2 Pop-Up Menus

Pop-up menus are floating menus that appear when specifically invoked by the user. The items displayed on the menu depend on where the pointer was located when the button was pressed; hence, pop-up menus are also called contextual menus. For example, if the pointer was positioned over selected text, the menu might include text-specific commands; if the pointer was on the title bar of a window, the menu might include commands for moving and resizing the window.

Pop-up menus provide an efficient way to access commands. Because they are presented at the pointer's location, they eliminate the need for the user to navigate to a menu bar or control bar. Furthermore, pop-up menus are only displayed on demand, so they do not take up dedicated screen space.

5.1.2.1 Appearance and Location

A pop-up menu follows the guidelines for standard drop-down menus discussed in section 5.2, except that it does not have a title (see Figure 5.3).

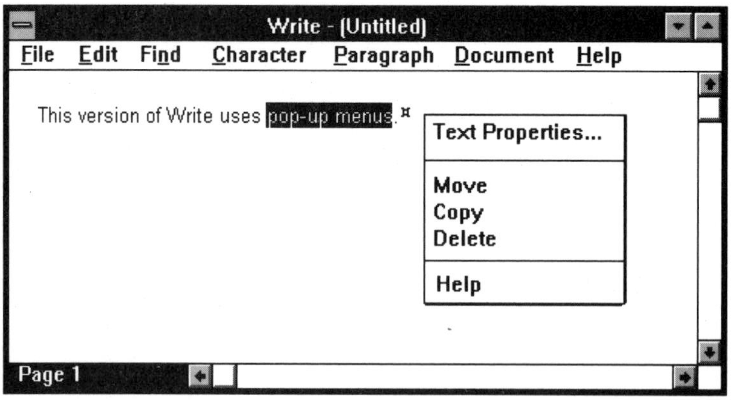

Figure 5.3 Pop-Up Menu

It is suggested that the pointer's hot spot be initially positioned close enough that the user can move into the menu easily; but not so close that the pointer is positioned on an item, thus selecting a command on the menu inadvertently. If the pointer is positioned in such a way that the menu would appear clipped or off-screen, the menu is adjusted so that it appears fully on the screen.

Pop-up menus are primarily designed for mouse users. At the present time, there is no defined keyboard interface, except for UP ARROW, DOWN ARROW, ENTER, and the ESC key, which can be used to cancel a pop-up menu. Consequently, menu items should not have mnemonic access letters or shortcut keys. For information on accessing pop-up menus with the mouse, see section 5.3.1.1.2.

5.1.2.2 Additional Guidelines

- Pop-up menus are designed to provide an efficient method for accessing common, contextual commands. For this reason, a pop-up menu should not include too many commands or multi-level cascading menus. Single-level cascading menus are acceptable and should follow the guidelines in section 5.1.3.

- If the pointer is positioned over selected text that contains heterogeneous items (for example, both text and graphics), at the minimum the pop-up menu should provide the commands that represent the intersection of pop-up commands pertaining to all items.

- Applications should not place individual property settings on pop-up menus. Commands for bold, italic, font family, style, and size are better presented in property dialogs or in special property viewers like control bars. (However, a pop-up menu can contain commands that result in property setting dialogs.)

- Applications should use pop-up menus for frequently used commands and not simply repeat the menu items from the menu bar. Pop-up menus may also include commands that logically apply to the limited context of the selected object. For example, a pop-up menu for a text selection can include separate items for a character properties dialog and a paragraph properties dialog, although these would be better presented as different "pages" of a single text properties dialog. Another example is Undo. This command may not apply to the particular selection, but to the domain to which that selection belongs.

5.1.3 Cascading Menus

A cascading or hierarchical menu is a submenu (also known as a child menu) attached to the right side of a menu item (called the parent item, in the parent menu). Figure 5.4 illustrates a cascading menu. Menu items that lead to cascading menus are marked with a right-pointing triangle after the menu item name. Cascading menus can be added to drop-down menus, contextual menus, or even other cascading menus. In general, however, the use of multilayer cascading menus should be avoided, because they compound the difficulties discussed in section 5.1.3.2 for single-layer cascades. The user drops down a cascading menu by selecting the parent menu item with any of the usual techniques for menu item selection.

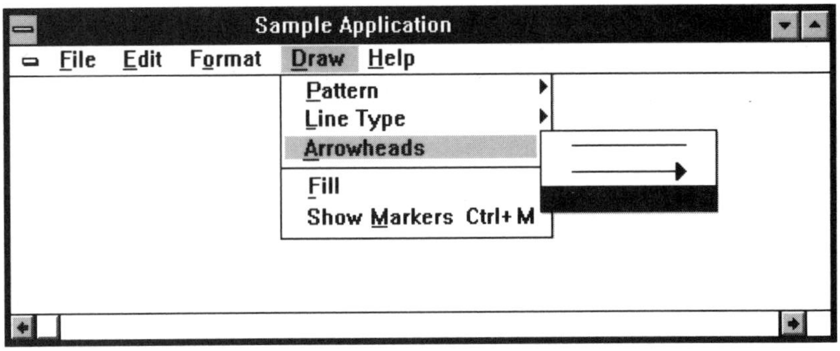

Figure 5.4   Cascading Menu

5.1.3.1 Advantages of Cascading Menus

- The top-level (parent) menus are simplified, because some commands are hidden in the cascading menu.

- More first-letter mnemonics are available. Mnemonics need only be unique within either the parent menu or the cascading menu, so there are fewer first-letter conflicts.

- High-level command browsing is easier. By dragging the mouse across the menu bar, the user can see important commands or command groups without being distracted by the details hidden in the submenus.

5.1.3.2 Disadvantages of Cascading Menus

- Access to submenu items is more difficult than access to top-level items.

  - Dragging to a submenu item requires extra coordination to negotiate the change in direction.

  - Accessing the submenu item by means of mouse clicks requires an extra click and a change in mouse direction.

- Keyboard access requires an extra keypress.

- Exhaustive command browsing is more difficult; the user cannot see all menu items by dragging the mouse across the menu bar.

Except for complex products with many commands, the disadvantages of cascading menus tend to outweigh the advantages. In general, cascading menus should be avoided whenever possible. If they are used, they are most appropriate for ordinary commands (for example, Insert Break -> Section), dialog box commands (for example, File Print -> Preview), and interdependent (one-of-N) settings (for example, Format Alignment -> Left). Cascading menus are less appropriate for independent (M-of-N) settings (for example, Format Character -> Bold), especially if users may want to choose more than one setting at a time (for example, Bold, Italic, and Underline). In such cases, it is preferable to place independent settings in a dialog or on a ribbon so that users who want to set multiple attributes can simply open the dialog once or directly access the ribbon buttons, rather than repeatedly working through two levels of menus.

5.2 Menu Components

Each menu consists of a menu title and one or more menu items.

5.2.1 Menu Titles

All drop-down and cascading menus should have menu titles. A pop-up menu typically does not have a title. Titles for drop-down and cascading menus should represent the entire menu and should reveal as clearly as possible the purpose of all items on the menu. In drop-down menus, the menu title is the term that appears on the menu bar. In cascading menus, the menu title is the name of the parent menu item.

Compound titles are acceptable (for example, Fontsize) but should be used sparingly because they may strike users as odd. The title may not contain numbers or spaces; spaces would increase the possibility of confusing a single two-word title with two one-word titles. Avoiding the use of spaces is especially important for systems that provide proportionally spaced system fonts.

As shown in Figure 5.1, each menu title should contain an underlined mnemonic access character that gives the user direct access to the menu through the keyboard. The access character should be (in suggested order of preference):

- The first letter of the menu title, unless another letter offers a stronger mnemonic link or the first letter conflicts with another menu title (for example, File and Format).

- A distinctive consonant in the title.
- A vowel in the title.

No two menu titles should use the same access character. If an application uses a non-Roman writing system (such as Kanji) but runs on a standard keyboard (such as an IBM® PC keyboard), the menu names can be given a Roman alphabetic character prefix as the menu access character.

Menu titles may be temporarily removed from the menu bar under the following conditions:

- Applications that support different document types may display different menu bars, depending on the document type that currently has the focus. In such applications, if no documents are open, there is no basis for deciding which menu bar to display. Accordingly, all menu titles should be removed from the menu bar, except for titles of menus containing commands that remain active even when no documents are open (for example, the Control and File menus).
- In applications that support only one document type, menu titles should not be removed from the menu bar when no documents are open. Instead, the titles of menus that do not contain any active commands should be dimmed.[2]

5.2.2 Menu Items

Menu items can be names of actions (for example, Cut or Paste), attributes (for example, Bold), documents (for example, "REPORT.DOC"), or windows (for example, "REPORT.DOC:2"). Menu items can also be graphical (for example, representing patterns or drawing tools). If an item has a keyboard shortcut, the shortcut should be listed on the menu next to the item. Shortcuts should be aligned with other keyboard shortcuts in the menu. By default, Windows provides left-alignment; however, applications may choose to right-align shortcuts to conserve space.

Whenever a menu contains items that fall into logical groups, the groups should be separated with a line (see Figure 5.5). The basic separator is a solid single line that spans the width of the menu. If a group has logical subgroupings, a dashed line can separate subgroups. People tend to remember information in chunks of three or four items. Accordingly, whenever possible, a menu should contain no more than four groups of items, with three or four items in each group. It is possible to implement scrolling menus that hold a very large number of items. However, such menus are not recommended, because the items are never visible at the same time and are therefore difficult to remember.

---

[2] Although the menu titles are dimmed (indicating unavailability; see section 5.2.2.3), they should still be selectable. This will allow the user to explore menu contents and to obtain help on a menu item.

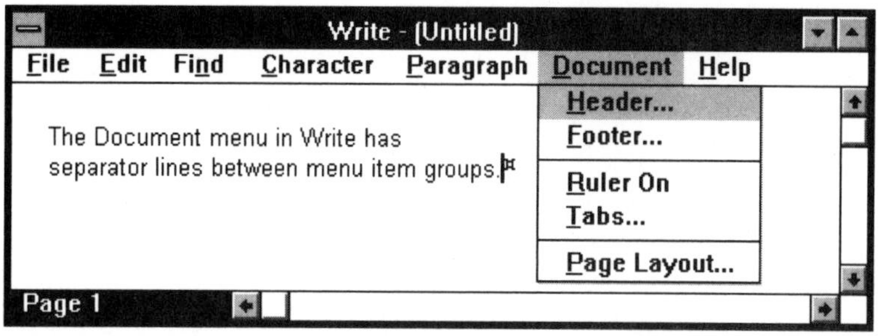

The Document menu in Write has separator lines between menu item groups.

Figure 5.5   Drop-Down Menu with Separator Lines Between Groups

5.2.2.1 Types of Menu Items

Some menu items take effect as soon as they are chosen, but others require further information before the command can be completed. Menu items that require further information are called dialog box commands, because the additional information that they require is obtained through a dialog box. The names of dialog box commands should be followed by an ellipsis ("...").[3]

Choosing a menu item results in the initiation of a process. For most menu items (for example, those for opening files, checking spelling, and so on) this is the most natural interpretation. Some menu items, however, are best understood in terms of properties rather than processes. Menu items that change attributes of data or properties of the interface are called settings. The two types of settings are independent (M-of-N) and interdependent (one-of-N).

■ Independent settings are the menu equivalents of check boxes in dialogs (see Chapter 6, section 6.2). For example, character attributes such as Bold, Italic, and Underline, if placed on a menu, would form a group of independent settings. Each of these can be changed without affecting the others, although they are related by virtue of being applicable to a single piece of text.

■ Interdependent settings are the menu equivalents of option buttons in dialogs (see Chapter 6, section 6.1.2). For example, alignment properties such as Left, Center, and Right, when placed on a menu, would form a group of interdependent settings. Selecting one setting deselects the others because a particular paragraph can only have one type of alignment.

---

[3] Some commands may or may not lead to a dialog, depending on the state of the data or on the setting of an application option. Although it would be possible to add or remove the ellipsis dynamically for such commands, the benefit to users is probably too small to justify the extra implementation cost. Instead, the ellipsis should always be omitted in such cases. This rule ensures that users will never see an ellipsis and mistakenly expect a dialog (which typically offers opportunities to cancel a command) and then be surprised when the command is executed immediately.

Groups of related (independent or interdependent) settings should be separated from other items on the menu with a single horizontal line. A group of independent settings can also include an item that turns off all the other settings in the group.

When a setting is selected, a check mark should be placed to its left, as illustrated in Figure 5.6.

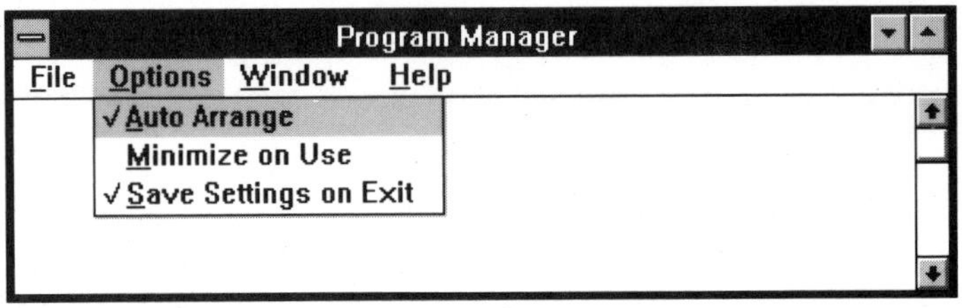

Figure 5.6   Current Settings Indicated with Check Marks

As an optional extension to this method, applications can use graphics other than check marks to distinguish between interdependent and independent settings.

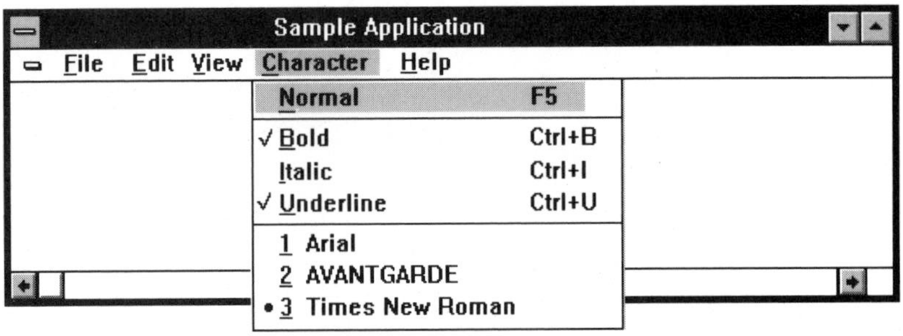

Figure 5.7   Independent and Interdependent Menu Settings

In some cases, it is appropriate to indicate the state of a setting by changing the name of the menu item rather than adding a graphic. As a rule of thumb:

■ If the two states of a setting are clear and obvious opposites, a graphic mark should be used to show the states. For example, a View menu item named Ruler should show a check mark when "on" and no check mark when "off."

- If the two states of a setting are not obvious opposites, a pair of alternating menu item names should be used to indicate the two states. For example, a naive user might guess that the opposite of a menu item called "Full Duplex" is "Empty Duplex." Because of this ambiguity, applications should pair "Full Duplex" with the alternative name "Half Duplex," rather than using graphics to indicate the alternative states. The item name does not represent the current state; it indicates the state that will be obtained by choosing the item. The same mnemonic access character should be used for both names whenever possible. This can often be accomplished by incorporating the same word as part of both names. For example, "Full Duplex" and "Half Duplex" both contain "Duplex," so D can be used for the mnemonic access character (if other menu items present no conflicts).

Sometimes the state of a setting is indeterminate—for example, when a text selection contains words with different attributes. Applications should remove the graphic marks from all groups for which the settings are indeterminate.

Applications should avoid menu items whose names and functions change depending on whether the SHIFT key is held down while the menu is opened. The shifted-state functionality of such items is normally hidden, thus it often remains undiscovered and unused. If possible, the shifted-state command should be added to the menu as a regular menu item. If this cannot be done because of limited menu space, a cascading menu that includes the unshifted- and shifted-state commands can be added as a last resort. Designers should carefully weigh the drawbacks discussed in section 5.1.3.2 before using cascading menus.

5.2.2.2 Names of Menu Items

Each menu item should be represented by a descriptive name or graphic. Applications should follow these guidelines when naming menu items:

- Item names should be unique within a menu, but may be repeated in different menus to represent similar or different actions.

- Item names may be single words, compound words, or multiple words (for example, Save As).

- Each item name should have a mnemonic access character for users who choose commands with the keyboard. The guidelines for selecting a menu mnemonic access character for menu titles also apply to menu items, except that mnemonics for menu items can also be numbers. Numbers are appropriate for menu items that are graphics or that are part of a varying list of items. For example, if a menu contains a list of file names, the names may vary, but numeric access characters for each position in the list provide constant, consistent user access to the items in the list.

- An ellipsis ("...") should follow the names of commands that require more information before they can be completed.

- Item names should be arranged in a single column. Multi-column menus are generally not recommended, except for menus that contain a long list of items (for example, sizes or amounts). If multi-column menus are used, the items should be presented in a logical order (for example, numeric ascending order would be appropriate for a list of font sizes), with the sequence organized by columns rather than by rows. For example, a numeric sequence would begin with the lowest numbered item at the upper left and proceed down all items in the first column before continuing to the second and subsequent columns.

5.2.2.3 Unavailable Items

Menu items that cannot be chosen meaningfully in the current state of an application should be disabled. To preserve the stability of the menus, applications should not remove disabled commands. Instead, the names of the commands should be dimmed to inform the user that they are unavailable. Similarly, if all items on a menu are temporarily unavailable, the menu title should be dimmed but not removed. Users can open a dimmed menu to explore its contents and to obtain help on menu items. If a user chooses a dimmed command, the application may optionally provide a brief message explaining why the command is unavailable. For example, if there is no current selection and the user tries to choose the dimmed Cut command on the Edit menu, the application could provide the message "You must make a selection before choosing Cut."

5.3 Menu Operations

Users can display menus and choose menu items with the mouse, with the keyboard, or with both methods.

5.3.1 Mouse Methods

Mouse techniques for menus rely almost exclusively on mouse button 1. The single exception is that mouse button 2 is used to display pop-up menus. The following discussion assumes mouse button 1, unless otherwise indicated.

5.3.1.1 Displaying Menus

The user must display a menu before selecting an item from it. Mouse techniques for displaying menus vary according to whether the menu is a drop-down, pop-up, or cascading menu.

5.3.1.1.1 Displaying Drop-Down Menus   To display a drop-down menu, the user uses the mouse to point to the menu title and presses the mouse button. This procedure highlights the title and opens the menu. If the user releases the button while the pointer is still on the menu title, the menu remains open so that the pointer can be moved to the desired menu item. Alternatively, the pointer can be moved to the item while the button is still held down. If the user moves the pointer to a second menu title before releasing the button, the first menu closes and the second menu opens. This lets users switch easily from one menu to another or see an overview of all menus by dragging the mouse across the menu bar. If the user drags the pointer out of a menu frame to any location other than a menu title, the menu remains open. However, if the user then releases the mouse button outside the menu frame, the menu closes without initiating any commands.

5.3.1.1.2 Displaying Pop-Up Menus   To display a pop-up menu, the user positions the mouse pointer over an object and presses mouse button 2 (for details, see section 5.1.2.1). If the user releases the button at the button-down point (or within four pixels of the button-down point), the menu remains displayed. If the user moves the pointer and releases the button outside the menu, the menu is canceled (removed from the screen). This is similar to the behavior of drop-down menus.

A pop-up menu is also canceled when the user clicks mouse button 1 or 2 outside the menu. Consequently, there can be only one pop-up menu displayed at any time. Clicking mouse button 1 outside the menu removes the menu and sets the selection to the clicked location.[4] Clicking mouse button 2 outside the menu only removes the menu.

Generally, a pop-up menu is invoked when the pointer is over an object selected explicitly with mouse button 1. (Explicit selection techniques are discussed in Chapter 3, section 3.1.2.) However, mouse button 2 can be used to select an object and display its pop-up menu simultaneously. For example, if icon A is currently selected and the user presses mouse button 2 over icon B, icon B becomes selected and its pop-up menu is displayed. Likewise, if there is no current selection, pressing mouse button 2 both selects an object and displays its menu.

If an object is selected implicitly, pressing mouse button 2 displays its menu. Implicit selection unifies the act of selection and action into one, but does not directly change explicit selections. For example, dragging a scroll box implicitly selects an object (the scroll box) and identifies its action (move). It is possible to get a pop-up menu for the scroll box by pressing mouse button 2 while the pointer is over the scroll bar. This does not result in scrolling, but simply displays the menu.

---

[4] Note that this may reset an existing selection.

5.3.1.1.3 Displaying Cascading Menus   To display a cascading menu, the user clicks on the parent item (this is the item with the right pointing triangle) or drags the mouse to that item. If the drag method is used, there is a brief pause before the submenu is displayed. This pause prevents the submenu from flashing when the user is dragging across the parent item on the way to another item. If the user releases the mouse on the parent item after the submenu appears, the submenu and the parent menu remain open. Alternatively, the user can drag the mouse into the submenu to choose an item from the submenu. If the user clicks on the parent item after the submenu has already been displayed, the submenu should disappear but the parent menu should remain open. The relationship of a submenu to its parent item parallels the relationship of a non-cascading menu to its menu title: The first click on the higher-level element opens the menu, and the second click closes the menu.

5.3.1.2 Choosing Menu Items

Mouse techniques for choosing menu items are the same for all types of menus. To select a menu item, the user releases the mouse button while the pointer is on the item. The release (that is, button up transition) is the second half of a mouse click. The press and release need not occur on the same item. In other words, the user may click on the item directly or may release the button there after dragging the mouse to the item from another location, either from the menu title or from another menu item. Whenever the mouse button is down and the pointer is over a menu item, the item is highlighted to indicate that it will be chosen if the mouse button is released.

If the menu is already open, the user can click a menu item to execute it. In drop-down and cascading menus, mouse button 1 is used for this purpose. In pop-up menus, the user can click mouse button 1 or 2.

5.3.2 Keyboard Methods

Table 5.1 lists keyboard techniques for drop-down and cascading menus. As explained in section 5.1.2.1, pop-up menus have no keyboard interface, except for UP ARROW, DOWN ARROW, ENTER, and the ESC key.

Table 5.1   Keyboard Techniques for Drop-Down and Cascading Menus

Key	Function
ALT	Toggles activation of menu bar (if inactive, activates it; if active, deactivates it and closes any open menu).
LEFT ARROW	▪ In menu bar, moves to previous menu; at extreme left, wraps to rightmost menu. ▪ In cascading menu, closes submenu but leaves parent menu open. ▪ In multicolumn menu, moves left one column.
RIGHT ARROW	▪ In menu bar, moves to next menu; at extreme right, wraps to leftmost menu. ▪ In multicolumn menu, moves right one column.
UP ARROW	▪ In open menu, selects item above current item; at top, wraps to bottom. ▪ In multicolumn menu, wraps to bottom of previous column.
DOWN ARROW	▪ If no menu is open, opens selected menu. ▪ In open menu, selects item below current item; at bottom of menu, wraps to top. ▪ In multicolumn menu, wraps to top of next column.
Mnemonic character	▪ When menu bar is active, chooses and opens menu with corresponding underlined mnemonic access character. ▪ When menu is open, chooses item with corresponding access character.
ENTER	Chooses selected menu item.
ESC	▪ If menu is open, closes menu but leaves menu bar active. ▪ If no menu is open but menu bar is active, deactivates menu bar.

A frequently used menu item may be assigned a keyboard shortcut (also known as an accelerator), which provides a single-step method of keyboard access, rather than the three-step method of ALT, menu title access character, and menu item access character. The shortcut key combination should be displayed at the first tab position after the name of the longest item in the menu that has a shortcut, and should be left-justified; spaces should not be used for alignment because they will not work properly with proportional system fonts. Key names should match those inscribed on the keyboard (for example, "CTRL" rather than "CONTROL"). CTRL and SHIFT key combinations should be displayed as "CTRL+*key*" (not "^+*key*"), "SHIFT+*key*", or "CTRL+SHIFT+*key*". As an optional alternative, applications can substitute graphical representations of key caps for the words "CTRL" and "SHIFT". If the application uses function keys for shortcut keys, the name of the key should appear as "F*n*", where *n* is the function key number. F is uppercase and there is no space between F and the number. Note that function key shortcuts (with or without modifier keys) are easier to localize than modifier+letter shortcuts.

When the user presses a shortcut key combination, the command is executed immediately; the menu that contains the command may appear highlighted but does not drop down.

Guidelines for assigning keyboard shortcuts are discussed in Chapter 2, section 2.2.5.

5.4 Standard Menus

Every application should include a set of standard menus, to give users a common starting point for each new application and to speed learning. The standard menus are Control, File, Edit, and Help. In the application window, the Control menu is represented at the left end of the title bar by a small box. For maximized document windows, it appears at the left end of the menu bar. On the menu bar, generally File appears first, followed by Edit (if supported). Help is generally the last menu on the bar. For application window Control menus, the access character is SPACE-BAR (that is, the user types ALT+SPACEBAR); for document window Control menus, the access character is HYPHEN. The access character for the File menu is F, Edit is E, and Help is H.

5.4.1 Control Menu

Every movable window (application, document, or dialog window) contains a Control menu at the left end of its title bar (see Figure 5.8). The Control menu is reserved for commands that provide keyboard control over the active window. Applications should avoid adding commands to the Control menu, unless no other menus are in the window and there are no suitable alternatives for providing access to the commands.

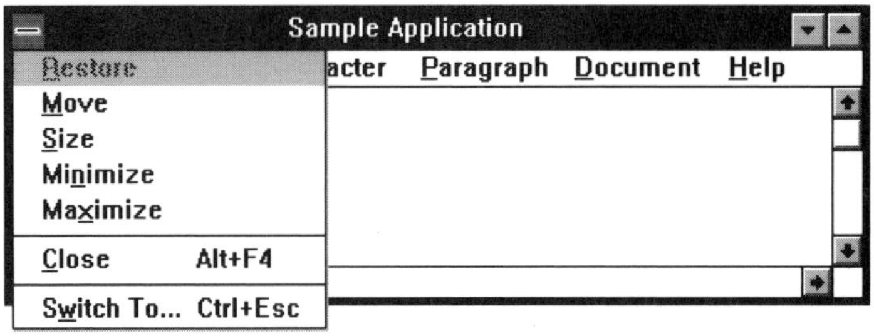

Figure 5.8   Control Menu

Control menus for dialog windows contain only Move and Close commands. The standard menu items on all other Control menus are Restore, Move, Size, Minimize, Maximize, and Close (in that order). Control menus for application windows also include a Switch To command for switching to other application windows.[5] Optionally, the Next command may also be included on the Control menu of MDI document windows to allow the user to switch to the next document window.

If one of the standard items is never used in an application, it may be removed from the menu. Tables 5.2 and 5.3 summarize Control menu items and keyboard shortcuts. Items in the first table appear on both application window and document window Control menus; items in the second table appear on only one type of Control menu. The items should appear in the order shown in the tables, with those in the first table preceding those in the second.

---

[5] The Control menu should not include a Run command. This command was included with applications delivered with runtime Windows, to allow the user to run other applications such as the Control Panel. With applications that depend on Windows version 3.0 or later, however, the Program Manager can be used to run other applications, so the Run command is no longer necessary.

Table 5.2   Control Menu Items Common to Application and Document Windows

Item	Function	Mouse Alternative*
<u>R</u>estore	Restores window from its maximum or minimum size to its previous intermediate size.	Click Restore button.**
<u>M</u>ove	Gray "ghost" window frame appears on top of regular frame; pointer changes to window movement pointer. Arrow keys move ghost frame. ENTER completes command and redraws window at new location.	Drag title bar.
<u>S</u>ize	Changes pointer to sizing mode pointer. Arrow keys move pointer to nearest border and change pointer to appropriate resizing pointer. Arrow keys then resize ghost window frame. ENTER completes command and redraws window at new size.	Drag window frame.
Mi<u>n</u>imize	Replaces window with its minimized representation (usually an icon). If window is an application window, all supplemental windows (document windows, dialogs, floating palettes, toolboxes, and so on) are hidden.	Click Minimize button.
Ma<u>x</u>imize	Expands window to maximum size.	Click Maximize button.**
<u>C</u>lose§	Closes window; displays a dialog asking user whether to save data if window contains unsaved changes. If window is an application window, all supplemental windows (document windows, dialogs, floating palettes, and so on) are also closed.§§ If window is a dialog window, committed transactions are accepted and uncommitted transactions are not accepted.	Double-click Control menu.

Note: Mnemonic access characters for menu items are underlined.

* The mouse can also be used to select menu items from the Control menu.

** Some applications support a double-click on the title bar as an equivalent shortcut for Maximize or Restore. This shortcut may conflict with future system-defined behavior for title bars and should not be documented.

§ The recommended keyboard shortcut for Close is ALT+F4 for dialog and application windows and CTRL+F4 for document windows. CTRL+ESC is the shortcut for Switch To (see Table 5.3). No other keyboard shortcuts are currently recommended for commands in this table.

§§ As a rule, the Close command removes windows from the screen, whereas the Exit command (on the File menu) ends the active application. Close is functionally equivalent to Exit when it is used to close the main application window.

Table 5.3   Additional Control Menu Items

Item	Function	Mouse Alternative*
S<u>w</u>itch To	Displays dialog that contains a list of running applications so user can switch to another application. This command is only available on application window Control menus. (Keyboard shortcut: CTRL+ESC.)	Click on desired application window; or double-click on desktop to show task list.
Nex<u>t</u>	Switches among open document windows and icons. This command is only available on document window Control menus. (Keyboard shortcut: CTRL+F6.)	Click on desired window.

Note: Mnemonic access characters for menu items are underlined.

* The mouse can also be used to select menu items from the Control menu.

5.4.2 File Menu

Applications that use data files should include a File menu, which provides all the commands the user needs to open, create, and save files. Figure 5.9 shows a standard File menu. If an application has a File menu, it should be the first menu on the menu bar (except for the Control menu for a maximized document window in MDI applications). The mnemonic access character for the File menu is F.

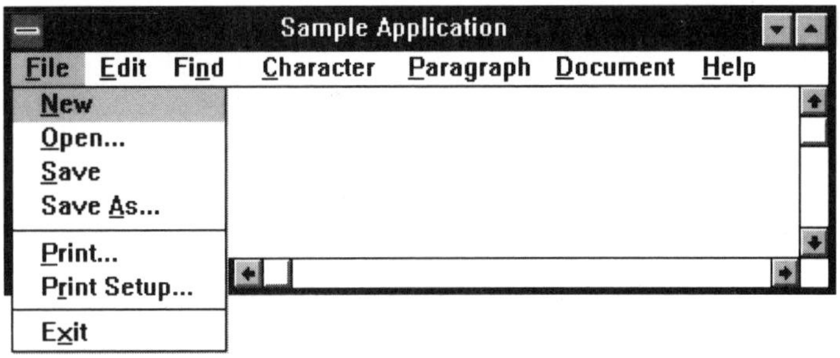

Figure 5.9   Standard File Menu

5.4.2.1 Standard Items

The File menu contains the following items in the order listed (other items may be interspersed): New or New (always the first item), Open, Save, Save As, Print or Print, Print Setup,[6] and Exit (always the last item). In applications that deal with multiple open document files (MDI), the Close command may optionally be added (after Open) to close the document file displayed in the active window. Table 5.4 lists the standard File menu items.

Table 5.4   Standard File Menu Items

Item	Function
New or New...*	Creates new document with default name such as Untitled, Document$n$, Sheet$n$, or Image$n$. Applications that can create different types of documents (for example, spreadsheets and charts) should display the standard dialog to allow user to choose type. Most common type should be default choice, and user-supplied file name should not be required; user should be able to create new document quickly by simply pressing OK after dialog appears.**
Open*	Leads to standard dialog that allows the user to open existing files, which may be located in different directories or on different storage devices.**
Save	Saves file displayed in active window. If file has never been saved, displays Save As dialog so that user can specify file name.
Save As	Displays standard dialog that allows user to save current file under a new name, in the same or different directory.
Print or Print...	Prints active document at currently selected printer; if appropriate, first displays standard dialog that allows user to set print options (for example, page range and number of copies) before printing.
Print Setup***	Displays standard dialog that allows user to switch from one printer connection to another and to specify settings for selected printer.
Exit*	Terminates application and closes all windows belonging to it. (In applications that do not include File menus, the Exit command should be the last command on the leftmost application menu, after the Control menu.)

Note: Mnemonic access characters are underlined. No standard keyboard shortcuts are currently recommended for File menu commands.

* If executing this command would cause information to be lost, the application should display a message dialog prompting user ("Save changes to *<file name>*?") before executing the command. This dialog should contain the Yes, No, and Cancel buttons for user response. For further information about message dialogs, see Chapter 7, section 7.1.4.

** If the New or Open command results in closing an existing file that has unsaved changes, the user should be queried to save the changes before the New or Open dialog is displayed.

*** Note that the name of this dialog is Print Setup, not Printer Setup. The latter name is now reserved for the system dialog that changes global printer settings.

---

[6] Not "Printer Setup"; see note to Table 5.4.

5.4.2.2 Common Optional Items

In addition to the standard items in Table 5.4, the File menu frequently includes optional items, such as the most recently used (MRU) list of files.

5.4.2.2.1 MRU List   The MRU list provides quick access to recently used files, without requiring the user to work through a dialog box to specify the location of the files. When the user chooses a file name from the MRU list, the file is opened immediately. (If the file is already open, a new window should not be opened; instead, the existing window for the file should be brought to the front.) If present, the MRU list should precede the Exit command, which is always the last menu item so that it can be easily located.

The number of files on the MRU list may vary between applications but should remain constant within an application.[7] The appropriate length for the list depends on the length of the File menu but should not be less than three or more than eight. When the user opens a file (or saves a new document in a file), the file name is placed at the top of the list, next to the number 1, which can be used as a mnemonic access character. The numbered list continues through progressively less recently opened files, with the least recently opened file at the bottom. The MRU list entry may also display all or part of the pathname, but it is preferable to display only as much of the pathname as is necessary for the user to distinguish between similar file names. Internally, however, the full pathname of the file should be recorded so that the file can be opened immediately without asking the user for storage information.

5.4.3 Edit Menu

The Edit menu follows the File menu on the menu bar. The mnemonic access character for the Edit menu is E. Figure 5.10 shows the standard Edit menu items.

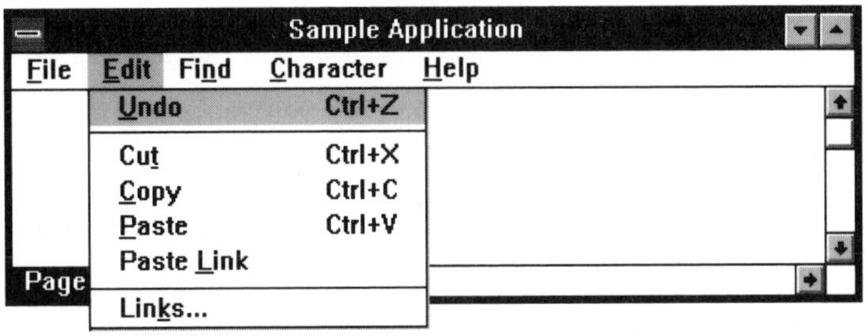

Figure 5.10   Standard Edit Menu

---

[7] Except for the first few times an application is used, when there may not be enough previously used files to fill the list.

5.4.3.1 Standard Items

The standard Edit menu provides commands for:

- Reversing the last action that altered the user's data (Undo).
- Moving, copying, and linking data and objects (Cut, Copy, Paste). These operations rely on the system clipboard, which is a common data buffer used to move data within and between applications.

Undo is always the first command on the Edit menu. The remaining standard items (which may be interspersed with others) appear in the following order: Cut, Copy, and Paste. Paste Link and Links are added in applications that support linking and embedding (see Chapter 9).

Table 5.5 lists the standard Edit menu items.

Table 5.5   Standard Edit Menu Items

Item	Shortcut	Function
Undo	CTRL+Z*	Reverses last action that altered user's data. (Applications may also provide more extensive Undo support.) Name of last action appears after "Undo" (for example, Undo Cut). If action can't be reversed, command is dimmed; optionally, name may also change to Can't Undo.
Cut**	CTRL+X*	Transfers selected data to clipboard and deletes data from current window or field.
Copy**	CTRL+C*	Copies selected data, objects, or references to clipboard; marks current selection for subsequent use in Paste Link operations.
Paste***	CTRL+V*	Pastes data, object, or reference from clipboard into document at current insertion point. Replaces current selection (if any).
Paste Link***	(none)	At insertion point in current document (that is, destination), creates link to item previously marked in source (by means of Copy).
Links...	(none)	Displays Links dialog for changing link properties and accessing linked objects.

Note: Mnemonic access characters are underlined.

* The shortcuts for Undo, Cut, Copy, and Paste are new in Windows version 3.1. For backward compatibility, we recommend that applications designed to run under Windows version 3.0 also support the old shortcuts: Undo = ALT+BACKSPACE, Cut = SHIFT+DEL, Copy = CTRL+INS, and Paste = SHIFT+INS. However, the old shortcuts should not be documented in user manuals or listed on the Edit menu.

** Command should be dimmed if there is no selection.

*** Command should be dimmed if the clipboard is empty.

5.4.3.2 Common Optional Items

Common optional items on the Edit menu include Paste Special, Repeat
<Action>, Find, Replace, Clear, and Delete. (The Paste Special command is
discussed in Chapter 9, section 9.3.2.4.)

5.4.3.2.1 Repeat *<Action>* Repeat *<Action>* repeats the most recent action.
The name of the action appears after "Repeat" (for example, Repeat Paste). If present, the Repeat command should follow Undo on the Edit menu.

5.4.3.2.2 Find and Replace Applications that provide Find and Replace commands for text search and substitution should place those commands on the Edit
menu (see Chapter 8, section 8.3).

5.4.3.2.3 Clear vs. Delete The Clear command applies only to container
objects such as text boxes and grid cells; it removes the contents of the object
without removing the object itself. The contents are not placed on the clipboard.

The Delete command is equivalent to the DEL key; it deletes the current selection
without placing it on the clipboard. If the user selects a container object such as a
text box or a grid cell, Delete removes both the object and its contents. The Clear
command, on the other hand, deletes only the contents of a selected object. If the
user selects only the contents of the object, Delete has the same effect as Clear; it
removes the contents.

Delete is the more common of the two commands because it can apply both to containers and non-containers, and because it can be used to accomplish the same purposes as Clear. If an application provides an interface in which a container and its
contents can easily be distinguished, the application need only implement the Delete command. If the distinction between the container and its contents is blurry
and the user needs a quick way to clear the contents of the container, the application should also implement the Clear command.

5.4.4 Help Menu

The Help menu is always the rightmost menu of the menu bar (see Figure 5.11),
immediately following the next-to-last item.[8]

---

[8] Some applications currently place the Help menu at the extreme right of the menu bar. The current recommendation is that the Help menu immediately follow the next-to-last menu item, for three reasons: (1) to
increase the accessibility of the Help menu; (2) to decrease the likelihood of pressing the Maximize or
Minimize buttons by mistake when trying to access Help; and (3) to make the space at the extreme right of
the menu bar available in MDI applications for a Restore icon for maximized child windows.

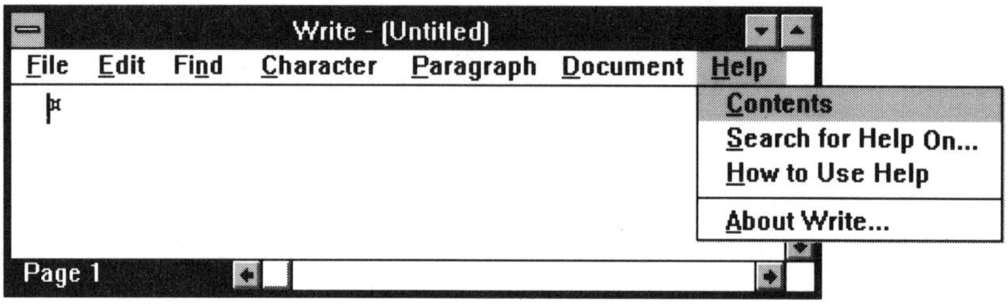

Figure 5.11   Help Menu in Windows Write

5.4.4.1 Standard Items

The Help menu contains the items Contents, Search for Help On, How to Use Help, and About *<Application-Name>* in the order listed. Other items may be interspersed.

Table 5.6   Standard Help Menu Items

Item	Function
Contents	Opens Help window and displays list of main topics.[9]
Search for Help On	Opens Help window and displays dialog that allows the user to search for Help topics containing specific keywords.
How to Use Help	Opens Help window and displays instructions for using Help.
About *<Application-Name>*	Displays standard dialog box containing application name, version number, copyright message, icon, serial number, and user's name; plus optional additional information such as amount of available workspace in memory or amount of storage space on active storage device. For more information on the About dialog, see Chapter 8, section 8.6.

Note: Mnemonic access characters are underlined.

---

[9] This item was called "Index" in Windows version 3.0. "Index" is now an optional item that leads to a full alphabetic index rather than a selective list of main topics.

5.4.4.2 Common Optional Items

The Help menu may also include additional items that access broad subcategories of Help (for example, Commands, Procedures, Keyboard), or that provide equivalents for commands used by other products in the same category. If the application includes an online tutorial, the menu can include a Tutorial item that starts the tutorial. This item should follow Search for Help on and precede How to Use Help; the mnemonic access character is T.

5.5 Common Optional Menus

In addition to the standard menus, applications frequently include the View and Window menus.

5.5.1 View Menu

The View menu includes commands for changing the user's view of the data in the window; these commands change only the view, never the data itself. For example, in a word-processing application, the View menu might include commands for switching between text and outline view; in a graphics application, the View menu might include Zoom In and Zoom Out commands.

The View menu may also include commands for controlling the display of interface elements, such as status bars and control bars that are a fixed part of the application window. (The display of movable control bars should be controlled by commands on the Window menu.) The View menu can also include commands for displaying specialized window panes (such as or annotation panes) or general-purpose panes. Applications that support general-purpose panes should provide a Split command on the View menu.[10] (For additional information on the Split command, see Chapter 4, section 4.2.5.) If present, the View menu typically follows the Edit menu.

5.5.2 Window Menu

The ability to open multiple document windows adds a requirement for additional menu commands that manipulate document windows as whole entities (for example, commands that place document windows in an orderly arrangement). MDI applications should include a Window menu for these commands. This menu should be the last menu before Help. A sample Window menu is illustrated in Figure 5.12.

---

[10]This command can also be placed on the Window menu.

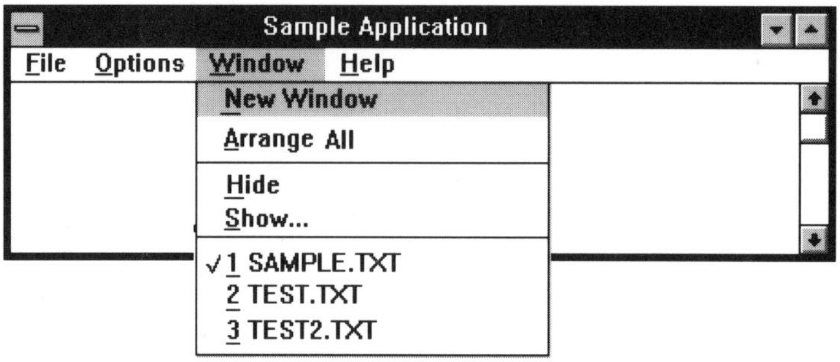

Figure 5.12   Sample Window Menu

5.5.2.1 Standard Items

Because document windows in MDI applications can overlap or even completely obscure each other, activating them by clicking on them with the mouse can become difficult or impossible. Consequently, the Window menu should contain a numbered list of open windows to allow the user to select and activate any window easily. When the user selects a document window from the Window menu, the currently active window is deactivated, and the selected window is activated and displayed on top of the other document windows.

The list of windows appears after all other menu items and is separated from them by a horizontal line. Each list item is preceded by a number, which serves as its mnemonic access character. An active window is indicated by a check mark before its number. The list shows the first nine open document windows. When more than nine document windows are open, the list contains a More command (with M as its mnemonic access character), which displays a dialog box listing all the open document windows, including those that were already shown on the Window menu. The application window, secondary windows, and dialog boxes never appear on the list. The order of windows in the list is the order in which the user opened the windows. When the user closes a document window, the list is renumbered.

5.5.2.2 Common Optional Items

Common optional items on Window menus include New Window, window arrangement commands, and the list of open windows. Applications that allow windows to be split into panes should include a Split command on the View menu. If the application has no View menu, the command should be placed on the Window menu.

5.5.2.2.1 New Window   The New Window command creates a duplicate window that opens another view on the active document.[11] When multiple windows are open for a single document, the title bar of each window indicates the document name and the number of the window. For example, if a spreadsheet application has a chart window named ChartA open, and the user selects the New Window menu item, the first document window containing ChartA shows "ChartA:1" in its title bar. The second document window containing ChartA shows "ChartA:2" in its title bar, and so on.

5.5.2.2.2 Window Arrangement Commands   Window arrangement commands are optional but highly recommended. As users open new document windows and resize old ones, the windows can overlap and eventually obscure or hide one another. Consequently, the user needs a way to arrange the windows so that all document windows are at least partially visible. This can be done in a variety of ways:

- The Tile menu item arranges the document windows in tiled style, with each window displayed in its own space within the application window.

- The Cascade command arranges the document windows in overlapping style, like offset note cards.

- The Arrange command (Arrange... or Arrange All) can be used for more general window arrangements.

You can also include arrangement commands that specifically affect minimized windows.

---

[11]The New Window command should not be confused with the File New command, which creates a new document.

Dialog Box Controls

This chapter discusses controls that appear primarily in dialog boxes (and in control bars, which are essentially modeless dialogs): buttons, check boxes, lists, and edit controls. Applications may also contain custom controls, but widespread use of such controls defeats the benefits of consistency. Before deciding to use custom controls, application designers should carefully consider whether existing controls can be used instead.

6.1 Buttons

Buttons are graphical controls that initiate actions and change data object properties or the interface itself. Users can choose buttons by clicking them with the mouse. Users can also choose most buttons using the keyboard, either through mnemonic access characters (for example, ALT+O for an Options >> button in a dialog) or keyboard shortcuts (for example, ESC for the Cancel button in a dialog or CTRL+B for the Bold button on a control bar).

Three-dimensional buttons that set properties should be shown in the depressed position whenever the specified property is in effect. For example, if a control bar contains a graphical button for turning on the Bold text style, the button should be shown in the depressed position whenever the current selection is in the Bold style. Similarly, a button that causes a drop-down control to open should remain depressed as long as the control is open.

When a button is inactive (that is, when the user cannot choose it because the associated action or setting is unavailable), the button label should be dimmed.

The standard interface uses two types of buttons: command buttons and option buttons.

6.1.1 Command Buttons

A command button[1] is a rectangular shape containing a label that specifies the action or response represented by the button, for example, "Assign" or "Cancel". Figure 6.1 shows a dialog containing several command buttons. Button labels are usually textual, but in control bars (for example, ribbons, palettes, or toolboxes), graphical labels may also be used. Graphical labels are particularly appropriate when the function of the button cannot be concisely represented with a textual label but can be summarized by a single picture. For example, buttons for setting text alignment can be labeled with miniature representations of appropriately aligned text instead of long textual labels, such as "Align Text with Left Margin." Graphical labels are also useful in reducing clutter when many buttons are presented in a small space, as in toolboxes.

---

[1] Also known as a push button.

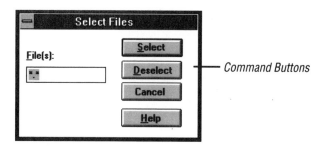

Figure 6.1   Command Buttons in Dialog Box

The user can choose a command button by clicking the mouse while the pointer is over the button. The action associated with the command button is initiated when the mouse button is released.[2] If the function of a command button changes depending on the state of the application, its label should change accordingly. For example, in transactional dialogs (also known as multiple-action dialogs), the user is allowed to perform several actions before closing the dialog. As soon as the user performs any action that cannot be canceled, the label of the Cancel button should change to Close, to reflect that the action cannot be undone.

A dialog box may contain several types of command buttons:

- Command buttons that initiate an action.

- GoTo[3] buttons, which close the current dialog box and open a related one.

- GoSub buttons, which open a related dialog box on top of the current dialog box without closing the current dialog box.

- Unfold buttons (such as Options >>), which expand the dialog to include additional options.

One command button in a dialog may be designated as the default. This button is pushed automatically when the user presses ENTER (see Chapter 7, section 7.3.2).

---

[2] Auto-repeat buttons (for example, scroll arrow buttons) are exceptions to this rule; their action is initiated as soon as the mouse button is pressed and continues until the mouse button is released.

[3] GoTo, GoSub, and Unfold are used descriptively; they are not the actual button labels. Applications should choose appropriate labels for these buttons.

6.1.2 Option Buttons

An option button[4] represents a single choice in a limited set of mutually exclusive choices. Accordingly, in any group of option buttons, the user can only select one at any time. Option buttons are represented by circles, as shown in Figure 6.2. When an option button choice is selected, the circle is filled; when the choice is not selected, the circle is empty. If the number of option buttons in a group exceeds four, the buttons can be replaced by a standard or drop-down list to save space. If space is not at a premium, however, option buttons provide easier access to choices.

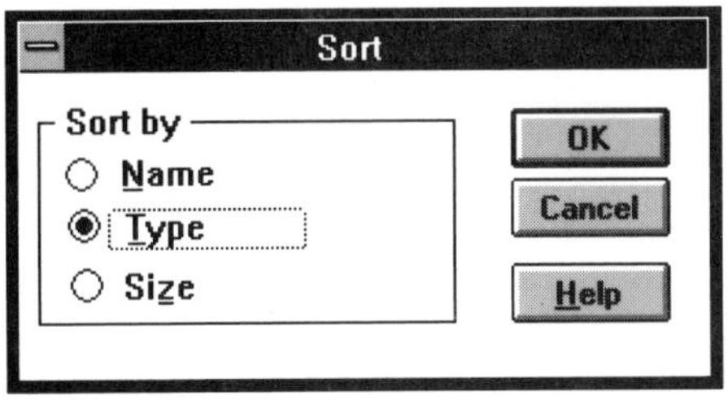

Figure 6.2   Option Buttons

A group of option buttons can be used to choose among a fixed set of attributes for a selection. Whenever the user makes a new selection, the option button group should indicate which attribute currently applies to the selection; that is, the option button corresponding to the current attribute should be filled, and the other option buttons should be empty. If the current selection is heterogeneous with respect to the set of attributes (that is, if more than one attribute is represented in the selection), all the option buttons in the group should be empty, as shown in Figure 6.3. Choosing any button applies the associated attribute to the entire selection.

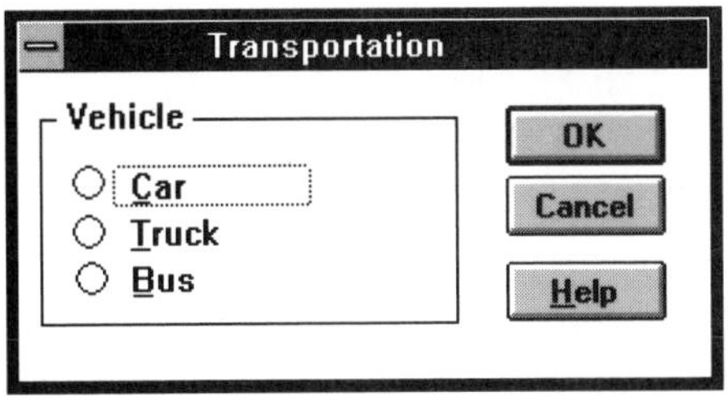

Figure 6.3   Option Buttons for Heterogeneous Selection

---

[4] Also known as a radio button.

In dialog boxes, double-clicking on an option button is an optional shortcut for selecting the button and choosing the default command button in the dialog, thus closing the dialog.

An application can also implement value sets, which are groups of adjacent rectangular option buttons in which the labels are contained inside the buttons. The labels may be graphical or textual. Value sets are particularly appropriate for options that can best be represented by graphical labels (for example, colors, patterns, or drawing tools), but they are also useful for options with textual labels that are short enough to fit within a small rectangle. When the user selects an item in a value set, the item should denote selection.

6.2 Check Boxes

Check boxes control individual choices that are either turned on or off. When the choice is turned on, the check box shows an X in it (see Figure 6.4). When the choice is turned off, the check box is blank. The user can toggle the state of a check box by clicking on the box or the label with the mouse or by pressing the Select key (SPACEBAR) when the check box has the focus.

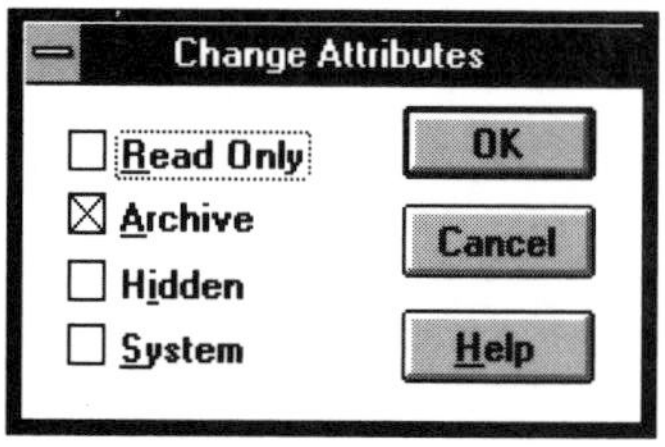

Figure 6.4   Check Boxes

Check boxes can be grouped, but grouping does not prevent the user from turning the check boxes on and off in any combination. Two exceptions to the independence of check boxes are allowed:

- If it is desirable to provide a quick way to turn off all check boxes in a group, an additional check box that performs that function can be added to the group.

■ Suppose that a large group of related, but in most cases independent, options (for example, type style options in a character properties dialog) contains two dependent options (for example, Uppercase and Small Caps). Applications should consider using option buttons or drop-down lists in such cases, but those alternatives do have some disadvantages. Option buttons force a third choice to be added (for example, Normal) to indicate that neither of the two options applies. Drop-down lists not only force this third choice to be added, but they hide all but one of the choices and make them harder to access. Accordingly, in crowded and complex dialogs, it is permissible to use check boxes for two dependent options that are in the middle of other independent options.

Check boxes may be used to set properties of a selection. As with option buttons, check boxes should correctly reflect the properties of each new selection. If the selection is heterogeneous, the check box for each heterogeneous property should be filled with a gray pattern, as shown in Figure 6.5. Grayed check boxes can be cycled through three states. Clicking a grayed check box once turns on the associated property for the entire selection (and places an X in the box). Clicking the check box again turns off the associated property for the entire selection (and removes the X). Clicking the check box a third time returns the selection to its original heterogeneous state (and restores the original gray pattern in the box).

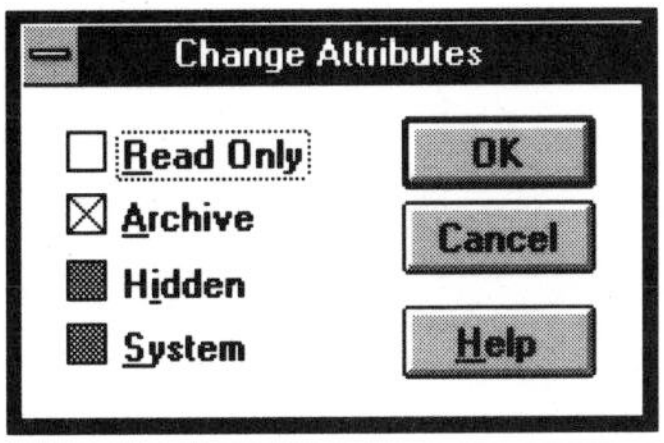

Figure 6.5   Check Boxes for Heterogeneous Selection

As with buttons, when a check box is inactive, its label should be dimmed.

6.3 List Boxes

List boxes are used to display choices for the user. The choices may be represented by text, color, or graphics (bitmaps or metafile graphic objects). Selected choices are highlighted according to the guidelines described in Chapter 3, section 3.1.1.1.

If a particular choice is not available in the current context, it should generally be omitted from the list. For example, if a certain point size is not available for the currently selected font, that size should not be displayed in the list. However, if it is important to communicate to the user both the existence and the current inaccessibility of a list item (for example, a file), the item can be dimmed rather than omitted. For example, in the standard File Save As dialog (see Chapter 8, section 8.1.2), the files in the current directory are displayed in the file name list so that users know which files already exist, but the names are dimmed and unselectable to reduce the likelihood of accidentally overwriting an existing file.

When a list box is inactive, its label should be dimmed. As an optional but recommended extension, applications can also dim textual list items when a list is inactive.

List boxes can be classified according to whether they permit the selection of one or multiple items. Single-selection lists are the most common.

6.3.1 Single-Selection List Boxes

The two types of single-selection list boxes are standard and drop-down.

6.3.1.1 General Characteristics

Because single-selection lists allow the user to select only one item, the items in the list are functionally similar to option buttons. Applications should use single-selection lists rather than option buttons in these cases: when the size or composition of a set of choices is variable, when the set of choices is large (more than four or five items), or when space or layout considerations make option buttons impractical.

The currently selected item in a single-selection list should be highlighted. The arrow keys can be used to move the selection highlight up and down in the list. The mouse may also be used to select items and to scroll the list with the scroll bar. If scrolling is not possible, either because the list is inactive or because all items in the list are already visible, then the scroll arrows should be dimmed, the scroll box should be removed, and the interior of the scroll bar shaft should be changed to the background color of the dialog box.[5] (For an example, see the illustration of the File New dialog in Chapter 8, Figure 8.3.) List boxes also support automatic scrolling (see Chapter 4, sections 4.3.6.1.2 and 4.3.6.2.2).

If the user presses a character key while a single-selection list box has the focus, the list scrolls to the first item that begins with that character (if there are any such items), and the item is selected. If no matching item is found, the list does not scroll, nor does the highlight move.

6.3.1.2 Standard Single-Selection Lists

Standard lists always remain the same size: tall enough to show from three to eight choices, depending on the available height in the dialog box, and several spaces wider than the average width of the items in the list. When the list contains an item that is too wide for the list, a horizontal scroll bar may be optionally placed at the bottom of the list. Figure 6.6 shows examples of standard lists.

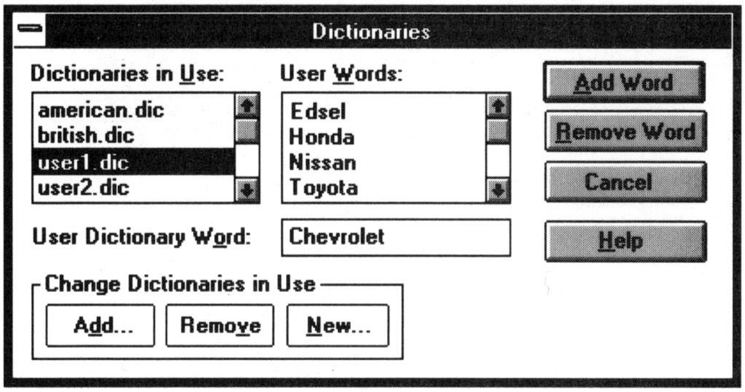

Figure 6.6   Standard Single-Selection List

In dialog boxes, double-clicking on an item in a single-selection list is an optional shortcut for selecting the item and choosing the default command button in the dialog, thus closing the dialog. This behavior parallels the shortcut for option buttons described previously.

---

[5] This is a new recommendation in Windows version 3.1.

If the choices in a list represent possible attribute values for a selection, the current value should be selected when the list is first displayed. If the selection is heterogeneous, no value should be selected.

When space is limited, standard lists may be replaced by drop-down lists.

6.3.1.3 Drop-Down Single-Selection Lists

Like a standard single-selection list, a drop-down single-selection list has a fixed width, which should be several spaces wider than the average width of the items in the list. As in a standard list, a horizontal scroll bar may be added at the bottom of a drop-down list if a particular item is too wide for the list.

Unlike a standard list, however, a drop-down list has two possible heights. When closed, a drop-down list is only tall enough to show one item. When opened, a drop-down list should be large enough to show three to eight items, just like a standard list. If the drop-down list contains more than eight or a variable number of items, it should have a vertical scroll bar. A drop-down list may drop outside the dialog box, but if there is not enough space on the screen for the list to drop down, it should open upward.

Figure 6.7 shows several drop-down lists. Note that the drop-down arrow button abuts the end of the associated list box. The lack of a gap between the list and the drop-down arrow is a visual distinction between a drop-down list and a drop-down combo box, which does have a gap (see section 6.4.1.2).

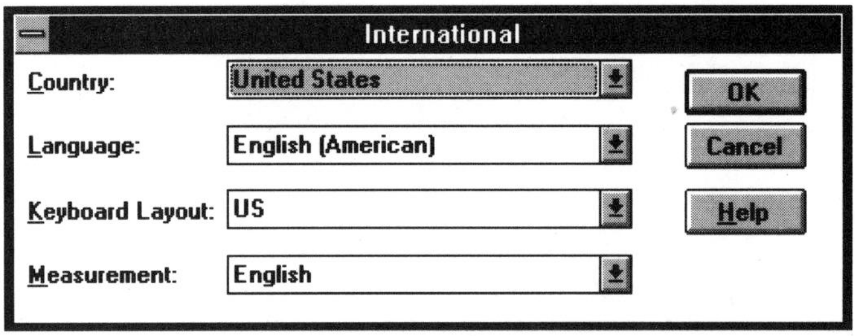

Figure 6.7   Closed Drop-Down Single-Selection Lists

When a drop-down list is open (see Figure 6.8), the list extends to the right edge of the drop-down arrow button, to allow the user to drag into the list.

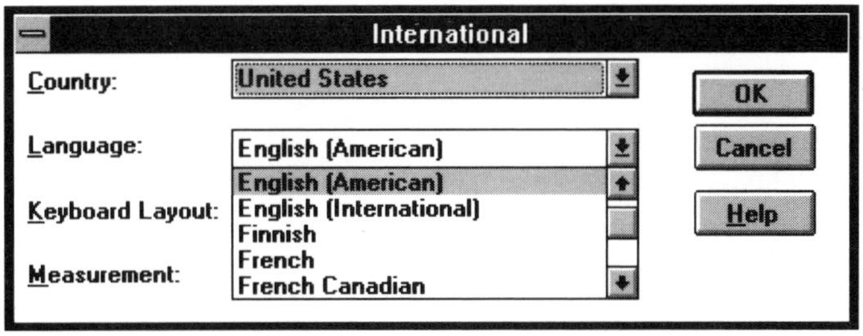

Figure 6.8   Open Drop-Down List

A drop-down list can be toggled between the closed and open state by:

- Clicking on the drop-down arrow.

- Pressing ALT+DOWN ARROW.

- Pressing ALT+UP ARROW.

- Pressing or clicking on the field at the top of the list.

When a list has the focus and is closed, pressing DOWN ARROW opens it. Scrolling is permitted only when the list is open.[6] Any new item selection made while the list was open is accepted and displayed in the list field.

An open list can be closed by:

- ALT+DOWN ARROW

- ALT+UP ARROW

- TAB or other navigation method

- ENTER (which does not close the dialog)

If the choices in a drop-down list represent possible attribute values for a selection and the selection is heterogeneous, no value should be displayed when the list is closed, and no value should be selected when the list is open.

---

[6] Windows version 3.0 allowed users to scroll and autoselect items from a closed drop-down list. This behavior was changed in version 3.1 to avoid delays associated with updating and processing information. For example, in a database application, changing the selection in a drop-down list may change the current query and thereby require a new database search. Similarly, scrolling the Drives drop-down list in the File Open dialog box would require the files list to be updated with each new drive selection.

6.3.2 Extended-Selection and Multiple-Selection List Boxes

Although most list boxes are single-selection lists, occasionally it is useful to let the user select more than one item. This functionality can be obtained with either extended-selection or multiple-selection list boxes.

Extended-selection lists should support the mouse and keyboard techniques for contiguous and disjoint selection described in Chapter 3, sections 3.1.2 and 3.1.3.[7] For example, pressing SHIFT+F8 turns on Add mode, which allows the focus indicator (the dotted box) to move independently of the selection highlight. Pressing SPACEBAR toggles the selection state of the item that has the focus and sets a new anchor point there, without deselecting other items. SHIFT+navigation or SHIFT+click propagates the selection state of the item at the current anchor point. Note that when no modifier keys or special modes are in effect, extended-selection lists behave just like single-selection lists.

Extended-selection lists are particularly useful under the following conditions:

- The user may want an action (for example, printing or deleting) to apply to more than one list entry at a time.

- Contiguous list entries are related in ways meaningful to the user. Because related entries are contiguous, extending a selection with the SHIFT key can easily pick out meaningful groups. This type of ordering frequently arises when the entries represent objects that have been created and named by the user.

When users want to select several entries from a list but the entries are not grouped in a way that makes extended selection useful, multiple-selection lists can be used. Whereas extended-selection lists provide easy range selection, multiple-selection lists are optimized for disjoint selection. The suggested appearance of items in a multiple-selection list includes a check box preceding each item, as shown in Figure 6.9.

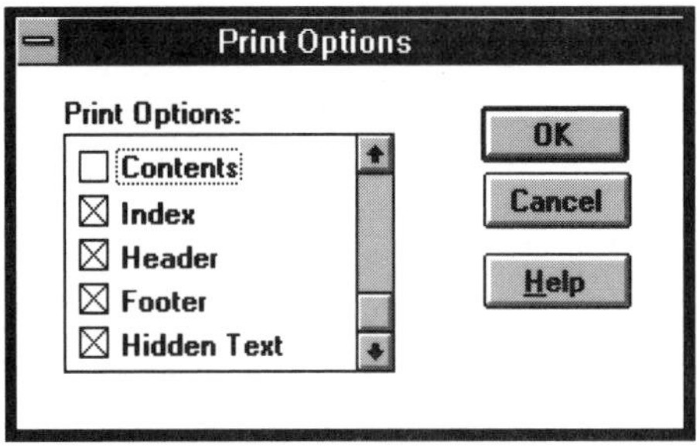

Figure 6.9   Multiple-Selection List[8]

---

[7] The directory windows in the Windows File Manager are examples of extended selection in lists.

[8] The multiple-selection list is not a predefined Windows program control.

The two main reasons for using check boxes rather than check marks are:

- Check boxes are a more familiar and widely used part of the interface.
- Even if no items in the list have been selected, the boxes are always present to indicate that the list is a multiple-selection list. This advantage outweighs the slight increase in visual clutter caused by the always-present check boxes.

When the focus moves to the list, the dotted focus rectangle surrounds the first item name (that is, the first check box label) but not the check box itself. Pressing the SPACEBAR toggles the state of the check box without affecting other items. The user can also toggle a check box by clicking on it (or its label) with the mouse. The behavior of check boxes in multiple-selection lists matches the behavior of free-standing check boxes (see section 6.2): If an item is selected, its check box has an X; if it is not selected, its check box is empty. Reverse video is not used to indicate selection.

6.4 Text Boxes

Text boxes are edit controls into which the user types information, as shown in Figure 6.10.[9] The user can accept the current text, edit it, delete it, or replace it. The LEFT ARROW and RIGHT ARROW keys move the insertion point within the text in a text box; when combined with CTRL, the same keys move the insertion point to the beginning and end of the text. Mouse and keyboard selection of text within text boxes follows the standard methods described in Chapter 3, sections 3.1.2 and 3.1.3.

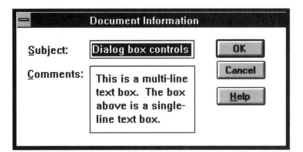

Figure 6.10 Text Boxes

---

[9] Text boxes are not the same as text frames, which are discussed in Chapter 3, section 3.9.

Most text boxes are only one line tall, but applications may also use multi-line text boxes, such as the Comments box in Figure 6.10. In multi-line text boxes, data that is too long to fit on one line may either wrap to the next line or extend beyond the right boundary of the box. Both single-line and multi-line text boxes should support automatic keyboard and mouse scrolling (see Chapter 4, section 4.3.6), to allow hidden data to be brought into view. Multi-line text boxes may also include scroll bars. To insert a carriage return in a multi-line text box in a dialog, the user can press CTRL+ENTER, because ENTER alone would perform its usual function of choosing the default button[10] and closing the dialog.

To activate a text box, the user either presses the access key combination or presses the TAB key to move the active control indicator into the text box. When a text box is activated in this way, its contents should be highlighted, and an insertion point should be placed inside the box at the end of the highlighted contents. If the text box is activated with a mouse click, an insertion point should be placed in the contents of the box as near as possible to the click location, but the contents should not be highlighted.

If a text box is inaccessible (for example, because it is associated with an unselected option), the label of the box should be dimmed.

In certain situations, fixed-length auto-exit text boxes can be used to speed up data entry. As soon as such a box is filled (that is, as soon as the last character is typed), the focus moves to the next control. For example, a five-character auto-exit text box could be used to facilitate entry of zip codes. As soon as the fifth digit is typed, the focus moves to the next control. Because the automatic focus shift can be unexpected and disconcerting, auto-exit text boxes should be used sparingly. In general, they are best limited to situations involving extensive data entry.

It is not unusual to link controls in a dialog box, such as a text box and a list, so that user interaction with one control also affects another. The standard File Open dialog box demonstrates the benefits of integrating a text box with a list box. This type of linking can be taken one step further by merging the two controls into one, called a combo box.

6.4.1 Combo Boxes

A combo box is a text box with an attached, integrated, and interdependent list. Combo boxes are useful when the application requires user input and can display a list of possible responses. The user can type a response in the text box if the correct one is not available in the list. Combo boxes can be classified into two categories, standard and drop-down, according to the type of list it includes.

---

[10]ENTER can be used if there is no default button.

6.4.1.1 Standard Combo Boxes

Standard combo boxes include a text box and a standard list, as shown in Figure 6.11. If the list is *never* expected to display more entries than can be shown at one time, the scroll bar may be omitted. The left border of the list is indented from the edit control by the width of a numeric digit in the character set. The entries in the list should be in alphabetic order unless there is a compelling reason to use a different order. For example, a list of file names should be in alphabetic order, but a list of dates should be in chronological order.

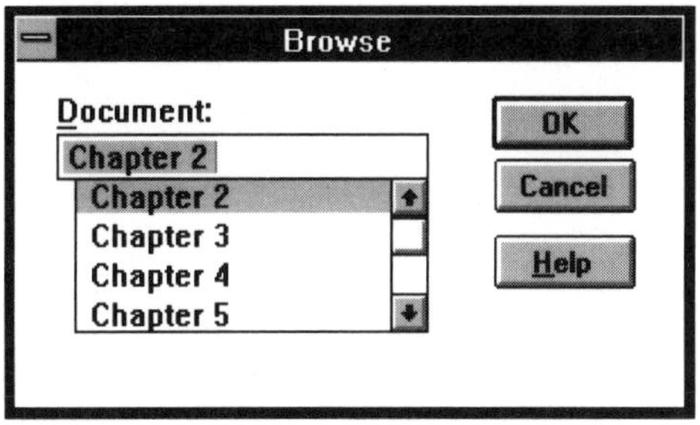

Figure 6.11   Standard Combo Box

When a combo box has the focus, the UP ARROW and DOWN ARROW keys move the selection up and down in the list and put the selected item into the text box. The LEFT ARROW and RIGHT ARROW keys move the cursor left and right in the edit field. The user can press character keys to enter characters in the text box. The list scrolls to the first item that begins with the characters in the text box. When the target item is brought into view, however, it is not automatically selected (as it would be in an independent list). Pressing the DOWN ARROW key selects the target item and places it in the text box.

When space is at a premium, standard combo boxes may be replaced by drop-down combo boxes.

6.4.1.2 Drop-Down Combo Boxes

A drop-down combo box includes a text box and a drop-down list. Figure 6.12 shows two drop-down combo boxes, one for changing fonts and the other for changing point size.

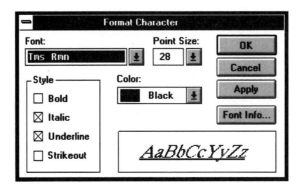

Figure 6.12   Two Drop-Down Combo Boxes

Note the gap between the end of the text box and the drop-down arrow button. This gap provides a visual distinction between a drop-down combo box and a drop-down list (such as the color control in Figure 6.12), which does not have a gap. When the list portion of a drop-down combo box is open, the list should extend to the right edge of the drop-down arrow button, to allow the user to drag into the list.

6.4.2 Spin Boxes

Spin boxes are specialized text boxes that accept only a limited set of discrete, ordered input values. A spin box consists of a text box with a pair of arrows (an upward-pointing arrow above a downward-pointing arrow) attached to the right side of the text box, as shown in Figure 6.13.

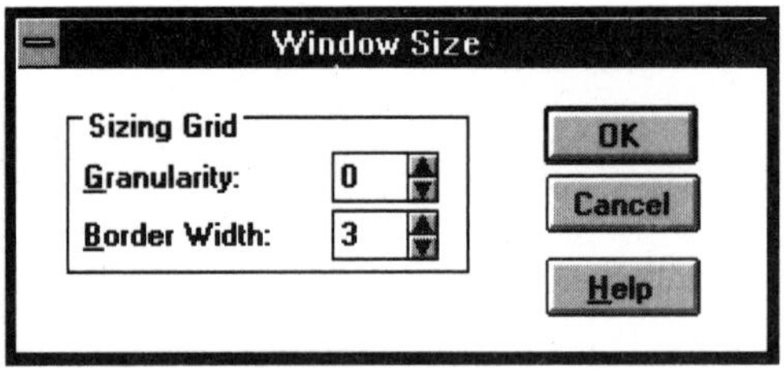

Figure 6.13   Spin Boxes

The user can type a new value into the text box, click the UP ARROW key to increase the value, or click the DOWN ARROW key to decrease the value. In effect, the arrows function like scroll arrows for a hidden list that is sorted in descending order (in contrast to actual list controls, in which entries normally should be sorted in ascending order).

Spin boxes may be used to display values that consist of several subcomponents (for example, time, which consists of hours, minutes, and seconds). In such cases, the text box is divided into several subfields and the subfields are separated by suitable separators (for example, in the U.S., ":" for time and "/" for date). The arrows affect the selected subfield; if no subfield is selected, the arrows affect the subfield representing the smallest unit of measurement.

A value typed into the text field of a spin box should be validated either immediately or as soon as the user navigates away from the spin box. For example, if the user types a letter into a spin box that is only meant to accept numeric values, the application may beep (or alert the user in some other appropriate way) and either remove or simply never display the letter. Optionally, the value can be validated when the user submits the dialog. At that time, if the value is invalid, the application should display an appropriate error message in a message dialog that contains a single OK button. Choosing OK to acknowledge the message should close the message dialog, but leave the original dialog open so that the user can change the invalid value. See section 6.10 for additional guidelines for validation of input.

6.5 Read-Only Pop-Up Text Fields[11]

Space limitations often restrict the amount of interface text that can be displayed. For example, long path names may not fit in a file dialog. Similarly, in Help text, it is usually impossible to include in-line definitions for every term. In such situations, applications can use the read-only pop-up text field illustrated in Figures 6.14 and 6.15.

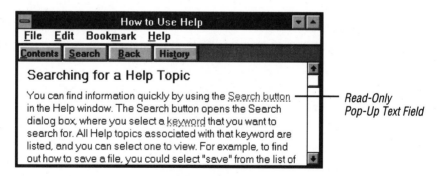

Figure 6.14 Closed Read-Only Pop-Up Text Field

---

[11]The read-only pop-up text field is not a predefined Windows program control.

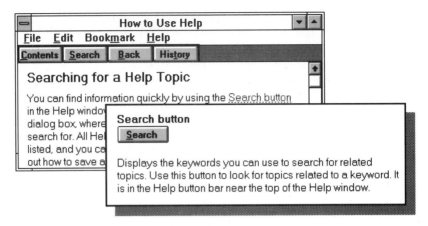

Figure 6.15   Open Read-Only Pop-Up Text Field

As shown in Figure 6.15, a dotted underline beneath the text contained in the text field indicates that the user can click on the text to obtain a pop-up with additional information. The pointer changes to a hand with an extended finger (as in Windows Help) when over the field, to provide an additional indication that more information is available. The pop-up opens when the user presses mouse button 1 over the text and remains open when the button is released. Clicking anywhere closes the pop-up.

From the keyboard, the user can navigate to the text field with TAB. If the field is labeled (as it should be, unless it appears in a continuous stream of text), the mnemonic in the field label can also be used to navigate to the field. To open and close the pop-up, the user can press the Select key (SPACEBAR) or any of the keys used for opening and closing drop-down controls (see section 6.3.1.3). When the pop-up opens, its top left corner appears at the same position as the top left corner of the original text. If the contents of the pop-up can change between invocations, the pop-up should be dynamically sized so that it is large enough to hold its current contents.

6.6 Sliders

Sliders are used to display and adjust values on continuous dimensions such as pitch, loudness, and brightness. A slider consists of a bar containing notches or measurement markings, plus an indicator perpendicular to the bar, as shown in Figure 6.16. The indicator shows the present value and can be dragged along the bar with the mouse to set a new value.

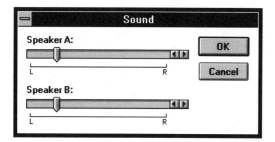

Figure 6.16   Slider

6.7 Static Text Fields

Static text fields are used to present read-only textual information (for example, the current directory location). These fields are static in the sense that the user cannot change the text in them; the application, however, can alter the text to reflect the current state of the application. Static text fields are often used to label controls that are not automatically labeled by the system (see section 6.9). When the user accesses a static text field using a keyboard mnemonic, the focus is passed to the next control in the TAB order. Accordingly, when a static text field is used as a label, it should immediately precede the labeled control in the TAB order.

6.8 Group Boxes

Group boxes, though technically considered controls, do not process any mouse or keyboard input; they may be used to provide visual grouping of related controls. Group boxes consist of a rectangular one-pixel frame with a label at the upper left, as shown in Figure 6.17.

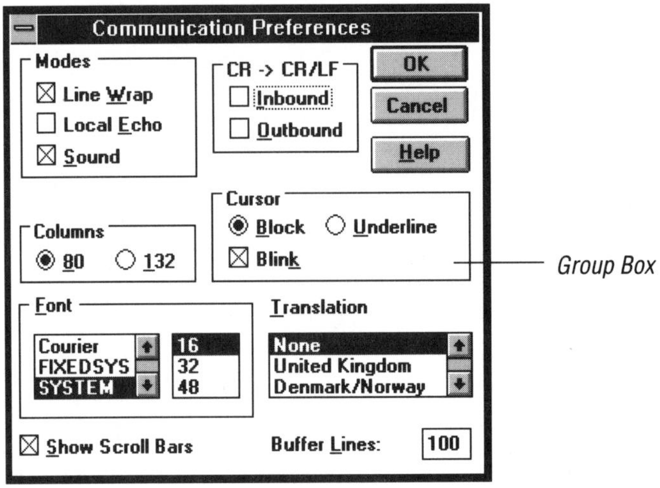

Figure 6.17   Group Boxes

6.9 Control Labels

Buttons, check boxes, and group boxes are automatically supplied with labels by the system; other controls can be labeled with static text fields (see section 6.7). Labels identify the function of the control and provide direct keyboard access to the control. The following guidelines are suggested for control labels:

- Capitalize the first and last words of labels. In addition, capitalize the initial letters of all other words in labels, except for articles (for example, *a*, *an*, and *the*), coordinate conjunctions (for example, *and*, *or*, *nor*, and *for*), prepositions (for example, *by*, *through*, and *with*), and the *to* in infinitives.

- Provide a unique mnemonic access character for labels of controls to which the user needs direct keyboard access. If possible, use the first character of the label as the access character. In the following cases, use another letter from the label:

  a. Another letter offers a stronger mnemonic link (for example, the letter X in Exit).

  b. The label contains multiple words, one of which is more significant than the first word (for example, "Process" in Set Process).

  c. The first character has already been used as a mnemonic for another control.

  Use consonants in preference to vowels because consonants are usually more distinctive and more easily remembered. Do not assign mnemonics to the OK command button because it can be accessed through the ENTER key.

- Dim the labels of unavailable or inapplicable controls.

- Use a bold font so that dimmed labels are not illegible.
- Position control labels according to the rules in Table 6.1.

Table 6.1   Position of Control Labels

Control	Label Position
Command button	Inside button.
Check box or option button	To right of box or button.
Text box, spin box, list, combo box, slider, read-only pop-up text field	Above or to left of control, followed by a colon, and left-aligned with the section of the dialog in which it appears.
Group box	On top of (and replacing) part of top frame line, starting just after upper left corner.

6.10 Validation of Input

Applications can validate input (or other dialog settings) immediately, after navigating away from a field, or when the dialog is submitted. Generally, the first two techniques provide better feedback because the user remains in the context where the information is supplied. However, these may not be appropriate when data fields cannot be processed individually.

Valid input can also be controlled by the type of control used to receive the input. For example, option buttons, check boxes, and drop-down lists limit the type of input that can be selected. Other types of controls (for example, those with text boxes) generally provide more flexibility for user input.

Using Dialog Boxes

Chapter 7

Some application commands require additional information from the user before they can be completed. For example, if the user selects File Open, the application needs the name of the file and where it is stored. If the user does not or cannot supply the information when issuing the command, the application can request the information by displaying a special window called a dialog box. A dialog box contains controls that collect the user's information and choices. These controls show the attributes of the selected data when the dialog box first opens. Dialogs do not generally contain menu bars, window scroll bars, split bars, resizing buttons, or status bars.

This chapter discusses types of dialog boxes and the use of command buttons in dialog boxes. For information on navigation in dialogs, see Chapter 3, section 3.3. Dialog box controls are discussed in Chapter 6 and several standard dialogs are described in Chapter 8.

7.1 Types of Dialog Boxes

Dialog boxes can be classified according to various characteristics:

- They may be movable or fixed in position.
- They may have a single size or two alternate sizes.
- They may be modal (that is, may require the user to respond before continuing), semimodal, or modeless.
- They may present simple messages with limited response options, or more complex transactional choices accompanied by a variety of controls.

7.1.1 Movable vs. Fixed Dialogs

The appearance of a dialog box depends on whether it is movable. A movable dialog box has a title bar containing a Control menu (which includes only the Move and Close commands) and a title. A dialog box that is not movable has no title bar. In general, an application should use only movable dialog boxes; the user can reposition these to view obscured data and maintain a sense of context because the name of the command or application is displayed in the title bar of the dialog. The title of dialog boxes that present messages should simply reflect the application name (or the source of the error, if the message represents a system or network error; see section 7.1.4 for details). The title of dialog boxes that represent completions of menu commands should reflect the name of the command that led to the dialog, without an ellipsis. The menu name should not be included in the dialog title, unless the same command exists on two different menus, or unless the command name alone is uninformative without the menu name.

7.1.2 Unfolding Dialogs

Whether they are movable or not, all dialog boxes have a non-sizable frame. Applications may, however, have dialogs of two sizes: a small size containing the basic controls and a larger size that includes advanced options. The user can expand the dialog from the small size to the large size by pressing an unfold button (a command button with chevrons, for example, "Options >>") included in the small form of the dialog. The dialog box may expand to the right, downward, or in both directions. The expanded form of the dialog contains both basic and advanced options.

After the dialog is expanded, applications may optionally leave the button active with the chevrons facing the opposite direction (for example, "Options <<") to allow the user to return the dialog to its original size. If the application does not allow the dialog to be returned to its original size, the button label should be dimmed. The next time the dialog box is displayed, it appears in its original (unexpanded) form; however, applications may provide options for using the expanded form instead.

7.1.3 Modal vs. Modeless Dialogs

Dialog boxes can also be classified according to whether they require the user to respond before continuing to work in the current application and in other applications. The four types of dialog boxes in this classification are: application modal, system modal, application modeless, and application semimodal.

Table 7.1 describes the characteristics of these dialog box types.

Table 7.1   Modal, Modeless, and Semimodal Dialog Boxes

Type of Dialog	Characteristics	Uses
Application modal	User must respond to dialog before continuing work in current application, but can switch to and work in other applications without responding.	Obtain information required before current application can continue. Should be used sparingly; modeless dialogs should be used instead whenever possible because the user can leave them open (for easier access) while continuing to work in the application.
System modal	User must respond before doing anything else in any running applications.	Obtain information required before any applications can continue. Should be used only for severe system problems, for example, impending fatal system error or unrecoverable error with active storage device.
Application modeless	User can continue work in current application without responding to dialog; dialog remains on display.	Display information or offer options that don't require immediate attention; obtain information for commands that need not be completed before proceeding (for example, Find). Useful for frequently used commands; user can leave dialog open rather than reselecting command from menu. When a movable palette or toolbox is implemented as a modeless dialog, it should always stay in a layer above the window to which it applies. In MDI applications, it should stay in a layer above all document windows.
Application semimodal	User can perform a limited number of operations outside the dialog as a means of responding to the dialog.	Offer alternative ways of responding. For example, a semimodal dialog in a spreadsheet might allow the user to specify ranges by clicking and dragging outside the dialog in the worksheet, as well as by using controls within the dialog.

Although semimodal dialog boxes are not part of the recommended minimum requirements of interface style, special situations within some applications may make such dialogs appropriate. Semimodal dialogs are similar to modal dialogs, in that the user must complete the dialog before continuing to work on a document in other ways.[1] Semimodal dialogs, however, permit a limited set of actions outside the dialog as a means of completing the dialog when the focus is on certain controls within the semimodal dialog. In particular, semimodal dialogs are appropriate in situations where it is convenient to accept mouse input or keyboard shortcuts from outside a dialog as a means of setting controls or defining attributes within the dialog. The user may only perform actions that set controls in the dialog but is not confined to using only the dialog box controls. For example, if column width can be set in a dialog text box, a semimodal dialog could also permit the user to drag columns to a new location with the mouse, with the text box echoing the measurements as the user drags the column border.

---

[1] Visually, semimodal dialogs should use the same window style as modal dialogs.

7.1.4 Message Dialogs

Modal dialog boxes that are used to display error messages and other important information are called message dialogs. Because message dialogs are modal dialogs, they require a response by the user before work with the application can proceed. Message dialogs for critical messages, which inform the user of serious system-related problems, are system modal dialogs. All other types of messages appear in application modal message dialogs. Message text should follow the guidelines in Chapter 3, section 3.6.1.2. An application should post messages only when it is the active application; when inactive, it should flash or beep for attention, as described in Chapter 3, sections 3.6.1.1.4 and 3.6.2.

Every message dialog has a title bar. The title is particularly important in a multitasking environment because it identifies the source of the message. The title of message dialogs in applications should consist simply of the name of the application. The title of message dialogs associated with system or network processes should contain the name of the system or network product, plus the word "Message" (see Figure 7.3). The reason for this longer title is that users are often unaware of the system and network processes that are occurring behind the scenes. The longer title "*<System or Network Product Name>* Message" helps clarify the purpose of the message dialog, which may have appeared unexpectedly while the user was working in an application. Message dialog titles should never include the word "Error," which has a negative effect on users.

Each message dialog also includes a graphical symbol that indicates what kind of message is being presented. The three types of messages are:

- Information messages
- Warnings
- Critical messages

Table 7.2 describes each message type and shows the associated symbol.

Table 7.2   Message Types and Associated Symbols

Symbol	Message Type	Description
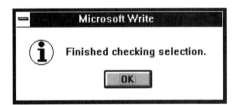	Information	Provides information about results of commands. Offers no user choices; user acknowledges message by clicking OK button.
	Warning	Alerts user to an error condition or situation that requires user decision and input before proceeding, such as an impending action with potentially destructive, irreversible consequences. The message can be a question (for example, "Save changes to REPORT.WRI?").*
	Critical	Informs user of a serious system-related or application-related problem that must be corrected before work can continue with the application.

* Some applications may find the question mark symbol more appropriate if the message is a question. However, note that the question mark is also used as the help symbol and may therefore confuse users.

Figures 7.1, 7.2, and 7.3 present examples of complete message dialogs.

Figure 7.1   Information Message

Figure 7.2   Warning Message

Figure 7.3   Critical Message

Message dialogs should contain only command button controls. If the application needs additional information, such as a file name, then a regular dialog box should be used instead of a message dialog. The standard command button combinations for message dialogs are discussed in section 7.3.6.

7.2 Dialog Placement

Dialog boxes are usually centered vertically and horizontally within the application window. If an application finds a more appropriate location for the dialog box, it may choose to place it elsewhere. On large screens, this rule could cause small dialogs to be positioned quite far from the menu bar at the top of the window, which is where users must focus their attention in order to obtain most dialogs.

7.3 Using Command Buttons in Dialogs

A command button is a rectangular shape containing a label that indicates what the button does (for example, Assign or Cancel), as discussed in Chapter 6, section 6.1.1. After the user presses and releases (that is, clicks) the command button, the action begins. A dialog box may contain several types of command buttons:

- Command buttons that initiate actions.
- GoTo[2] buttons, which close the current dialog box and open a related one.
- GoSub buttons, which open a related dialog box on top of the current one without closing the current dialog box.
- Unfold buttons, which expand the dialog to include additional options.

---

[2] GoTo, GoSub, and Unfold are used descriptively; they are not the actual button labels. Applications should choose appropriate labels for these buttons.

7.3.1 Recommended Buttons

Every dialog box contains at least one button that closes the dialog. Message dialogs that require only an acknowledgment from the user (rather than a choice) contain a single button labeled OK. All other dialog boxes contain at least two buttons: One closes the dialog and initiates an action; the other closes the dialog without initiating any action. The button that initiates the action is usually labeled either OK or *<Action-Name>*. The button that closes the dialog box without initiating an action is usually labeled Cancel. Some dialogs (called multiple-action dialogs) include additional buttons that allow the user to initiate actions without closing the dialog. In these dialogs, if the actions performed by the additional buttons irreversibly change the user's data, the label of the Cancel button should change to Close as soon as the first such action is carried out. Whether the button is labeled Cancel or Close, the keyboard user can press this button by pressing ESC. (The OK and Cancel buttons do not have mnemonics.) If the label is Close, C is underlined and serves as a mnemonic access character. This additional means of access helps users who know that ESC presses the Cancel button, but who may not realize that ESC also presses the Close button after Cancel changes to Close.

7.3.2 Default Buttons

One command button in a dialog box may be designated the default button, which will be pushed when the user presses ENTER. The default button should be distinguished from the others with a heavy border. In multiple-action dialogs, it may be appropriate for different buttons to be the default button at different times, depending on the current state of the data and the user's interaction with the dialog. In general, the button that indicates the most likely next action at any given time should be designated the default. However, a button that initiates an action with far-reaching and potentially destructive consequences should never be the default. For example, in a text search and substitution dialog, the Replace All button should never be the default.

If the user navigates to a command button that is not usually the default, the new button is temporarily designated the default (that is, the heavy border moves from the original default to the new button, and ENTER now pushes the new button rather than the old one). If the focus moves away from the temporary default button to a control that is not a command button, the button that was originally the default becomes the default again. For additional information on keyboard navigation to controls, see Chapter 3, section 3.3.2.

7.3.3 Dynamic Button Labels

The labels of individual buttons can change in two ways to reflect the possibilities currently available to the user:

- If the action represented by the button is not currently available, the label should be dimmed.

- If the nature of the action represented by the button changes depending on circumstances, the button label can be modified to reflect that change. For example, as mentioned previously, the label of the Cancel button should change to Close after any actions that cannot be cancelled have been carried out. When the dialog closes, however, the button label should be reset to Cancel for the next time the dialog appears.

7.3.4 Navigation to Related Dialog Boxes

As an application becomes more complex and provides additional features, the need to display options in a consistent and efficient manner becomes increasingly important. For example, if the application allows the user to set character properties from several dialogs, there is no need to complicate each dialog by repeating the controls for setting those properties. Instead, each dialog should provide a means to navigate to a single, uniform character properties dialog.

To provide for consistent presentation of controls and to keep individual dialogs simple, applications may use GoTo and GoSub command buttons to let the user navigate to related dialog boxes. A GoTo button typically closes the original dialog before opening the new dialog, whereas a GoSub button leaves the original dialog open and returns to it when the new dialog is closed. When a GoTo or GoSub button leads to a dialog that is also associated with a menu item, the dialog should have the same title as when it is invoked by selecting the menu item; typically this title will be the name of the menu item. The labels for GoTo and GoSub buttons should include a trailing ellipsis ("..."), which indicates that the commands represented by the buttons require additional information (the information collected in the new dialog) before they can be completed.[3]

If the user invokes a GoSub dialog and then returns to the original dialog, the Cancel button in the original dialog should cancel all changes that were made in both dialogs if the transaction has been committed and cannot be undone at that point.

---

[3] The ellipsis implies that the command leads to a dialog, but the reverse is not always true; commands that lead to message dialogs should not be followed by an ellipsis.

7.3.5 Arrangement of Buttons

Before users can decide which buttons to press in a dialog, they must first take in the information presented by the dialog. This information is scanned by eye movements that typically proceed as in normal reading; that is, from left to right and from top to bottom. Accordingly, the most appropriate places for buttons in dialog boxes are at the right or at the bottom, where the buttons will be seen after the user has already scanned the relevant information. Whenever possible, buttons should be arranged in one of two ways:

A. Stacked along the right border of the dialog, starting in the top right corner (see Figures 7.4, 7.5, and 7.6). In this case, buttons should generally be the same width—as wide as necessary to accommodate the longest button text. Group the command buttons according to whether they initiate an action (that is, Add, Remove, Find) or not (that is, GoSub, GoTo, or unfold buttons). If there is an OK button, OK and Cancel should be grouped together, separated from the other action verbs (see Figure 7.5). If there is no OK button, Cancel should be grouped with other action buttons (see Figure 7.6). Leave at least 3 dialog units (DUs) between the bottom of one button and the top of the next within the same group.[4] Between groups, do not use horizontal lines, which simply clutter the dialog; instead, insert at least an extra 5 DUs of white space, for a minimum total of 8 DUs between groups. Leave at least 6 DUs between the edge of the dialog and the edges of the buttons (that is, the top of the first button, the bottom of the last button, and the right edges of all the buttons).

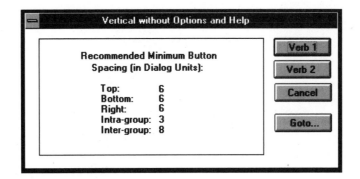

Figure 7.4   Vertical Button Layout Without Options and Help

---

[4] The measurements mentioned in this section are based on the use of 8-point MS Sans Serif Bold in the Windows Dialog Editor.

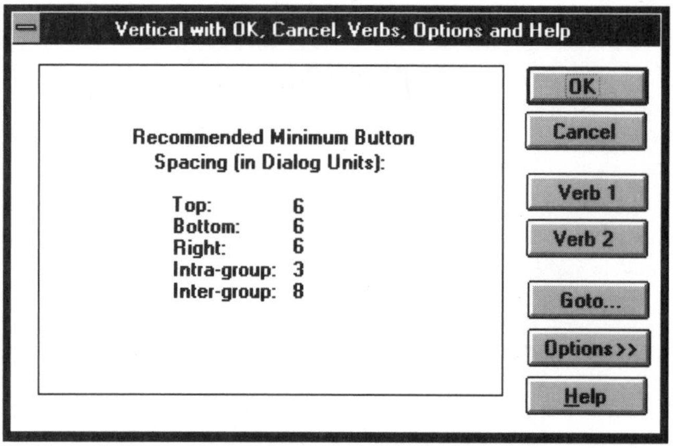

Figure 7.5   Vertical Button Layout with OK, Cancel, Verbs, Options, and Help

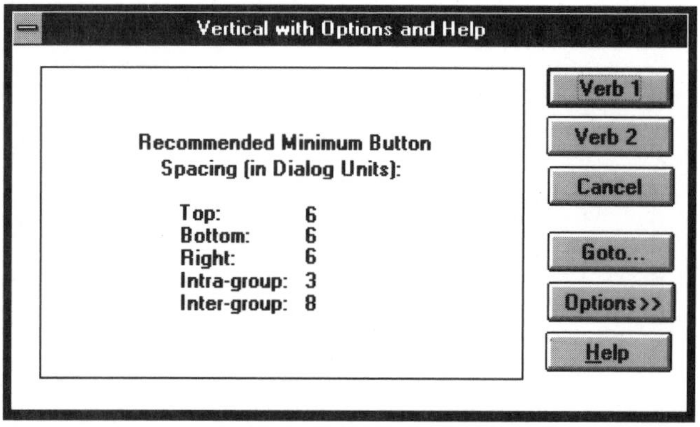

Figure 7.6   Vertical Button Layout with Options and Help

B. Line buttons up across the bottom of the dialog (see Figures 7.7, 7.8, and 7.9). Group the command buttons according to whether they initiate an action (that is, Add, Remove, Find) or not (that is, GoSub, GoTo, or unfold buttons). If there is an OK button, OK and Cancel should be grouped together, separated from the other action verbs (see Figure 7.8). If there is no OK button, Cancel should be grouped with other action buttons. Space the buttons evenly within each group, leaving at least 4 DUs between the right edge of one button and the left edge of the next. Between groups, do not use horizontal lines, which simply clutter the dialog; instead, insert at least an extra 5 DUs of white space, for a minimum total of 9 DUs between groups. Leave at least 6 DUs between the edge of the dialog and the edges of the buttons (that is, the left edge of the first button, the right edge of the last button, and the bottom of all the buttons). Normally the buttons should all be the same width, but individual buttons may be made wider to accommodate exceptionally long text (see Figure 7.9). It is not necessary to align buttons with other dialog controls, because the buttons should form their own visual group rather than being grouped with the other controls.

Figure 7.7   Horizontal Button Layout Without Options and Help

Figure 7.8   Horizontal Button Layout with Options and Help

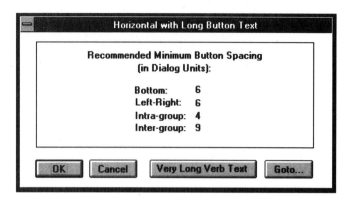

Figure 7.9   Horizontal Button Layout with Long Button Text

Additional guidelines:

- The most important button—typically, the default command—should be placed at the top (if arrangement A is used) or at the left (if arrangement B is used), followed by other command buttons that initiate actions, followed by remaining command buttons (if present) in this order: GoTo or GoSub button, unfold button, and Help button (see Figures 7.6 and 7.8).

- The Help button is placed after all other buttons so that it will be located near the bottom right of the dialog, where it will be visible to users after they scan the dialog.

- If an OK button[5] is present, place the Cancel button immediately after it; otherwise, place the Cancel button after all other command buttons, but before GoTo or GoSub, unfold, and Help buttons (see Figures 7.6 and 7.8). If OK is not the default button, it should still be placed first. (This will keep its location consistent with the large number of dialogs where it is first because it is the default.)

- If there is not enough room to fit all buttons in a single location, use arrangement A for the most important command buttons and arrangement B for all other command buttons.

---

[5] If there is a single, obvious default action in the dialog box, use OK rather than a verb. For example, to access the File Open dialog, the user selects Open from the File menu, and Open appears in the title bar of the dialog. In this case, it is clear that the default action is to open something (a file or a directory), so there is no need to repeat "Open" as the default button name; "OK" is sufficient. In contrast, if the nature of the interaction in the dialog makes the intended action ambiguous (for example, if there are several possible actions, none of which is clearly the default), consider replacing "OK" with a verb.

- Except in message dialogs, arrangement A (vertical stacking at the right) is more common than arrangement B (horizontal alignment at the bottom). Accordingly, if either method would work equally well in terms of dialog layout, arrangement A should be given priority because it will be more familiar to users. Message dialogs are an exception to this rule; buttons in message dialogs should be placed at the bottom (arrangement B), where they will not interfere with the left-to-right flow of message text.

- The recommended minimum size for OK and Cancel buttons is 40 x 14 DUs. The recommended minimum space between the left or right edge of a button and the nearest edge of the text within the button is approximately the width of a lowercase "n".

- Other arrangements may be used if there is a compelling reason, such as a natural mapping relationship. For example, it would make sense to place buttons labeled North, South, East, and West in a compass-like layout.

7.3.6 Command Buttons in Message Dialogs

Command buttons are the only controls used in message dialogs; they represent the responses or choices offered to the user. The safest or most typical response should be designated the default command button.

If a message requires no user choice and only needs acknowledgment, the message dialog should contain only an OK button and (optionally) a Help button. (If this type of message appears as the result of a dialog submission, acknowledging the message should dismiss the message but leave the dialog open, so that the user can correct the error.) If the message requires the user to make a choice, the dialog should contain a button for each option. The clearest way to present the choices is to ask the user a question and provide a button for each response. When possible, questions should be phrased to permit Yes or No answers, which can be represented by Yes and No command buttons. The use of OK and Cancel buttons in place of Yes and No is permissible. However, Yes and No are preferable, because OK and Cancel can be ambiguous for questions that imply cancellation, such as "Interrupt file transfer?" or "Delete reservation?" If the message cannot be phrased unambiguously for Yes or No responses, the command buttons can instead be labeled with the names of the relevant actions (for example, "Save" and "Delete").

Some message dialogs offer the user the following three choices:

- Performing a preliminary action (for example, saving data) before carrying out the process that led to the message dialog (for example, closing a document).

- Not performing the preliminary action before carrying out the process.

- Canceling the process altogether.

The appropriate buttons for this type of message dialog are Yes, No, and Cancel. Yes means "Perform the preliminary action and then carry out the process"; No means "Don't perform the preliminary action, but do carry out the process"; and Cancel means "Don't perform the preliminary action, and don't carry out the process either."

Help buttons in message dialogs are optional but highly recommended, especially for warning and critical message dialogs.[6] They allow the user to obtain further information or suggestions about the problem described by the message.

7.4 Fonts in Dialogs

As mentioned in Chapter 6, section 6.9, a bold font is suggested for control labels in dialogs, so that the labels remain legible when dimmed to reflect unavailability. The font used for control labels in the dialog box is also typically used for other text, but different fonts may be used if there is a good reason to do so. For example, if a dialog displays a sample of text from another document, the text could be displayed in its original fonts. If reproducing the original fonts is too difficult, the text could be displayed in a single font that is different from the font used in the rest of the dialog. The use of a different font emphasizes that the displayed text represents data from another document, rather than standard elements within the dialog.

7.5 Samples in Dialogs

Dialog boxes are frequently used to change visual properties or attributes. If the changes selected in the dialog are not reflected immediately in the document, it is helpful to provide a sample inside the dialog that shows the effect of the changes. For example, the standard character properties dialog includes a text sample that reflects changes to the font, type style, point size, and color (see Chapter 8, Figure 8.10).

---

[6] The user can also press the F1 key to obtain help.

Common Dialog Boxes

This chapter describes common dialog boxes for the following operations:

- Opening and saving files (sections 8.1.1 and 8.1.2)
- Creating new documents (section 8.1.3)
- Printing files (section 8.2)
- Searching and replacing text strings (section 8.3)
- Setting character properties (section 8.4)
- Setting page margins (section 8.5)
- Displaying information about an application (section 8.6)

The dialog boxes discussed in this chapter provide a starting point for applications; they can be customized depending on an application's specific needs.

8.1 File Operations

The next three sections describe the new standard for File Open, File Save As, and File New dialogs. Applications that use other dialogs that involve file browsing (for example, Insert File) should model them after the File Open dialog.

8.1.1 File Open Dialog

Figure 8.1 shows the File Open dialog.

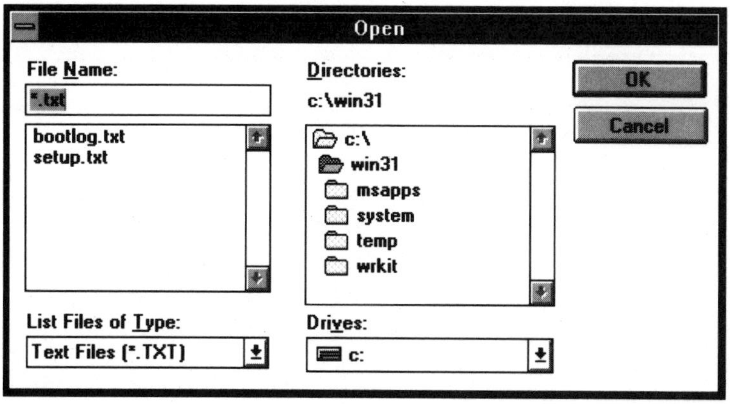

Figure 8.1   File Open Dialog

8.1.1.1 Directories Control

The Directories control is a list box that displays:

- First, the parent directories, preceded by 🗁
- Next, the current directory, preceded by 🗀
- Finally, the child directories of the current directory, preceded by 🗀

The directory icons and names are indented according to their depth in the directory tree. To move to a directory, the user double-clicks the directory name or icon, or selects it and then chooses OK (or presses ENTER). If the indentation causes directory names to be clipped at the right, a horizontal scroll bar appears at the bottom of the list.

If the current directory contains so many child directories that there is not enough room in the list box to display all the parents, the immediate parent is displayed at the top of the list, followed by the current directory and its child directories. Displaying the immediate parent helps the user maintain a sense of orientation in the directory tree, and allows the user to move up at least one level in the directory tree without having to scroll the list.

When the user switches to a new drive, the directory list box should always show the root directory at the top, even in the rare case that the active path directory is so far down in the directory tree that it is not visible. Displaying the root directory at the top helps users orient themselves to the directory structure of the newly selected drive.

Note that the Directories list box contains no ".." entry because the parent directories are shown. Note also that the root directory is indicated by a drive letter followed by a backslash (for example, "c:\"), not by the backslash alone.

After the user switches to a new directory, the keyboard focus may optionally move to the File Name text box so that the user can type a new file name immediately. This automatic shift of focus away from the Directories control makes repeated directory navigation slightly more difficult for keyboard users. However, most users will change directories only once (if at all) during each dialog invocation and will want to type a file name immediately after changing directories.

8.1.1.1.1 Directory Tracking Text The non-editable text item above the directory list box should show not only the current directory name (for example, "xyz") but rather a longer string (for example, "c:\..\xyz") that indicates the current position in the directory tree. To truncate this string when pathnames are long, use the following rule: If N is the maximum number of wide characters (for example, W is a wide character) that can fit in the available space after an initial "c:\..", the string should show as many entire nodes as will fit into N characters. It should not show parts of nodes unless the number of entire nodes that will fit is less than one; that is, unless even the last node will not fit. In that case, the beginning of the last node should be truncated.

Table 8.1 lists truncation rules. Note that increasing N from 10 to 11 changes the tracking text in all cases; increasing N from 11 to 12 changes the first two cases; and increasing N from 12 to 13 only affects the "GammaAndDelta" case.

Table 8.1 Truncation of Directory Tracking Text

N	Path	Tracking Text
10	c:\Alpha\Beta\GammaAndDelta	c:\...maAndDelta
10	c:\Alpha\Beta\Gamma\Delta	c:\..\Delta
10	c:\Alpha\Beta\Gamm\Delta	c:\...Gamm\Delta
11	c:\Alpha\Beta\GammaAndDelta	c:\...mmaAndDelta
11	c:\Alpha\Beta\Gamma\Delta	c:\...Gamma\Delta
11	c:\Alpha\Beta\Gamm\Delta	c:\..\Gamm\Delta
12	c:\Alpha\Beta\GammaAndDelta	c:\...ammaAndDelta
12	c:\Alpha\Beta\Gamma\Delta	c:\..\Gamma\Delta
12	c:\Alpha\Beta\Gamm\Delta	c:\..\Gamm\Delta
13	c:\Alpha\Beta\GammaAndDelta	c:\...GammaAndDelta
13	c:\Alpha\Beta\Gamma\Delta	c:\..\Gamma\Delta
13	c:\Alpha\Beta\Gamm\Delta	c:\..\Gamm\Delta

Showing a small number of whole nodes rather than parts of a larger number of nodes is recommended for two reasons:

- First, whole nodes (for example, "Report" as opposed to "ort") are recognized and understood more easily.

- Second, if parts of two nodes are displayed, the ellipsis between them is somewhat ambiguous. Unless the user knows the truncation rules, it is not immediately apparent that the last ellipsis represents truncation of only one node. For example, "c:\...Beta\...amma" could represent "c:\a\b\Beta\Gamma", "c:\a\b\Beta\Foo\Gamma", "c:\a\b\Beta\Foo\Bar\Gamma", and so on.

The recommended minimum length for N is 12. Because N does not include the initial drive letter, colon, backslash, and ellipsis, 12 is enough for an 8-character directory name, followed by a period and a 3-character extension. If possible, N should be larger than 12 to allow more of the path to be displayed.[1]

8.1.1.2 Drives Control

The drives are displayed in a drop-down list box labeled Drives. This list displays the drive letter followed by the volume name (or server+share names), not the drive letter alone. The suggested format for volume names is "c: [*volume*]" (with two spaces after the colon, and the *volume* name in square brackets). For server+ share names, the format is similar, except that the brackets are omitted to save space (for example, "f: \\server\share"). Each drive name should be preceded by an appropriate drive icon (floppy, hard disk, or network), as in the File Manager. If the drives list is open and the selection is changed with arrow keys, the files list is not updated until the drives list is collapsed, because on-the-fly updates would take too long. The drives list can be collapsed with ALT+DOWN ARROW, ALT+UP ARROW, TAB (which also navigates to the next control), or ENTER (which does not close the dialog so the user can see the effect of changing drives).[2]

8.1.1.3 File Name Control

This control consists of a text box labeled File Name and a list box immediately below it. The list box shows the existing files in the current directory. It should be tall enough to contain at least eight items. The list box should track typing in the text box, and selecting from the list should replace the contents of the text box.

---

[1] *N* should be easily modifiable by product localizers so that it can be changed for different languages on systems supporting long file names.

[2] As explained in Chapter 6, section 6.3.1.3, drop-down lists no longer allow scrolling and autoselection in their closed state. This prevents delays associated with processing or updating information.

8.1.1.3.1 Entering a String in the File Name Text Box   In the text box, the user can type a file name, a filter, a drive, a directory, a complete path in the form "drive:directory\...\filename", or a universal naming convention (UNC) pathname.

When the user types a string in the text box and presses ENTER, the following algorithm is used to process the string:

- If the string is a filter, filter the list accordingly.

- If the string is not a filter, try to open the storage location (drive, directory, or file) represented by the string.

  - If successful, update the controls (if the string represents a drive or directory) or close the dialog and display the file (if the string represents a file). The updating of controls proceeds as if the new drive or directory had been chosen in the drive or directory controls.

  - If the open fails, divide the string into two parts (internally, not in the text box): the part before the last backslash (\), which represents a drive or a path, and the part after the last backslash. If the string contains no backslashes but does contain a colon (:), divide the string at the colon, and leave the colon attached to the first part of the string. (For example, "c:\foo" is divided into "c:" and "foo"; while "c:\foo\bar.txt" is divided into "c:\foo" and "bar.txt"; and "c:foo" would be divided into "c:" and "foo".) Try to change to the drive or directory represented by the first part of the string. In other words, eliminate the part of the original string that might represent a file name, and try to change to the drive or directory where the user thought the file was located.

8.1.1.3.2 Effect of Navigation on Contents of Text Box   Suppose that the user types a string in the text box, but then decides to navigate with the drive or directory controls (without first pressing ENTER to confirm the string). Any initial part of the string that could represent a drive or path is deleted, leaving only the part that could be a file name. In practice, this means that characters from the text box are deleted up to and including the last colon or backslash. The current filter is always shown in the type control, so there is no need to reproduce it in the text box and destroy a file name typed by the user.

8.1.1.4 Type Control

This control is a drop-down list labeled List Files of Type displayed below the list of files. Selecting a type modifies the contents of the files list box so that only files of the selected type are displayed. As an optional extension, applications can precede each type description in the list with a distinctive icon. The same icons can be used in the files list to distinguish between files of different types.

The purpose of the type list is to allow users to view all files that match a set of criteria, such as parent application (for example, Write), document category (for example, spreadsheet or template), or file format (for example, TIFF). (The set of criteria may be empty, in which case all files match it.) The type list adds the filter name in parentheses after the class description, to acknowledge that the resulting file list is based on name matches only, not on the more abstract class description. For example, the type list may contain items such as TIFF Files (*.TIF), Write Files (*.WRI), and so on. An application can include any filter that is appropriate.

There are two additional optional extensions:

- User-supplied types can be added to the type list. If the user types a filter in the text box that is not already included in the type list, the new filter becomes the first item in the type list, but is not given a label. If the user types in another new filter, this filter replaces the previous one; thus, the type list never includes more than one user-defined filter. The user-defined filter is preserved in the list in subsequent invocations of the dialog (but not in subsequent invocations of the application); but the dialog always opens with the type set to the default filter for the application.

- The type can optionally be preserved as the default during the current session. For example, if the user changes the extension to *.TXT, this remains as the filter until the user changes it or reruns the application. This allows the user to browse for files of a particular type without having to reset the type filter between invocations of the File Open command.

8.1.1.5 Layout

Most layout guidelines are shown in Figure 8.1. The following points deserve explicit mention:

- Align control labels with the left edges of the controls, not with the text inside the controls.

- Align the left edge of the List Files of Type control with the left edge of the File Name text box and list.

- Align the left edge of the Drives control with the left edge of the Directories list.

- The layout of the command buttons follows the recommendations in Chapter 7, section 7.3.5.

- Add application-specific controls either at the bottom of the dialog or under the Cancel command button.

8.1.2 File Save As Dialog

The File Save As dialog (see Figure 8.2) is similar in appearance to the File Open dialog, except for the following differences:

- The dialog contains the File Name text box and the list box underneath, but the list box items are dimmed and nonselectable, although still scrollable.

- The type control is labeled Save File as Type instead of List Files of Type. Selecting a type specifies the format of the file to be saved. It also filters the list of files, but does not affect the files directly. The type control contains only format descriptions, such as Normal, Text Only, Windows Write, and so on. Changing the type does not affect the contents of the File Name text box. Applications should provide appropriate extensions for each format and supply the extension if the user does not specify one in the File Name box. The format indicated by the type control overrides the extension specified by the user in the File Name box.

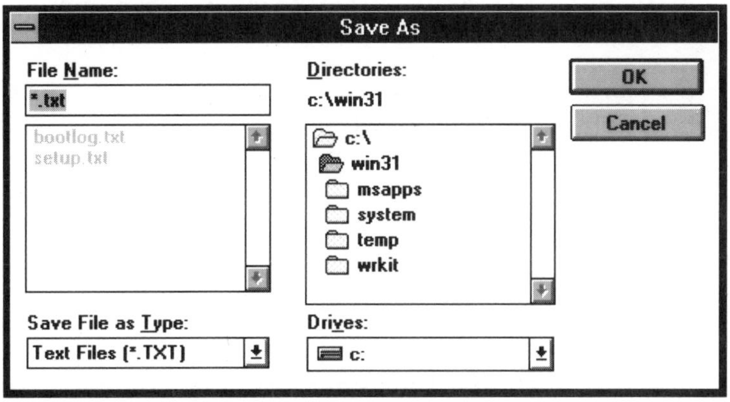

Figure 8.2   File Save As Dialog

8.1.3 File New Dialog

Applications that allow the user to create more than one type of document may provide a File New dialog similar to that shown in Figure 8.3.

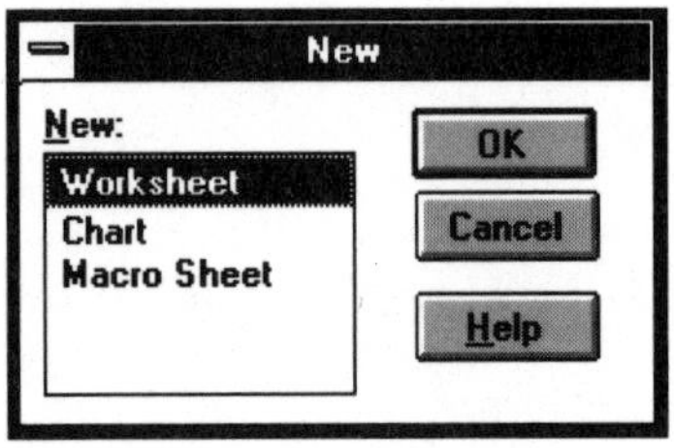

Figure 8.3   File New Dialog

The New list contains the predefined document types for the application, as well as any document types that the user has created. When the dialog opens, the most common document type should be selected as the default. When the user presses the OK button, the dialog is closed, and a document based on the selected type is created and displayed in a window. The File New dialog should not slow down the process of document creation by requiring a user-supplied file name, because the user may create a temporary document without intending to save it as a file.

8.2 Printing

As discussed in Chapter 5, section 5.4.2.1, the Print and Print Setup commands are common items in the File menu. These commands lead to the common dialogs described in sections 8.2.1 and 8.2.2. The Print dialog allows the user to set properties for a particular print job (for example, page range and number of copies). The Print Setup dialog allows the user to set printing properties that will be stored with the current document (for example, paper type and orientation). Both dialogs are modal.

8.2.1 Print Dialog

The recommended format for the Print dialog is shown in Figure 8.4. The printing properties set in the Print dialog last only for the duration of a particular print job; they are not stored with the document.

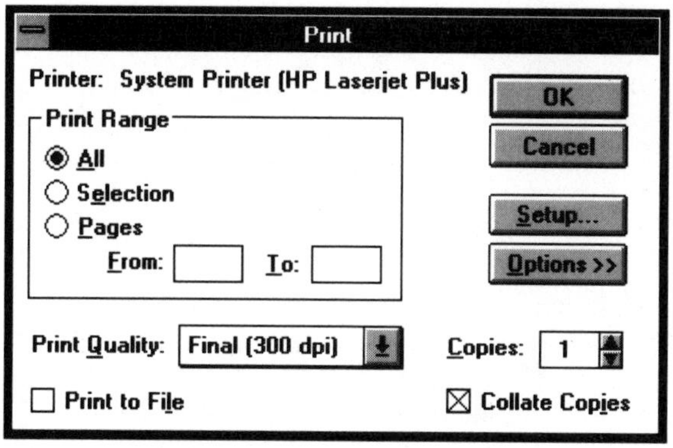

Figure 8.4 **Print Dialog**

Most features of the Print dialog are self-explanatory, but a few deserve comment:

- In the Print Range group box, the Pages option button allows the user to print specific pages (or units) by typing the appropriate numbers in the From and To text boxes. You can enter ranges of pages as well; and leaving a box blank results in the printing of all remaining pages (or all preceding pages). Examples are shown in Table 8.2:

Table 8.2 **Printing Ranges**

From:	To:	Print Result:*
1	1	Page 1
3	-	Page 3 to end of document
2	3	Pages 2 and 3
-	5	Beginning of document to page 5
3	1	Pages 3 to 1 in reverse order

* In pages or in other appropriate document units.

- The Print Quality drop-down list box allows the user to choose from the list of printing resolutions provided by the printer device driver.
- If the Print to File check box is checked, a new dialog appears after the user presses OK and asks for the name of the file to which the print output should be sent. A file created in this way will print properly only on the printer for which it was generated; it is a device-dependent file, not a metafile.

- The Collate Copies check box is turned on by default. When printing multiple copies of multipage documents on page-oriented printers, users can turn off this check box to speed up printing.[3] On printers that do not support the printing of uncollated copies, the Collate Copies check box should always be checked, and the check box and its label should both be dimmed.

- The Setup button allows the user to reach the Print Setup dialog without going back to the File menu.

- The Options button unfolds the dialog to include application-specific options, such as controls for reversing print order, printing hidden text, and so on, as described in Chapter 7, section 7.1.2. This button may be omitted if the application includes no printing options. Applications that include only one or two printing options may also omit this button and simply add the options at the bottom of the dialog.

When the user chooses Print from the File menu, the following two conditions are tested before the Print dialog opens: Is the printer that was stored with the document currently available? If not, has the current printer already been explicitly chosen or acknowledged by the user? If neither of these conditions is met, a warning message (see Figure 8.5) is displayed with the text:

```
This document was previously formatted for the printer "<stored
printer name>", but that printer is not available. Use system printer
"<default printer name>"?
```

The message dialog contains three buttons: Yes, No, and Setup. Pressing any of these buttons closes the message dialog. Yes opens the Print dialog, No returns to the document, and Setup opens the Print Setup dialog so that the user can choose a different printer. The same tests are used if the user chooses Print Setup from the File menu, but the resulting message dialog contains no Setup button, and the message text is:

```
This document was previously formatted for the printer "<stored
printer name>", but that printer is not available. The initial
settings shown in the Print Setup... dialog are for the current
system printer "<default printer name>".
```

---

[3] On page-oriented printers, printing all the copies of the first page before going on to the second page is faster than printing the entire document once before going on to the second copy of the document.

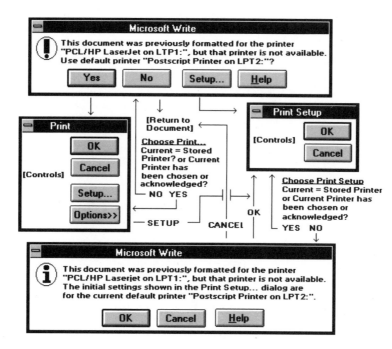

Figure 8.5   Message Dialogs for Printing

A message is also provided if all the following conditions are met when the user chooses Print or Print Setup:

- The document was previously stored with the default printer as the printer.

- The default printer was subsequently changed from the Control Panel.

- The new default printer does not support one of the settings (for example, landscape) that was previously stored with the document.

This "default printer changed" message does not change to reflect the condition; there is just one general-purpose message, with slight variations for Print versus Print Setup. For the Print dialog, the message is:

```
This document was previously formatted for a different default
printer, "<stored default printer name>". Use current default printer
"<current default printer name>"?
```

This message appears in a message dialog that contains Yes, No, and Setup buttons, like the "Non-default printer not available" message described previously (see also Figure 8.5). If the user presses Yes, the default settings of the new default printer are used wherever the ones stored with the document aren't available.

For the Print Setup dialog, the "Default printer changed" message is:

> This document was previously formatted for a different default
> printer, "*<stored default printer name>*". The initial settings shown
> in the Print Setup... dialog are for the current system printer
> "*<current default printer name>*".

This message is displayed in a message dialog that contains OK and Cancel buttons, like the Print Setup version of the "Nondefault printer not available" message described previously (see also Figure 8.5).

The user is not warned if the current printer matches the stored printer, but the current orientation or paper type do not match the stored settings. This situation is rare but could occur if a driver-specific dialog was used to modify the list of available paper types for a particular printer. In this case, the application should simply provide the best possible match to the stored values.

8.2.2 Print Setup Dialog

The recommended format for the Print Setup dialog is shown in Figure 8.6.[4] The printing properties set in this dialog are stored with the current document; they do not affect systemwide defaults, which can be changed only from the system Printer Setup dialog. Applications may expand the Print Setup dialog downward to include controls for document-specific properties such as margin settings.

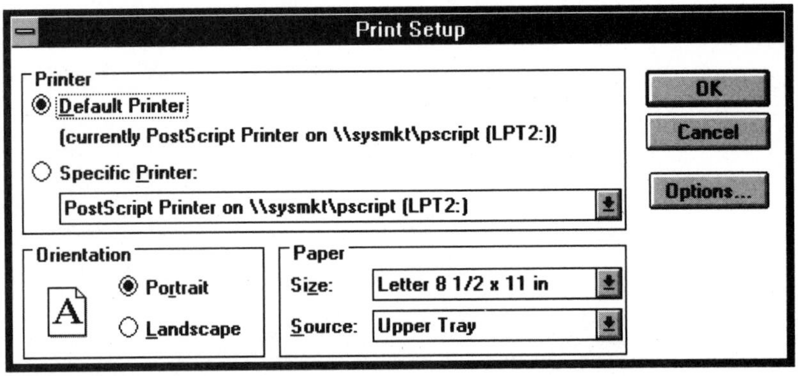

Figure 8.6   Print Setup Dialog

When the user chooses Print Setup from the File menu, the application should test the same conditions that are tested when Print is chosen (see Figure 8.5). The Print Setup dialog operates as follows:

---

[4] Note that the name is Print Setup, not Printer Setup. The latter name is now reserved for the system dialog that changes systemwide printing defaults.

- If the Default Printer option button is selected, the document is printed on the printer established as the default by the system Printer Setup dialog. As a result, if the user changes the system default printer, all documents that were stored with the default printer setting will automatically print on the new printer. For some documents, however, users may want to choose a particular target printer and store that choice with the document so that the document will always print on that printer, even if the system default printer is changed. This capability is provided by the Specific Printer option button and its associated drop-down list. The list entries are in the form "PCL / HP Laserjet on LPT1," "PostScript Printer on LPT2," and so on.

- The Orientation controls allow the user to choose portrait or landscape printing; the icon changes to reflect the choice. In portrait mode, the lines of text or the tops of the graphics are parallel to the short edge of the page; in landscape mode they are parallel to the long edge. If one of the modes is not available for the current combination of printer and paper type, the label and option button for that mode are dimmed, and the option button for the available mode is selected.

- The Paper Size drop-down list allows the user to choose from the list of paper sizes provided by the printer device driver. This list specifies the paper sizes that can be loaded into the printer, not the sizes that are actually loaded at the time of printing. The list may also include custom forms added in the printer properties dialog provided by the printer device driver. If the current printer does not support the paper size that was stored with the document, the default size for the current printer is used.

- The Paper Source drop-down list specifies the source of the paper (for example, Upper Tray, Lower Tray, or Manual Feed).

- The Options button leads to a dialog that allows the user to select additional driver-supplied printing options (for example, duplex printing) that will be stored with the document. This button is dimmed if no such options are provided by the current printer driver.

8.3 Text Search and Substitution

Most of the recommendations and design decisions for the common Find and Replace dialogs are shown in Figures 8.7 and 8.8; the key points are summarized below. The recommendations have the following order of priority: (1) Command names; (2) Names and behaviors of controls within dialogs; (3) Type of dialog (modal versus modeless) and menu location of commands.[5]

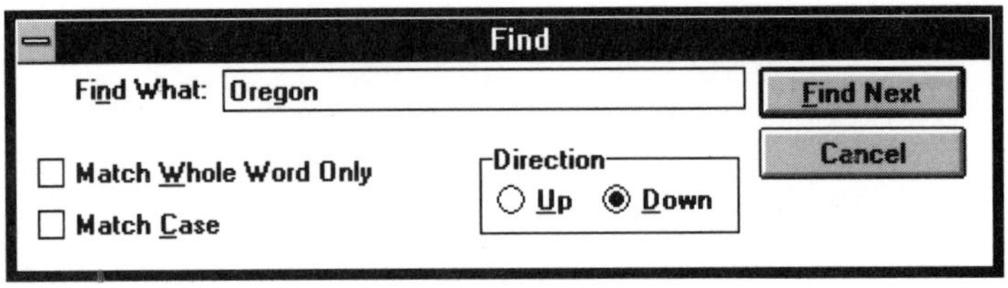

Figure 8.7   Find Dialog

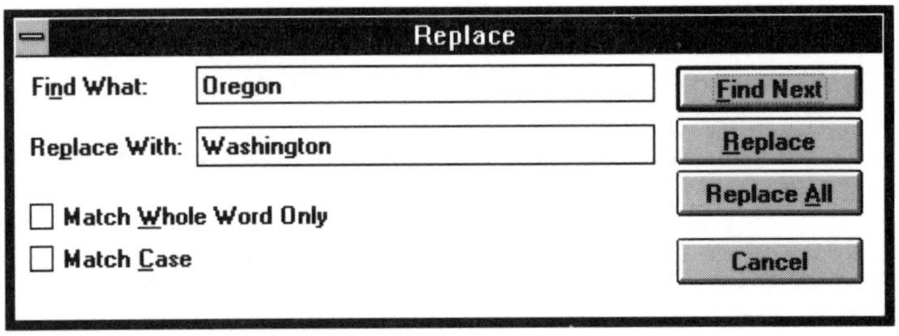

Figure 8.8   Replace Dialog

8.3.1 Command Names and Menu Location

The text search command should be named Find (rather than Search) in all applications. "Find" is a more common, familiar word. The substitution command should be named Replace (rather than Change, which is too vague).

The Find and Replace commands should both be on the Edit menu. Replace is clearly an editing operation; Find is less so, but is placed on the same menu as Replace because it is a logical component of that command. Placing both commands on the Edit menu, which is present in all applications, will make the commands easier to find for users of many different applications.

---

[5] As shown in the illustrations, the Find and Replace dialogs are very similar. Applications may consolidate the two dialogs and provide access to these functions through a single command called Find/Replace on the Edit menu. If a single dialog is used, its design should be consistent with the guidelines for the Find and Replace dialogs.

8.3.2 Dialog Type and Operation of Commands

If possible, the dialogs invoked by the Find and Replace commands should be modeless. If making the dialogs modeless is too difficult, they should at least have a title bar and be movable, to let the user expose text hidden by the dialogs.

8.3.2.1 Operation of the Find Command

Searches in the Find dialog may proceed forward or backward, according to the option chosen with the option buttons at the bottom of the dialog (see Figure 8.7). Searches begin at the current insertion point or at the beginning of the current selection. The top command button in the Find dialog is always labeled Find Next. This button causes the search to proceed in the specified direction until the next instance, if any, of the search text is found. Each time an instance is found, the document is scrolled behind the dialog box to show the text and some context before and after the text.

When a forward search reaches the end of the document or a backward search reaches the beginning, a message is displayed. For forward searches, the following text is suggested: "No matches found. Continue search from beginning of document?" (where "document" may be replaced by "spreadsheet," "presentation," and so on as appropriate). For backward searches, the text reads, "Continue search from end of document?" In both cases, the message dialog contains two buttons below the text: the default button Yes on the left, and No on the right. Pressing either button closes the message but leaves the Find dialog open. Pressing Yes continues the search from the appropriate boundary of the document. If the other boundary of the document is reached again, another message is shown, with the text "No matches found. *<Boundary>* of document reached" (where *<Boundary>* is "Beginning" or "End" as appropriate). This message contains a single button labeled OK beneath the text. Pressing OK closes the message but leaves the Find dialog open.

8.3.2.2 Operation of the Replace Command

The Replace command invokes a single four-button dialog that stays open until the user has finished replacing text. The single-dialog model allows easy adjustment of replacement text in the middle of a series of replacements, without requiring the user to start over again.

The Replace dialog uses the document-boundary messages described for the Find dialog. If the user changes the search string in the middle of a series of replacements so that it no longer matches the current selection, the search is considered to have restarted from the beginning of the selection. This new starting location is used to determine document-boundary messages.

The four command buttons for the Replace dialog are arranged as shown in Figure 8.8.

- The top button is always the default button and is always labeled Find Next. This button finds the next instance, if any, of the search text without replacing the current instance.

- The second button is labeled Replace. This button replaces the current instance of the search text and finds the next instance. The button is active when a selection matches the search string; otherwise it is dimmed.

- The third button is labeled Replace All. If there is a selection when the dialog opens or is reactivated, the button replaces all instances of the search text in the selection and retains the selection. If there is no selection when the dialog opens or is reactivated, this button replaces all instances of the search text from the current location to the end of the document. The document-boundary message discussed previously allows the user to continue the replacement operation from the beginning of the document.

- The bottom button, Cancel, closes the dialog. The label of this button should change to Close after the first replacement if replacements cannot be undone.

If the user uses the Find or Replace command to search for text, changes the cursor location, and then continues the search, the next search starts at the new location. If the user switches to another document window, the search proceeds from the current cursor location of that window.

8.3.3 Labels

The Search text should be labeled Find What. Replacement text should be labeled Replace With.

The check box for limiting matching to whole words should be labeled Match Whole Word Only. The check box for turning on case sensitivity should be labeled Match Case.

8.3.4 Other Controls

8.3.4.1 Direction Controls

All applications should include options for forward and backward searches in the Find dialog. The simplest case will have only two such options (labeled either Up and Down, or Forward and Backward), represented by option buttons in a group box labeled Direction. Applications that include variations on these options (for example, Forward from Start, Forward from Here) may use a drop-down list in place of option buttons.

8.3.4.2 Application-Specific Options

An Options button can be placed beneath the Cancel button in the Find dialog and to the left of the Cancel button in the Replace dialog. This button unfolds the dialog to include application-specific options (see Chapter 7, section 7.1.2). If these options are used frequently, the application can provide easier access to them by omitting the Options button and simply adding the options to the bottom of the dialog.

8.4 Character Properties

Figure 8.9 shows the recommended format for the dialog used for changing character properties such as font, size, type style, and color.

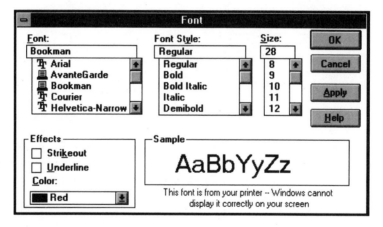

Figure 8.9   Basic Version of Character Properties Dialog

Applications that require advanced features can add them at the bottom of the dialog. Figure 8.10 shows an example of how such features can be added.

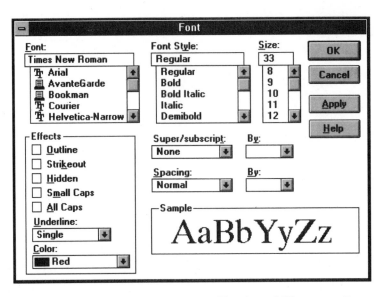

Figure 8.10   Example of Enhanced Version of Character Properties Dialog

Adding features may involve adding new controls, altering old ones, or repositioning otherwise unchanged controls to make the best use of space, but the overall structure of the dialog should be preserved as much as possible. In Figure 8.10, for example, the Underline check box has been changed to a drop-down list to allow more underlining options, and the Sample box has been moved to make room for the Super/Subscript and Spacing controls, but the appearance and position of the buttons and the Font, Size, and Color controls remain essentially unchanged from the basic dialog.

Applications that offer advanced features should use an expanded dialog rather than an unfolding dialog, for two reasons:

- First, for many users, the only reason to invoke the dialog at all is to access the advanced features because the basic ones are usually available in other ways (for example, from menus, from a ribbon, or through keyboard shortcuts). Accordingly, the advanced features should be immediately available without the intermediate step of pressing an Options button.

- Second, it is difficult to construct a space-efficient basic dialog that neatly unfolds into an advanced version through simple addition of elements. As Figures 8.9 and 8.10 show, the basic dialog has to be somewhat reorganized to accommodate new controls. Having this reorganization suddenly occur after the user presses the Options button would be visually disruptive.

8.4.1 Character Dialog Box Controls

8.4.1.1 Choice of Controls

The font and size controls are combo boxes rather than lists for two reasons: speed, because users can quickly type in names rather than seeking them in the lists; and flexibility, since users who don't currently have a particular font or size available can type its name, even though it doesn't appear in the list; the name will be stored for later use.

8.4.1.2 Font Combo Box

This combo box lists font family names. If the user selects a printer font, the following message is displayed under the sample box: "This font is from your printer—Windows cannot display it correctly on your screen." If the user selects a screen font, the following message is displayed: "This is a Windows screen font—it may not print correctly on your printer."

8.4.1.3 Font Style Combo Box

When the user selects a font style (that is, a particular weight, slant, or combination of weight and slant), the system attempts to provide a built-in typeface corresponding to the selected style. For example, if the current font is Helvetica and the user checks Bold and Italic, the system uses the built-in Helvetica Bold Italic typeface. If a built-in font is not available, the system synthesizes it and displays the following message under the sample box: "This font style is simulated by Windows—it may not print correctly on your printer."

8.4.1.4 Size Combo Box

This combo box contains a list of point sizes. Users may type any size, but the list box should provide the following sizes for TrueType™ and vector fonts: 8, 9, 10, 11, 12, 14, 16, 18, 20, 22, 24, 26, 28, 36, 48, 72. (For fonts that are not infinitely scalable, only actually available sizes should be listed.) Applications may alter this list to suit the needs of their users; for example, desktop presentation programs may want to include additional large sizes.

8.4.1.5 Effects Check Boxes

These check boxes allow the user to choose effects such as strikeout and underline, which do not involve weight and slant, and typically do not correspond to built-in typefaces.

8.4.1.6 Color List

This drop-down list may contain color patches followed by color names. Using a list rather than a palette is recommended, because a palette would give too much space and emphasis to a relatively infrequently used part of the dialog.

The list will contain the eight most commonly used standard system colors (black, white, red, green, blue, yellow, cyan, and magenta) and additional colors if the application provides them. On monochrome systems, the color patches will be mapped to patterns. The choices available in the list should be independent of what is currently available on the printer and on the display. Optionally, applications may include an Auto list entry, which means "Use black on the printer and the system default text color on the screen."

Applications that provide a large set of colors may replace the color drop-down list by a patch of the current color next to a button labeled Color, which leads to a color selection dialog. The form of the dialog is not addressed in this guide.

8.4.1.7 Sample Box

The sample box contains the string "AaBbYyZz" displayed in the selected type-face with all the selected attributes. "AaBbYyZz" includes one character with an ascender and one with a descender, and will present fewer internationalization problems than a sample word. The sample box should be at least large enough to accommodate a 24-point font.

8.4.1.8 Command Buttons

The dialog contains two required command buttons (OK and Cancel) and two optional buttons (Apply and Help).

- The OK button accepts all changes and closes the dialog.

- The Apply button applies all changes but leaves the dialog open. Although this button is optional, we suggest including it whenever possible. The Apply button is useful whether the dialog is modal or modeless. In modal dialogs, it allows the user to see the effect of changes one step at a time; this makes it easier to reverse a decision by resetting the property that was just changed. (The sample box also shows the effect of changes but isn't sufficient by itself; the user must press Apply to see the changes. Also, the sample box shows only a few characters.) In modeless dialogs, Apply is useful for the same reasons. In addition, it allows the user to apply changes to one piece of text and then select a different piece of text and apply different changes, without having to close and reopen the dialog.

- The Cancel button changes to Close once any changes have been applied. This button closes the dialog, ignoring any changes made since the last Apply command but accepting all previous changes.

- The optional Help button allows the user to obtain further information about the current font family or about the current combination of font family, size, and attributes. For example, the Help information might provide advice on the most appropriate uses for particular fonts. The exact content of Help information is determined by the application.

8.4.1.9 Effect of Undo

If the dialog is modeless, it would be difficult for Edit Undo to restore all character properties to their state before the dialog opened; too much could have happened in the meantime. Instead, Undo should have one of the following effects (for consistency, the same recommendations apply if the dialog is modal):

A. Reverse all formatting changes made to the last selection.

B. Reverse all formatting changes committed by the last Apply or OK. (If the user commits some changes with Apply and then presses OK without making further changes, Undo should cancel the changes made by Apply rather than doing nothing.)

Option A is preferable, but B is acceptable if implementing A is too difficult. Here is an example of how the two options would work:

1. User makes selection, opens dialog, checks Bold, presses Apply.

2. Bold formatting is added to the selection in the document window.

3. User checks Italic and Underline, presses Apply.

4. Selection is italicized and underlined.

5. User activates document window, either by clicking on it or by pressing OK or Close to close the dialog.

6. User chooses Edit Undo. (Undo is dimmed if document window isn't active.)

7. In case A, the italics, underlining, and bold formatting are removed from the selection; in case B, the italics and underlining are removed, but the bold formatting is left intact.

8.5 Page Setup Dialogs

There is no common dialog for setting page margins, but there is a standard layout for text boxes used to set top, bottom, left, and right page margins. Consider the following two layouts:

Option A: Top   Left
             Bottom   Right

Option B: Left   Right
             Top   Bottom

Option A is the suggested layout because it places the two members of a natural pair (two opposites) closer to each other. The arrangement also makes it easier to compare the values of pair members. This is useful because the user often wants to set paired margins equal (for example, top and bottom margins of 1 inch, left and right margins of 1.25 inches).

8.6 About *<Application-Name>* Dialog

Figure 8.11 shows the common About *<Application-Name>* dialog. This dialog should be accessed by an About *<Application-Name>* item on the Help menu. Some elements of the dialog are recommended; others are optional.

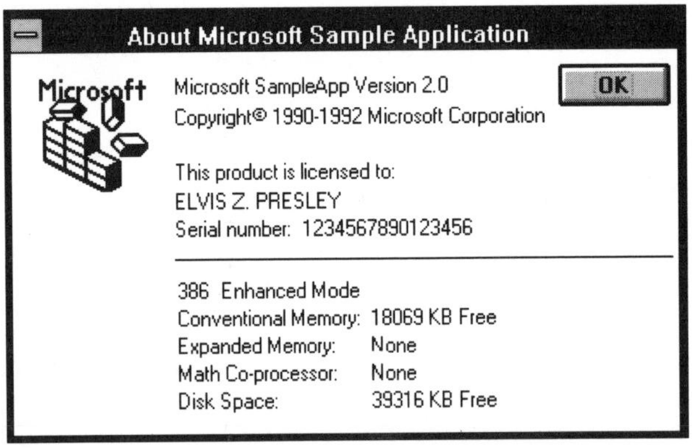

Figure 8.11   About *<Application-Name>* Dialog

8.6.1 Recommended Elements

The dialog has a title bar that includes a title in the form About *<Application-Name>*, where *<Application-Name>* is the official name of the application. The first line of the dialog repeats the official name of the application. The second line displays the version number. The next line contains a copyright statement in the form "Copyright (c) 19xx-19xx *<Corporation-Name>*." An icon (or other graphic) associated with the application appears to the left of these lines; this is typically the icon used to identify the application on the desktop, but other icons may also be used. An OK button appears in the top-right corner of the dialog.

8.6.2 Optional Information

The licensing information above the horizontal black line in the dialog is optional. The system information below the line is optional but highly recommended. If present, it should be formatted as shown in Figure 8.11. Note that the labels are left-aligned, following standard dialog box style. If this information is not present, the black line should be omitted. Applications may also add graphics, animated icons, and logos, as appropriate, to the dialog box.

Object Linking and Embedding

This chapter introduces object linking and embedding (OLE), which is the process of creating compound documents that contain embedded and linked objects. OLE can best be understood through the concept of the compound document.

9.1 Compound Documents

Over the last decade, productivity applications have become sophisticated managers of specific types of information; for example, spreadsheets, databases, charts, richly formatted text, and so on. This specialization has resulted in an inability to create documents that integrate different types of information; in general, it is difficult to include charts in a spreadsheet, or tables and figures in a text document.

This frustrates users who want to create documents that integrate several types of information through one graphical interface, without switching between applications and without using cumbersome methods to assemble and to maintain integrated information over time. Users want a consistent way to manipulate a given type of information without dealing with different interfaces. For example, it is difficult enough to master one drawing tool, let alone different tools for different applications; users want one drawing capability that they can access from all applications.

The answer lies in the concept of compound documents. A compound document is a container document that includes components from various source applications. The compound document provides the framework for housing different components and for invoking their respective applications.

In a compound document, users can point to any location and insert any kind of information—for example, text, a table, a picture, or a chart. If the user wants to insert a chart, the container application invokes a charting application. If the user wants to insert a table, the container application invokes a spreadsheet application, and so on.

In an ideal implementation of compound documents, the user is unaware that different source applications are being invoked. The process of browsing, selecting, and editing information is seamless; users can manipulate various types of information within the body of a single document without the inconvenience of switching from one application to another. They can create a single document that either links (references) or embeds different packets of information (objects); hence the term "object linking and embedding."

OLE is the process of creating compound documents that contain embedded and linked objects. These objects can be of the same type or of different types. For example, the bulk of a Microsoft Word for Windows document (client.doc) shown in Figure 9.1 is probably text, but it also contains a link to a Paintbrush™ object illustrating the company's logo and embeds a Microsoft Graph object summarizing the company's monthly expenses over the last year. Objects and their applications come in all shapes and sizes—voice objects, audiovisual objects, equation editors, graphic designers, and so on. The power of OLE, however, is limited only by the user's imagination (and perhaps by hardware).

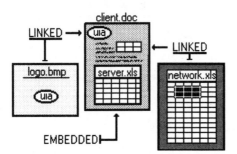

Figure 9.1   Linked and Embedded Objects in Word Document (client.doc)

9.2 OLE Concepts

- **Object.** Objects are information entities (for example, text, graphics, sound, video, and so on) that are the components of a compound document. An object is like an opaque package that contains the source application's data (or a linked reference to that data) and the name of the source application. OLE objects are "opaque" because the container application never looks inside the object and therefore doesn't need to understand its contents or its format. Instead, the container application simply calls application programming interfaces (APIs) in the OLE dynamic link library whenever it needs to display an object or wants to invoke the object's source application program.

- **Class.** The object class describes the type of information contained within an object and is assigned by the server application. Examples of Microsoft object classes include Drawing (Microsoft Draw), Picture (Microsoft Paintbrush), Worksheet (Microsoft Excel), Document (Microsoft Word), and Chart (Microsoft Graph).

- **Client.** The client is the container application that produces the container document. The use of the term "client" in OLE is similar to its use in network terminology. That is, the application that receives and stores the object is the client. For example, if a Microsoft Excel chart is embedded within a Word document, Word is the client application, the Word document is the container document, and the Microsoft Excel chart is the embedded object.

- **Server.** The server is the source application that produces the embedded or linked object. The use of the term "server" in OLE is similar to its use in network terminology. That is, the application that remotely creates, edits, and displays (or plays) the object is the server. For example, if a Paintbrush picture is embedded within a Word document, Paintbrush is the server application and the Paintbrush picture is the embedded object. In object linking, the server produces a source document from which the container document can extract information (or an image thereof).

- **Package.** A package is a special type of OLE object that contains an OLE object, a file, or a command line. It is represented by an arbitrary and selectable icon or other graphic. Double-clicking a packaged object activates the object inside the package. Packages present compact tokens of large files or OLE objects. They also provide some of the functionality associated with hyperlinks.

- **Embedding.** Embedding is the process of inserting a new or an existing object into a container document (see Figure 9.2). All information normally stored in a file created by a server is instead embedded into the body of a file created by the client. This allows all components of a compound document to be stored in a single file. The user can spend more time composing and updating a single document and less time dealing with the bookkeeping of multiple source documents. For example, embedding a chart within a Word document is easier than remembering the location of the chart on disk.

- **Linking.** Linking achieves the effect of copying information from one document into another without actually making a physical copy (whereas in embedding the actual information is stored within the document). When the user links information from a source document into a container document, the information appears inside the container as if it had been physically copied there. In fact, the container simply contains a link, that is, a reference to where the information exists in the source document and where the source document can be found. The container document uses the link to get this information when needed—for example, when updating the display (sometimes a bitmap or metafile will be placed into the container as a facade). Links provide an effective way for documents on a local drive or documents distributed over machines on a network to share information. For example, Figure 9.3 shows how a Microsoft Excel worksheet that contains a summary of monthly financial transactions can be used for linking. The user can link the summary lines (omitting the raw data) into an end-of-month document for the manager and link all the data over a network into a database at corporate headquarters. Updating the monthly transactions automatically updates the end-of-month document and the corporate database.

Compound documents can contain any number of embedded and linked objects.

Figure 9.2   Embedding (Microsoft Excel Worksheet Embedded Within Word Document)

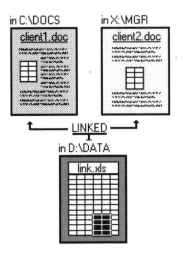

Figure 9.3   Linking (Separate Word Documents Link Fragment of Microsoft Excel Worksheet)

9.3 OLE Interface

The OLE interface provides easy methods for inserting, editing, viewing, and activating linked and embedded objects, and modifying the properties of such objects.

9.3.1 Clients and Servers

The OLE process requires a dialog between client and server. Any application is capable of being a client, a server, or both. In addition to the changes in functionality, there are several key differences in the interface of clients and servers.

- Clients have four commands added to the Edit menu below the Paste command: Paste Special (and/or Paste Link[1]), Links, Object, and Insert Object, (see Figure 9.12). If there is an Insert menu, the Insert Object command may be placed there as Object instead.

- There are two types of servers: full servers and mini-servers. The title bar for both server types should read: "*<Server> - <Descriptive-Class-Name>* in *<Container-Document>*" (see Figure 9.4). An object class must always be presented to the user (in window titles, list panes, dialogs, and so on) in the human-readable format provided by the registration database. The client application must supply an appropriate *<Container-Document>* string to the server. Because link servers open the source document, their title bars display the standard information: "*<Server> - <Source-Document>*".

9.3.1.1 Mini-Servers

A mini-server looks like a dialog box and requires three command buttons: OK, Cancel, and Help. (The example mini-server in Figure 9.4 includes an optional Apply button.)

---

[1] Paste Link is optional if you have the preferred Paste Special command discussed in section 9.3.2.4.

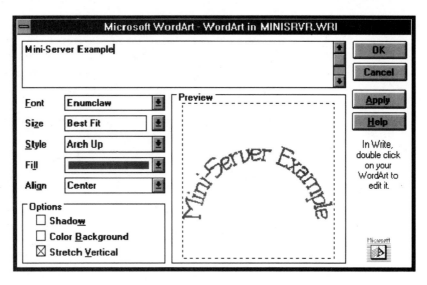

Figure 9.4 Mini-Server Interface

9.3.1.2 Full Servers

A full server is a stand-alone application with a full set of menus. In a full server (or in a server window in an MDI application), the File menu should be modified as follows (see Figure 9.5):

- The Save command should be replaced by Update *<Container-Document>*.

- The Close command (MDI applications) should be replaced by Close & Return to *<Container-Document>*.

- The Save As command should change to Save Copy As.

- The Exit command should be replaced by Exit & Return to *<Container-Document>*. The client application must supply the appropriate *<Container-Document>* string to the server.

Additional note: SDI applications should not implement New and Open when running as servers. It is recommended that these commands be replaced by the Import command, which would allow the loading of an existing file (object) without severing the connection with the client. (See section 9.3.5.1.)

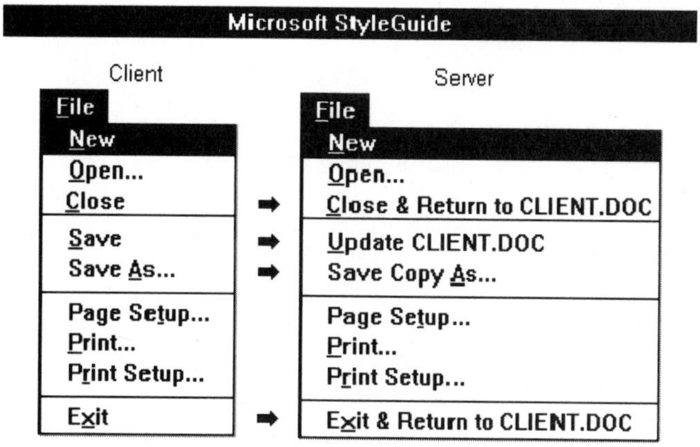

Figure 9.5   Full Server Interface Changes

If the user attempts to launch a server (for example, a mini-server) that cannot be run as a stand-alone application, the error message shown in Figure 9.6 should be issued.

Figure 9.6   Warning Message When a Server Cannot Be Run Stand-Alone

9.3.2 Inserting Objects

The basic user interface for inserting linked and embedded objects relies on the familiar Cut, Copy, and Paste commands on the Edit menu, plus one additional command—Paste Special (and/or Paste Link)—for inserting linked objects and for providing additional control over data formats. To accelerate object embedding, applications should implement the Insert Object[2] command. The use of Copy and Paste is not limited to selected document fragments. Entire files may be linked or embedded into documents and displayed as double-clickable icons (that is, packages) with Copy/Paste or by using drag/drop from the File Manager.

---

[2] Paste Special and Insert Object are optional only if a cogent argument can be made for their omission. Paste Link is optional if the preferred Paste Special is used.

9.3.2.1 Inserting Embedded Objects with the Insert Object Command

To accelerate the procedure for embedding new objects, applications should implement an Insert Object command. In applications that include an Insert menu, the
command should appear on that menu and should be called Object. In applications
that do not include an Insert menu, the command should appear on the Edit menu
and should be called Insert Object. The command leads to the dialog shown in
Figure 9.7.

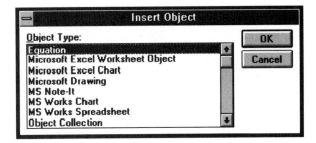

Figure 9.7   Insert Object Dialog Box

The Object Type list box in the Insert Object dialog contains the descriptive object
class names drawn from the registration database maintained by Windows. The
client application must sort and display the list in alphabetical order. To embed an
object, the user selects its name from the list and presses OK. This results in the
following:

- A rectangle (default size is determined by the client application) immediately
  appears at the insertion point as an interim placeholder until the new object
  image is available. The rectangle is masked with the open visualization (see
  Figure 9.13) to indicate that its server is currently open.

- The server application is launched for the selected object type. The server displays a blank or default window in which the user can create or edit the object.

If the client application fails to locate the requested server when the user selects
the entry from the Insert Object dialog or double-clicks on an object, the following
error message should be displayed.

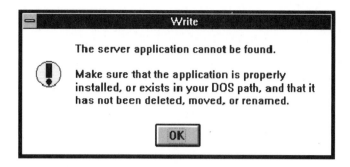

Figure 9.8   Warning Message When Server Application Cannot Be Found

While editing, the user may select the Update *<Container-Document>* command from the server's File menu at any time to place the current rendition of the embedded object in the client at the current cursor location. (This will replace the placeholder if it is the first update.) After editing is complete, the user selects the Exit & Return to *<Container-Document>* command from the File menu of the server. This command closes the server and returns focus to the container document. If the user does not choose the Update command for a modified embedded object before exiting, the prompt shown in Figure 9.9 is displayed.

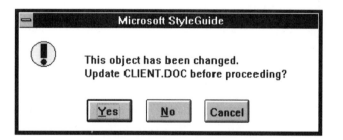

Figure 9.9   Warning Message When Exiting Server with a Modified Embedded Object

9.3.2.2 Inserting Embedded Objects with Cut, Copy, and Paste

Although the Insert Object command for embedding objects is preferred, most users are familiar with the Cut, Copy, and Paste commands and will want to use these commands. The basic procedure for inserting embedded objects with Cut, Copy, and Paste is simple. For example, inserting a drawing into a text document requires the following steps:

- In the server application for the drawing, select all or part of the drawing and choose the Copy (or Cut) command from the Edit menu.

- Switch to the text application.

- In the text application, position the cursor as desired and choose the Paste command from the Edit menu.

This procedure inserts the drawing at the current cursor location in the text document.

In general, for applications that support OLE, the Paste command will embed the object that is on the clipboard. Under some circumstances, however, the application may choose not to embed the object. In particular, if the object is represented on the clipboard not only by the embedded object format but also by an alternate format that completely represents the original data and that the application knows how to edit, the application should insert this editable data rather than embedding the object. Most applications, however, will not be able to provide full editing capabilities for alternate formats, so they will simply embed the object and allow the source application to later function as a server.

Thus, in most applications that support OLE, the Paste command will embed the object in the current document when the clipboard contains an object from another application. Note that in applications that do not support OLE, the Paste command simply inserts a static copy of the data without providing easy access to the tools required to edit the data.

9.3.2.3 Inserting Linked Objects with Copy and Paste Link

Inserting linked objects is as easy as inserting embedded objects. To continue the previous example, suppose that instead of embedding the drawing, the user wanted to insert a link to the drawing. The following steps would be required:

- In the drawing application, select all or part of the drawing and choose the Copy command from the Edit menu. (Do not use Cut because it eliminates the source.)

- Switch to the text application.

- In the text application, position the cursor as desired and choose the Paste Link (or Paste Special) command from the Edit menu.

Note that the only difference between linking and embedding an object is the selection of Paste Link instead of Paste in the final step.

This procedure inserts a linked object to the drawing at the current cursor location in the text document. The drawing is displayed in the text document but stored in the original drawing file. The link is an "automatic" link; in other words, whenever the drawing file changes, the drawing in the text file is updated automatically. Automatic and manual links are described more fully in section 9.4.

9.3.2.4 Selectively Inserting Linked and Embedded Objects with the Paste Special Command

Some applications will need only the simple methods discussed in the preceding sections for inserting linked and embedded objects. Most applications, however, may want to provide additional control with the Paste Special command.

Some applications can interpret and edit data in a variety of formats—for example, formatted text (that is, rich text format or RTF), ASCII text, bitmaps, and object-oriented picture formats. These applications may provide a Paste Special command on the Edit menu to provide greater control over the format to be pasted.

By default, the standard Paste and Paste Link commands look on the clipboard for a format that completely represents the original data and that the client application can edit with its own tools. If such a format is found, the original data is translated into that format and inserted into the client; if not, an image representing the original data is usually inserted. In some cases, however, the user may want to override the default format. For example, special tools or editing operations (for example, rotation, translation, applying format) might be available only for a nondefault format (for example, copying the format, but not the contents, of a paragraph to another paragraph). Alternatively, the user might want to force the data to be inserted as an embedded object so that the tools of the original creator application can easily be invoked to edit the object. These format choices are supported by the Paste Special dialog shown in Figure 9.10.[3]

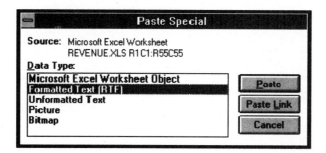

Figure 9.10   Paste Special Dialog Box

---

[3] Although not shown, a Help button may be included in the Paste Special dialog box if elaboration on data types or paste behavior is useful.

The Data Type list in the Paste Special dialog shows the formats available on the clipboard that the client can process. The names of these formats should clearly suggest the resulting capability of the pasted information. The list also includes one additional entry, *<Descriptive-Class-Name>* Object (for example, Microsoft Excel Worksheet Object). When the dialog opens, the format that would have been used if the Paste command had been selected from the Edit menu is highlighted. The dialog contains two command buttons, Paste and Paste Link, which operate as follows:

- The Paste button translates the data into the selected format and inserts it into the document without establishing a link to the original source of the data. (If the user does not change the default format that is originally selected in the list, pressing Paste in this dialog is equivalent to choosing Paste from the Edit menu.) If the user selects *<Descriptive-Class-Name>* Object instead of a data format, the data is not translated into a native format, but inserted as an embedded object.

- Like Paste, the Paste Link button translates the data into the selected format and inserts it into the document. (If a particular data type cannot support a link, the Paste Link button is dimmed.) Unlike Paste, however, Paste Link establishes an automatic link to the original source of the data. Because the Paste Special dialog provides a superset of the functionality provided by the Paste Link command, applications that include Paste Special need not also include Paste Link. The Paste Link button should be dimmed only when the clipboard does not contain an object link format. Paste-linking *<Descriptive-Class-Name>* Object behaves like any other link—that is, it inserts a facade into the container document along with a reference to the source file.

9.3.2.5 Copying Linked Objects

When a linked object exists in one document, it can be inserted in other documents with Copy and Paste (not Paste Link). For example, suppose that Document1 contains Link1, which refers to a bitmap in a graphics file (see Figure 9.11). If Link1 is selected, the Copy command copies Link1, not the bitmap that is the source object. The Paste command then inserts a copy of Link1 (which we can call CopyOfLink1) at the current cursor location. Like Link1, CopyOfLink1 refers to the original bitmap. If Paste Link is used instead of Paste, a link to (not a copy of) Link1 is inserted. This new link (LinkToLink1) refers to Link1, which in turn refers to the original bitmap. Link1, CopyOfLink1, and LinkToLink1 all yield exactly the same visual presentation (a representation of the original bitmap) in their client documents, but Link1 and CopyOfLink1 refer directly to the bitmap, whereas LinkToLink1 refers to the bitmap only indirectly, through Link1.

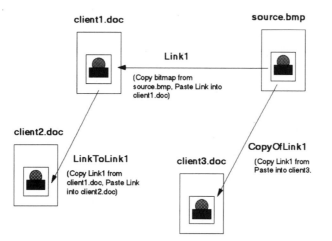

client1.doc

source.bmp

Link1

(Copy bitmap from source.bmp, Paste Link into client1.doc)

client2.doc

CopyOfLink1

LinkToLink1

client3.doc

(Copy Link1 from Paste into client3.

(Copy Link1 from client1.doc, Paste Link into client2.doc)

Figure 9.11   Transferring Links: Paste vs. Paste Link

Just as linked objects can be copied from one location to another with Copy and Paste, they can also be moved with Cut and Paste. In this respect, linked objects behave like all other objects that can be manipulated from the clipboard.

9.3.3 Viewing Objects

Compound documents may contain several OLE objects interspersed with objects that are native to the document. Because OLE objects support operations different from those supported by the native objects, it is convenient to be able to visually distinguish the two. For this purpose, applications should provide visual indications of OLE object boundaries. The boundaries for a particular object should appear whenever the object is selected. In addition, applications should provide a way for all object boundaries to be turned on or off at once, to facilitate easy viewing of all OLE objects in a document. For example, applications can reveal object boundaries and other normally hidden information with a Hidden Structure command on the View menu or a Show All check box in an Options dialog.

Figure 9.12 shows recommended boundaries for linked and embedded objects.

Linked object with dotted borner   *Embedded object with solid border*

Figure 9.12   Recommended Boundaries for Linked and Embedded Objects

In addition, when an embedded or packaged object is open in the server application, its appearance should be masked in the container document. The masking is also applied to objects whose representation is an icon (like sound). There is no masking for open linked objects.

Figure 9.13 shows recommended visuals for the inactive, selected, and open (embedded or packaged objects only) states of an object.

Inactive

Selected

Opened

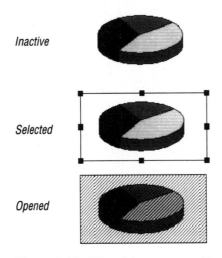

Figure 9.13   Visual Appearance Recommendations

9.3.4 Activating Objects

When OLE objects are inserted into a document, the standard user interface provides two methods for editing the objects: by double-clicking and through the Edit menu *<Descriptive-Class-Name>* Object command.

9.3.4.1 Double-Clicking

Double-clicking on the object boundary (or selecting the object and pressing ENTER[4]) invokes the server application associated with the object. If the object is unitary (that is, if only the whole object can be selected in the container document) the user can double-click anywhere on the object to invoke the server.[5] If the server is an SDI server, a new instance of the server is started, even if one is already running. This tight connection between the new instance and the current object helps promote the impression that the object is an integral part of the compound document in which it is displayed.

There are three exceptions to the rule that a new instance of the server should be started to edit an object. No new instance is necessary in the following cases:

1. The object is already open in an existing instance of the server. In this case, the existing instance should be surfaced.

2. The server application is an MDI application and is the same as the client application (that is, the editor for the object is the client itself). The appropriate behavior depends on whether the link is external or internal.

   a. External links: For example, suppose that one Word document contains a link to another Word document. In this case, double-clicking on the linked object should not start a new instance of Word. Instead, if a document window for the source document is already open within the current instance (case 1 above), that document window should be surfaced. Otherwise, a new document window should be opened for it within the current instance of Word.

   b. Internal links: If the link refers to another part of the same document, double-clicking on the linked object should scroll to show the source of the link.

3. If the server is an MDI application that does not use memory efficiently when multiple instances are running, it should make an intelligent decision about what to do. For example, the application can check available memory to see whether running one more instance is likely to cause problems. If so, the application can issue a warning and/or offer the user a choice between starting a new instance or loading the file into an existing instance.

---

[4] Selection+ENTER need not be implemented in a single or multiple-edit line because, by default, this should replace the selection with a carriage return and a line feed. In this case, the user can activate the object by using the *<Descriptive-Class-Name>* Object command discussed in section 9.3.4.2.

[5] The double-click or (selection+ENTER) starts the server and invokes the primary verb for that object. Sometimes the primary verb is not Edit. Instead, it is an Activate-type verb such as Run (for a script), Play (for a voice note), and so on. The distinction between primary and secondary verbs is described further in the discussion of the *<Descriptive-Class-Name>* Object command in section 9.3.4.2.

9.3.4.2 The *<Descriptive-Class-Name>* Object Command

If an object supports only one verb, it appears as *<Verb-0> <Descriptive-Class-Name>* Object on the Edit menu. If an object supports multiple verbs, they appear within a cascading menu; selecting *<Descriptive-Class-Name>* Object from the Edit menu displays a submenu for *<Verb-0>*, *<Verb-1>*, and so on. Scripts, videos, and voice notes are examples of objects that may support multiple verbs such as play, edit, and rewind.[6] The commands should change dynamically in the menus to reflect object class-specific verb names retrieved from the registration database. The menus must access the verbs from the database; no fixed commands should be used. These verbs should be registered as mixed-case strings and follow the general style of menu commands described in Chapter 5. Each registered verb should also have an assigned mnemonic (underlined letter) for keyboard access. Also note that each verb should be a single word to ensure that the status bar messages and menus in the client application (described later) will read correctly.

If a selection contains multiple objects of the same class or of different classes, the object verbs should not be available to the user. The object verbs should appear only when there is exactly one object in the current selection; no attempt should be made to join verbs of multiple objects in a selection.[7]

The most frequent operations for an object should be registered as its primary verb (*<Verb-0>*). Mouse users can invoke the primary verb through double-clicking; keyboard users can invoke the primary verb by selecting the object and pressing ENTER.[8]

Figure 9.14 shows an example of a *<Descriptive-Class-Name>* Object submenu that leads to dynamic, object-specific menu items. The primary verb is accessed by the first (topmost) item, followed by subsequent verbs in order.

---

[6] When such an object plays, if possible, it should provide a way for the user to interrupt playing and start editing. For example, a voice note can display a control panel with buttons for stop, rewind, and so on.

[7] Verbs are not displayed even if the selection contains objects of the same class, because applying a verb concurrently to the whole set would have ambiguous results.

[8] Selection+ENTER need not be implemented in a single or multiple-edit line because, by default, this should replace the selection with a carriage return and a line feed. In this case, the user can activate the object by using the *<Class>* Object command.

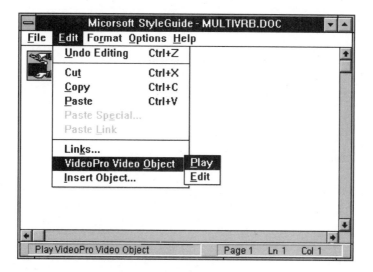

Figure 9.14 *<Descriptive-Class-Name>* Object Command with Object-Specific Verbs

For packages (which are always embedded, never linked), the primary verb is the primary verb of the object inside the package; the primary menu item name is Activate Contents. This means that the mouse user can invoke the primary verb of the object inside the package by double-clicking on the package icon.

The secondary verb for a package is Edit Package. Selecting this verb invokes the Packager. Some objects (for example, text objects) have no secondary verb. For such objects, the *<Descriptive-Class-Name>* Object command does not lead to a cascading menu; the command simply executes the primary verb. The verb is prepended to the menu item: *<Verb> <Descriptive-Class-Name>* Object. For example, if the object is a Word document, the menu item is Edit Word Document Object.

9.3.4.3 Busy and Unavailable Servers

A server may be busy or unavailable for several reasons. For example, it may be busy printing, it may be waiting for user input to a modeless error message, or it may be hung or accidentally deleted. If the server is not available, the warning message in Figure 9.15 should be displayed. The recommended time between the first request and displaying the dialog is 2-3 seconds.

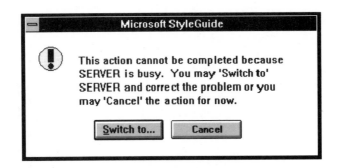

Figure 9.15   Server Busy Warning Message

Three different cases can cause the warning message in Figure 9.15 to be displayed: Busy, Blocked, and OLE_BUSY. Table 9.1 describes the behavior of the buttons in each case.

Table 9.1   Behavior Caused by Different States

State	Caused By	Button Pressed	
		Switch To...	Cancel
Busy	Client receives OLE_QUERY_RETRY callback notification	Will invoke Task Manager	The OLE operation is discontinued. The dialog is dismissed.
Blocked	Client timed out before getting OLE_RELEASE	Will invoke Task Manager	The OLE operation will continue. The dialog is dismissed.
OLE_BUSY	OLE libraries returned OLE_BUSY from an API call	Will invoke Task Manager	The previous OLE operation will continue. The dialog is dismissed.

9.3.5 Editing Objects

When the server window opens, the object is loaded into the window. For embedded objects, the window is initially sized to show only the portion of the object that was displayed in the client.[9] The user can resize the window to display additional portions of the embedded object. In the case of linked objects, the entire linked file is loaded, and the linked portion is selected. If possible, the server should not come up maximized and should obscure as little of the object in the container document as possible.

---

[9] Some embedded objects such as spreadsheets may include portions that are not displayed. These hidden portions are included only if the displayed portion draws data from them.

The user can modify the object with the editing tools provided by the server. The process for updating the object in the container file varies depending on whether the server supports the single document interface (SDI) or the multiple document interface (MDI).

9.3.5.1 Updating Objects from SDI Servers

9.3.5.1.1 The Update Command

When an SDI application functions as a server for an embedded object, the Save command on the File menu changes to Update, as illustrated in Figure 9.5. (This change occurs only for embedded objects, not for linked objects.) The Update command updates the object in the container document, but (like Save) does not close the server; the server is left open to allow the user to make further changes after seeing the effects (for example, repagination) of the update in the client. If the user tries to exit the server without updating the object, the warning message shown in Figure 9.8 is displayed.

9.3.5.1.2 The Save Copy As, File New, and Open Commands

When editing an embedded object, the user can choose the Save Copy As command from the File menu to save a copy of the embedded object in a separate file. Save Copy As does not sever the connection with the client. The inclusion of the New or Open commands in the File menu is not recommended for SDI applications. These commands should be replaced by the Import command, which allows the user to load an existing file (object) into the server application without severing the connection between the server and the client application.

If an SDI application implements the File New and File Open commands, which sever the connection to the client, the warning shown in Figure 9.16 should be displayed.

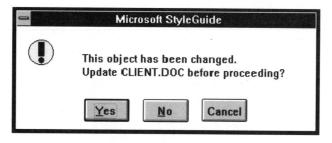

Figure 9.16   Warning Message when Terminating OLE Connection with Modified Object

9.3.5.1.3 Closing (Exiting) a Server or a Client

When the server closes, the focus returns to the client. If the user closes a client while servers for that client are still open, the usual client application save confirmation appears. (The container document is considered modified as soon as any object is opened.) If the user chooses to save the container document, all objects are updated without prompting before the file is actually saved. Declining to save the file will likewise discard any modifications made to the objects.

9.3.5.2 Updating Objects from MDI Servers

The procedure for editing and updating objects from MDI servers is similar to the procedure for SDI servers, with the following exceptions:

- If the focus changes from the embedded object window to a "normal" document window (that is, a window containing an existing file or a new document), the File menu reflects that of a client (see Figure 9.5). If the embedded object window regains focus, File menu reflects that of a server again.

- When the user chooses the File New or File Open command, the window containing the embedded object remains open. Therefore, it is not necessary to display any warning messages about updating the object.

- When the user chooses the File Save As command, the client application is informed and the link follows the newly saved file.

9.3.5.3 Operations in Clients Containing Open OLE Objects

9.3.5.3.1 Save Command

When the user saves the container document with the File Save command, all open objects are automatically updated in the container document before the document is saved. The server application remains open.

9.3.5.3.2 Delete Command

Deleting a selection destroys objects (whether or not they are open) just as it destroys native data. Servers of deleted objects close silently. The client should request an update from the server before deletion so that the user can get the latest updates in the case of an undo.

9.3.5.3.3 Close (Exit) Command

The case of closing a client containing an open object was discussed in section 9.3.5.1.3.

9.3.5.3.4 Cut and Copy Commands

When the user chooses the Cut or Copy command, open objects will silently update and the updated versions will be carried to the clipboard. Copying open objects leave their servers open and connected to the original object; cutting open objects close their servers.

9.3.5.3.5 Paste Command (Dropping on, Inserting over, Typing over, etc.)

Pasting over objects (whether or not they are open) replaces them just as it replaces native data. Pasting over open objects also closes their servers. Before closing the server, the client should request an update to prevent data loss in the case that the user wants to undo the paste operation.

9.4 Links and Link Dialogs

Links are "displayed" references to data stored in external documents (or sometimes to data stored within the same document), as illustrated in Figure 9.1. Because linking relies on a dialog with source documents, an interface for maintaining and updating such links is necessary. Figure 9.17 shows the Links dialog, which allows users to change the type of updating (automatic or manual) for links, update linked objects, cancel links, and repair broken links.

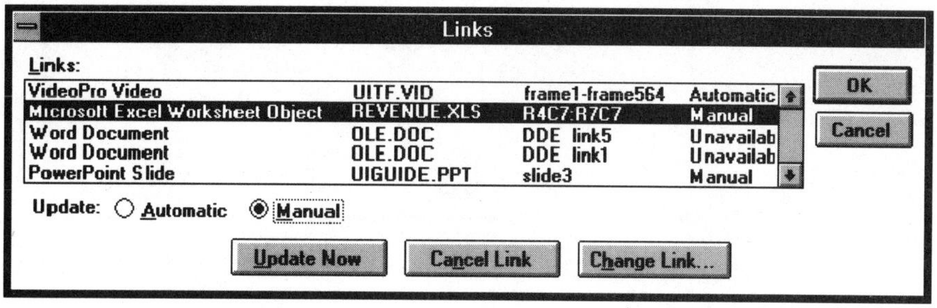

Figure 9.17   **Links Dialog**

When the Links dialog first opens, the Links list shows each link contained in the document. Links contained in the current selection in the document are initially selected in the list. (Embedded objects are not shown in the list.) The list is an extended-selection list; the user can select one or several links by using SHIFT+click for range selection and CTRL+click for disjoint selection, as described in Chapter 3, section 3.1.2.1.

9.4.1 Update Option Buttons

Below the Links list, the Links dialog contains two Update option buttons: Automatic and Manual. When the dialog opens, these buttons reflect whether the currently selected links are automatically updated whenever the linked file changes, or whether they must be manually updated. If the selected links have different update rules, neither button is selected. In this case, choosing one of the buttons changes all the selected links to have the corresponding update behavior.

9.4.2 Link Command Buttons

At the bottom of the Links dialog, three push buttons allow the user to update, cancel, and change the selected links.

- Update Now updates all links selected in the Links list. In other words, the presentations of the linked objects in the client are updated to reflect the current data in the linked files. Suppose that the selected links are all associated with a file called SOURCE.DOC. It is possible that the client contains other, currently unselected links associated with the same file. In this case, after the selected links are updated, the message dialog shown in Figure 9.18 is displayed. If the links selected originally are associated with several files and if the document contains other unselected links to those files, the message dialog is displayed once for each file.

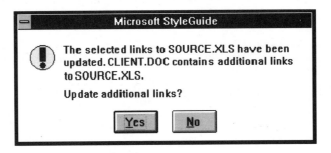

Figure 9.18   Message for Updating Additional Links to the Same File

- Cancel Link permanently breaks the link between the client and the server. The linked object in the container document is changed to a picture that can no longer be updated or edited with the standard OLE techniques. The picture can still be edited with the older Cut, Copy, and Paste techniques, but it is unlikely that the picture will retain all the data present in the original linked object. When the user presses the Cancel Link button, the entry for the link disappears from the Links list in the Links dialog. Offering the option of changing an embedded object into a picture should be part of an application's own controls (like a menu or a button).

- The Change Link button is dimmed if the selection in the Links list includes multiple links that are not all linked to the same file. Otherwise, the button is active and leads to a dialog exactly like the File Open dialog, except that the title is Change Link (see Figure 9.19). The standard File Open dialog is described in Chapter 8, section 8.1.1.

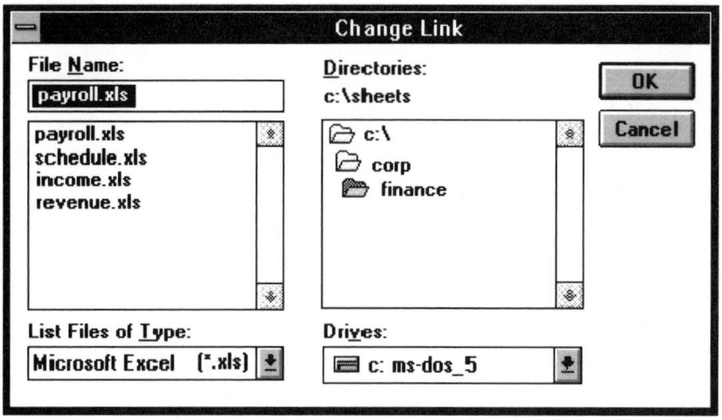

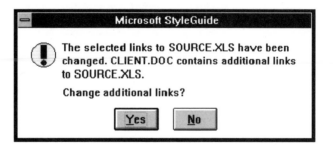

Figure 9.19   Change Link Dialog Box

The Change Link dialog allows the user to change the file to which a link refers. For example, if a linked file is renamed or moved to a new location, this dialog lets the user reconnect the link in the container document, using the new name or the new location of the linked file.

When the user chooses a file and presses OK in the Change Link dialog, the links that were selected in the Links list are disconnected from their previous file and connected to the newly chosen file. It is possible that the previous file was also associated with other, currently unselected links in the container document. In this case, after the selected links are changed, the message dialog shown in Figure 9.20 is displayed. This message is analogous to the one shown in Figure 9.17.

Figure 9.20   Message for Changing Additional Links to the Same File

9.4.3 Dialog Control Buttons

- The OK button confirms the changes that the user made in the dialog and closes the dialog.

- The Cancel button discards all the changes that the user made and closes the dialog.

9.4.4 Link Status Entries

The link status entries in the Links list box consist of four parts: the human-readable form of the class name, the source file for the link, the item name for the link, and the status of the link.

- The human-readable form of the class name is the string that is registered in the registration database for that object class.

- The source file for the link contains the full pathname for the link. If the full path is too long to be displayed, the entry should be truncated.

- The item name contains the server-specific item name for the object.

- The status of the link can be Automatic, Manual, or Unavailable:

  - An *automatic* link is updated automatically when it is changed in the server or when the linked object is loaded and the server is open with that object. It is also updated when the linked object is loaded and the user responds "Yes" to the Link Update Message Dialog (Figure 9.21).

  - A *manual* link is a link that the user must explicitly update through the Links dialog. The update takes place when the link is selected and the user presses the Update Link button in the Links dialog.

  - The link receives an *unavailable* status when the attempt to update the link (upon loading the file or requesting OleUpdate) fails.

9.4.5 Other Dialogs for Link Updating

When the user opens a file containing links (manual or automatic[10]), a message dialog is displayed to ask the user whether to update the links (see Figure 9.21). If the user presses the Yes button, the application updates all of the links.

---

[10]Automatic links are not automatically updated unless the server is open and the source of the link is loaded, because this could make simple viewing of the file cumbersome.

Figure 9.21   Link Update Message Dialog

The progress indicator shown in Figure 9.22 may be displayed while the links are being updated. The Cancel button interrupts the update process and cancels all updating that has already been carried out.

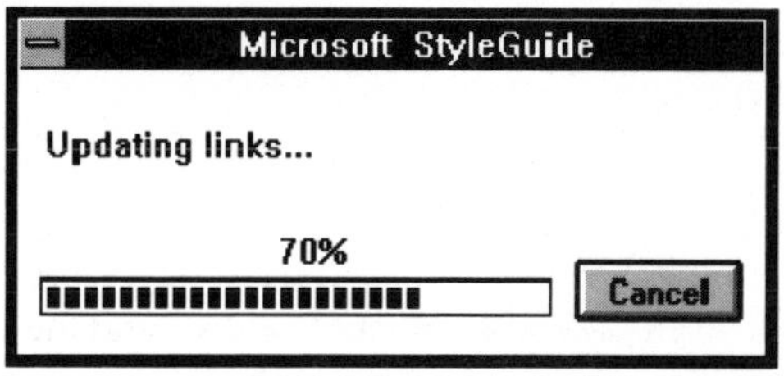

Figure 9.22   Progress Indicator for Link Updating

If some of the linked files are unavailable, the warning dialog shown in Figure 9.23 is displayed. This dialog contains two buttons, OK and Links. The OK button closes the dialog without updating the links. The Links button displays the Links dialog (see Figure 9.17) with all the links listed. Unavailable linked files are marked with the word "Unavailable" in the third column of the list. The user can attempt to locate the unavailable files by using the Change Link dialog (see Figure 9.19), which is available from the Change Link command button in the Links dialog.

Figure 9.23   Warning Message for Unavailable Links

9.5 Status Line Message Recommendations

If a client application uses the status line to elaborate on menu commands, the messages below can be used for OLE commands.

Table 9.2   Status Line Messages

Menu Commands	Status Line Message
File Menu	
Update	Update changes in *<Container-Document>*
Save Copy As	Save a copy of *<Descriptive-Class-Name>* in a separate file
Exit & Return to *<Container-Document>*	Exit *<Server >* and return to *<Container-Document>*
Edit Menu	
Paste	Inserts clipboard contents as *<Default-Data-Type>*[11]
Paste Special	Inserts clipboard contents as a linked object, embedded object, or other format
Paste Link	Inserts a link to *<Descriptive-Class-Name>* Object from *<Source-Document>*
Insert Object	Inserts a new embedded object
<Verb>[12]*<Descriptive-Class-Name>* Object	None
<Descriptive-Class-Name> Object	Apply the following commands to *<Descriptive-Class-Name>* Object
<Descriptive-Class-Name> Object *<Verb>*	None
Links	Allows links to be viewed, updated, opened, or canceled
Options (Preferences) Menu	
Show Objects	Displays the borders around objects (toggle)
Mouse Interface	
When an object is selected	Double-click to *<Primary-Verb>* *<Descriptive-Class-Name>* Object

---

[11] *<Default-Data-Type>* is identical to the initially highlighted value in the Paste Special Data Type list. This status line message indicates the data format used to paste clipboard contents.

[12] If no verb in the registration database is specified, "Activate" should be used as the default.

The Pen Interface

Pen-based computers let users provide input by tapping or writing on the surface of the computer screen with a special pen. The pen provides a natural and intuitive way of interacting with the computer. The number of pen-capable computers and applications is expected to grow rapidly in the next few years. Any application that makes good use of menus and graphical controls has a head start on a good pen interface.

10.1 Pen Input

The pen can be used for both pointing and writing, depending on where it is placed.

10.1.1 Pointing

When the pen is moved over menus or controls, it becomes a pointing device and lets the user select menu commands, choose buttons, or perform other mouse-like operations. Tapping[1] the pen once on the screen is equivalent to clicking mouse button 1 once. A double-tap is equivalent to a double-click. If the user holds down the barrel button of the pen while tapping, the tap is equivalent to a click with mouse button 2.

10.1.2 Writing

When the pen is over an edit control or a text area, it becomes a writing tool and the pointer changes into a pen shape. When the tip of the pen touches the screen, the pen starts "inking"—that is, tracing lines on the screen. The user can draw shapes, characters, and other patterns; these can remain on the screen exactly as drawn or can be recognized, interpreted, and redisplayed.

10.1.3 Dragging

The pen retains the power of the mouse even in contexts where it normally functions as a writing or a drawing tool. If the user presses the pen tip down on a text area and holds it steady for a certain period before moving it, the subsequent pen movements are interpreted as mouse movements. Thus, the pen can be used for drag selection of text, outline selection of graphical objects, object movement, and other mouselike operations.

---

[1] To tap, the user presses the pen tip on the screen and releases it without moving the pen.

Table 10.1 summarizes the principal pen techniques described above and gives a few examples of their use.

Table 10.1   Pen Techniques

Technique	Examples of Use
Tap	Select object or menu command; set insertion point in text; push command button.
Double-tap	Open object; select word.
Drag	Move object (for example, to move a window, drag its title bar); resize object (for example, to resize a window, drag its border; to resize a graphical object, drag its resize handles).
Press/hold/drag	Select text from pen-down location to pen-up location; perform drag operations (for example, object movement or marquee selection) in contexts where the pen normally functions as a writing or drawing tool.
Write/draw	Enter text or graphics; execute gestural commands (see Table 10.2).

10.1.4 Gestures

When the pen is used for writing, certain ink patterns are interpreted as "gestures" —special symbols that issue a command, such as deleting text, or produce a non-printing text character, such as a carriage return or a TAB. For example, the "∧" shape is equivalent to the Paste command. After a gesture is interpreted, its ink is removed from the display. Table 10.2 lists the 12 standard pen gestures.

Table 10.2 Pen Gestures

Name	Glyph	Hot Spot	Acts Where?	Granularity	Effect	Equivalent**	Comments
Space					Insert space where drawn.	Space character	Don't replace selection. (For non-positional operation, which replaces selection, use on-screen keyboard, menu, or circled letters.)
New Line		First point			Insert new line where drawn.	New line character	
Tab				Insertion point	Insert tab where drawn.	Tab character	
Paste		Top	Positional		Paste where drawn.	SHIFT+INS***	
Extend Selection	1↓ ↑2	Center			Extend selection from anchor point to gesture.	SHIFT+click	Start downward to avoid confusion with *l*.
Backspace		Lowest point		Character	Delete character under gesture.	BACKSPACE	Start in either direction.
Delete Words		Left, right		Word	Delete words under gesture.	Double-click +DEL****	
Edit Text		Inside center of lower "v"	Act on selection if one exists; otherwise positional* (always positional in boxed edit controls).		Put selection (if any) or word into Edit Text dialog.	—	
Cut		First point		Selection or word	Cut selection if any, otherwise cut word under gesture.*	SHIFT+DEL***	
Copy		Center of bounding box			Copy selection if any, otherwise copy word under gesture.*	CTRL+INS***	Feedback: copy pointer flashes.
Delete		Lowest point		Selection or character	Delete selection if any, otherwise delete character under gesture.*	DEL	Start in either direction.
Undo		None	Non-positional	Operation	Undo last operation.	ALT+ BACKSPACE***	

* Cut, Copy, and Delete never act positionally in Windows applications that were not designed for the pen. If there is no selection, they act at the insertion point. For Cut and Copy, this usually means that no operation is performed.

** This column specifies keyboard and mouse equivalents used in Windows applications that were not designed specifically for the pen.

*** This column is not intended to represent the recommended shortcuts for Cut/Copy/Paste, but to show the mapping that Windows for Pen Computing uses for compatibility with Windows version 3.0 applications.

**** Note that double-click+DEL deletes only one word, whereas the Delete Words gesture is capable of deleting multiple words.

10.1.4.1 Positionality of Gestures

Most gestures act positionally. They contain a "hot spot" that can be used to determine where the gesture should act. For example, the hot spot of the Paste gesture is at the top of the "^" shape. When the user draws the Paste gesture, the pasted data is inserted at the location of the hot spot.

Undo is the only gesture that never acts positionally. Regardless of where the user draws it, this gesture cancels the last operation. Positional, object-specific Undo functionality is a possible extension for future interfaces.

10.1.4.2 Basic and Advanced Gestures

To reduce the amount that new users must learn, the gestures are divided into two sets: basic and advanced.

The basic gestures are Edit Text, Backspace, Space, New Line, Cut, and Undo. Cut is included instead of Delete for two reasons:

- In handwriting edit controls and in pen-centric applications, Cut can be used to delete one word at a time.

- Delete is only necessary when the user doesn't want to destroy the contents of the clipboard. This is an advanced situation that beginning users don't need to know about.

Undo is included in the basic set, despite its availability on the Edit menu of many applications. Rapid gestural access to Undo functionality makes the interface seem more forgiving and approachable.

The advanced gestures are Copy, Paste, Delete, Delete Words, Extend Selection, and Tab. Copy and Paste are included in the advanced set instead of the basic set for two reasons:

- Copy and Paste commands are available on the Edit menu of most applications.

- Users can remember the basic set more easily if it is limited to fewer commands.

Pen applications should support both the basic and advanced gestures. However, documentation should focus on the basic set, and pen application designers should ensure that their applications can be used productively with the basic set alone.

10.1.4.3 Circled-Letter Gestures

The pen interface also allows users to define gestures consisting of circled letters that can be mapped to specific functions or key equivalents. Four circled-letter gestures are assigned default meanings: C (Copy), P (Paste), U (Undo), and X (Cut). These gestures are non-positional in handwriting edit (hedit) controls and in Windows applications that were not designed specifically for the pen. In boxed edit (bedit) controls, the circled-letter gestures are positional.

10.1.4.4 Advantages of Gestures

Pointing, drawing, and text input are important functions already supported by current mouse-based and keyboard-based applications. A unique virtue of the pen is its ability to specify a selection (the "noun" for an operation) as well as an action (the "verb" for that operation) directly through a gesture. Gestures eliminate the "select object then select operation from a menu" interface enforced by the mouse and by the keyboard. With the pen, users make a single gesture at the object. The application then determines which data to change and which operation to perform.

The rapidity and naturalness of gestural commands are among the key advantages of the pen interface. However, applications should not rely on gestures as the only way to perform commands, because gestures are hidden from the user. As a supplement, applications should also provide menu commands or buttons to carry out the functions performed by the gestures. Applications can put a bitmap of the gesture next to the corresponding menu command. This bitmap helps the users learn gestures; it replaces the keyboard shortcut text that appears on standard Windows menus.

10.2 Designing Pen Interfaces

These guidelines ensure that pen applications take advantage of the strengths of the pen while avoiding its weaknesses.

10.2.1 Simplicity and Directness

10.2.1.1 Keep The Interface Simple

Pen applications are often used by unsophisticated users on machines with small displays and limited storage space, so simplicity is especially important for pen interfaces. Pen applications should forego kitchen-sink interfaces in favor of streamlined simplicity: short menus, small dialog boxes, uncrowded control bars, few overlapping windows, and simple metaphors. Many pen applications can dispense with some of the standard interface elements altogether. For example, the Microsoft Windows for Pen Computing tutorial uses a simple interface with no menus or dialog boxes.

10.2.1.2 Exploit Direct Manipulation

Direct manipulation is particularly useful in pen-based systems for two reasons:

- First, dragging objects with the pen requires less coordination than dragging them with the mouse, because the user does not have to press a button while manipulating the pen.

- Second, manipulating objects with the pen is even more direct than manipulating objects with the mouse. The mouse is located on the user's desk, separated from the pointer on the screen, whereas the pen points directly to the object on the screen. To drag objects with the pen, the user presses the pen tip onto the screen over the object and then moves the pen along the surface of the screen without lifting it.

Pen applications should provide adequate hot zones around small areas that will be targets for pen taps or drag-and-drops. In general, the minimum area of the target plus the hot zone should be at least five pixels. Hot zones are especially important for pen systems because the thickness of the display surface can cause distortion and make precise positioning difficult.

10.2.1.3 Take Advantage of Positionality

One of the great strengths of the pen is its ability to specify a spatial position as it draws a gesture, a character, or a graphical object. Pen applications can take advantage of this feature to process pen input intelligently. For example:

- A gesture typically affects the object underneath it; however, if the user does not draw the gesture directly on any object, the application can apply the gesture to the nearest appropriate object.

- In free-form input, a character can be inserted where it was written; in formatted text, it can be snapped into alignment with the nearest neighboring character.

- In flow charts or organization charts, a square drawn in empty space can be left at the drawing location, whereas a square drawn near an arrow can be moved to abut the arrow (see Figure 10.1).

- In an application that supports both shape and character recognition, an "o" shape can be interpreted as a character or as a circle, depending on whether it was closer to other characters or to other graphical objects.

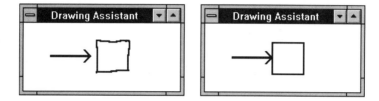

Figure 10.1   Using Proximity to Determine Placement After Recognition

Some pen hardware can detect the proximity of the pen to the display surface. Applications can use this information to provide feedback about the operations that will be available if the user taps or draws on the display. One way to provide this feedback is with pointer changes, as described in the next section.

10.2.1.4 Use Pointers to Increase Accuracy and to Provide Feedback

Because the pen (unlike the mouse) points directly at the screen, graphical on-screen pointers may seem superfluous; however, they do have an important role to play. Usability tests show that pointers help pen users select small targets faster. Moreover, changes from one pointer to another provide useful feedback about the actions supported by the object under the pen. For example, when the pen moves over a resizable border, the pointer can change from a pen (indicating that writing is possible) to a resize pointer (indicating that the border can be dragged to resize the object). Pen applications should use this type of feedback whenever possible to help users understand the actions that are currently enabled by the application. For a list of suggested pointers, see Chapter 3, section 3.6.1.1.1.

In principle, pen applications could dispense with pointers altogether and instead provide target feedback by changing the object under the pen. However, this approach has some disadvantages. First, it can easily lead to a larger number of distracting display changes than are required with pointers. For example, when the pen is moved over a tool bar, the pointer approach only requires one small change (from pen to arrow pointer). The object-change approach, however, would probably require either one, much larger, change (such as highlighting the whole tool bar) or many small changes (such as making each button flash as the pen passes over it). Another potential disadvantage of the object-change approach is its lack of real-world intuitiveness; real objects typically don't change when we approach them. The pointer approach is slightly more realistic in that respect; our hands (analogous to pointers) can undergo changes (for example, sensations of heat and cold) when moved near objects. For these reasons, the object-change approach cannot be recommended without further design work and usability testing.

10.2.2 Recognition Issues

10.2.2.1 Minimize the Need For Writing and Recognition

Because handwriting recognition takes extra time and may occasionally result in errors that must be corrected by the user, pen applications should minimize the need for the user to write text that must be recognized. Two general rules for minimizing writing and recognition are (1) avoid text boxes and (2) preserve ink where appropriate.

10.2.2.1.1 Avoid Text Boxes   Text boxes can sometimes be replaced by lists, combo boxes, or spin boxes; these controls present entries that the user can select without typing or writing. If your application has some knowledge of possible values for the text box, you can use:

- Standard or drop-down lists, if the entire set of possible input values is known (for example, list of available macros or templates or see Figure 10.2). For additional information on lists, see Chapter 6, section 6.3.

- Standard or drop-down combo boxes, if likely field values are known but others are also possible (for example, font names). For additional information, see Chapter 6, section 6.4.1.

- Spin boxes, if likely values are known but others are possible, if the values are intrinsically ordered, and if the user typically only wants to make small increments or decrements (for example, margin settings or month names). For additional information, see Chapter 6, section 6.4.2.

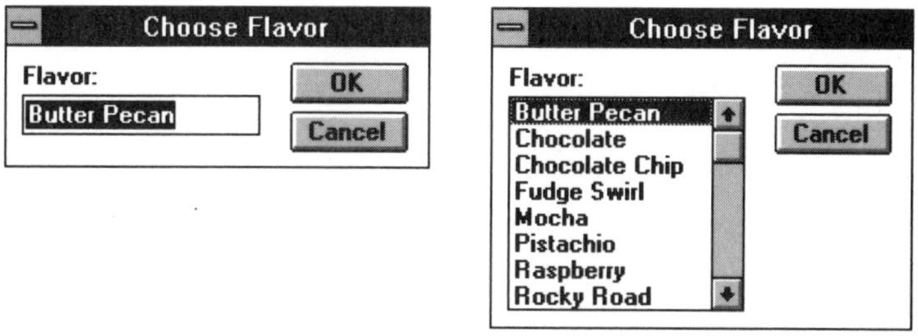

Figure 10.2   Replace a Text Box (Left) with a List (Right) Whenever Possible

10.2.2.1.2 Preserve Unrecognized Ink When Appropriate   In situations where writing cannot be avoided, it is sometimes appropriate to avoid recognition by preserving the ink exactly as written. For example, in applications involving personal notes, annotations, or electronic mail, uninterpreted handwriting is a simple and natural means of expression (see Figure 10.3). Handwriting edit controls and boxed edit controls both support the ability to accept and preserve ink input without recognizing it. Inking capabilities can be added to existing window classes without much effort.

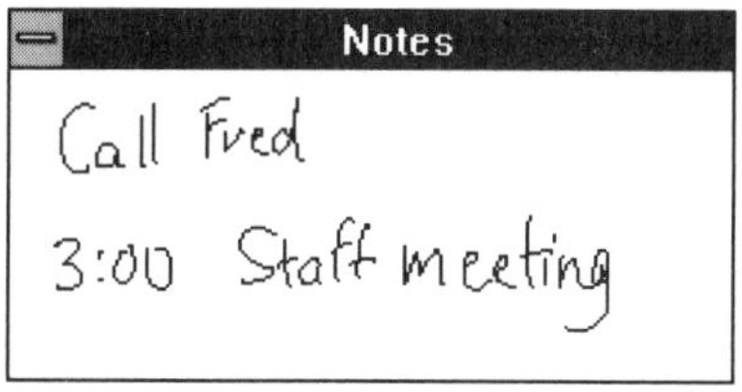

Figure 10.3   Ink Need Not be Recognized to Be Useful

Many of the convenient features of traditional word processors—alignment, cut/paste, bold versus plain styles, and so on—are equally valuable for uninterpreted ink. Ink also opens up many new possibilities such as free-form sketches, annotations, ink erasure, selective recognition for indexing, and more.

10.2.2.2 Aid Recognition By Providing Input Areas for Neat Handwriting

When the need for recognition cannot be avoided, applications can improve the accuracy of recognition by providing input areas that encourage neat, well-segmented handwriting.

10.2.2.2.1 Use Boxed Edit Controls Use boxed edit controls (see Figure 10.4) to get handwritten input from the user whenever possible. Users write more neatly when constrained. Moreover, boxed edit controls provide excellent segmentation and baseline information for the handwriting recognizer. Boxed edit controls function best when the input length and type are known, for example, in a social security number, a phone number, a first name, and so on. Boxed input is less than optimal when the amount of user input cannot be predicted or restrained.

10.2.2.2.2 Provide Large Areas for Handwriting Input Applications can improve recognition in boxed edit controls and in handwriting edit controls by providing plenty of space (see Figure 10.4). In general, larger handwriting is recognized more accurately. People write more neatly and deliberately in large spaces as opposed to small spaces. Ample space also makes selection, correction, and other modifications easier.

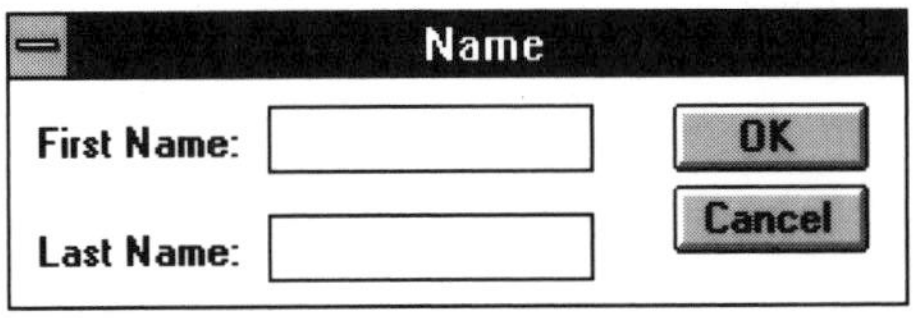

Not recommended

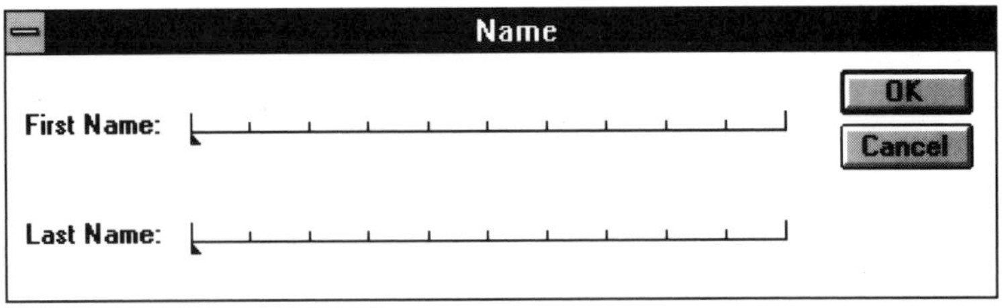

Recommended

Figure 10.4   Replacing Small Text Boxes with Spacious Boxed Edit Controls

10.2.2.3 Use Contextual Constraints to Improve Recognition

Applications can improve recognition accuracy by telling the recognizer what type of data to expect. For example, an address book application can constrain fields, such as phone number and zip code, to contain only numbers. Applications can also constrain recognition by supplying lists of acceptable values (for example, currently registered license plates). In addition to providing strictly defined constraints to the recognizer, applications can apply their own, more flexible, heuristic constraints after the recognizer returns a set of possible results. For example, suppose that after the user writes text in a spreadsheet cell, the recognizer returns "25", "2s", "z5", and "sz" as possibilities. Because the spreadsheet cells can contain text as well as numbers, all four choices are potentially valid, but the spreadsheet can select "25" as the most likely choice.

10.2.2.4 Use Recognition for Graphical Input

Recognition is not limited to writing. Special recognizers (such as the shape recognizer that is included with Windows for Pen Computing) can convert drawn graphics to application-specific or context-specific input. Examples include a drawing package that can snap a rough circle or square to a perfect one (see Figure 10.5) and a CAD/CAM application that can recognize the symbols specific to that industry.

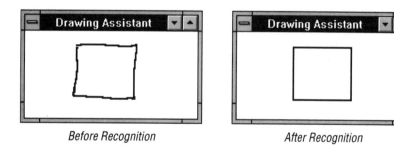

Before Recognition   After Recognition

Figure 10.5   Recognizing Graphical Objects

10.2.3 Hardware Constraints

Pen application designers should take the constraints imposed by pen-capable hardware into consideration.

10.2.3.1 Economize on Storage

Many early pen machines have limited RAM and disk space. As a result, simple, streamlined applications are preferable to large, feature-laden applications. Simple applications not only require less storage but also tend to be easier to use, and ease of use is a key factor for the pen market.

10.2.3.2 Provide Configurable Layouts

A pen application interface should be adaptable to the variety of screen sizes, shapes, and orientations that will be available on pen machines from different manufacturers. Most computer screens adopt a horizontal (landscape) orientation. Clipboard-style pen computers can also be used in a vertical (portrait) orientation. This is a result of how we traditionally hold clipboards. The impact on applications is that the display, which is 640x480 when held horizontally, suddenly becomes 480x640 when held vertically. Pen applications should provide layouts that take both orientations into account. Dialog boxes and control bars must also be designed to fit in both orientations.

Pen applications should also take different screen sizes into account. Hardware manufacturers will soon be providing a wide range of display sizes for pen machines, including some displays as small as 320x200. Pen applications can prepare for this market—while also increasing their simplicity and usability—by streamlining their interfaces (for example, by keeping menus short and dialogs small), and by making interface elements scalable or resizable whenever possible.

10.2.3.3 Don't Rely on Color   ??

For at least the next year or so, clipboard computers will not provide color displays; instead, most will provide 16 shades of gray. For this reason, pen applications should not rely on color to distinguish interface elements or to provide other essential information.

10.2.3.4 Don't Assume An Auxiliary Keyboard   ??

Pen-based clipboard computers will often be used without a keyboard. Accordingly, pen application designers should ensure that the application can be driven entirely from its menus, dialog boxes, and control bars. The most important actions should be directly available through on-screen buttons or easily remembered gestures.

10.2.3.5 Minimize Setup and Startup Time ⧗

Because pen computers are frequently used by people on the go, pen applications should minimize setup and startup time. One helpful technique is to restore the interface settings that were in effect the last time the application was used. For example, applications can automatically restore the previous window location and layout. In some applications, it may also be appropriate to reload the most recently used data and to scroll the window to the most recently viewed portion of the data.

10.2.3.6 Conserve Power

Although power management is not strictly a user interface issue, pen application designers should be aware of the power implications of interface decisions and minimize power consumption whenever possible. For example, features such as automatic background repagination substantially increase power consumption and thus reduce the operating time of a portable pen-based computer. In general, when waiting for user input, pen applications should simply wait in the Windows message loop rather than trying to accomplish numerous background tasks.

Miscellaneous Topics

11.1 Loading and Initialization

The following list shows the suggested sequence of steps for an application after it is invoked:

1. Display the application window.

2. Display the startup message.

In general, additional initialization tasks may be performed any time after the application window is displayed—either before or after the startup message. These tasks typically have no visible results. If they take a long time to complete, they should be divided into two groups. The first group should be performed before the startup message is displayed; the second group should be performed after the start-up message. The appearance of the startup message between the two sets of tasks serves as a progress indicator that makes the lengthy initialization seem shorter.

11.1.1 Memory Check

Generally, if insufficient memory is available when the application is invoked, the system posts a message informing the user. However, once the application code is executed, it becomes the application's responsibility to inform the user if insufficient memory is available for performing specific operations.

11.1.2 Display of Application Window

The application should display the application window as soon as possible, rather than leaving the screen blank until the application is fully started and ready for user interaction.

11.1.3 Display of Startup Message

After the application window has been displayed, the application should display a modal dialog window that includes copyright, version, and user identification information. (The dialog window need not include a title bar.) Figure 11.1 shows the standard format for this information. The startup message window may also contain an icon or other graphic that identifies the application; typically this will be the same icon that is used in the About *<Application-Name>* dialog box (see Chapter 8, section 8.6). Once the application is loaded and ready for user input, the startup window should be automatically removed.

Microsoft SampleApp Version 2.0
Copyright© 1990-1992 Microsoft Corporation

Spelling Checker and Thesaurus
Copyright© Soft-Art, 1987-1990

This product is licensed to:
ELVIS Z. PRESLEY

Warning: This computer program is protected by copyright law and international treaties. Unauthorized reproduction or distribution of this program, or any portion of it, may result in severe civil and criminal penalities, and will be prosecuted to the maximum extent possible under law.

Figure 11.1   Startup Screen

11.2 User Levels and Customization

To accommodate user preferences and skill levels, applications may provide means for the user to customize the interface. When the user quits an application, the current customizations should be saved so that they can be set up in the same way the next time the user invokes the application.

Customization methods differ widely in how much flexibility they offer the user. Some only allow the user to choose from a limited set of predefined possibilities, whereas others allow the user to rearrange parts of the interface in a virtually un-limited number of ways, or even to create completely new commands.

11.2.1 Unfolding Dialog Boxes

Large, complex dialog boxes can intimidate new or inexperienced users. To pro-vide simple, easy-to-understand dialogs for these users while retaining advanced functionality for experienced users, applications can implement dialog boxes that have two sizes—small and expanded. Whenever the dialog is invoked, it should initially appear in the small size, which includes the basic controls necessary to provide the most common functions in the dialog. The small size also includes an unfold button (typically labeled Options >>), which the user can press to expand the dialog. The expanded form of the box contains both basic and advanced con-trols. For more information on unfolding dialogs, see Chapter 7, section 7.1.2.

11.2.2 Customization Dialogs

Applications may also allow users to customize the interface by providing one or more customization dialogs. For example, such dialogs may offer options for displaying or hiding interface elements (such as special characters, gridlines, or horizontal scroll bars) or for changing interface behavior (such as whether typing replaces an existing selection). Customization dialogs may also let the user change the location of menu commands or even add new commands (for example, commands created with macros).

11.2.3 Considerations for Disabled Users

Some customization methods provided by the application (for example, menu reconfiguration) or the system (for example, mouse, keyboard, and volume adjustments) allow disabled users to adjust the interface to suit their needs. Applications can further accommodate disabled users by observing the following guidelines:

- Use multiple perceptual input channels.
  - Avoid using only audio cues, such as beeps, for any situation that absolutely requires attracting the user's attention.
  - Don't rely on color alone to provide essential information.
- Do not require rapid responses.
  - Avoid time-out situations that require a quick response, except in games. If time-outs are used at all, either make the time-out period long (at least one minute) or permit the user to run the application in a "slow" mode.
- Avoid rapid flashing on the screen.
  - Avoid using high rates of flashing for any interface elements or data items. Rapid flashing can cause seizures in some users.

11.3 Help

Applications can facilitate users' tasks by providing small amounts of helpful information automatically while the user is working, either through the message bar (see Chapter 4, section 4.2.6) or through message dialogs (see Chapter 7, section 7.1.4). However, the scarcity of screen space and the need to keep the application window uncluttered limit the amount of helpful text that can be displayed during the user's normal interaction with the application. Applications should therefore provide a way for users to access additional help whenever they need it.

11.3.1 Access to Help

Users may access help from the Help menu, the Help key (F1), or Help mode (SHIFT+F1, followed by a mouse click on the element for which help is desired). For information on the Help menu, see Chapter 5, section 5.4.4.

11.3.1.1 Help Key

When the user presses the Help key (F1), the Help application window appears. Whenever possible, the information initially displayed in the Help window should be context-sensitive; that is, it should reflect the currently active interface element. For example, if a menu command is selected, the Help window should provide information about the command; if a message dialog is being displayed, the Help window should provide additional information about the message. If the application cannot support context-sensitive help, the Help window should initially display a list of possible help topics when F1 is pressed.

11.3.1.2 Help Mode

As an optional extension to Help, applications may implement a Help mode. To enter Help mode, the user presses SHIFT+F1, which changes the mouse pointer to the Help pointer (the standard selection pointer joined to a question mark; see Chapter 3, Table 3.9). To cancel Help mode, the user presses ESC. In Help mode, the user positions the pointer over the interface element for which help is desired. When the user clicks mouse button 1, the Help window appears with information appropriate to that element. As a rule of thumb, applications should always provide the most specific help possible for the context, to the extent that the context can be determined.

Keyboard access to menu items is also available in Help mode. Choosing a menu item with the keyboard in Help mode displays Help information for the menu item instead of initiating the item. If a dialog box is open when the user initiates Help mode, the Help window and appropriate information should appear without further user intervention; that is, the user should not have to close the dialog first.

11.3.1.3 Help in Dialogs and Messages

When using dialog boxes, users can always obtain Help by pressing F1. For more visible access to Help, applications may also provide a Help command button in the dialog box. The "H" in the button label should be underlined to indicate that it is a mnemonic access character. The keyboard user can press the Help button with F1 or ALT+H. Although the ALT+H method is somewhat redundant, it provides two advantages over the F1 method. First, the H mnemonic is more visible. Second, it is easier to remember because H is the first letter in Help and because ALT+H is also used to access the Help menu outside dialog boxes.

Help buttons in message dialogs are optional but highly recommended, especially for warning and critical messages. They provide additional information or suggestions about the problem described by the message.

11.4 International Concerns

To compete successfully in international markets, applications should ensure that their interfaces can be easily adapted to accommodate differences in language, culture, and hardware.

11.4.1 Interface Text

The process of internationalizing an interface starts with translating the interface text. Interface text includes title bar titles, menu names, menu items, control labels, list items, and messages. For easy localization, such text should be stored as resources in the resource file rather than being included in the source code for the application.

Translation of interface text from English to other languages typically increases the length of the text by 30% or more. In some extreme cases, the character count can increase by more than 100%; for example, the word "restore" becomes "zurückspeichern" or "wiederherstellen" in German. Accordingly, if the amount of space for displaying text is strictly limited, as in the status bar, the length of the English interface text should be limited to approximately one-half the available space. (Mode indicators in the status bar, such as NUM, may use all the available space because localized versions try to use the same number of letters as the U.S. version.) In contexts that allow more flexibility, such as dialog boxes, the interface design should allow for text expansion of at least 30%; message text in message dialogs, however, should allow for expansion by about 100%. Applications should never rely on the position of text in a menu, dialog box, or window because translation might require that the text be moved.

11.4.2 Hardware

Outside the U.S., display hardware is not dominated by EGA or VGA standards. Accordingly, dialog boxes and other interface elements should be designed to maintain their aesthetic appeal on various resolutions and screen aspect ratios.

International keyboards may also differ from those in the U.S. installed base. In particular:

- ALT+key combinations should be chosen carefully because some international keyboards use them to enter certain characters.
- Function key accelerators are easier to localize than modifier+letter accelerators.

- Shortcuts that use punctuation marks should be chosen carefully because some punctuation marks (for example, braces and brackets) are frequently not found on international keyboards or are only available in combination with the ALT key.

- All international applications should support multiple code pages and sorting tables to allow for the use of different extended character sets. For sorting and case conversion, applications should use system-supplied rather than application-specific routines whenever possible.

11.4.3 Formats

Different countries often use substantially different formats for dates, time, money, measurements, and telephone numbers. As a result, international applications should allow these formats to be changed easily. The setup program for the application should initialize the formats to the default values obtained from the system Control Panel. The application itself may also allow the formats to be changed whenever necessary during normal use of the application. Such changes may be saved on an application-specific or document-specific basis, but should not affect the system defaults.

Table 11.1 lists the most common format categories.

Table 11.1   Formats for International Applications

Category	Format Considerations
Date	Order, separator, and long/short formats
Time	Separator and cycle (12-hour vs. 24-hour)
Physical quantity	Metric vs. English measurement system
Currency	Symbol and format (for example, trailing vs. preceding symbol)
Separators	List, decimal, and thousandths separators
Telephone numbers	Separators for area codes and exchanges
Paper sizes	U.S. vs. European paper sizes

Index

W

Y

Z